# The Buchanan Bastard

### Dedra L. Stevenson

Blue Jinni Media

**The Buchanan Bastard**

Edited by: Lene Pieters
Production by: Rodney W. Harper

Blue Jinni Media
https://bluejinnimedia.com

*For all the lonely ones, those that don't quite fit, for they are the ones that break the wheel and change everything.*

# AUTHOR'S FOREWORD

This novel is the result of a very long and turbulent journey. Three years in the making, through one personal crisis after another, this project kept me steady and gave me purpose. My husband and I celebrated our honeymoon in New Orleans, and somewhere deep down, I've always wanted to pay homage to this very unique city. Deeply rooted in French origins, it's tenacity, liveliness, and mystery, not to mention the delicious food, gives New Orleans an edge that makes you want to return again and again. Once you've experienced the magic of Mardi Gras, you'll be hooked.

The 1970's was an interesting and somewhat transitional decade in American history. I was a kid in the 70's, and I remember our collective innocence was still alive, but only by a thread. After all, it was a decade of activism and political awakening. While it wasn't all serious, thanks to Star Wars, Scooby Doo, shag carpets, massive sideburns, and smiley face buttons, we also learned that we couldn't leave our doors unlocked anymore or let our children play outside unsupervised as the emergence of the serial killer also reared it's ugly head.

The Buchanan Bastard takes the reader to the crawfish boils and Cajun barbecues, as well as the Southern Charm and deep family ties while exposing the dark underworld of New Orleans. The journey of the Buchanan family is similar to most posh families of the American South, rich with dark secrets and wrought with controversy. I hope you enjoy their journey.

I couldn't have gotten through this without a team. A family of supporters and friends who selflessly gave of their time and effort to guide me into making this book the best book I've ever written. I'd like to take this opportunity to acknowledge and thank them. First of all, my family, for their constant support has meant the world, especially my son, Abdullah Kayyani, for reading my drafts multiple times and criticizing his mom's writing mercilessly without fear, as this made me a better writer. I know it came from a place of love.

My beta readers, Richard Dee, Luke Hinds, H.K. Frost, and Rodney Harper deserve a huge thanks for their guidance and encouragement. Making a great book means getting through your beta readers, for they are the gatekeepers and the voice of your target audience. I thank them with all my heart.

To Lene Pieters, my editor, I offer my sincere thanks for her thorough evaluation of my book, catching each mistake, each error in logic and each flawed plot and sub-plot. This process was tedious and she got through it with the strength of a gladiator. My book is polished and pristine thanks to her.

And finally, I'd be nowhere without my cousin and mentor, Rodney Harper, who has been a constant supportive force in my journey. He's my partner at Blue Jinni Media, my family, my friend, my advisor, and the one who makes sure my books are laid out with care and precision and distributed to each and every platform in the world as eBooks, Paperbacks, Hardcovers and Audiobooks.

Enjoy my new book, and please drop a review on one or all of the online stores and stay in touch by connecting with me on all my social media pages.

Sincerely,

Dedra L. Stevenson

# PRELUDE

*February 1977, New Orleans, LA, late night somewhere in the French Quarter*

In a dark alley, he punched the wall. She winced, holding an arm up to protect her face. He wanted to scream at her, but he couldn't be sure of their surroundings. Cajun bands blared music from clubs around the French Quarter, masking their sound, but he still wasn't taking any chances.

"There's no purpose to this. Leave it. You and I can run. We can start over... get away from here. My sweet one, you are not ready for such darkness."

"I am ready," she said firmly.

In such a dark alley, he could barely see her face, only that she wasn't covering it anymore. She sighed. "I *can't* let this pass. He ruined everything for us, took away any chance I had to be happy, and he'll *pay*."

"Let me do it. I'm already soulless," he said as he tucked a loose hair behind her ear.

He reached out to take her into his arms, making her flinch at first, but then she allowed it. Her perfume filled his nose with the smell of sweet jasmine. *I can't let her do this. I love her, and I don't love anything. She's my world. Without her, I'm empty.* He pulled her closer and breathed in the smell of her hair. The fresh smell always reminded him of their childhood together. Her carefree laughter.

How her blonde streaks glimmered in the sun. He stroked her hair and whispered, "I can do it with no problem, and I *won't* get caught."

She pulled back, cocked her head to one side and glared at him, almost snarling. "And I will?"

"Shhhh...lower your voice, or this is over before it starts." He looked at the street, then back into her eyes.

She clicked her tongue. "Fine...but you've done nothing to convince me. This is happening, and everything is ready. By tonight, they'll both be dead. It's already begun, and I *won't* screw it up." She stroked his face and gently kissed his cheek. "You can help me...that way you can be sure that I won't back down...finish the job. I know you'll protect me."

"You've killed before for hire darling, but *this* is personal. *Personal* gets messy. Especially love and family," he sighed. "I guess you leave me no choice. I'll be there, dorogaya."

She kissed him. "You've always been there, watching over me. You're my dark angel."

# BRIAN

BRIAN BUCHANAN NEVER EXPECTED TO FALL IN LOVE SO SOON AFTER entering the university. He often remembered the first time he saw her, laughing with a group of her friends and how it made his heart melt. He'd met women before, but no one like Laura Lynn Beauford, an Economics major, minoring in Political Science.

Laura seemed to be a freak of nature in many ways, Brain thought. A girl who's great with numbers, but beautiful and charismatic? Her existence didn't seem fair to the other women. She had it all, especially her beautiful smile.

Her smile made his chest swell. She was an all-American beauty. Blonde, green eyes, petite, sweet face and an adorable laugh, but that was only the beginning of her beguiling nature. She was witty and charming, smart, and sexy. If the world would ever be able to accept a woman for president, that would be Laura.

Brain was raised as a manly man, but a gentleman as well. He knew he should focus on her intellect, but all he could think of was how much he wanted to kiss those lips and hold her in his arms, but there was competition, heavy competition. She was in the debate club, and being the feisty character she was, she caught the attention of more than one major player on campus, some from his own fraternity.

He watched as she turned down one after another. *How is she gonna see me as different from those other clowns? I can't get shot down. That would not be cool.*

One fateful morning, four weeks ago, he caught her staring at him as they waited in line for breakfast at the campus cafeteria. *Bye Bye Miss American Pie* was playing over the speakers, and she was wearing the cutest pink bell bottom jeans and a lacy white peasant top. Her hair was blonde and feathered, and she wore a shimmery lip gloss that accentuated her full lips, lips that definitely got his attention. Her face turned as pink as her jeans when she realized that he noticed her, more like *stared* at her. She bit her bottom lip and looked away. *Is she interested in me? Don't let your imagination run away with you, Buchanan.*

One of his fraternity brothers, Martin, sat down to eat with him. "Hello, old sport. How are we this fine morning?"

Martin, wearing the latest plaid leisure suit from Fashion Beat magazine, styled himself as an old-fashioned gentleman. He cut his bagel with a knife and fork, after spreading a pat of butter over it, ever so gently, and winced when he saw Brian chomp into his bagel, dropping a dollop of jam on the table.

"So, who is she?" Martin asked, with a knowing smile on his face.

"Who's who?" Brian asked.

Martin smiled and shook his head. "The blonde Southern debutante you can't seem to take your eyes off of."

He smiled at Martin and blushed. "Okay, fine. I admit it. I'm lost, lost in that bewitching creature."

"So, what's so special about her?" Martin asked, taking a delicate bite of his bagel.

"She's different. Classy...Most women here are pretty much guilty of professional husband-hunting, but not her," Brian said, pausing to smile at her. "She's here to learn. Maybe to even go into politics like her father...I'll admit that would be a reach for an accounting major, but by God, it would be nice to have leaders that wouldn't sink the economy. Most things that are important come down to numbers, right? Anyhow, the last thing she wants is some heathen who only wants to get in her pants."

Martin grinned. "Is that what you're doing? Getting into her pants?

Brian scoffed. "No, of course not! This gal is gonna be the mother of my children."

"Groovy. That's so far out!" Martin said. "So, what are you waiting for? Talk to her."

"Working on it," he replied, scratching his sideburns.

Later on, after working up his courage, Brian finally tried something, something different. He left a rose and a card taped to her dorm mailbox, after which he waited nearby, hidden behind an azalea bush.

After an agonizing hour, she arrived back at her dorm. He watched her read the card, scribble a reply and tape it back to the postbox before disappearing inside. His heart leaped when he retrieved the card and saw her neat handwriting say "yes". He felt like the king of the world, so victorious. Now, it was just about planning a great first impression.

As far as he knew, she wasn't aware of the fact that he had significant means. *I'll keep it simple, romantic. She'll appreciate this. She's not about status, so I'm not gonna try anything flashy. I'm just a regular guy who happens to be interested in kissing those pouty lips all night long.*

"Stop that," Brian said out loud to himself. "This is not *just* a conquest."

He remembered his father warning him about gold diggers. Jack Buchanan III would always say, "son, have fun out there, but be careful. They're around every corner. Hussies that'll spread their legs for the almighty dollar."

*No! She can't be like that...could she?* Just thinking about it made his hands shake. What a disappointment that would be. He took a deep breath. "Don't worry, everything's groovy. I'll just enjoy the evening and see where it goes. Keep it chill. No big deal."

He arranged a romantic night for Laura. It was impressive, but not expensive. He looked down at his trembling hands. *Here goes nothing*, he thought as he showed up at her doorstep with a single flower in hand and a picnic basket. He grinned when he saw her in her colorful Mexican peasant blouse and her frayed jeans with a beaded purse strapped across her body. Her dress style was so fresh and fun.

She looked at the basket and her lips curled into a sweet smile. Luckily for him, she resided close to the location he'd been planning for their date. "My lady, shall we?"

"It's about time," she smiled.

"Beg your pardon," he murmured.

Laura giggled. "I've been waiting for you to ask me out forever."

He couldn't believe how much time he'd wasted on nerves. *She's wanted me all along. I'm such a space cadet.* He cleared his throat. "Well, I guess I've got some lost time to make up for."

She smiled and took his hand. He led her on a lovely stroll around Big Lake. They got there just in time to watch the sun go down and the streetlights switch on. The scenic circular path was an easy stroll and the weather was anyone's dream. The perfect temperature with a light breeze in the air. He held her hand and blushed. *Why am I blushing? Please don't look at me, Beautiful. You may see a twelve-year-old here.* "So, where are you originally from?" He asked, clearing his throat.

"Alabama," she said, looking down.

He grinned.

"And what's wrong with being from Alabama?"

"Nothing, it's far out," he chuckled. "Well, there is that song...*Came from Alabama with a Banjo on my knee...*ha!"

"Ah! I see. So, what you mean is that I'm a redneck?" She said, smirking at him.

"Naaa. Not a redneck for sure. You're far too classy. Too glamorous. Too poised and graceful." he said, looking at her with starry eyes.

"I am a spaz though," she said.

"Why? What makes you say that?"

"I read a lot," she said, grinning.

"Well, if that makes a spaz, count me in! What kind of books?"

"I love spy thrillers," she said.

He raised an eyebrow. "Wow. I never thought I could be more impressed with you. You're a righteous babe alright. Smart, beautiful, and you love spy novels. Did you drop from Heaven just for me?"

She blushed. He got a peek of her fresh pink glow from the corner of his eye. His hands stopped trembling. They reached their picnic spot and spread out. He set out the plates, napkins, and food. She sat down and he served her a tuna sandwich and a dixie cup of fresh-squeezed lemonade that he poured out of a flask. "I made this all myself. I hope you like it."

She took a sip and smiled. He sat opposite her and noticed the look on her face. She seemed to be staring. He checked his pants for fear that he'd left his zipper down.

"What? Something wrong?"

"Oh...nothing...Well, it's just that most boys that ask me out take me to fancy restaurants, theaters. Stuff like that. This is *new*. I dig it." She took a bite of her sandwich.

He grinned. "I'm glad you feel that way. It's not the same when you're not a man of means. But I can tell you this. I am a man who stands up for people I care for, and for what I believe in."

"Really?" She asked as she took a sip of lemonade. "Wow! This is really good, by the way."

"Thank you," he said.

"Tell me about the people you care for, your family," she asked, taking another bite.

"That's easy. I have two older brothers. They're about the most awkward guys anyone could ever meet, but if they love you, they'd take a bullet for you," he said, then took a sip of his lemonade. "My mother...well, she's had a lot of hard times. I was actually born in a trailer park."

Laura almost choked on her sandwich. "What?"

"Yeah," Brian said, nodding. "My mother had almost no money as I was growing up. Times were hard. My brothers and I actually stole now and then to try and help...which is ironic now, considering one of my brothers turned out to be a cop. My mother is so proud."

Laura stared. Brian felt the mood chill and shifted. "Is there a problem?"

She put down her food and folded her arms. "Yeah. I'd say there's a problem! You're a liar."

Excuse me?" His head tilted as his eyes bore into hers. "I've been nothing but brutally honest. Look, I'm sorry if I'm not one of your rich playboys! Guess I should get my trailer park ass out of here, huh?"

"You can drop the act, Brian...*Buchanan*." She stood up and her brow furrowed.

"You know about my family?" He asked.

"Do you think I'm stupid? That I wouldn't find out?" She blurted.

His eyes darted back and forth as he stammered. "No. I didn't mean...come on!"

She began to gather her things to leave. He took her by the arms. "No, please. You don't understand...Yes, I'm Brian Buchanan, but for years, I was Brian Higgins...but where I started out... that part, which was the truth. I swear to God."

"Go on, I'm listening," Laura said, sitting back down on the picnic blanket.

Brian sighed. "My mother had me out of wedlock, so for the first fifteen years of my life, I was only with her, living in a trailer park, until my father decided to acknowledge me as his son and adopt me. Call me crazy, but I don't like how rich people show off with fancy things. I thought we should just talk on our first date. Get to know each other for real."

Laura looked down and smiled. "Well...I guess you have a point. About the way rich people are pretentious. I've always hated that too...I just didn't know what to think. I mean, I knew who you were, and when I saw how good looking you are, I thought you may be cocky, so I found out all I could about you. When I found out you're from such a family, I thought..."

"That I just wanted to get in your pants...right?" He said, smiling. He hoped she didn't notice how his heart quickened at the compliment. His face felt hot and he felt giddy. *Don't be a dork. Don't be a dork. Be cool.*

She chuckled. "Well...yeah, something like that."

"Well, your virtue is safe with me, young lady. I really just wanted to get to know you. That's all."

He looked around the lake. "Hey, if it's okay with you now, I did plan a second part of this date. Look over there. There's a gondola ride we can take around the lake, just like in Italy. What do you say?"

"I like it," she said, as she reached out for his hand. He helped her back up. "I say, Mr. Buchanan, you are quite the romantic!"

"Baby, you have no idea."

# LAURA

LAURA SMILED AS SHE UNPACKED DISHES, PUTTING THEM INTO THE white kitchen cupboards of her new home. *Content...so that's what it feels like?* Someone gently hugged her waist from behind. How she loved his hands, strong and capable, and so loving.

"Hey there, beautiful. Let me help you with those," Brian said as he softly kissed her on the cheek.

"Thank you, sweetheart," she said, then whirled around to kiss his lips before handing him the box. "This place is so great. Thanks for agreeing to live away from our parents for a while, well, away from *my* dad."

"No problem. You're right. We need to have some time alone before we give in to all their expectations for us. I'm a Buchanan. You're a Beauford. I just wanna be *us* for a time, or maybe forever? Ha!" He smiled. "Who knows if we're ever gonna go back?"

"Your daddy won't let us have that option for long. He needs you to be there for the company at least." She took his hand as he put the last plate away.

"That's what I've been doing for the last eight months. I'm sure my father will be home anytime now. I don't believe he's gone. They just want to consider him dead? Bastards...They don't know him like I do," he said.

*Is Jack ever coming home? Brian puts on a brave face, but I have a bad feeling.*

The phone rang, making her forget her doubts for a moment. "Hello. Buchanan residence," Laura answered.

It was Larry, Laura's father. His voice boomed so loudly that it was easy for Brian to hear what he was saying. Brian smiled, shaking his head.

"Oh, my sweet girl. You haven't been a Buchanan long, only a year. Can't I believe that you're still a Beauford too? Hmm?"

"Well, I'll never forget that I'm a Beauford, Daddy. No way, no how," Laura said.

Larry chuckled. "I just called to check in, darlin'."

"We're doing fine out here," she said. "I really like Baton Rouge."

"I bet you miss Alabama though, don't ya? There's nothing like wakin' up to the smell of biscuits and grits," he said. "That's some good eatin', little gal."

"You do know that I can make my own grits, right?" She sniggered.

"I'm just messin' with ya," he said. "Are you sure you're not bored to death out there?"

"No, Daddy," she replied. "I'm right as rain. Got my dream boat, and a good life with him."

Brian smiled at her. She winked at him.

"You're still my little princess," her father chuckled softly. "Don't forget that... And no matter how much money that bozo has, he's still not good enough for you. Got it?"

Laura giggled. "Daddy, no one's good enough for me in your opinion."

"Damn right!" He blurted. "Okay, serious talk time now. I can't have you putting my grandchild at risk doing all that housework. Let me hire you a maid."

"Oh, come now, Daddy. You know I've never been any stranger to hard work. Why should it be any different now? I'm not made of glass, you know. We didn't always have means, and I helped out a lot, remember?"

Larry paused. Laura knew that he remembered indeed. She was his only child, and he had lost her mother to cancer many years ago, when she was still a little girl. Even then, she was strong. She cooked and cleaned and brought him his coffee in the mornings. But ever since he started making a comfortable living, he just wanted to keep her in splendor.

"I remember, sweet girl. Well, you take care of each other. We'll be in touch soon."

"Yes, Daddy. Good night."

Laura looked at her husband as he smiled at her. *His dimples are adorable. Look at his hair! Oh, I love running my fingers through that thick, black hair. It's so soft. He loves me so much. God, I'm dying to get him in bed right now.* She grabbed his face gently and said, "You're going places, love. And not just because of your father. Because of you, your imagination, and your integrity. You're a good man, with a strong heart. I can't believe how lucky I am." She grinned. "You're pretty freakin' sexy too."

He pulled her in close and gave her a long slow kiss. Her toes curled and her body was in flames. She melted into his kiss and softly sighed when he grabbed her head and rested his forehead against hers, looking deep into her soul. "Oh, I'm the lucky one," he whispered. "I love you so much. You bring out the best in me and make me believe in myself. How did I ever survive without you?"

"Let's hope you don't ever have to find out." Laura said.

He let go, then grabbed both her shoulders. "Well, Mrs. Buchanan. What do you say to having dinner with me and then helping me make sure that this home is filled with the right conditions for the pitter patter of these little feet soon? Hmm?"

He touched her belly. Her heart pounded and she smiled. "We have our whole lives together. I love you," he said.

"Aces. I'd love that, darling," she said. "And I love you too."

The crashing sound of thunder broke their embrace. Storm clouds suddenly loomed ominously overhead, casting the room in shadow. Hail balls the size of marbles clattered against the roof of their home. She shuddered. "Seems like it's gonna be a vicious storm." Laura hurried to the living room to close the open window.

"Yeah...never seen the sky turn black like that so quickly." Brian said, as he turned on the light. He put his arms around her, pulling her close.

She noticed a black Mercedes parked across the road from their home. The glint of a set of binoculars caught her attention. "What in the..." Laura murmured.

"What's wrong, sweetheart?" Brian asked, squinting to see what she saw through the rain-streaked window.

Laura saw a woman dressed in black throw the binoculars in the passenger seat and drive off in a hurry. *What in the world was she doing?*

"Sweetheart, can you check all the locks for me? That didn't feel right," Laura said.

Brian kissed her on the head. "I was thinking the same thing. Don't worry, I'm on it."

Thunder clapped and lightning streaked through the sky as she tried to look across the street again. The car was gone. No trace. She thought of notifying the police, but to report what? She shrugged her shoulders, getting back to organizing the kitchen.

# LAURA

MR. AND MRS. BRIAN BUCHANAN ARRIVED AT THE GRAND *CHATEAU Versailles*, one of the most iconic hotels in the French Quarter, with luxurious rooms, stunning views, and balconies to die for. This would be a wonderful getaway for them, a last hurrah before they welcomed a baby into their lives. They only had a couple of months left before the baby came, but Brian rarely got a few days off from work to do anything like this, and he'd just get busier with Buchanan Oil.

Jack's funeral had been hard on everyone, especially Brian. They had become so close. The thought of what he must have gone through when he saw that empty casket being lowered down into the ground was heartbreaking for Laura. From the time they had made the crushing choice to declare Jack legally dead, to the takeover of Buchanan Oil, and the Buchanan home, Brian was forever changed, more serious, and far more stressed out. Jack's belongings were covered with dust cloths, to be dealt with later, after the baby came, as it was just too painful for them to sort through it now. Brian's lack of time was also a major factor. Laura worried that he wouldn't have time for them, and this baby was going to grow up feeling his absence.

Laura looked over their beautiful balcony, wondering how she could make sure they got chances for getaways like this after the delivery. *Brian will be such a good dad. I just know it. If he gets the chance.*

Even though she barely saw Brian lately, she chose to remain hopeful. Surely, he'd take them back to the hotel again after the baby comes, at some point, she reckoned. *The next time we come here, we'll probably be three.* She smiled as she imagined Brian with a toddler on his shoulders, watching the Mardi Gras parades with them. The thought was heartwarming, and her negative thoughts were temporarily quieted, and painful memories tucked away. It was time to get ready for their first night out on the town, and she wanted to look perfect.

Laura stepped out of the elevator to the floor of their hotel room wearing a flowing asymmetrical one shoulder evening gown with exquisite beading and fringe throughout. The frilly neckline only accentuated her diamond necklace and her dangling diamond earrings, a birthday gift from her romantic husband last year. The gown was one of her first maternity purchases. She bought it especially for the trip, figuring that it would hold up for quite a while because of its non-constrictive style. That did little to relieve the pressure exerted by her step-in maternity girdle, however. It was either that or back pain, as Laura's small frame was already feeling her center of gravity shift.

However, despite her considerable discomfort, she was on cloud nine. They had just come back from a lovely dinner on Bourbon Street. Walking next to the man she loved, she grinned like a giddy girl and walked with a spring in her step. She looked at her perfectly manicured hand, sporting a diamond ring that was bigger and more luminous than she'd ever seen. She held it up to see it closer. Such a pleasing sight. She smiled at him, thinking of the peach baby doll nighty that she planned to wear for him tonight.

————

THE NEXT NIGHT, Mardi Gras began. The spectacle was amazing, a perfect way to celebrate the love she had for her husband. The colors, the masks, the band music, the smell of bourbon and crawfish in the air. It was Fat Tuesday, traditionally, the day that one must use up all the fats in their cupboard before Catholic Lent. New Orleans made it a party, one in which all the decadence of life was to be enjoyed and savored before fasting, not just the fat, but the very nectar of life. It felt right that Laura was there, celebrating that very concept with her dreamy man.

They took in the sights. The parades began in mid-morning and were to last all day. Even though they had only been married for a short time, this trip was planned from the day they said, "I do". She breathed in deeply and truly took in her surroundings. She and Brian had their challenges, but this was a blissful time, and her heart soared, until suddenly, it didn't.

The afternoon had been going well, but after lunch, Brian looked unwell. He felt winded and said he needed to lie down for a while. *Is he okay? We've been looking forward to this trip forever.* It wasn't just that they were in New Orleans, but in a hotel that overlooked the best Mardi Gras action around.

She put him to bed that afternoon and she didn't want to leave him, but they were due to attend a charity dinner function that evening, and now Laura would have to make excuses for him. She wished she could just blow it off completely, but it was important for the company that Buchanan Oil was represented.

"Sweetheart, I really wish I could stay here with you, but I won't be long. Just a few hours, I promise," she said.

"It's okay, ma darlin'. I think it's a little bug or something, nothing serious. Go ahead and enjoy your night. I'll be fine. Just gotta get some rest."

"Are you sure? I just hate leaving you." Laura said. She kissed his feverish head.

He took her hand into his and kissed it. "Yes, I'm sure, honey. To tell ya the truth, I'm worried you're gonna catch this if you stay around me. It feels like the bubonic plague. Just God awful. I'll be sick every day of the week and twice on Sunday if I never have to see you feeling bad, particularly now...You know good and well what I mean. We have to protect your precious cargo."

She squeezed his hand and a tear rolled down her cheek. "I'll make excuses to leave early. I can't be away from you long."

"Okay darlin'," he said weakly, shooing her off. "Now go on and get outta here."

She sighed, picked up her wrap and bag, and blew him a kiss. Her brows furrowed. "I swear though, if you're any worse when I get back, we're going to the emergency room, okay?" She wagged her finger. "Never mind, that's not a question, Brian Buchanan. I won't take 'no' for an answer."

"Yes, ma'am...Love you."

"Love you too, sweetheart." She said, taking one last look at him, huddled under the covers.

# LAURA

*February 1977, New Orleans, Louisiana, Chateau Versailles...Mardi Gras*

HOURS LATER, LAURA RAN OUT OF THE ELEVATOR. "OH MY GOD. So late....so late!"

She'd lost count of how many hands she'd had to shake that night and how many nincompoops she'd spent painful moments in conversation with. All she could think of was her Brian. This evening had left a bad feeling in her stomach, a sinking feeling, and she made mental plans to pack him up and take him to the nearest hospital, whether he liked it or not. As she briskly walked towards their room, she turned a corner and bumped into a brunette woman, another guest, carrying an ice bucket. Some of the ice cubes spilled out on the floor.

"Oh, excuse me! I'm so sorry," Laura said. "Guess I wasn't looking where I was going."

The young woman looked over the rim of her thick glasses and replied with a quiver in her voice, "No...no problem. Have a good night, ma'am."

Laura reached down to pick up the ice, but the young woman blurted, "Leave it. Really, no worries."

Laura nodded. "Well, okay hun. Sorry again."

"I'm sorry," said the young woman.

Laura noticed the young woman's sullen face, and even as she left her, she noticed that the girl had *following* eyes. A chill ran through her, but she didn't give it much thought. All she wanted was to get back to Brian.

She turned the key to their beautiful suite and walked in. It was dark, so she switched on the light. "Brian? Sweetheart? I'm back. I'm sorry it took me so long."

She walked past the bathroom, checking herself in the mirror along the way. "Sweetheart!"

There was no answer. Once she reached the bed, her blood ran cold, and she froze in her tracks. Her heart sank into her chest, as she whimpered. She trembled, unable to process what she was seeing. Brian lay in bed, alongside a strange woman. They were completely naked and there were ugly bullet holes in their heads and chests. The walls seemed to be closing in on her. *What is this? He was just here, alive...what is this?! How? Who the fuck is that? Did they have sex? Did she kill him? Oh God!*

She sobbed and held her stomach as though an invisible boot had just kicked her, making her step back. She took a deep breath. Her eyes darted around the room. *Oh! This can't be real. God, Laura, get your shit together. Your husband's dead. Oh my God!* She screamed loud enough to cut through the raging sound of the Mardi Gras outside.

Their blood stained the sheets and pillows red and was splattered all over the headboard. Laura couldn't move. Her eyes scanned the floor and she saw a revolver lying near the bed. With trembling hands, she picked up the gun, by the barrel, careful not to touch the grip. It was still warm. She looked around, breathing in shallow bursts, tears forming in her eyes. She shivered when she realized that she may not be alone. *Is the killer still here?*

Someone banged on the door. She flinched.

"Please sir, call the police!" She sobbed. "My husband and a woman are murdered in here."

"Miss! Open up," the hotel manager shouted. "Do you need help?"

"Just call the police! The son of a bitch could still be in here!"

The manager's voice wasn't heard again. Laura heard the sounds of the crowd outside, but it was surreal. She didn't feel a connection with her body at this point, almost looking at the scene as an observer. She touched Brian's hand. It was so cold. She sobbed uncontrollably. Suddenly, there were fists pounding on the door.

"Open up! It's the police!"

Laura sobbed and wailed, dropping the gun. "It's my husband! Oh my God! Help me!"

She turned towards the door, struggling to step forward. The stress of the situation made her sick. She wanted to throw up, and the baby was moving actively due to the adrenaline. This made her back wrench with pain. She was too late to open the door willingly. The officers crashed through, scanned the crime scene, then restrained her in cold steel handcuffs. Her mind reeled and she sobbed softly. Everything seemed surreal. *Why? My life was perfect... What's gonna happen to my baby? He or she's never going to know his father. What did we ever do to deserve this? God...why have you done this to me?*

Many people opened their hotel room doors to glimpse the action. Laura, flanked on both sides by officers, noticed the endless stream of open mouths, furrowed brows and shaking heads. She kept her head down, too ashamed to look any of them in the eye. The local press must have gotten wind of a double homicide and couldn't pass up the chance to snap some photos for the morning paper. Laura shuddered as she imagined the headlines. She shook her head. "This wasn't me! Please! This wasn't me!" She muttered to herself.

*Why do they think I could shoot the love of my life, my whole world? I could never hurt him. I lived for him. Who would want to kill him? He was wonderful.*

Just as she got on the elevator with the officers, Laura spotted a brunette woman, the woman with the ice bucket. Hey eyes were red, as someone who had been crying. Laura blinked, then she was gone.

She clenched her teeth at the sight of it all. "God, someone, please help me!" She sobbed, "I ... I ... didn't do anything, and *someone* just killed my husband...Oh God!"

# LARRY

ALREADY, THE SUN HAD SET, AND THE RISING FULL MOON LOOMED over his outdoor shooting range and knife-throwing targets, set up in his sprawling garden. But it was never too late to keep practicing. Larry S. Beauford squeezed the trigger of his vintage ArmaLite AR18, hitting the heads and the hearts of his paper targets without fail, expertly handling the recoil.

His advanced age came as a shock to most, as Larry kept in shape. He was muscular, but had a grizzled war beaten face, a mustache and well-kept beard that framed his square jaw perfectly. Despite large sideburns being all the rage at the time, Larry thought they were for hippies, and kept his sideburns small and well-trimmed. As a former military man, Larry Beauford believed in order, but those close to him saw the kindness in his eyes. He knew it and didn't mind the fact that his soft side showed to those he loved.

Nothing was more important to him than his family and friends. He vowed to take care of them, especially financially. Before he entered politics, his law practice had thrived. He had a head for business as well, and thanks to some well-placed investments, he enjoyed a comfortable lifestyle in his later years.

He didn't let the lifestyle of a wealthy man spoil him. He kept up with his training. After all, he had to stay sharp. War with the Soviets or the Iranians could break out any year now and he couldn't afford to let himself become soft, like so many soldiers turned politicians.

"Sir!"

He turned, only to spot his housekeeper rushing into his garden. "It's an urgent call regarding your daughter," she said.

Larry lowered his rifle. "My daughter? What the hell?"

As his assistant approached him, a posterboard of an SS officer popped up. Larry gritted his teeth. Briefly, his mind flashed back to when he found those ditches filled with frozen corpses of American POWs, their faces locked in silent screams. *Damn Krauts.* He grabbed one of the throwing knives off his table, and without looking back to aim, he threw it into the posterboard, hitting the Nazi right between the eyes.

He hurried inside his posh mayoral mansion, which resembled a hunting lodge, thanks to his love of the great outdoors. Deer and bear heads hung on the walls, alongside mounted prize fish and pictures galore of men gathered for hunting trips and mock training camps. Even though he knew he wouldn't be mayor forever, he strived to make the place perfect for him, customized for a man of his tastes and proclivities.

He picked up the phone.

"I don't understand." He snapped. "She did *what*?! Who's been murdered? Lord Almighty, not Brian! Okay, I'm coming! Don't do anything until I get there. Tell Laura I'm coming."

Larry hung up, then picked up the receiver to access his head of security. "Mr. Thomas, prepare the car. I'm headed to New Orleans. Yes, it's an emergency. Activate emergency protocol. Yes, make sure my staff know what to do to keep the town safe while I'm gone, and what to do in case I don't return...Yes, thank you. Please send someone to help me prepare my personal items."

He hung up, then went upstairs to start packing. His hands were shaking. He looked in the mirror. "Calm down now, Larry. It's alright. You're not just a mayor. You're a criminal lawyer, just what Laura needs now."

His housekeeper helped him get his bags together, including a medicine bag with many bottles of pills, and Larry proceeded to the car that was waiting for him. Just before he stepped outside, he spotted the family portrait over the fireplace. His beloved late wife stared tenderly back at him. Laura's teenage face held a hint of the beauty she would become. He was so proud of her. "Hold on darlin'. Daddy's coming."

# CORAL

"CORAL! CORAL! WHERE ARE YA, GIRL?"

Stella's scratchy voice grated on the ears as she called from outside the trailer window. Coral finished pinning the old towel diaper on her newborn son, swaddled him in the mothball smelling blanket and laid him in the old crib with peeling paint distorting the row of ducklings parading around the edge. She peeked outside and spotted Stella smoothing her mousy brown hair, pulling a few sticks from her old sweater, admiring her reflection in the window. Coral was too busy with her newborn to care that Stella had been messing around with Daryl Rae even though she'd promised to be there to watch over her *very* pregnant best friend.

"In here!" Coral called out, as she dunked the dirty diaper into a nearby bucket, to be rinsed outside later.

Stella stepped in hesitantly, quiet as a mouse, which was unusual behavior for Stella. She reeked of Daryl Rae's cheap aftershave. It confirmed what must have gone down. Stella started making excuses. *I can't really blame her,* Coral thought. *He's a sight for sore eyes, tall and fit. Oh boy, is he fit! Mmmm...and that hair! What a fine ducktail!*

As she carefully lowered herself into the creaky rocking chair next to the crib,

Coral tuned out Stella's ramblings to remember the awesome nights they'll all had around the trailer park. When they hung out around the fire in the steel barrel trash can, which kept them warm as they drank homemade hooch. They usually listened to Elvis with a little Johnny Cash now and then, smoked a little pot, and played poker on a folding steel table, balancing precariously on rusting metal folding chairs cast off by one of the rich families in town. The cats and chicks who gathered at these nightly events were not much to look at, but they were a family of sorts.

She shook her head and smirked as she remembered how many of them were fat, bald, and missing teeth. Daryl Rae was the only cool cat worth a second look, compared to the other greasers who darkened their doorsteps at the trailer park on Linden Highway 17.

"Coral! Coral! Are you listening to me?" Stella blurted, snapping her fingers in front of Coral's face.

She blinked her eyes, exhausted from labor. "Yeah, I hear ya! Where the hell were you?"

"I...um...I..." Stella muttered.

"You know what?" She said, her voice getting louder and louder. "It's okay. I know you were banging Daryl Rae, and I don't blame you. He is good to us, but still. You should've been here."

Stella's mouth opened. "Yeah...he is."

Coral glared at Stella, too tired to argue.

Stella fidgeted and looked at her feet. "You delivered three weeks early! How was I supposed to know that last night was the night? I'm sorry, hun. Daryl Rae just kept kissing on me, and God knows I ain't had nothing for a month now. But I am sorry I wasn't there to help this cute little critter come out. How on Earth did you cut the cord anyhow?"

"I used my kitchen knife, ran it under boiling water to kill the germs, just like the doctor told me years ago with my first. Tied it off with a shoelace, then cut it myself. It wudn't my fault. If you'd been here instead of catting around, I wouldn't have had to do it alone." Coral said. Her eyes softened, looking at her new boy. She sighed. *Come on, she's your best friend. Do you really wanna be friendless right now? All alone?*

"Look, I'm sorry for the catting around comment. Like I said, it's okay. I don't blame you for being with Daryl Rae. I just had another man's baby, so everything's different. I can't be thinkin' about anybody but the father of this little prince," she said softly, stroking his head tenderly.

Stella sighed and held her hands out. "I'm sorry I wasn't here. I know we always check up on each other, and I said I was gonna do it and I didn't. I just didn't think you were gonna give birth so early! I mean, really! Who knew, right?"

She nodded. "Yea, I reckon that's true."

"What are the other two doin'?" Stella asked as she got up to turn on the radio.

"Ike! Jim! Y'all get in here and say hi to your Aunt Stella!" She shouted towards the bedroom.

Stella settled on a station playing an Elvis tune, something soft. Love Me Tender played as Ike and Jim, her two sons from two different fathers, poked their heads around the bedroom door. Jim's eyes darkened as he watched his mom fuss over the infant. She felt his glare and feigned a smile. "Come over here, baby. You ain't spent hardly any time with him. He's your new brother. His name is Brian."

Ike wandered closer to the crib, and she smiled as he stroked the baby's soft hair. "That's so good, Ike. That's my good boy. You know, thanks to this baby, the toys around here are gonna get a lot better soon."

"How come, Mama?" Ike asked, wide-eyed.

She kissed Brian's head. "His daddy is really rich, baby. He's gonna give me a lotta money soon. I can get us nice, new house and new clothes for you and your brother. Maybe even a nice gold tooth to fill this hole in my mouth...It's not like your trucker daddy is ever gonna give us anything except a few bucks here and there. He don't want that wife of his finding out, now does he?"

Jim grabbed Ike by the hand. "Come on Ike. Let's go play. We don't need rich daddies. We just need each other," he said, glaring at Coral.

Coral grumbled under her breath, then slapped her hand down on the rocking chair's armrest. "Ok Daddio! We sure ain't gonna get any help from your daddy either. He can't even sell vacuum cleaners like he's supposed to! He ain't good for shit."

Her tirade woke the baby, so she plopped him on her breast to suckle and be quiet.

Jim pulled Ike back inside the bedroom that they all shared and slammed the door. The noise startled Brian and his lips came unstuck from her breast, which made him squeal again. The shrill sound of his cry, the stress of the day in general, got to her. Tears flowed down her cheeks. *I can't do this no more.*

Stella picked baby Brian up and tried to comfort him while patting Coral's shoulder. "Now Coral, honey, you don't need to be second guessing yourself. You did good here. This little goldmine is gonna get you and those boys out of this dump...I just hope you're gonna take me with you, or at least help me out a little."

Coral sneered. *That's all she's doing here. Making sure her meal ticket is secure, me.*

"Don't worry about it. I got your back," Coral said.

She lit a cigarette and took a deep drag. "That shitbag, Gus, used to call me his Truck Stop Beaver Delight. Can you believe that? Hmppff... I mean, I was just a waitress, but at least that's honest work. I never turned tricks, like some of the other girls." She sighed and looked out the window. "I thought that piece of shit loved me. He said he'd leave his wife."

"They never leave their wives," Stella said.

"No shit," she blurted. "Well, at least he pays up every now and then to keep me from telling the old ball and chain."

"Do you ever get anything out of Jim's daddy?" Stella asked, making funny faces for the baby.

She saw Stella playing with Brian and smiled. She crushed out the cigarette and sat down on her dirty sofa. "Nope. Truth is, I never even knew his name."

They both sniggered.

"Well, at least Jim is gonna grow up big. Maybe he can be a ball player one day? His grades don't suck. He even gets a C now and then," she said.

Stella nodded. "Yeah, I can see that. Poor Ike will be lucky to graduate high school. I'm sorry to say it, darlin', but that one's dumb as a stump."

Coral lit another cigarette and cracked open a beer can. "Yeah, I know...want one?"

"Always," Stella sniggered. "But I reckon we need to change this little rich baby again. He's startin' to get ripe."

Coral threw her an old T-shirt and a cut-up towel. Stella changed him, wincing from the stink, then wrapped him up in the T-shirt. "He sure is a cutie pie. You better not let him call me anything but Aunt Stella."

"Yeah, he will," she said, pulling out her other breast for him to suckle on. "Look at how good he is, Stella. Nothing like those two squawkers in there."

"He's just perfect," Stella said, chugging her beer.

She looked down at him, such a sweet baby, enjoying his mama's milk. *Maybe one day I'll be a fine New Orleans lady, a mama you can be proud of. Wouldn't that be nice, sugar?*

# JACK

*November 1952, New Orleans, LA, Buchanan Oil*

LITTLE BRIAN WAS THE PRODUCT OF AN UNFORTUNATE EVENING FOR Jack Buchanan III, yet another problem on his laundry list. He took a long drag from his Montecristo Cuban cigar. *Damn it! What should I do?* He gulped down the last of his Ballantine Scotch, then slammed the solid crystal glass on the bar. "What's my daddy gonna do to fix *this*?"

He gazed out the window and looked back to the night he met Coral. He poured himself another drink and sat down. *She got pregnant to trap me. I'm not gonna fall for it. Finer minxes than her have tried that and failed. There's no way this trailer trash hussy is gonna bag herself a Buchanan by spreading her legs... Shouldn't piss her off though. I may actually want the little rugrat. He may have a purpose.* "Guess it would be nice if she had a boy."

*Coral, you were a hot little number, a real sex pot, but what have you done to me?* Taking another sip of his drink, he closed his eyes and let his mind drift to that night. It was the Mardi Gras to end all Mardi Gras. He was freshly divorced and free, ready to find some fun for the night. He certainly didn't intend to get a gal in trouble. All he wanted was to party.

# JACK

*March 1952, New Orleans, LA, French Quarter, Mardi Gras*

"Let's go boys! So many racks, so little time!" Jack shouted as he parked his convertible Corvette C-1.

"Hey baby! Look at this!" a woman shouted as she flashed her tits to the spectators on the balconies. He grinned as he saw the strings of beads seemingly pouring from the sky. His ears pricked up and his skin reeled when he heard the girls howl with pure decadent pleasure. Their voices harmonized with the bands that played wild sounds of pleasure and joy. Costumes were bright and shiny, like a parade of glittery sin. *We can be anybody we want here. I love Mardi Gras!*

He headed on to a Mardi Gras party in the French Quarter, with a few of his buddies. "We got enough beads, right guys?"

"Yeah buddy! Let's get some!" one of his friends shouted.

He never missed a Mardi Gras. He always relished in its delights, especially the women. And tonight, would be no different, except for one major thing. He was divorced and finally free of the latest bitch he married. Tonight, was a celebration.

He spotted a gorgeous waitress just a few feet away. Brunette beehive hairdo with big tits and a round ass. Not to mention her small waist with pouty lips. That's all it took for him to latch onto her like a tractor beam. *I'm gettin' me some of that. Get ready, baby. Here comes Big Jack.*

He smiled and stared at her as she waited tables, bending over seductively, showing off her assets. *Poor little thing. She's probably hard up for money. This is gonna be too easy, like taking candy from a baby. Look at her! She's sending me signals.*

He raised his drink to an air toast to her as she circulated among some of New Orleans elite. Little numbers like her were abundant as the rich and powerful reveled in a night of complete debauchery. Every fat cat in the city was there, from Congressmen to prominent entrepreneurs. Coral brought a bottle of champagne to one of the most respected businessmen in New Orleans, James Debouche, the owner of a marvelous little coffee shop he frequently visited. *Damn if his French coffee and French Dip sandwiches aren't the best I've ever eaten. Even my nanny, Ms. Beulah, can't hold a candle. And she's always been the best cook in three counties.*

He shook hands with a few people and lit his cigar. Coral approached. "Can I bring you something, sir?"

Jack smiled and clicked his tongue. "Now that's a dangerous question, sugar pants. I might ask you to bring me a glass of *you.*"

Coral blushed. "Well sir, at least for now, can I get you a drink? I need to get a few more drinks and some crawfish over there for that guy."

She pointed at James, who was now getting a lap dance from Foxy Blue, the town's most notorious stripper. He smirked. "Yeah, I'll bet he's working up a powerful appetite."

Coral chuckled.

"I'll take another Scotch, neat, darlin'."

"Yes, sir. Right away," she said, looking back at him as she walked away.

*Oh yeah, you already want me, don't you? Well, baby. Tonight, your dream is gonna come true.*

He took a deep drag of his cigar as he watched Coral approach James with his tray of crawfish. He and his posse dug into their meal, feeling young and free. He shook his head. *Tsk. Tsk. Tsk. Enjoy it while it lasts, buddy.*

James had nothing to worry about. Despite him being a family man with four lovely children and a wife that he doted on, no one would dare violate the gentlemen's agreement. He also felt relief that none of them would mention his wild nights, especially in the boardroom.

He laughed when he saw Foxy cranking up her new dance number. She gyrated and entertained her overly enthusiastic audience. *No doubt this is a good payday for her too.*

James slapped Foxy's bare backside, shouting "Shake it baby! Shake it!" Jack stepped out onto the balcony to watch the tail end of the parade.

He loved the sound of the marching bands, how the floats glided down the street, and the smell of bourbon and crawfish in the air. The necklaces were made from beautiful glass and plastic beads, inherently worthless, but there was an undeniable competitive feeling the men enjoyed as they raced to throw down all they had to bare-chested beauties. *We threw more beads out than anyone here, I reckon.* He noticed that his glass was completely empty. *Where's that little number? She said she'd bring me a Scotch.*

And there she was, with a fresh glass of Scotch, neat, just like he asked for. Jack smiled, taking the glass. She smiled back, then bit her lip.

There was something about her, he thought. She was genuinely sweet, for trailer trash. The way she batted her eyes at him, the blush of her cheek. Not the kind of thing you usually see in women of low standing.

Physically, she was stunning. It wasn't just her hourglass shape or her round ass. Her hair was pitch black and her eyes were as blue as his mother's favorite sapphire ring. He stared at her full lips.

"Is there anything else I can get you, sir?" She asked.

"Well sugar, you can get me a minute of your precious time as soon as I'm done with this here party! I do declare that you are the prettiest thing I've seen here all night."

She giggled and blushed. "You are the charmer, ain't ya? I mean, *aren't* you?"

He grinned at her. "Baby, you have no idea," he said, handing her a room key. "Now, why don't you take this room key and meet me in there, in an hour. I'm gonna bring you a bottle of this fine champagne and some juicy strawberries with whipped cream!"

"Mr. Buchanan, I don't know what you've heard, but I'm not a *working* girl, if you catch my drift."

"No darlin'. You got me all wrong!" He stood closer to her. "I just wanna spend some time with a friendly face who isn't here to kiss my ass. You know, I just wanna spend time *talking* to you, honey. I need a friend tonight. I don't mean that I'm trying some funny business or anything."

He followed his declaration of innocence with another beautiful bright smile, followed by a wink. *Oh, she's swooning. You still got it, Big Daddy. Better get some rubbers though. Dollars to donuts this gal knows about my money. She's picked up on the scent of that, along with a little Buchanan charm.*

She accepted the key and their hands touched for a moment, both looking into each other's eyes. She blushed and giggled. "I'll see you later...Jack."

Jack nodded with a wink. Coral's blush turned crimson. She went back to work and finished the hour, clocked out, then went to his room. Tonight, was going to be a night to remember.

# JACK

*November 1952, New Orleans LA, Buchanan Oil*

JACK TOOK ANOTHER LONG DRAG OF HIS CIGAR. *I WAS HAMMERED that night, otherwise I wouldn't have let the rubber break. What the hell was I thinking?*

That night was fun, but it changed his life in a way he didn't expect. She was cute, no doubt about it, sexy too, but in a low-class kind of way. *Damn it! I'm not gonna lose my stake in a multi-million-dollar company for a great "piece of ass".*

Of course, he only had himself to blame. He had had too much to drink, and he knew it. He didn't remember much after she sashayed into his room, still wearing her uniform. He took a long drag of his cigar. "I've gotta take control of this. Daddy can't do this. If he pays her off, I may never get the kid."

Jack's former wives and mistresses never gave him any sons. He wondered if he was shooting blanks. The last thing he wanted to do was get married *again*. He was already pushing forty, and he didn't want the drama of another failed marriage. Besides, he reckoned that he and marriage were just not meant to be, otherwise one of the other three would have worked out. He exhaled as he thought of his father. *The old bastard will never let me hear the end of it if I never have a son to inherit the family name and legacy. Can't believe it was her to make it happen.*

He enjoyed being in control, so his lack of memory of the night bothered him.

"Oh yeah Coral. You were quite the little honey pot, so eager to please me. I didn't see it coming, literally...Now, what the hell am I gonna do with you? How am I gonna get that child, especially if it's a boy, without having to take you too."

He entered the drawing room to find Jack Senior, patriarch of the Buchanan Oil legacy, chewing on his fat cigar, dressed to impress. His waistcoat was cut from the finest cloth, custom made, and his watch cost more than most people make in a year. Jack Junior gulped. His father didn't even look back at him. "Explain yourself boy! What's this about you knocking up some trailer trash?"

Jack squirmed as his father puffed on the cigar in his mouth. "Are you gonna let her raise your heir in squalor?"

"No Daddy," he said.

Jack Sr. crushed out his cigar in the ashtray, "Here's what's gonna happen. You're gonna pay the little bitch off, and I ain't never gonna see her in this house. You understand?"

"Yes sir," he said. "Excuse me, Daddy."

Jack burst out of the room. That old bastard always knew how to make him feel small. "Maybe I'll just marry her to spite you, but I'll have my heir to Buchanan Oil, and he'll be raised by *me*, not *you*!"

Jack poured himself another glass and walked in front of a full-length mirror. He toasted himself. "Here's looking at you, Jack. It's gonna be okay."

# LAURA

*February 1977, New Orleans, City Jail*

LAURA LYNN BEAUFORD BUCHANAN, FORMER ALABAMA SOCIALITE, sat on the bed of her New Orleans city jail cell, clutching her belly. If her daddy failed, she'd be charged with the murder of her husband and Delta Dawn Johnson. She didn't know the woman. *Who was Delta Dawn? Why was she there?*

An investigator had questioned her earlier. She was so distraught, she forgot one of the cardinal rules of her father–never let them question you without your lawyer present. The interrogation stopped right there. She took a drag of her cigarette and sighed.

*My life's gone with the wind. I suppose,* she thought, blowing a puff of her cigarette through the bars of her cell. Her nails were still freshly polished in red nail varnish, but her rings and other jewelry had been confiscated when the police booked her. *Did he make love to her?* She asked herself. It was only natural to assume they were lovers, for the woman was laying naked in bed with *her* husband. She reminded herself that it was okay to be curious. After all, maybe it was a murder/suicide? Yes, knowing who Delta Dawn was seemed rather pressing at the moment, she figured.

*Why would he do that? Did he love me at all?* She took another drag of the cigarette. *He was happy with me. I know he was.* After all, they had been together

for years, but married for only short six months, still in the honeymoon phase...
except for the pregnancy. Sure, to get pregnant that quickly felt a little trashy, but
looking back on it, she was grateful to have this child on the way, a bit of him that
will live on with her. *Unless I go to prison for the rest of my life.* Laura sighed, then
sobbed uncontrollably for a few minutes.

She thought for a moment and her brow furrowed. *Did Coral have anything to
do with this? Surely not! That old bat never liked me, not from day one.* The
memory of that meeting would never leave her mind. It was a hot day in June, and
she must have gone through twenty dresses that day, hoping to impress Brian's
mother, the one who made it through such strife.

Laura was no stranger to strife. She lost her mother early and had to become
very mature, very quickly. Her father was almost destroyed when he lost the love
of his life. Cancer is, after all, one of the most painful and slow deaths that one can
face. Even still, it felt small compared to growing up with seven siblings, living on
crops and arts and crafts. Coral was never truly someone until she snagged Jack
Buchanan, but oh my, what a thing to be known for! *Poor lady*, Laura thought.
*I'm going to do my best to make her happy.*

# LAURA

"I can't believe I'm gonna meet the famous Coral today," Laura said, as applied the finishing touches to her makeup.

Brian combed his hair. "Yep. I hope you wanna stay married to me after you meet her."

Laura giggled. "She can't be that bad."

"Oh, sugar. You ain't seen nothing yet," he said.

Since Brian and Laura were newlyweds, and still in college, they thought it best to move into Brian's family home, for a couple months at least, a place where they'd be supported. It was like living in a fairytale, plus they even had their own entrance to the property, which meant privacy. Laura was ready for their first visitor. *Well, almost ready,* she thought. *Just one final check.*

She looked in the mirror and smiled. She wore a yellow floral blouse, bell bottom pants to match, and platform shoes to make her look taller, as she always felt sensitive about being only five feet tall.

As she came out of the room, she gulped when she saw Coral. Laura smiled, hoping she wasn't looking too eager. She immediately offered Coral some refreshments and invited her to sit down.

Was she trying too hard to make her mother-in-law feel welcome? She hoped no one noticed how nervous she was. Coral herself seemed to be in good spirits, and all Laura wanted was to help Brian bridge the terrible gap that had grown between him and his mother.

"Oh, I'm so happy to meet you, Miss Coral. Brian has said wonderful things about you." she said, shifting her position, and slightly grasping her hands.

"Has he now?" Coral snipped. "Well, I hope he's had at least a *few* nice things to say. Our last communication wasn't so *nice*."

"Mother!" Brian blurted.

"Oh...*mother*? Since when do you call me, *mother*? I've always been 'mama' before, before your hoity toity daddy got his hooks in you! Since you turned your back on your brothers! Have you ever thought of them, as you were spending time at your fancy school?"

"Oh, of course I thought about them! I still think of them. I've spent a lot of time with them lately, but I'm sure they didn't tell you that. It's *you* that ended things between us! Don't you forget that. After you came to the house that night, I knew that you *gave me away*, and I also know that you thought you were doing what's best for me."

Coral's bottom lip quivered. Brian held her hand and kissed it. "I had privileges, and that was nice. But I grew up without a mom, and that hurt. I've tried to reach out to you, but you never replied.

"I just didn't know what to say," Coral murmured.

Laura nodded. "Ms. Coral, Brian loves you."

Everyone seemed to relax for a moment. Coral smiled. "I'm so glad my son found a fine lady such as yourself."

"Thank you, ma'am," Laura said.

The peaceful reprieve Laura provided them didn't last, for only a half hour later, as they had their first course, the conversation turned dramatic once again, when Coral brought up a painful memory that everyone would have preferred to forget.

"I thought at least you'd want a friendship with me," Brian said as his eyes welled with tears. He looked away, then cleared his throat. "I did it because I felt sorry for you."

"Sorry for me!?" How dare you, you smart ass little shit! How fucking dare you!" At this, Coral stomped away, muttering loudly to herself. "I never should've come back here! What was I thinking? Tell that fancy butler to call me a cab! You can afford it."

Brian ran after her down the driveway, but before he left, he did as she asked. "Call a cab for my mother, please."

"Yes, sir," the butler replied.

Laura watched in shock as Coral stormed out. *What a classy dame! My poor husband. Look what he puts up with.*

She'd never seen such ill manners in all her natural born life, but at the same time, she felt a little sorry for Coral. Things had going well until they started talking about the night of their drunken visit to the Buchanan home, and it seemed as though none of them were willing to let it go. *Stubborn Southern families. Uff!*

She looked at Brian and grasped his arm. "I'm so sorry, honey. I really wanted her to like me and for you both to make peace. Why did she say all that? And why on Earth did you encourage her to talk about *that* visit? I made her a lovely dinner, and she just walked away."

"Don't worry about it, baby. I've turned my back on that side of the family, except for Jim and Ike, and some of them aren't incredibly happy about it. That's all you gotta know. They're toxic, always have been. Don't need that in our lives."

Brian kissed her. She wouldn't pursue this conversation any further. Still, it bothered her. Family shouldn't have bad blood. At least, that's how she was raised.

# LAURA

LAURA WINCED AS SHE REMEMBERED. SHE HAD LEARNED TO ACCEPT that Coral was in her life, but she never felt comfortable around her. Still, could she have? She shook her head. *No! A mother wouldn't do this to her child. She's an ill-mannered skank, but I do believe she loved him. But who would hate Brian so much?*

To accuse anyone of anything, proof would be required. She looked at the clock on the wall. "When's Daddy gettin' here?"

She felt sick, then remembered that she needed to eat. Ever since she got pregnant, she had to remind herself to eat at regular intervals to avoid nausea. She felt worlds better if she spread out her food into small snacks all day, instead of three-square meals. Of course, at the moment, under the current circumstances, she didn't feel hungry at all. If she weren't pregnant, there'd be no way she'd think of food at all.

She looked around at the other cells. Many of the women didn't look much different than she did. One may not even be able to tell that they had done something illegal at first glance. Well, except for the prostitutes, she figured.

They seemed the only ones capable of laughing at a time like this. But were they laughing for real? Or just covering up for their feelings. Laura banged on her bars to get the officer's attention.

"Hey! Excuse me?"

The officer on duty approached. "Yeah? What can I do for you, princess?"

Laura sighed. "When I was arrested, they were told that I'm pregnant."

"Congratulations," the officer blurted. "So, what do you want from me? A baby shower?"

"Just a little food would be good, if that's no bother," she said.

"Fine, I'll see what I can do, but this ain't no five-star restaurant, so you eat what you get."

"I understand. Thank you," she said.

Somehow, she had to distract herself, at least until her food came. She wanted to think of Brian and the early years of their relationship, but first, she thought of her father. "Maybe I should have listened to Daddy?"

# LAURA

*September 1973, New Orleans, LA, University*

THE EARLY DAYS AT LOUISIANA STATE UNIVERSITY...

The first day of orientation was one she'd never forget. Her father pulled the last of her luggage out of the car. He looked at her, then at the ground, then back at her. "Darlin', I wish you'd stay close by. I mean it looks like a nice place and all, with fine people, but I could've gotten you into any Alabama college you wanted. The University of Alabama was just dying to take you! And you know what?"

"What, Daddy?" she asked, amused.

Larry put his hands in his pockets and took on his politician's stance. He began one of his talks, trying to convince her into coming back to Alabama. She didn't listen, but she was damn amused at how hard he tried. After all, he was so adorable when he acted so protective.

"The women in our hometown could've used a role model like you. They still live in the dark ages there. Lord, you would have gotten me every female vote in town!"

She smiled. "Oh Daddy. A girl's gotta grow up some time! I know it's hard to let me go, but you're a brave man to let your only daughter leave home and have some adventure. I'd say that's mighty progressive Daddy! And don't forget that you taught me how to fight, to shoot, to camp. Heck, you even taught me Morse code! Ha!"

Her father shooed her away playfully. "You are a politician in the makin'! Aren't ya?"

She giggled.

"Your mother would have been so proud of you." he said, looking down at the ground. "She was a strong independent woman too. God rest her soul."

Her father teared up. She grabbed his arm and squeezed. "Oh, Daddy. Mamma would have also been proud of *you*. You've been everything a young girl could want in a father and more."

"If I hadn't left her alone that night," Larry sniffed. "If I had been home, I could've said goodbye, told her I love her one more time."

"Don't do that to yourself, Daddy," Laura said. "Come on now. It wasn't your fault that you weren't there when she passed, and you told her you loved her almost every day. I heard you."

Larry sighed. "Well, at least I get to be here to see you off properly."

Laura squeezed his shoulders. "Exactly! Now, let's go see what my dorm room looks like! Your little girl is in college, so let's focus on that."

Just a few months later, she met Brian, and the rest was history. He stood out among the other frat boys, and she became totally smitten. "That's one far out looking dreamboat," she muttered to her friends. He was so handsome and had such a beautiful smile, but there was something *vulnerable* about him.

Every day after that, she hoped that he'd ask her out. She made eye contact, smiled. Sent all the right signals that she would be interested, without looking like a tart, of course.

He finally worked up the nerve to ask her out, and only then did it occur to her that she really didn't know him very well, so she began to ask around. Finding his story wasn't hard. After all, it's not easy hiding the fact that you're sitting pretty, Buchanan style. That's why it surprised her when he went for the humble approach for their first date.

She remembered what he said about that date once they were married. "You were so banging that night," he mused. "A straight up fox. And when you called me out, oh God, I thought I may lose you. My heart almost stopped beating."

Looking back on that tender memory, a tear streamed down her face, and she looked up to Heaven. "Why? Why, God? Why him?"

The few tears turned into many as she curled up on her cot into a fetus position, pulling the scratchy blanket over her. She sobbed uncontrollably, wiping her tears into the pillow.

She prayed for a little sleep.

# Laura

*July 1974, New Orleans, LA, University*

Any woman would have been taken with how handsome Brian was, his black curly hair and his perfect white teeth. She always beamed when she thought of his million-dollar smile. Brian looked so much like his father, Jack Jr. at his age. She thought of how it was to meet Jack Buchanan II. Brian's father was far more pleasant to meet than his mother. After all, he was a walking legend, like Jack Sr. and his great grandfather, Tobias Buchanan, before. *What a character that man was!* She reminisced.

Tobias Buchanan, as everyone learned in history class, was a famous explorer, discovered one of Louisiana's first oil reserves. He was as old as dirt at that time, after enjoying a fruitful career as a gold miner in Alaska in the 1800's, during the Yukon gold rush.

Her first introduction to Jack was at a family dinner. As they ate that evening, Jack told her the entire story of Brian's life, even though it wasn't exactly a fairy-tale.

This revelation was perfectly paired with a meal of barbecue chicken and red wine. Jack had waiters there, serving the meal, so that everyone could relax. She listened with great interest and intensity whilst enjoying the Southern cuisine.

Jack was surprisingly handsome, given his history of alcohol consumption. One may have expected him to be red faced or have a paunch, but no. There before her, she saw a stacked silver fox. Dark hair with streaks of grey in just the right places, and a well-groomed mustache to make him appear quite the debonair dish. *I can see that Brian is gonna hold his looks well as he ages. Good to know.* She thought.

He was digging in as though he hadn't eaten or drank in decades. He gulped down the last of his wine. "Yes Laura, I saved this young man, saved him from a life of debauchery."

"Debauchery? Surely, you're not serious. Not your son," she blurted, putting out her cigarette.

"Baby," Brian said. "I wish you wouldn't smoke so much."

She sipped her water and looked at him.

"Leave this beautiful young woman alone, son. I'm sure she'll quit when she's expecting my first grandson," Jack said with a smile.

She almost choked on the water. "Grandson? Well Sir, he's gotta pop the question first I reckon."

"Now, you two nosey bodies...I'll do it when I'm ready. No rushing," Brian waved his fork for emphasis before continuing.

"Daddy, maybe Laura doesn't need to hear all that gnarly history?"

Jack slammed his hand on the table. "Nonsense, son! If she's gonna be a part of our family, she should know about that mother of yours and your mongrel brothers. She needs to go in with her eyes wide open."

Jack then made absolutely sure her eyes were open about it all, at least *his* version of it. He let her know he couldn't be happier for his son, how he loved seeing Brian this happy. This was the culmination of all his efforts to be sure Brian would lead a great life, not the life Coral would have given him. Brian had lived with Jack since he was fifteen years old, because under Coral's influence, Brian wouldn't have amounted to anything.

She nodded, noticing a few pictures on the wall, as he yammered on. Jack with at least two women, wearing wedding attire. "Were those your former wives?" she asked, pointing to the pictures.

"Yeah," Jack grunted. "I was married twice before and engaged once to another woman. None of them gave me children...I guess, in a weird way, Brian's mother was a blessing to me, no matter what grief she caused. I needed a son to pass down this family legacy. It's all gonna be *his* one day."

"Yep." Brian blurted. "He did actually marry my mother for a short time though, so technically you were married three times, Daddy."

Jack stared at him, and they all paused while the waiters cleared the table and served coffee. Once they were out of earshot, he felt comfortable to carry on talking about personal matters.

Jack rolled his eyes. "Yes, you are right. I made a prenup deal with her, when he was about fourteen, so all she'd get out of me was a small settlement. We were only married for six months." Jack looked at her, and for a split second, she noticed a softness in his eyes that made her heart swell.

"She made good on that and opened her own restaurant with the money. Agreed to the settlement and to give me full custody of Brian, so I could bring him up right," Jack said.

She took a sip of her coffee and lit another cigarette. Brian rolled his eyes, but she ignored him and turned to Jack. "So, she just gave him up? After living here with you?"

"She tried to fight, but all I had to do was offer her a little more money. She signed those papers real quick." Jack noticed Brian's face. "I'm sorry son. But you really were better off without her."

She squeezed Brian's hand. He lifted it and kissed her hand.

"Yes, Laura," Jack said. "I'm so proud of my boy, for getting through all that, and finally getting to live his destiny as my rightful heir."

"Sounds like you're talking about royalty," she replied with a chuckle, flicking her cigarette ashes.

He put down his cup and spoon and looked at her sternly. "Yes, we are... Southern royalty, and we take care of our offspring."

Her eyebrow raised. "So, that's why you never adopted Brian's brothers when you were married to his mom?"

Jack gulped down the last swallow of coffee and snapped his fingers so that a waiter would bring him a shot glass of whiskey. Brian winced.

"Damn right...They're not my concern. I'm not their father." Jack said, taking the shot of whiskey.

"Does Brian have any siblings on your side, Jack?" Laura asked.

"No!" Jack barked, slamming the whiskey glass on the table, nearly shattering it.

Laura and Brian looked at him, eyes widened, but he swallowed, smiled, and checked himself. "Sorry about an old coot like me. I lose myself when I drink Wild Turkey...No, Laura, not to my knowledge."

He clearly wanted to change the subject and told her about Jack's early days in his home. "Once Brian was under my roof, the first thing I did was buy the boy a proper wardrobe," he said, smiling.

She watched Jack's face soften as he recalled that first shopping trip. "All those years of paying Coral child support hadn't done anything for his poor wardrobe choices. I'll never forget the look on his face when I got him into his first suit."

"He looked great, and this was an important step in learning what it takes to become a Buchanan. 'One must always dress like a boss!' That's what I told him, Laura. It's what my daddy told me."

"Well, you certainly did a good job, Mr. Buchanan. Brian always looks amazing." Laura said.

"For heaven's sake, young lady. Call me Jack! Well, at least until *after* the wedding. Then, you can call me Dad," he said with a wicked smile, winking at Brian.

"Ha, okay Dad," Brian said, rolling his eyes and sinking into his chair.

"Don't slouch, son. A man should always be standing up straight. You're large and in charge. Have *that* attitude and the gals will all think you're the cat's pajamas. Remember that?" Jack said with a smile. "Remember when I told you that?"

"Yes, Daddy. I remember. I guess I was slouching so I could get away from this story. Do we have to rehash *everything*?" Brian sighed.

Jack continued telling the story to Laura, determined to fill her in on it all, as if it were a member's initiation. Brian sunk into his chair, trying to disappear. Jack went on, explaining how that first shopping trip turned out to be great. This look on his face was one of pure bliss, as he reminisced about that happy day.

Laura winked at Brian, as they both settled in to hear the tale. What a joy it was to be with them that day, to witness how proud Jack was of his son.

As the story went, the day started out well...

# JACK

*March 1966, New Orleans, LA*

HE TOOK BRIAN TO HIS FIRST SUIT SHOP TO GET HIM FITTED. BRIAN grinned throughout the whole experience, making Jack's heart swell with pride. He'd make his son feel good about living with him, because Ike and Jim had certainly gotten their claws into his way of life.

Night after night, the three boys would go out, drink alcohol, smoke pot, and associate with the wrong types of teenagers. He did have a private eye looking in on Brian's activities, hoping to use that against Coral later when a custody arrangement had to be made.

She held out so hard. She didn't just want a settlement without marriage. The only way she was giving him Brian was to be Ms. Jack Buchanan, even if it was just for a little while. Once she finally got him to agree to marry her, his private eye reported that she was continuously purchasing ingredients for Hoodoo spells, trying to make him fall hopelessly in love with her. *I guess that one backfired on her ass*, he thought, chuckling.

Jack only loved his boy, but unfortunately Coral was part of the package, at least for a few months. Long enough to give her a little money and social status, the two things that she always wanted, minus the opportunity to live in the Buchanan mansion and have marital relations with him.

The thought of that still made him angry. Thankfully, he cut short his involvement with her and got his prize at last. A son of his own, an heir, a boy he could teach and guide.

Indeed, the boy's first day under his roof was a special day, the first day of Brian's *real* life, when he'd find out who he was destined to be. They got home from a long day of shopping, getting their shoes shined and enjoying a trip to a proper barbershop. Brian's face lit up with sheer excitement when he saw Jack's sprawling lush mansion in broad daylight. "I still can't believe I live here now."

"Come on son, let's go get you properly moved into your quarters," Jack said, putting his arm around his son's shoulder.

"My quarters? But I thought..." Brian asked.

"Yes! You didn't think you're just getting a bedroom, did you?" Brian looked puzzled as his brow crinkled. "Oh no son, you've got a small apartment in the house that's all yours. You have a TV, a sitting room, and a small library just for you!"

Jack loved the look of wonder on his face, followed by a warm smile. "Dad, do I really get to live here now? Always?"

Jack put both hands on his shoulders to address him face to face, "Yes. I'm only sorry I didn't do this sooner. Should've gotten you as far as possible from all that trailer trash a long time ago."

Brian winced at the reference to *trailer trash*. "I just didn't wanna face my daddy for a long time cuz he and I have had a...well, a rocky past when it comes to my *relationships*. But I finally stood up to the old man, just before he died. Daddy was sorry he never got to meet you."

Jack regretted that most of all, the fact that he could never get the old coot's approval. Tough old bastard. A part of him knew he'd never have it, but it mattered less when he had his own boy.

# LAURA

*July 1974, New Orleans, Buchanan mansion*

AFTER HEARING ABOUT BRIAN'S EARLY DAYS WITH HIS FATHER, LAURA put her hand on Jack's arm. "Thank you for sharing that sweet story with me, Jack. I'm so happy to be here right now. Brian introduced me to Coral, but I don't think she liked me very much."

Jack rolled his eyes. "Don't worry about her. All she needs is a little money waved in front of her nose, and she'll come around."

Laura and Brian glanced at one another uncomfortably. Jack didn't seem to notice. *God I'm glad Brian doesn't say things like that. Her sweetheart couldn't think like that. How the hell did I get so lucky?*

# LAURA

LAURA'S THOUGHTS DRIFTED BACK TO THE PRESENT. SHE STRUGGLED to look at the clock on the far wall. Still no sign of her father. She lay on the hard mattress on the cramped steel cot, wrapped up in a thin scratchy blanket, thinking of every moment of the past, searching for anything that could lead her to the truth. A tear streamed down her red face.

Her back hurt. Her earlier requests for an extra pillow fell on deaf ears. *No special privileges for pregnant ladies here. Savages.* "I can't sleep. God, please let me sleep."

She looked at the bucket in the corner, placed there for her toileting needs. Her brow furrowed. *I have to pee so badly. That looks so gross.* She thought. "No choice."

Carefully trying not to attract attention, she lifted her dress enough to perch upon the bucket and relieve herself. Pregnant women pee a lot, so she didn't feel that there was any getting out of that embarrassing situation. *They could at least give us some toilet paper. Unacceptable! Just because I'm in jail doesn't mean I'm a farm animal.* She scoffed.

She grunted and threw the blanket off, stood up. There was no window, nowhere to see the outside world, and her heart started to race. After she did her thing, she lit her next to last cigarette and scoffed.

"Where's Daddy? What's taking him so long?"

She stretched and tried to get comfortable on the cot again, though it was a futile endeavor. She teared up, clenching her fists, scared to sob out loud and ... If only Brian was here to spoon her gently as she slept. She knew he was gone, but she could still feel him. He had always made her feel so loved, so wanted. *Now he's gone! God, if they only knew how much I loved that man.*

Now's not the time for tears. No. She'd need to be strong. She wiped away her tears and remembered their college days, when they had become so close, sharing everything, even their secrets. The sordid history of his family, his mother, their poor living conditions, and how much he loved his brothers. Their devotion to one another made her wish for a sibling. Her heart sank when she thought of what they must be going through right now. *Who could have done this? Brian was the sweetest man alive, wouldn't hurt a fly. God, why? Why did you take my love from me?*

# LAURA

LAURA REMEMBERED BRIAN TELLING HER THAT HIS FIRST YEAR OF college brought many changes. After spending two years with his dad, training to manage the company, he felt like a true Buchanan. He'd learned much about the oil business when he interned at Buchanan Oil in the summers to learn the ropes. His father had insisted that a business degree would teach him modern strategies and give him the credentials to command a great deal of respect.

One night they talked about having children, and it was the sweetest night of their courtship. Laura Lynn smiled through her tears when she remembered that starlit night, when they sat on the porch of that little Baton Rouge bed-and-breakfast that they loved to stay in.

"I think we'll have a boy and a girl. The girl will be 'Rosemarie' and the boy will be 'Ronald'." Laura said, lying in his arms.

He winced. "What is it with you and 'R' names? Those are horrible! No, I won't have that for my *fine* offspring. No ma'am. First, these lovely hips are gonna provide me with three sons and two daughters." He held her close and stroked the hips in question in a very distracting manner.

"Five kids! Why Mr. Buchanan, that's a lot of children! You better get me a cook and a nanny to help out with all that work," Laura had joked.

Brian gave her a long, slow kiss. She grabbed his head, running her hands through his hair. When their lips parted, he looked deeply into her eyes. "Whatever my queen wants. That's what she'll get. Our children will be princes and princesses. We're gonna have an amazing life, baby."

# LAURA

"LAURA BUCHANAN!" THE GUARD, A BURLY WOMAN WITH A VISIBLE mustache, called out.

"Yes?" Laura replied.

"You have a visitor. Come with me." The guard commanded.

The guard led her to a visiting area, where her father stood waiting. Her breath hitched "Oh Daddy!" she yelped, rushing to throw her arms around him.

They embraced for a moment. The moment was short lived. "No contact!" The guard barked. "Sit down at the table."

They sat down. "Are you and the baby okay?"

She nodded.

"Don't you worry, little gal. I'm gonna get you out on bail, and we're gonna prove you didn't do this! My girl could never do such a thing! I know you loved that boy so much. And I *know* what a gentle girl I raised. How dare they accuse you!"

"Well, guess I was stupid enough to be in the wrong place at the wrong time," Laura said.

"You think you were set up to be there, darlin'?" Larry asked.

Laura Lynn looked up at the corners of the wall. Her brow furrowed and her eyes darkened. "Yes! Definitely. I can't be sure of who would do this, but my mind keeps going to his brothers. I'm not saying they did it. God knows, it would be unthinkable."

"Why do you think it's a possibility?" Larry folded his arms. "I thought he got along well with his brothers."

"He did. I just wonder if it was a *jealousy* thing. I dunno, Daddy," Laura groaned. "Even as I say that out loud, it's hard to wrap my mind around."

"You think they were jealous enough to want him dead?" Larry asked.

"I don't wanna think so," she said as doubt clouded her mind.

"They never let their jealousy show to Brian, but I saw the side glances they flashed at him when he wasn't looking. He really missed those days when they were kids, and those two made him feel at home again. I think it was because his mother gave him to his daddy."

Larry winced. "Well, Coral really did him a favor by getting him out of that trailer park. Surely, he knew that...didn't he?"

"He did. He didn't blame her too much for taking the settlement and making something out of herself, but still. He still felt like she gave him up for money and status. That hurts a boy, even if you understand the reason. His brothers made him feel accepted and important, maybe even to her?"

Laura's eyes started to water at the thought of it.

"Daddy?" Laura said, her voice shaky.

Larry took her hand, despite the guard's dirty look. "What baby? What is it?"

Tears streamed down her cheeks, the thought boring into her mind. "Do you think his mama had anything to do with it?"

Larry exhaled. "It's unthinkable! What kind of mother would do that? Even one as selfish and gold diggin' as her? She got that settlement money. Was she gonna get more if he died?"

"He left everything to me, but if I fry for his murder, that only leaves his mother and those two brothers to take it all."

Laura sobbed. "They could be plotting my death right now, the three of them, rubbing their grubby hands together, imagining all the money they'll end up with once I'm electrocuted for this heinous crime."

He grabbed both her hands, but the guard consciously looked the other way and let it happen. "Don't worry darlin', I'm gonna defend you myself, and we are gonna get through this together! I'm not gonna let those trashy pieces of shit destroy my daughter or our family. Do you understand me?"

"Yes, Daddy. I do need your help. I don't have anybody else...But just so you know, I *do* believe his brothers loved him, but they've always followed a desperate path. The promise of that kind of money could outweigh family. Happens all the time. People have killed for a lot less," Laura said.

"But what about Brian's father, Jack?" Larry asked.

Laura looked up and her lips pressed into a hard line. She whimpered. Jack still had to be told about his son's murder. No one knew his whereabouts or even if he was alive to tell him about anything. She looked at the floor and sighed, "There has not been any contact or sightings. He's been gone so long there's talk of declaring him as missing, presumed dead."

Supposedly, Jack was in the Middle East, but no one knew for sure exactly where he went. All they knew was he was on a special mission for the U.S. government to try and calm political tensions, to finally end the OPEC oil crisis. He was one of many influential men representing the American oil industry. "Brian's been heading up Buchanan Oil for a little over a year now."

"I didn't know he had that much responsibility on his shoulders," Larry said.

Laura smiled. "He bore it well, the crown. He was the prince, after all," she sighed and folded her arms. "I couldn't believe that he wanted to take a couple days to get down to 'Nawlins with me, but he said we deserved a break."

Larry rubbed his chin thoughtfully. She nodded, knowing what he was thinking.

"Before Jack left, he put Brian in charge of *everything*, the whole operation," she said. "Brian was proud to accept the challenge from his father, and I was there when he shook his father's hand to seal the deal. But now, after the rumors that the American delegation was attacked and many were possibly killed, everyone fears the worst. There's no confirmation. No one's found a body or reported any evidence he's dead."

"Dear Lord Jesus," Larry said, shaking his head.

"I reckon it's time I told you about the last day Brian saw his Daddy," she said.

Larry sat up straighter, bracing himself for a sad tale.

# LARRY

*February 1977, New Orleans, County Jail*

LARRY SIGHED AND SAT BACK AFTER LAURA TOLD HIM. HE SHOOK HIS head.

"Lord have mercy."

"Did anyone else know that Brian was in charge, that he was the sole heir to Jack's fortune? Oh, and who was that woman he was in bed with?"

Laura shook her head and bit her bottom lip. Larry winced. *She must be thinking of something awful. I shouldn't have mentioned that girl. Dammit! God help her.* He hated seeing what this was doing to his baby girl.

"The woman. Her name was Delta Dawn. But that's all I know. As for who knew? I'd bet anything his brothers knew about him being in charge, although I can't think of a time, they let on about it. Must be a lot smarter than they look. Everyone in the company knew, though. Jack signed papers to give Brian all the necessary authority."

"Delta Dawn, like the song?" Larry asked.

"Yeah, I reckon that's just like the song. Wow...anyhow, I haven't been able to find out anything about her, not really," Laura said. "Imagine that. I'm accused of murdering a girl I don't know from anyone, and no one in here will tell me a goddamn thing."

She looked at her father, then sighed. "Poor Jack. I wonder where he is. I really don't feel like he's dead. Don't have any proof, but surely some evidence would have surfaced by now. Ever since he went to the Middle East... We knew his location and itinerary were classified, so we weren't allowed to contact him. Poor man doesn't know what's happened to Brian. Imagine the horror of coming back, just to find out your child is not just dead...murdered."

She sobbed. "I'm going to prison for the rest of my life! If I don't fry. God help him if he comes back, and I'm gone too. If he finds Coral raising my baby."

Larry's eyes watered, so he cleared his throat and sucked up his fear, just like a good soldier.

"Nope. No ma'am. We are *not* going to do this! We are the Beauford family, and we don't just lay down and die, right?"

Laura squeezed his hand, nodding. The expression on his face changed as he grabbed his chest and coughed. Not an ordinary cough, but a severe coughing fit, as if his lungs were full of sand. Everyone stared.

He doubled over and pulled his handkerchief out of his breast pocket. He held it against his mouth and tried to stop but kept coughing, his face turning a dark shade of red. The guard spoke into her walkie talkie, "Can someone bring a glass of water right away? And possibly a paramedic? There's a visitor here with severe coughing, and he is struggling to breathe."

Within minutes, a cafeteria worker brought Larry a glass of ice water. Everyone watched as he took a couple of deep swigs. He exhaled loudly, struggling to sit upright on the chair. "Well, I do apologize to everyone in here. Don't know what came over me. I didn't mean to alarm, y'all."

"Are you all right, Daddy?" Laura asked. "That sounded horrible! Have you been to a doctor?"

Larry stuffed the handkerchief into his pocket, then shooed her away. "Yes, oh, lordy, yes, I am fine. Don't fuss over me. Reckon I'm only tired, and my throat was just really dry. This water has got me feeling right as rain! Now, let's get on with things."

Laura looked at him, another tear rolling down her cheek. "Oh Daddy. What would I do without you?"

"Well, hopefully, you won't have to know that darlin," he said, standing to indicate it was about time to go.

They looked at each other for a moment. "Are you sure this wasn't something serious?" She asked him again.

He smiled, holding her hand. "I've got this, little gal. Spend all your energy on staying healthy for that child's sake and getting out of here. That's what you need to focus on now, not your old fart of a father. I'll go check in with the warden and get you a doctor's visit scheduled and some vitamins."

"Oh, my goodness, you're not an old fart." Laura blurted. "You're a stubborn old codger! The worst patient ever, too! I bet you didn't go to any doctor."

Larry looked straight into her eyes. He knew that she knew that he meant business when he gave her this look. He'd shown her that face a million times when she was little and she was inches away from him *skinning her hide*, as he put it. "This is handled. What isn't handled is *your* situation. Understand? Drop it."

"Yes, sir," she replied.

Once he'd laid down the law with her, he went right back to being the big teddy bear she always remembered when things were good. "I wanna hug you so bad, honey. But that guard would probably have a hissy fit. Guess it's good they let me clutch your hand...Hey, now where's that strong woman I raised? Remember, I'm the only feminist in our town!"

Larry's mouth curled into a playful smile as he tried to cheer Laura up. She appreciated the gesture, and there was something about his face and the way his eyes twinkled that filled her with hope. She managed to smile through her tears rolling down her cheeks.

"Thank you, Daddy. Thank God you came. I do feel better, but please don't let those boys or Coral know you're helping me. Just stay away from them. Remember, we're talking about millions *of dollars* in inheritance. There's probably nothing they won't do for that money! Including killing you...maybe?" She sighed, obviously not convinced of what she was saying.

"Please get some security guards. Take some precautions, Daddy. You're a mayor. You can pull some strings, right? Promise me, Daddy."

His eyes softened. He nodded, "Yes, little gal. I will stay safe to be here for you. I promise I'll bring a security guard to protect me."

Laura exhaled, as if she'd been holding her breath for ages. She smiled. "Thank you, Daddy. You're all I've got. Can't let them take you too. I wouldn't survive if they sent me to prison, and if you're gone, they'll get me next and have their disgusting hands all over my baby's inheritance."

"Time's up!" The guard barked.

Getting up to leave, Larry glanced at her one last time, then squeezed her hand. He slipped her a pack of cigarettes that she quickly put into her sleeve.

Larry smiled cautiously. "The docs used to tell your mother that smoking would calm her nerves, and I know they still say that, but I just don't know...guess you gotta do what you can to get through this."

"I definitely do," she said. "Thank you for being here for me, Daddy. I love you."

Larry grinned. "Love you too, Darlin'. And don't you worry. I'll get to the bottom of this, no matter what! Those trailer trash scum bags aren't gonna hurt my baby girl anymore. No one is. I'm gonna see to that. Just remember I love you, and I'm here now."

# LAURA

*February 1977, New Orleans, County Jail*

LAURA NODDED AND PUT ON A BRAVE FACE, WAVING GOODBYE AS THE guard escorted him out of the visiting area. Another guard took Laura back to the cell, and she shivered as the door shut behind her with a loud clang. She cringed at the sound every time. Thankfully, the other women didn't stare quite as much this time. Even if they did, she didn't care. She lit a cigarette from the new pack her father had brought her and took a deep drag. She blew the smoke between the bars. *God, please get me out of here, and please look after my father.*

# CORAL

IT WAS A FINE DAY TO HAVE A GRADUATION. THE SUN WAS BRIGHT, and everyone was dressed up in their finest. Coral was in attendance, front, and center, beaming a smile that said, proud mother. It wasn't the college she'd imagined but becoming an officer of the law was still quite impressive, she reckoned. Jim looked out at the attendees, searching for another face, probably his brother's.

"I can't get off work, Mama!" Ike had said, twelve hours earlier.

She heard Ike sigh into the phone receiver. "You know I shouldn't be around all those cops. I wouldn't know what to do with myself."

Coral's brow crinkled. Her eyes filled with tears. "But your brother is gonna be so upset! If this were your graduation, he'd be there for you. You know that."

His voice cracked as he said, "Well, we both know I ain't graduating from nothin'! Ain't that what you always told me, Mama? You knew I was good for nothin' even before I did."

She looked out the window and clasped her hand over her mouth. Ike's breath hitched as he heard Coral sob softly. "Mama, I'm sorry. Didn't mean to snap at you."

Coral looked up at the sky and sniffled. "It's okay, son. I may not have been the best mama in the world, but I love y'all. Just hope you know that."

"Course, I know that," he said, in a cheerier tone. "Now, you've got a meeting with the fuzz! Better high tail it out of here, young lady!"

Coral chuckled. "Well yeah, I reckon there'll be an awful lot of 'Nawlins' finest out there. Maybe it's better if you see your brother afterwards."

"Tell him I'll be here after work if he wants to swing by," Ike said. "Love you."

Coral nodded, then kissed into the phone receiver. "Love you, sweet boy."

Ike blurted. "Bye Mama. Go support your golden boy."

"Uh, huh," Coral said, then hung up. She rolled her eyes, determined that nothing was going to spoil her day.

She watched the ceremony with joy in her heart as Jim walked up to the podium to receive his badge. "Oh! My baby boy is an officer of the law today! Whoo!" She squealed loudly, as people looked on with disapproval.

*Fuck these hoity toity assholes! They don't know what it's like coming from nothing. We do. Lord, how I love that boy. God knows I worried about him. But now look at my son. Keep staring, assholes. I'm gonna cheer for my baby. My sweet Jim.* She announced to those seated next to her, "That's my son up there...yep, that tall handsome one over yonder."

Many of her friends from Linden Highway 17 never believed she'd have an officer in her home, considering all the nights they spent playing poker and smoking weed, but some of them were there as well, wearing their Sunday best to support Jim.

None of them really believed Ike or Jim would ever do anything worthwhile, not that they could judge, least of all, Daryl Rae. He was in and out of jail for one minor violation after another, like skipping out on child support payments to his *many* illegitimate children. Nevertheless, Daryl Rae was right there beside her, the only father figure Jim ever had, clapping as Jim received his badge.

"Yeah! That's my boy! That's an officer over there! Yeah!" Daryl Rae boasted.

At the reception, she stood beside her fine young officer, Jim, for one photo after another, and when she was done, she lifted her glass of champagne to toast her son. "I'm so proud of you, darlin'! I just knew you'd do this."

"Thank you, Mama. I told you I wudn't gonna end up a loser like Ike, and even he's not really doing bad now. Like, he's working at least."

Jim looked out over the visitors there that day, sad that he didn't see Brian out there. Jack must have kept him away.

"We can't all be spending the day with our rich daddy or getting ready to go to a fancy university."

She wiped the dandruff flakes off Jim's shoulder and straightened his tie. "Now Jim, don't you think about anything today but your great success! I'm just so proud of you, my boy! Hey, let's go out for a drink! What do y'all think?"

Jim patted her on the shoulder. "Well Mama, I don't think a drink would be right, not in broad daylight, especially with my new boss and cop friends around, do you? But you go ahead. Just don't get wasted in front of everybody."

Coral's face dropped. She sighed, blushing. "Oh, silly me. Yes, you're right darlin'. You go ahead with your new team over there and me and Daryl Rae will go on and get outta here."

Jim gave Daryl Rae a judging glance. "Mama, can I talk to you *alone* for a second?"

"Sure, baby." Coral replied.

They stepped out of earshot, Daryl Rae looking very annoyed. Jim looked at Coral, and his brow furrowed. "Mama, don't you think you'd better stay clear of Daryl Rae? He's bad for ya. I know me and Ike have done a lot of partying with y'all, and it was a blast, but now that you have your restaurant, and Ike's finally workin', you don't need that bastard anymore. I'm a cop now. We just took his bullshit cuz he kept you entertained."

Coral's eyes widened with anger. She bit her bottom lip. A part of her mind felt as though it was boiling over. Coral tried to contain it. "Why you little..."

"Mama! I'm sorry. I'm only trying to look out for ya. You know he's probably still got Stella on the side, or God knows who," Jim pleaded.

"After all I've been through with you kids! None of y'all get to tell me what to do. None of ya! Hear me? Not even Brian! Sittin' up in his mansion with his rich daddy, and by God, at least I got a little restaurant out of it. So what? ... I do the best I can, baby. That's all I've ever done. I'm not a fancy lady, and I get lonely sometimes. Daryl Rae keeps me company."

"Okay Mama." Jim said. "I understand. I'm sorry." He grunted and turned away. "Do you see what Brian causes? Damn that little shit! If it weren't for him, Mama, we'd all be happy. We'd all be satisfied to live as ourselves, but that pretentious little shit and his fat cat daddy make us feel like shit by comparison. You deserve more. Brian's even changed with him. He used to be a cool brother. I didn't feel any difference between us, but Jack's got him thinking we're all trash."

Daryl Rae interrupted. "Hey baby, we gotta get going. Come on. Shake a leg!

Gotta work later. Yesterday, Skeeter hooked me up with a painting gig. I can't pass that up, baby. You may be some fancy businesswoman, but I'm just a working stiff."

Coral snickered. "You are a 'stiff' something or another, baby!"

It took Daryl Rae a minute to figure it out, but his simple wit finally let him get the joke. "You little vixen! Come here!"

She giggled and he snickered like a schoolboy, grabbed her by the waist, then waved back at Jim as they made their way out of there to the car. Coral turned back. "Bye darlin'! I'll call ya!"

# JIM

Jim's face turned red. He scoffed. *She can't help how trashy she is, but if that bastard was better to her, she could've been a real lady and had stuff. Jack may have even treated her better. A leopard doesn't change his spots. He's cheating on her for sure, and there she is, shacked up with him.*

He forced himself to forget about it and enjoy the day, whether Ike had been there or not. He spent some time celebrating with his colleagues, then headed straight for Ike's trailer. He pulled up in the gravel driveway, in his new Ford pick-up truck, still wearing his dress uniform. Ike was lying in a foldout lawn chair, smoking a cigarette. When he caught sight of his brother, he smirked. "Well, well, well, look at what the cat dragged in."

Jim got out of the truck and walked up to Ike. "Hey bro. I missed ya at the ceremony today. Mama was there with that shitbag, Daryl Rae."

Ike scoffed, "Ha! Yeah, he's a real shithead alright, but at least he puts a smile on Mama's face. God knows she ain't had enough of those. You and me both know that."

"Yeah." Jim answered. "I reckon that's true."

Ike stood up in front of Jim, or rather, *looked up* at him. His brother towered over him, as Ike was always the skinny, lanky type.

"I'm sorry I didn't get to come out there. You know I had to work. I had just got back five minutes before you came here. Was just thinking about going to get me a burger for dinner. You wanna come?"

Jim patted him on the shoulder. "Yeah, I'll drive us. It's on me."

"Why thank you, officer." Ike sneered and feigned a curtsy.

"Shut up, dickhead! Get in the car, and maybe I'll get you a better meal than what you were planning for," he said.

"Oh, la, la! How fancy shmancy." Ike chided.

They got in the car and drove off to Jim's favorite crawfish place, The Crawdaddy. They were seated in a booth, and the waitress brought some bibs to keep the fish juice from dripping over their clothes. Ike smiled. *It's about time we spend some time together. He'll never know how much I've missed him.*

Despite all the fights they'd gotten into over the years, Ike needed him, especially since that dipshit Brian abandoned the family. But did he? He didn't want to think his brother threw their relationship away, even if he was rich now. Maybe it's all Jack? Ike seemed to be having fun, which made Jim happy.

"Wow! Didn't know you were taking me somewhere so fancy. Would've dressed better." Ike said, licking his lips.

"Don't worry about it, bro. Let's just have a good time." Jim said as he strapped on his bib.

The waiter plopped down a heaping tray of crawfish on the table, and both men took a deep whiff of the aroma. "By golly, this smells like Heaven on Earth! Whoo!" Jim hooted.

Of course, nothing washed down crawfish like a couple of ice-cold beers, so the two had quite a time, eating and talking about everything in life.

"To us!" Ike declared, holding his beer up for a toast.

Jim reciprocated and their beer bottles clanked, but his face dropped. *If only Brian was here.* Ike frowned. "What's up? Boy, you always have a stick up your ass about somethin'. Why can't you just have a good time anymore?"

"Just keep thinking about Brian. We used to have a lot of fun together, and now we can't even see him. It's been two years, for God's sake! He doesn't even call us. I'll bet it's Jack, cuz Brian wouldn't do that to us."

He pounded his fist on the table. "How can they keep us from our own blood? Brian's our brother! We can't just sit by and be treated like this!"

Ike slurped down a crawfish head and sputtered, "Yeah, but they're all in that rich mansion, with guards and shit. How the hell are the likes of us gonna get past all that?"

"I'm a cop now. I'll come up with something. You wanna see him, right?" Jim asked.

"Yeah, but what if he's *different* now?" Ike asked.

"What? You mean snobby? Like he's too *good* for us?" Jim narrowed his eyes. "Well, guess we'll have to teach him he ain't better than us, won't we?"

"Whatever you say, man. But money like that has a way of changing folks. Just saying." Ike said as he took a deep gulp of his third beer.

———

AN HOUR LATER, Jim was seeing double and the room swayed back and forth. Those last shots of Jack Daniels were brutal. He giggled. Ike elbowed him and stumbled to the ground. Both laughed hard at the sight of Ike on his ass. "I reckon I better call Mama to pick us up. I ain't lettin' either one of us get behind a wheel tonight." Jim vaguely remembered that he was a cop now.

Ike burst into fits of laughter. "Yeah man, you do that! Dollars to donuts she brings Daryl Rae with her."

Jim returned from the pay phone to find Ike passed out on the curb. "Hey man! Come on! Get your ass up now."

Ike could barely focus but managed to come alive again. "Hmm...okay I got it. I'm up."

He looked at his little brother and sniggered. *Such a dipshit, but I love this little coot! Hope Mama's gonna get here soon.*

He and Ike stood outside on the street, singing, when Daryl Rae's truck pulled up. In unison, the brothers sang.

*Well, in the North of Carolina, way back in the hills*
*Me and my old pappy and he had him a still*
*He brewed white lightnin' till the sun went down*
*And then you'd fill him a jug and he'd pass it around*
*Mighty, mighty pleasin', pappy's corn squeezin'*
*Ssh, white lightning!*

CORAL JUMPED out of the car, huffing, and puffing. "You two heathens get in this car right now!"

*Oh shit, Mama's mad.* He looked at Coral's face and saw her tapping her foot. What a crock! She's not worried about us. *We were responsible enough not to drive drunk. We called. Instead of being proud of that, she's worried about her precious reputation. I don't give a fuck what she thinks. Me and my brother had the time of our lives.* He looked at Ike and burst out laughing until both their faces turned red. Daryl Rae chuckled a little. Coral whipped her head around and gave him a cold stare. Daryl Rae straightened up and nodded. Again, she focused on her sons. They stumbled into the car, still giggling like 12-year-old boys who had just seen their first dirty magazine.

"Oh Mama" Jim said, "you sure are something, ain't ya?"

"What the Hell is that supposed to mean?" Coral snapped, folding her arms and tapping her foot in annoyance.

Ike slurred his words. "What my cop brother here is saying is that you ain't got no right to judge either one of us! You got bought by that rich asshole and sold your own son for the money to open your place. Me and Jim just miss Brian, that's all."

Ike passed out with his head in Jim's lap. He rolled his eyes. "Ike didn't really know what he's saying, Mama. But he's right about us missing our brother. We just don't know why you gave him up so easily. Do you even know if he's happy? That rich asshole might be beating on him or torturing him. You'd never know because you *sold* him."

Coral's eyes watered upon hearing this, and Daryl Rae squeezed her hand, eyes fixed on the road. Daryl Rae knew better than to utter a word at a time like this, but his sympathetic glances said it all.

She choked out a feeble response. "I'm sure he's got a better life than he ever could've had with me, right? ... So why shouldn't I have taken a little something for myself? It's not like Jack can't afford it. I did a lot for him."

"Whatever you say, Mama...Why don't we go and pay him a visit now?" Jim asked.

"What? Now?" Coral's eyes widened. "You're both wasted, and you wanna go see Brian, like this?" She was silent for about a mile.

Coral raised an eyebrow, then nodded. "Okay boys. Guess it'd be rude not to tell him about your graduation. That's big news after all."

Ike stirred. "What's going on?" he croaked.

"Wake up, dickhead. We're gonna go see Brian now," Jim blurted.

# BRIAN

BRIAN SIPPED HIS COFFEE, SITTING ACROSS FROM HIS FATHER IN A classic English wingback armchair, basking in the warmth of the nearby fireplace. It was their custom after dinner. Brian relished coffee time, the only time he got to *hang out* with his dad. It made him feel normal. He'd be off to college soon, and he looked forward to learning about business, to being more helpful to Jack, and about taking on the responsibilities of the company one day. Lofty thoughts for a fifteen-year-old, but he was no ordinary teenager.

"The roast was really good tonight. God knows I was craving some meat. I feel a lot better now," Brian said.

Jack smiled. His own father firmly believed that real men needed meat. After all, it was something that a *true boss* would take part in regularly. Another ritual that was just for *real* men was cigar smoking. Soon, Jack had promised, he'd teach Brian the art of enjoying a fine Cuban cigar made right in New Orleans, in the French Quarter. *The Cuban*, a cigar factory that had been around for ages, was where his great grandfather had gotten his Cubans. In fact, his great grandfather Tobias had introduced the art of cigar smoking to Jack Senior at about this age.

"Son, it's about time you learned about something else men enjoy," Jack said. He exhaled a stream of twisting smoke.

Brian leaned forward and looked his dad right in the eye. Initially, he thought his dad was talking about women, and his imagination was already running wild. "Um, okay Dad, I'm ready for that," he said, face turning slightly red.

Jack laughed. "No son, I'm not taking you to a whore house or anything ... at least not tonight. No, I'm talking about Cubans, Montecristo's!"

"Cubans?" Brian asked, confused.

The corners of Jack's mouth turned up into a grin, as if enjoying the amusement of his clueless son. "Cubans are the finest cigars in the world, son. Montecristos were our favorite before we started manufacturing our own, right here in New Orleans. Onassis loves Montecristos, as do many men of our class, but we make one just as good, if not better. Here, go on and take one. Let's get you lit so you can enjoy it."

He got a cigar from the hand carved humidor on a side table and clipped one end, before putting the other in his mouth. He took his first draw. "There ya go, son! Now take in a few little draws to get that fire started."

Brian didn't want to disappoint his father, so he followed Jack's instructions. On the very first puff, he coughed, choking on the smoke. *Dad's gonna think I'm a loser, just a little boy. Oh shit, here it comes. He's gonna laugh at me now. Ugh.*

Jack howled with uncontrollable laughter, and Brian shifted and looked down at the floor. His cheeks flushed. Then his dad slapped him on the back.

"Oh son, it's okay. I didn't expect you to get hold of this on the first try. Maybe we should open a little Scotch? That always makes a fine Cuban taste better. What do you say? You're fifteen now. I'd rather you take it in with me than with anyone else."

Brian beamed. His smile was hard to dial back as he bonded with his father over manly things like roast beef, cigars, and fine Scotch. All good things must end, however, and he knew this good night was over the second he heard the tires screech outside. Jack rolled his eyes.

"Excuse me, my boy. I gotta see what in the blazes is happening out there."

He followed his dad out the front entrance to find them all there. Loud, stumbling, and drunk. Every one of them. Coral leaned on Daryl Rae, Ike and Jim leaned on the car. His stomach churned. *Oh God, please don't let them embarrass me. Dad and I were really bonding. They may be here to take me back! No...they can't do that. Can they?*

He looked at his father. Jack held his glass of Scotch on the rocks, so he did as well, wanting to appear strong and in control. Jim's eyes darkened at the sight of them, and he crushed the beer can he was holding, spewing the remaining beer all over the driveway. "So, we thought we'd come see our little brother, but it seems like he's turned into a hoity toity asshole, like his rich daddy!"

Jack scoffed and pointed to Brian's brothers. "Look at this trash you came from, son. Put this image in your mind. Remember the fate I saved you from when I bought you from your mother."

Jack leered as he took another long drag from his cigar. Watching Brian looking at Coral, Jack chuckled to himself. Coral gasped and clutched at her chest. Brian's mouth hung open.

"What? ... Bought?... What does *that* mean?... Mama? What does that mean!"

"Uh...Um...I'm..." Coral stammered.

"What? Can't you even explain yourself?" he blurted angrily.

Coral had tears in her eyes as she stared up at her son.

"You ain't got no right to judge Mama for anything!" Ike snapped. "This old bastard knocked her up, and even when he knew she had two kids, no money, and no family. What could she do?"

Brian couldn't find the voice to respond. His whole life felt like a lie, a business deal. Flashbacks of hearing his mother's voice refer to him as a *payday* to Stella and her other friends made him doubt if she'd ever really loved him. *Have I always been a meal ticket for her? Did she want to keep me?*

"Brian?" Coral said weakly, her face turning red as tears rolled down her cheeks. "Baby, Ike's right. I didn't have much choice. I...I did what I did cuz I thought you'd be better off here with your daddy."

He looked down, struggling to hold back the tears. He couldn't risk letting his father see him as a wuss. He threw his glass, shattering it against the wall. He turned to look at her, his eyes darkening.

Coral continued in a firmer voice. "You've had three years with him now. Your life's been rich, with all kinds of advantages I could never give you...Sometimes I do feel like it was a mistake though. Especially now, after getting a good look at him! He's gonna teach you how to be a selfish bastard like him."

Brian opened his mouth to speak but noticed the blood streaming down his hand from the broken glass. "Sorry about the mess, Dad."

His father snapped his fingers and the butler immediately brought out a towel for his hand, then started picking up broken glass. Jack put his arm around him and sneered at Coral. Brian's bottom lip quivered. He cleared his throat. "I guess we all got what we wanted then. So, don't worry about it, Mama. I'm staying."

Coral stumbled back. Jim scooped her up and put her in the truck. Daryl Rae fanned her with a hunting brochure as Jim approached Brian. "Hey, listen, just because you're held up here with him doesn't mean you can't spend time with us now and then. Me and Ike miss the old days. Don't you?"

"I do...but I have to learn a business now, learn to be in a whole new world," he said.

His father nodded and put a hand on his shoulder.

"That's my boy."

Brian rolled his eyes and feigned a smile. *He thinks he can buy anything, even love and loyalty. It's not right. I wanna make him happy, but it's not right to keep me from who I really am.*

He glanced over at Coral, and his eyes softened. He looked at Jim again. "Take care of Mama. Maybe I'll see you around sometime...Oh, and hey, heard about your graduation from the servants. Congrats."

He shook Jim's hand, took one last look at Coral, Daryl Rae, and Ike, then turned to go inside. Just before he stepped into the house, he stopped and glared at his father, without saying a word. His eyes darkened with contempt. Then he dropped his head low and went into the house.

Brian watched from a window in his room upstairs as Jack smashed his scotch glass against the wall. He opened his window slightly to hear better as Jack shouted at Coral.

"You miserable bitch! You were a sweet piece of ass back in the day, but it's not right to keep on making me pay for that over and over. You've done nothing but stalk me for two long years now, and that wasn't part of our deal! I paid you in one lump sum and you agreed to leave me alone with *my* son. If not for him, I would prosecute you and your *mongrel* brats."

Ike leapt forward and tackled Jack to the ground. They struggled, but Ike was too drunk to do much damage. Jim jumped on Ike to pull him off.

"Ike! He ain't worth it! He ain't worth it!"

"Stop! No!" Brian called out, but his voice landed on deaf ears. His eyes grew sullen as he watched this drama play itself out, somehow knowing that it would be a night burned in his memory for a very long time. He was relieved to see Jim put a stop to things before they turned tragic.

*Thank God for Jim. Why did they do this? It can't be just because they miss me. They're drunk...Still, I've seen them in better control than this when they're drunk.*

Ike panted, still clenching his fists when he stood up next to Jim. They both watched as Jack pulled himself up from the driveway as the security guard from the gate ran up to them, nightstick at the ready. Jack put his hand up, to stop the situation from escalating. He dusted off his jacket, wiped some blood from his nose, then cleared his throat.

"White trash! Yep, you can take the trash out of the trailer park, but you can't take the trailer park out of the trash! Ha!"

Brian scoffed, still hidden by the window. *That's fucked up. I'm from a trailer park. Am I trash too?*

Jack smiled at the lot of them, more confident now that he had backup. Coral began to cry. Jim looked back at the state she was in and spoke to Ike.

"Live to fight another day, bro. Let's go. I have plans for him, but you can't help me if you're locked up. Let's get the fuck out of here before he calls for help and embarrasses me in front of the other cops."

Ike snorted and nodded in agreement, but couldn't resist the chance to say, "Fuck you, asshole!"

"Ah! Spoken like a true vulgarian," Jack said, smiling and folding his arms.

The butler interrupted the scene. "Sir, *she's* on the phone again."

"Who?" Jack asked, not wanting to miss a moment of the humiliation.

The butler answered, "The same one as before, sir. She's quite adamant."

Jack rolled his eyes, waved at the group. "See yourselves out, won't you?", turned his back and went inside.

Brian winced. *What's that? Walking away from a good backstabbing? For a phone call?* He looked out the window at his mother. Tears still streamed down her cheeks, and she sobbed again when she looked up and saw him peering through the window from his new suite. She nodded and half-waved at him. He simply nodded in return.

Brian fell back on his bed, processing what just happened. Would he ever feel as though he belongs? Or would he perpetually feel torn between the posh world of his father and the simple world of his mother? He decided to leave that decision for now and simply relax. Tomorrow would certainly be a better day.

# CORAL

*April 1967, New Orleans, later that night.*

AS DARYL RAE DROVE CORAL AND HER SONS BACK HOME, SHE PEERED out the window. The night was humid, smelling like rain was just about to pour. She cracked the window slightly, as she enjoyed the smell of fresh cut grass. Somehow, it was a comfort to her after what had just happened. She hadn't really contemplated how she'd lost him ... sold him, or sold him out, until she saw his searching eyes looking down from the window. *What kind of life would he have had with me*, she wondered? She remembered her own mother, and what a terrible home she came from.

*I don't know how I survived Delilah for so long. I'll survive this too, hopefully.*

# CORAL

CORAL'S LATE MOTHER, DELILAH, HAD A REPUTATION OF BEING ONE of the most foul-tempered skank hillbillies in town. She lived in an old shack out near an almost abandoned Uniontown farming area in Alabama, covered in overgrown shrubs and grass. Delilah didn't seem to mind that the tall grass attracted rattlesnakes. Coral, along with her nine brothers and sisters, were always in awe of how their ballsy mother could snatch a garden hoe and chop the head off of a coiling, hissing rattlesnake without blinking an eye. Once that happened, it was no surprise what was for dinner that night.

"Them rattlers are good eatin'!" Delilah would say indignantly. "We ain't gonna waste this good meat. What do you think we are? Rollin' in money?"

She would drag the long rattlesnake to her kitchen, then gut it, skin it, and chop it into chunks. Once it hit the fat in the frying pan, the aroma wasn't half bad, or so the kids thought at the time. Truthfully, Coral didn't mind it so much, as rattlesnake really did taste like chicken. It was better than the slop Delilah fed them most nights.

Delilah had the family mostly living off her little crochet dolls she made to sell, as well as her corn, peas, blackberry, and peach crops she worked. Of course, all the kids pitched in to pick crops, arrange them neatly into baskets, and man the table at the farmer's market. Delilah managed the sales of her dolls herself at the market, as she fancied herself somewhat of an artist. She'd dress up to be as dainty looking as she could manage for those markets, and occasionally, she'd catch more than a doll sale.

Yes, occasionally, she'd catch a "gentleman caller" as she'd call him. This occasional man would follow her home, where she'd pretend to be a woman of class and leisure, but no one was getting fooled. Before she'd entertain her guest, she'd lock all the kids into the one room they shared, and instead of a kiss on their foreheads, they got tucked in with a threat. Through tightly gritted teeth that hissed smoker's breath, she'd growl, "If any of you screws up for me, I'll tan your hide! Do y'all understand? I'm trying to find y'all a new daddy. Now keep quiet! He ain't gonna stay if he knows that wild heathens live here."

Coral tried to hum herself to sleep on nights like this. She dreamt of living in a better place, around better people. Some nights she'd hum to entertain her brothers and sisters, but sometimes they'd just whisper to themselves.

Indeed, Coral dreamed of a better life. She was already quite the oddball compared to her friends. Most had dropped out of school by now, opting for the simple life of raising kids and housekeeping. Coral wanted more, despite how much her mother and everyone around her mocked her for it.

"Just let me get to be sixteen, and I'm leaving this place. I'm not gonna stay here and be her slave forever. I hope y'all are gonna get out too. This ain't the way mommies are supposed to act," the then fourteen-year-old Coral explained, hugging her sisters tight.

*One day*, she thought, as sleep was about to take her, *I'll be a woman of taste and style, and I'll finally get away from this sorry excuse for a mother.* As she tried to ignore the animal-like sounds of Delilah's evening pursuits, she fell asleep with dreams of a better life in her mind, complete with a charming prince that would take her away from all this.

Her high school years didn't bring much more good fortune. Although there weren't many girls her age in school anymore, Coral was hard-headed. She studied hard, hoping she'd go to college and make something out of her life. Nursing was always an interest of hers, and even as a child she pretended to bandage injuries on her brothers and sisters. Delilah wasn't supportive of her imaginative adventures in medicine, however, and would often remark, "Little girl, what the hell are you doing?! You ain't nothing. You ain't ever gonna be nothing. None of you sorry ass kids are gonna amount to diddly squat! You may as well be pissin' in the wind!"

Coral didn't pay much attention to her negativity at the time, and studied as hard as she could, but her dream was shattered when her grades didn't qualify her for any scholarships. Delilah would never pay for tuition, even if she could. She always saw school as a waste of time.

"You need to get your ass to a good trade school," she would say. "Learn a trade that will get you a job in a factory or a salon. Now *that's* a steady paycheck! That's what this here family needs."

As Coral got older, her hopes of an education and a proper life blew up around her. She often wondered if her mother was right, but something always held her back. In her heart, she still wanted the fairy-tale.

# CORAL

*April 1967, the outskirts of New Orleans*

HER HEART CAVED IN AS SHE IMAGINED THE LOOK ON BRIAN'S FACE. *He must hate me now.* Tears welled in her eyes.

As they sped off, back to her fine new brick home, Ike and Jim pretended not to notice the sobbing from the front seat. They didn't even look at each other and spent the car ride in silence. As they got closer to her home, Daryl Rae spoke up.

"Sorry about how y'all were treated back there. That ain't right," he said as he turned to Coral. "Baby, I know he might've been exciting back in the day, but what he said ain't true."

Daryl's words caused her heart to swell with emotion. She sobbed even louder. He looked in the rear-view mirror and cleared his throat. "I've known your mama since before y'all were born. She's a good woman with a heart of gold. She used to wanna be a nurse. Did either of y'all know that?"

"Stop, Daryl Rae," she said, putting her hand over his on the steering wheel.

"No, sugar," Daryl said. "They need to know you were doing the right thing by that boy, cuz he'd have a better life there."

"They know," she said, turning back to look at them through red eyes and running mascara.

"I know Mama. I'm sorry I thought of doing any of this. Tonight was a disaster, but I don't think Brian is better off, necessarily. He's gonna lose himself there," Jim said, dusting some fuzz from his jacket.

Ike nodded, then winced. "Well, we just gotta figure out ways to see him now and then. When he went back in the house, he did say he'd see us around. That's gotta mean he *wants* to see us again, right?"

"Right!" Jim agreed. "I've got a plan. I'll come by tomorrow and talk to y'all about it. But for now, I think we could all use a good night's sleep. I'm pretty wiped out, and I think we'll all think clearly in the morning."

"Ha! I don't think I'm gonna be up before noon!" Ike blurted.

Daryl Rae put his free arm around her, and she nuzzled into him, enjoying the supportive embrace. She was so lucky to have him, even if he was a part-time lover she shared with Stella. She allowed herself a small smile. A memory came to mind of a particular night. Daryl Rae had just won fifty dollars in a poker game. He knew how down she was, staying up with the baby night after night, so he came by one night with a daisy taped to a gift certificate for a hairdo with a manicure and pedicure from their neighbor, Ellie, a cosmetologist. That little salon visit was just what she needed. Once her services were done, Daryl Rae returned to see his handiwork. "You look like yourself again. I just hated seeing you looking so run down. You're a beautiful gal. You know that?"

No one had ever been so sweet to her in her whole life. She threw her arms around him and kissed his cheek. That Aqua Velva smell, his clean-shaven face, his soft long hair. How could she resist? She put baby Brian to bed and thanked her man properly. What a night!

As happy as that memory made her, she couldn't help but feel her heart sink, and her eyes droop. Why couldn't she get over Jack? *Was it because he rejected me?*

She had read so many self-help books. So many friends had told her to "get over it" and "move on", that she was "better off". *Why can't I do that? Why do I let his rejection hurt me, again and again? What's wrong with me?* She tried to force the questions out of her head, holding Daryl Rae even tighter. By the time they pulled up into her driveway, she felt a bit better.

They got out of the truck and took a moment to stare at the stars. It was just the two of them, and it felt good to let Daryl Rae hold her and kiss her on the head.

"I can stay tonight if you don't wanna be alone," he said.

She kissed his lips. "Yes, please do. Alone is the last thing I wanna be. I need you."

Without another word, Daryl Rae scooped her up in his strong arms and carried her through her front door.

# BRIAN

BRIAN BEAMED WHEN THE FAMILY LIMOUSINE PULLED INTO THE parking lot of Louisiana State University's fraternity row. He'd spent his first semester in a dorm, but now, he'd get to relish the chance to finally find a place in an esteemed fraternity. He peeked through the tinted glass as his limo pulled up to the only fraternity he'd join, without a doubt. Delta Beta Kappa, the same fraternity all Buchanan men had been members of. The Buchanan chauffeur, Ronald, a small black man with a thick mustache, hopped out of the driver's side. His polished black shoes hitting the pavement, and with the stature of a naval officer, he opened Brian's door with a flourish.

"We've arrived, sir. I'll help you with your bags."

"Thank you, Ronald."

A representative from the fraternity rushed up to the car to assist. A blonde guy, about Brian's age. His blue eyes widened as they met.

"We're so honored you're here, sir. We're honored to welcome your family into our halls."

"Thank you. What's your name?" Brian asked, trying to be polite.

"Barry, sir ... Barry Peterson."

"Why do you call me sir? We're around the same age."

Barry sighed, "I'm a pledge, sir. It's my first year. New pledges must perform services for the fraternity, so that we can later be worthy of a membership." His eyes lowered.

*How unfair he must think this is! Just for being a Buchanan, I don't have to go through pledge duties.* Ronald unloaded his suitcases and Barry snapped to attention to grab them. Brian took the handle of the biggest case and patted Barry on the back. "It's okay. Just relax. We have this, okay?"

Barry smiled. "You're a swell guy. I do hope I get picked."

"I'll put in a good word," he said as they both rolled the brand new fashionably wheeled suitcases up to the front steps. Barry beamed. "What's your major? Oh wait, of course it's business, right? What am I thinking? Well, maybe we can study together sometime?"

Brian nodded, "Yeah, why not? You a business major too?"

"I wish," he sputtered. "I'm pre-law, thanks to my dad. He's a personal injury lawyer, here in New Orleans. He wants me to be better."

"Well, I'm sure you'll make him proud. I know something about wishing to make a father proud, trust me," Brian said, grinning.

Barry's eyes lit up. He opened the front doors, then stepped into a lavish foyer with a winding staircase trimmed in dark wood, complete with a fireplace beneath and lush leather sofas. The entire room was paneled with bookcases and potted plants on carved wooden stands. It all looked so dignified and fancy, like something straight out of a gentleman's magazine.

A stylish young man approached Brian. Handsome chiseled brunette, with dimpled cheeks, a groomed mustache and close stubble beard. He pulled out a gold engraved cigarette case, put a cigarette between his lips, then waited for his personal pledge to come and light it for him. His name was Richard Parker, of the Baton Rouge Parkers, famous for a number of businesses, including a chain of Italian Restaurants called Gusto. Brian recognized him from the fraternity brochure.

The pledge was a tall lanky fellow from Charleston, South Carolina. Brian recognized him from articles about the Wellington family in the financial magazines. *That was Ernest Wellington!* Ernest's father had made his fortune in peaches. Wellington Farms was the finest name in peach production for the last fifty years, and Ernest was poised to take over the keys to the kingdom very soon. Many articles hinted that Charles Wellington was nearing the end of his life. *That boy's soon gonna sit on a bloomin' fortune!* Brian smiled and gave a little nod to Ernest.

"Leave us!" Richard snapped, shooing off Ernest, who scurried away to some nearby hiding place.

Brain looked him over. Richard stood about six feet tall, slim, and well dressed in an expensive Neiman Marcus button up with pleated black slacks. No groovy duds for this guy.

"I'm Richard Parker. I'd like to welcome you to your new home," he said, smiling. Brian played along. *It's power play time, I guess.*

Richard put an arm around Brian's shoulder and led him into the parlor. "Have a seat, Mr. Buchanan."

Brian sat down as Barry arrived with coffee, served on a silver platter, with cups, saucers, sugar cubes, and freshly baked cookies. "Well? Aren't you going to pour for us?" Richard blurted.

Barry jumped to duty, nodding. "Sir, yes sir. I'm sorry."

*Poor bastard. Look how this pompous ass is treating him. Is this even worth it?* Brian thought.

Barry poured the coffee and placed a cookie on each saucer next to the coffee cups. Richard took a drag of his cigarette, then finished up. Barry lowered his head. "Can I do anything else for you, sir?"

Richard scoffed. "No. Wait, yes, you can. Take Mr. Buchanan's luggage up to his suite in the west wing."

"The west wing, sir? But I thought that was only reserved for senior members of the fraternity." Barry's brow furrowed.

"When I give you an order, you just do it!" Richard snapped again.

Barry flinched, and without another word, did as he was told. Brian reeled. *I'd tell this piece of shit to go fuck himself. Ha, that's probably Jim and Ike talking through me...Miss those guys. None of us ever talk shit like this. Rich people suck.*

Once Barry was out of earshot, Brian cleared his throat. "Excuse me, why was that boy treated like that? I'm a new pledge, like him. I understand that the quarters for senior members may not be appropriate for me."

Richard smiled and shook his head. "No. No. Brian ... May I call you Brian? You are lucky enough to be from a family that's more than *just* an alumnus. Your father, and his father before him, are legends at this university, practically royalty. Everyone is honored to have you in this fraternity."

*This guy's tripping! He really thinks he's got real power. He's getting off on this. What a spaz!*

Brian thought for a moment, then scratched his sideburn. "But that doesn't explain why poor Barry and the other ones are getting treated like servants."

Richard smiled without moving his eyes, giving off a "political" vibe. "Brian ... we'll have plenty of time to discuss this later. I'm sure you're exhausted. Perhaps you'd like to hear about the curriculum requirements before you see your suite?"

Brian was, indeed, exhausted. He bookmarked this conversation in his mind for another day. *I'll deal with you later, fancy pants.*

After Richard had spoken excessively about the subjects and various professors, Brian was finally alone in his new suite. He stood for a moment, taking in the grandeur of his new surroundings. The suite was spacious, with an oak bed, desk, walk-in closet and bathroom, more luxurious than New Orleans' finest hotels. "I don't think the other guys get rooms like this. Something isn't right," he said, opening his first piece of luggage.

He stopped with the bag long enough to walk to the window to open it for some air. He froze when he saw Jim on the street, looking up at him, waving. "What the hell is *he* doing here?"

Brian walked outside to greet him, and to his surprise, Jim seemed friendly, despite that unpleasant scene at the house, years ago, back when Brian was only fifteen. As Brian approached, Jim put his hands up, as if guilty, and smiled.

"Hey little brother! Don't worry, I come in peace. Just felt pretty shitty how things went down before. Thought I could try to make it up to you."

Brian folded his arms, then tapped his chin. "It was pretty bad...But, why should I believe you? You're just here to make things right? Since when do you care about that? And, how did you even know where I was?"

"Cops can find out things, little brother. Don't think I haven't been watching out for all of you, the whole time...But yeah, about that night...all I know is that as soon as I sobered up, I wanted to fix what happened. I started with Ike, but he's so pissed at me. He's scared he's never gonna see you again! You know he's always looked up to you...and...if I'm being perfectly honest..."

"What?" Brian asked.

Jim cleared his throat. "I think you're perfect in every way. To tell you the truth, I was always jealous of that, of how I lost Ike to you, his admiration, even when we were just kids."

Brian's eyes softened, but his arms remained folded. "Come on man, I know you two are as thick as thieves! What do you want me around for? You said it yourself that I'm *snooty falooty* like my rich daddy...And come on? Here you are, three years later? What took you so damn long? Huh?"

Jim sighed. "Well, you graduated and then you spent a year interning for your daddy. He'd have me and Ike run off the property if we tried to get close to you. And, for a while, we couldn't even find out what school you'd gone to. No one would tell us. Like some damn national secret!"

Jim paused, but Brian stood silent. "What about Mama? Didn't you care about trying to reach her through these years?"

Brian stuck his hands firmly in his pockets. "She was done with me a long time ago it seems."

Jim smiled and put a hand on Brian's shoulder. "You know that's not true. She's always loved you. She really did feel that you'd be better off with Buchanan. So, what if she got a little something for herself? Poor gal has been through hell. Can you honestly say that if you were in that situation, you'd do it any differently?"

*She did have it rough. Damn...who am I to judge her? People are so shitty to each other sometimes. At least she means well.*

He shrugged his shoulders. "Well, I guess I wouldn't know...hmm. Well, okay you're here. So, what do you want from me?"

Jim scoffed, "Shit, man! I just wanna go out or something. Bury the hatchet. Come on! I'll buy you a beer."

Brian's lips slowly curled into an approving smile. He raised an eyebrow. "Well, I don't know many places, but I do know of one place we can go. It's pretty darn cool. I think you'll like it. But maybe we should go in my car so Ronaldo can drive us? I don't think we'll be in any shape to drive afterwards."

Jim nodded and pounded his chest with his fist like a warrior. "Yeah baby! That sounds perfect! Let's do this!"

Jim put an arm around Brian's shoulder and they went to find Ronaldo. Many of the fraternity had limo drivers. They even had their own rooms, albeit smaller. Ronaldo was just about to turn in for the night, but not particularly bothered by the late-night request of his young superior.

Once they got into the French Quarter, Brian had Ronaldo drop them at a small hotel overlooking Bourbon Street.

I'll be just down the road, sir," said Ronaldo.

"Very good," Brian replied. "We'll come to you when we're done."

Jim grinned when he saw the place. Brian chided. "What are you smiling like a monkey about? Huh?"

Jim took a pocket comb out. "This isn't your first time here, is it?" Jim grinned, combing his hair and sideburns.

"You got me, big brother. The Park Hotel is kind of known around these parts for the topless talent, if you know what I'm saying."

*If you only knew, brother.* Brian nodded.

Jim patted him on the back. "Yeah, I've heard that too. I'm glad we're here... Oh! But did you also know that the draft beer is imported from Ireland? It's so strong, it can get up and walk out the door!"

"Really?" Brian snorted.

When they were escorted in, Brian looked at Jim and flashed a wolfish grin. "Well, brother? What do ya think?"

"I think you wanna get fucked up on your first night as a fraternity boy, right?" Jim blurted.

"Well... maybe?" Brian said with a devilish grin.

Jim's smile dropped to a frown, suddenly changing the mood. Brian saw his brother fold his arms and look down at the floor. "Man, I hate that your daddy thinks that this is the kind of shit I lead you to. How about we have *one* drink, only one, and then get you back to your fraternity?"

"Wow! Now I've heard everything... Officer Jim doesn't wanna party."

Brian stared into his eyes for a moment, trying to read his face. "Gosh, you're making me think you really mean what you said about us getting along."

"Yes, I do, dickhead!" Jim blurted with a grin on his face. "I really want us all to be brothers, not just party buddies." Jim smiled and reached for a hug. "I'm a cop, you know. Gotta be a good guy and all."

Brian hugged his brother. Having his brother in his life, this way, was exactly what he wanted. His heart warmed. "I'd like that. Maybe next time we go out, bring Ike?"

"Sure! If the little shit can stay off the sauce long enough! Ha!" Jim snorted.

Jim suddenly looked at a woman staring at them from the corner of the bar. Her blue eyes peeked out through her bluntly cut brunette bangs, but when she caught sight of him, she left the bar. Brian cleared his throat. "Hey man, what's up?"

Jim murmured, "Never mind, little brother. Thought I recognized someone, but I was mistaken."

"A girl?" Brian asked.

"Yeah, but not what you think. Forget it. Let's just have fun," Jim said.

They sat for a while, chatting, shooting the breeze. For both, it was the most fun they'd had in a while. Brian took a last sip and looked at his watch. "Ok, Let's go. I'll go to the front desk and phone Ronaldo."

"How's he gonna answer? Where is he?" Jim asked.

"You do realize he's got a car phone in there, right?"

Jim's eyes widened. "It's so far out, thinking of you with all that bread, man."

They both sniggered, and once Ronaldo picked them up, they headed back to the fraternity. Once they reached, however, Brian had concerns about letting Jim drive.

"Hey, you cool to drive?" Brian asked.

"Yeah man, don't worry," Jim said. "Just had one drink. I'm dyno-mite! Still under the legal limit. I'm a cop, remember?"

"You said that already," Brian said, grinning.

He watched as Jim got into his truck and drove off, but before he sped away, he rolled down the window to say one last thing.

"Thanks, man," Jim said. "This was pretty cool."

Brian smiled. "See you on the flip side, brother."

# BRIAN

OVER THE NEXT COUPLE YEARS, HE ENJOYED MANY SIMILAR OFF-color visits with his brothers, and to his surprise, neither tried to influence him to misbehave as they had done before. They truly bonded as brothers and watched sporting events, shot pool, and sometimes just hung out talking. They even encouraged him to keep up his grades.

On one such visit, he spotted Richard Parker watching him from the window as Ike dropped him back off at the fraternity. Ike got out of the truck to hug him goodbye, and Richard sneered. Ike got Brian's polo shirt dirty as he held him. "Oh, damn, man, sorry! Didn't mean to get you all scuffed up."

"It's okay. Don't worry about it," Brian replied.

"Well, it's just so fancy shmancy in there. I don't wanna be the reason anyone laughs at you or anything," Ike said, looking at the ground.

"Look at me brother."

Ike looked at him. He put his hand on Ike's shoulder. "Hey, you're my brother. I don't care how *fancy shmancy* those spoiled brats are, nothing can change that. You hear me?"

Ike beamed. "Well, I reckon I'd best be getting back to work. Glad we had a chance to hang out today though."

"Me too."

Ike drove away and he made his way into the house. Richard was still standing by the window, smoking a cigarette. He could feel those judging eyes. "Hello Richard. What are you doing there?"

"Oh, nothing really. It's just that when you stand still and watch, life can be rather surprising, wouldn't you say?"

He took another drag of the cigarette.

Brian winced. "What are you talking about? If I may ask?"

"When you first came to this house, you were treated like a prince—a crowned prince of a vast empire. Imagine my surprise discovering you aren't a *pure* royal? You've got the blood of rednecks, and not just any rednecks, the lowest that society has to offer. Well, all except the cop, of course." Richard said, sneering.

Brian scoffed and pointed. "You know what? You're right about me being a crowned prince. I do hold the keys to the kingdom, and with that kind of backing, I could tear this fraternity to the ground, or lift it up to heights never achieved by our order. It's all up to you, man."

"Um, I didn't mean..." Richard stammered.

"You didn't mean what?" Brian snapped. "To insult my brothers? Look, I know you've been raised with a silver spoon in your mouth. That's great for you, but fortunately for me, I know what life is like on the other side of the tracks, and that's not a bad thing. That's going to help me be a better businessman and a stronger human being."

"I was only surprised. That's all I said," Richard blurted.

"I get it. You made a mistake! Well, old boy, anyone can make a mistake once, so let's just forget it, ok?" Brian said, smiling.

Richard nodded. Still smiling, Brian put his hand on Richard's shoulder, then looked him directly in the eyes. "Never say anything derogatory about my family again. I hope I've made myself clear. Or I'll have to tell everyone you're not really a Parker, but the bastard son of the guy who used to drive the ice cream truck in your neighborhood."

Richard gulped and his eyes bulged. "How did you...?"

Brian said, "We've got more than a few highly skilled intel agents of our own? Don't worry, I'll never tell. Be nice to me and my family and I'll be nice to you." He patted Richard on the back. Richard gulped audibly, giving Brian a feeling of funky satisfaction.

# RICHARD

*1974, New Orleans, LA, University*

RICHARD SMILED NERVOUSLY AS BRIAN RELEASED HIM AND SPRANG upstairs to his quarters. Richard sipped his drink and sat down in a leather armchair. *That little shit. If he thinks he's going to usurp me, he's sadly mistaken.*

His eyes dropped and he sighed as he sat alone in the dark room like an injured wolf licking his wounds. Suddenly, a female voice emerged from the next room.

"I told you so. Are you *in* now?"

He lowered his head and muttered, "Yes."

"Good. One day I'll call on you. Your family owes my mentor many favors. Don't be surprised when I come to collect one," she said menacingly.

"Look, I get it, okay. You won't have anything to worry about. When the time comes to bring him down, I'll do whatever you ask...not just to save my family, but because I'll truly enjoy it."

The woman sneered. "Such a noble heart."

A moment later, Richard turned. He realized she was gone and sighed.

"Bitch."

# LARRY

*February 21, 1977, New Orleans, Orleans County Courthouse*

LARRY TAPPED HIS FINGERS ON THE DEFENDANT'S TABLE, SITTING next to Laura who was dressed in a dark blue frock he had picked up from her maid. Today was her arraignment, and his heart was pounding. *What if I can't do this? What if I don't have time? Time...sweet Jesus, such a luxury. Do any of us truly appreciate the gift of time?*

He exchanged glances with the District Attorney, Charles F. Barrington, who, along with his Deputy District Attorney, Richard Huntington III, were representing the State of Louisiana themselves, because after all, this was a high-profile case. It's not every day you get justice for a Buchanan. *They didn't even offer us a deal, not really. What was that about? Amateurs!*

"Daddy, please stop looking at him," Laura whispered. "Didn't you once tell me to never let anyone see your weaknesses?"

"I'm not," Larry blurted.

"You're looking at him too much, so he can tell you're nervous."

He scoffed. "The student became the teacher. Yes, that is what I said. Okay, I'll just focus on you."

"That's better," Laura snipped, resting a hand on her bump.

Larry looked at his daughter's pale face. His eyes softened, and he let himself take a good look at her body. Even though she had a small baby bump, she was otherwise frail and looked almost green around the gills. *Poor little thing.* She covered her nose and mouth with a handkerchief and looked nauseous. "Honey, you don't look well. When's the last time you've eaten anything?"

"I guess it was yesterday, if I'm being perfectly honest." Laura said, noticing the concern in his face.

He sat back and stared, with that all too familiar face.

"What?!"

"It's only because prison food is disgusting, Daddy."

"A holding cell, not prison, which is the Ritz by comparison...Look, I don't care, darlin'. You look a mess right now. I can't be worried that you're gonna keel over in the middle of all this." He called a court officer and whispered in his ear.

The officer left and Larry straightened his jacket. Laura whispered nervously, "Well, what did you tell him?"

"I asked him if he'd get my pregnant daughter a chocolate milkshake before she passes out and wastes the honorable judge's time," he said, flashing her a grin.

"I guess you make a fair point and thank you," she said, touching his arm.

"Really?" Larry asked. "I know you, darlin. You're reacting just how your mama did when she was carrying you. You need nutrition...and I'm gonna use your condition to get you out of jail today. Just watch and see."

The officer brought Laura a milkshake from a nearby diner and she carefully took a few sips, thinking it the best milkshake she'd ever had. Larry breathed much easier as he witnessed the color coming back to her cheeks. He said, "Okay, now let's talk for a second about our strategy."

"Okay Daddy," she said, slurping up the last of the chocolate.

Larry grinned and patted her on the back. He got his papers in order. "Okay, so if this went on as you said, I don't think we're gonna avoid a trial. You were right there at the scene and caught with the murder weapon right in your hand." He shook his head. *I can't believe she walked into that trap. Good God in heaven!*

Laura rolled her eyes. "Yes, I know. I know. I picked up the murder weapon, but I panicked. I didn't know if the killer was still in there or what. I froze. I didn't know what was going on. Time was a blur."

He cleared his throat and nodded. "I got that, darlin'. We'll figure this out, but I need to do some investigating of my own to see who could have orchestrated such a thing. I just hope that the judge gives me enough time."

The bailiff walked in. "All rise! The honorable Judge Edward Sherwood, presides!"

Everyone stood up and the judge, a well-groomed mustached gentleman in his early fifties took the stand. *Lord, help us all. I can see him in his country club now. Lord have mercy.*

The judge sat down, and everybody rearranged themselves on their seats. Everyone in the courtroom followed. Since this was only an arraignment, it was a mere formality to establish that enough evidence existed to take the case to trial, depending on how the defendant pleaded.

Judge Sherwood began. "The defendant in this case. Mrs. Laura Lynn Beauford Buchanan is accused of two counts of murder in the first degree, for Brian Allen Buchanan and one for Delta Dawn Johnson. How does the defendant plead?"

Larry stood up. "You Honor, my client pleads not guilty."

"I understand that you'd like to post bail for Mrs. Buchanan?" Judge Sherwood asked.

The Deputy District Attorney, Richard Huntington III, was a short and portly man from Baton Rouge. His fat nostrils flared alarmingly as he looked Laura up and down. "Your Honor, this woman has been accused and arrested for an exceedingly violent crime! I move for bail to be denied."

Judge Sherwood looked at the tiny frame of Laura. "Mr. Beauford, does your client pose a threat to society?"

Larry scoffed. "Your Honor, most definitely not. In fact, she's expecting a child. She's small, but we reckon she's close to six months along now. Her frail condition requires medical assistance, and any violent behavior is most assuredly not going to happen."

"Motion denied," Judge Sherwood said. "Bail will be set for fifty thousand dollars."

"God damn," Larry whispered.

He pounded the gavel. "Now, as for the trial. I have reviewed the evidence in this case, and it's compelling. I believe that there's cause for a trial, and I will set the date for two weeks from now, to give us time to assemble a jury and for you two to get your cases together. Court date is set for March seventh, in the year of our Lord, nineteen seventy-seven."

Larry jumped up. "Your honor, may we request a later court date? We have an investigation to bring underway, my daughter's pregnancy to attend to, a trial to prepare for as well as a funeral. We kindly request more time."

"Request denied," said Judge Sherwood.

"But your Honor!" Larry blurted.

"Mr. Beauford don't test me. I said denied! This court is adjourned." He pounded the gavel and quickly left.

Larry turned to Laura. "Well, at least I can get you out of here. At least we know that."

"That bastard is tough, too tough!" he said as he folded his arms.

"You got that right, Daddy," she said.

He rolled his eyes. His daughter smiled and put a hand on his shoulder. "But thank you. Hey, fifty thousand dollars is a lot of money. Is that okay?"

"Darlin', don't you know better than to ask me such questions? When it comes to you, that judge could've said a million dollars and I'd have paid it. I'd have to hock everything I own, but no one is more important to me in this whole world than you. Your mother, God rest her soul, would've wanted that."

He stroked her cheek, then snapped his briefcase closed. With his arm around her shoulders, they walked to the bailiff, but he began to falter. He coughed so hard that it felt like he was coughing up a lung. He heaved and fell to his knees on the floor, struggling for breath. Blood dripped on the floor, startling a few onlookers. Feeling the cold stares, he held a handkerchief to his mouth, managed to clear his throat enough to speak. "Water, please!"

Laura scrambled to get his water and other onlookers rushed in to see if there was anything that could be done. He continued to cough deeply. When he reached for it, the blood on his handkerchief became visible to everyone. One female bystander gasped and covered her mouth, jumping back. Laura looked at the handkerchief. "Daddy! Oh no! Daddy, what is this?"

Larry took a long drink of water, before speaking carefully. "Sweetheart, can we finish posting your bail? Then, you and I can sit down to a nice slice of pecan pie and discuss everything. Okay?"

He cleared his throat, breathing heavily, then smiled. He swept away a few strands of hair covering Laura's tear-filled eyes. She nodded. "All right then," he said. "Let's get going. We don't wanna make a bigger scene here."

# LAURA

*February 21, 1977. New Orleans, Café Fleur De Lis*

AFTER HER FATHER PAID THE BAIL, LAURA WAS FREE FOR THE TIME being, albeit on a short leash, so they had lunch at a little café downtown. This was in the heart of the French Quarter, as this particular cafe had been in business since the 1880s. He ordered their famous Big Easy Breakfast with iced tea. She sniffed. "I don't think I can eat. My stomach's in knots, Daddy."

Larry took her hand. "Darlin', I'd feel better if I knew you're staying healthy. Have a sandwich, a shrimp po'boy, a salad, anything. Please."

"Fine, I'll have a bowl of chicken soup and some crackers."

"Oh, come on," Larry said. "How 'bout a little gumbo. It's mighty fine here."

"You heard what I said about my stomach. The smell of seafood would make me barf," she said.

The waitress wrote it down and went to round up their food. "Now, tell me what's really wrong with you. Don't you dare lie to me. If I'm gonna get through this, I need nothing but truth telling all around." Laura said firmly, taking a sip of her water.

Larry blotted up the sweat from his shiny forehead, coughed a bit, and let his shoulders relax as he exhaled. "Okay, I can't hide this from you anymore, so I'm just gonna come out with it... I've got lung cancer. It's terminal."

Laura's eyes welled up and her bottom lip quivered. "Oh, Daddy! Why didn't you tell me earlier?"

She sobbed and hugged him. He held her and stroked her hair. She buried her face in his lapel, feeling like a little girl again being comforted after a nightmare. She remembered the nights when she'd run into those big arms, crying about a monster in her sleep. Cancer was a much more sinister beast, able to defeat anyone, even her invincible father, just as it had taken her mother. How could she survive this? Even though she was small, she remembered that sick sinking feeling, knowing that her mother would never brush her hair again, never pick out her clothes or make her breakfast. *Oh God, how she would have been over the moon right now to meet this baby.*

She sobbed. The thought of losing her father, her rock, for all those years, was devastating.

"Just like Mama," she whimpered. "How can I lose you too? Oh Daddy, I ..."

He took her face in his hands and wiped away a few tears with his fingers. He got a tissue from the table and cleaned her nose.

"Aww now, sweetheart, you had just gotten married, and I didn't wanna do anything to put a damper on your happiness. It was such a joy to me to walk you down that aisle and see that smile on your face. Good Lord, child. When I see your mother, I'm sure she's gonna tell me she's proud I was there for that. I lived long enough to see my baby girl happy."

Laura wept. She wasn't a quiet crier.

*This can't be happening! I'm losing my father now. I just lost my husband. God, please don't let me lose him too. Please, God. I can't do this alone.*

Her thoughts were wild with prayer, as she begged for her father's life. Laura's face turned red when she was upset, so customers started to notice the ruckus as the crying made her face as red as a tomato.

"Now hun, I don't want you to be this sad," Larry said, holding her face in his hands. "This dang condition runs in my family like gangbusters! I reckon it was only a matter of time for me too. I had a lot of joy in my life. God knows I did, but I can't go anywhere until I make sure you're free, and ready to start over with your life, you and that sweet baby."

"Daddy, I can't believe you didn't tell me though. Maybe we could've done something? Did you try any treatments?" Laura asked as she took another sip of water.

Larry chuckled. "Oh, yes, I did. Lord knows I tried everything, even surgery."

Laura's eyes opened wider, and her mouth fell open. "Remember that vacation I said I was going on? Well, that *was* the vacation," Larry said.

"Oh, dear God," Laura said.

"They got some of it, and I tried the chemotherapy, but all it was doing was making my hair fall out and making me sick. I couldn't stop vomiting. My poor housekeeper was so sweet to me, and worked overtime taking care of me, but I decided I don't wanna spend what I have left like that. I wanna spend it as *me,* for as long as I can," he said with a smile.

Laura smiled through her tears, as there was something charming and sensible about his words. She couldn't help but think that if it were her, she'd do the same exact thing. She wouldn't want to live the time she had left as a sickly and bedridden invalid. She'd want to do all the things she'd always wanted to do while she still had time. *We always tell ourselves we'll have tomorrow, or I'll do it later. Problem is, sometimes there is no later.*

She took her father's hand and looked into his eyes. "I understand that, Daddy. I just wish we could be enjoying what you have left. How long did the doctors say, anyway?"

"Well, the doc says that it could be anywhere from a year to eighteen months, so I reckon that's something, as long as I try to be as healthy as possible until then. I guess by not tempting fate, I can stretch it out as long as possible if God's willing and the creek don't rise!" He laughed. "At least I'll get to meet my grandbaby."

The waitress arrived with the food, and the two of them began to eat. Laura enjoyed her chicken soup, lapping up spoon after spoon, much to Larry's surprise. She blotted her lips with a napkin long enough to comment, "Thanks for making me order something. Didn't realize how hungry I was! I guess I was a little starving after eating that slop that they fed us in lockup."

Larry grinned, then took a sip of his iced tea. "Your mama always had a big appetite too, especially when she was carrying you, in between her morning sickness... Lord, I do love to see a woman eat well."

"So, what's our first move? How are we gonna prove I didn't do this? I don't wanna spend my father's last days behind bars. I wanna spend time with them enjoying your company and watching you spend time with my baby. That's all I care about right now."

Larry smiled. "Well, I reckon we need to interview all the witnesses. The police have a list of people that were in the hotel that night, both before and after the time of death. We need to find out what they know and what they saw. That's number one."

"That sounds good. What else? Oh boy, this baby sure is hungry right now!" Laura said. She was suddenly quite distracted by a fierce hunger for more food. Her father didn't seem to mind. He chuckled a bit as she called the waitress over to order a sandwich and an iced tea.

"Well, you're gonna need to take me through the whole week leading to the deaths," Larry continued. "Be as specific as you can. A minute-by-minute account if you can manage it, everything from what you two said, to where you went, and who you met with. I'm thinking it would be best if I interviewed you and we recorded your day-by-day account of things,"

Larry bit down on his breakfast sausage, then called attention to the waitress, who'd just arrived with Laura's food.

As soon as the waitress set down the plate, Laura took a big chunk out of Larry's omelette and gobbled it down, then licked her lips. She couldn't remember the last time she'd taken so much pleasure in eating anything. "Why didn't you tell me your omelette was that good? Maybe I will have a shrimp po'boy."

Larry looked at her and smiled. "Guess everything tastes better when you're eating for two?"

She bit into the toast that accompanied Larry's omelette and groaned. "Mmmm..."

"I'm so glad to see you eat something for the baby." Larry smiled. "We'd better get that list and get to these interviews today. We can't afford to waste any time."

Laura gulped down the last bite of her toast and licked her fingers. "I'm ready now. Let's get to work. I'll get a sandwich to take away. I may need a snack later."

Larry looked at his empty plate and grinned awkwardly. "Make it two, please."

"Oh shucks, Daddy. I'm sorry."

Larry chuckled. "It's all okay, darlin'. Never mind me. You just keep eating."

# CORAL

*February 1977, On the outskirts of New Orleans*

CORAL WEPT. SHE WAS LYING ON HER SIDE, OVER A MASSIVE PILE OF used tissues, clutching on to Brian's faded baby blanket. She cuddled with it, now and then sneaking a smell. *He always smelled so sweet. What a perfect baby! My sweet boy...those little toes. Oh God. I'll never see him again. How will I live? I can't take this. I can't.*

That perfect baby smell only made her cry more. At least Daryl Rae was taking care of her, bringing her soup, and giving her a strong shoulder to cry on. He made the pain at least bearable.

The doorbell rang. "Ike, I hope that's you, son," Daryl Rae called out as he opened the door. "Your mama needs more Tylenol and I'd really like to stay here with her."

He looked surprised when a feminine voice replied, "I'm not Ike, whoever that is."

Coral came to the door, sniffling and still clutching the baby blanket. The young woman at the door was very pretty, and she definitely didn't recognize her. *Who in the hell is this?*

"Oh, I'm sorry. Thought it was my girlfriend's son at the door. How can we help you, ma'am?" Daryl Rae asked, standing up straight.

"I'm looking for Coral Buchanan," the woman said. "I'm a reporter for The Bayou. Excuse me, are you Ms. Buchanan?"

Coral smoothed her hair and wiped her nose. "Yes, but I'm not married to Jack Buchanan anymore."

*Now, who the fuck are you?*

"I don't recollect if I've ever heard of The Bayou, ma'am." Daryl Rae blurted.

Coral stared and folded her arms. *Neither have I. Good point Daryl Rae.*

The young woman gave them a tight-lipped smile, and slowly took off her dark sunglasses, revealing her striking blue eyes. "Let's start over," the woman said. "My name is Jane Wheeler, and I'm a reporter for a small women's magazine, The Bayou. We do pieces on women of means and style. I've been following Ms. Coral's news for a long time now, and I was saddened to hear of her son's passing. I really hoped I could get the scoop on this story before others start pounding on her door. Will you help me please? I'd love to write about you, Ms. Coral."

She spoke with softness in her voice and ended her words with a flirtatious glance up at Daryl Rae. *Damn, she's good at getting the men to notice her. Got my boyfriend eating out of the palm of her hand already.*

Daryl Rae cleared his throat and coughed. "Well, I reckon it won't hurt. What do you think, darlin'?"

"Sure, why not?" Coral murmured, sniffling. "I'm not in a great mood for any of this, though."

"Great!" She said, stepping inside. Her reply certainly caught Cora's attention.

Jane looked around eagerly, almost hunting for something. She sat on Coral's sofa and crossed her long legs. *Wow, those are some sexy legs. I'm sure Daryl Rae isn't gonna miss the chance to stare at those.*

Coral clicked her tongue and gave Daryl Rae a dirty look, because sure enough, he reacted exactly as she predicted. He couldn't peel his eyes away, not for a second. *That's my man, predictable as the day is long.*

"Baby, why don't you help me get this sweet lady something to drink, and a snack? What do you think? Maybe some coffee and chocolate chip cookies? Some of my kind neighbors brought some over. Come to think of it, I think I've got about every casserole ever made in here if you're hungry."

"You don't have to go to all the bother," Jane said.

"Oh honey, it's really no bother," Coral said. "You'll be doing me a favor by eating some of this. It's just how it's done in the South. There's a death in the family, then everyone brings a casserole, so you don't have to cook until the cows come home!"

"Well, the cookies sound good," Jane said.

"Huh?" Daryl Rae mumbled.

Coral pinched his arm. "Ow! Um, okay. Yeah, I'm sorry. Let's get that snack," he said.

Coral was nervous but wanted to make sure Daryl Rae didn't mess anything up. She accompanied him to the kitchen. "You make yourself comfortable, hun. We'll be right back."

# JANE

WHEN THEY WERE OUT OF SIGHT, JANE SNOOPED AROUND. SHE spotted several picture frames holding photos of Brian with his mother and brothers. She picked up one that seemed to be a particularly happy occasion, one in which they were all smiling.

"What made you so special?" she whispered, looking at Brian's eyes. *Was it just because you were a boy? You made him forget me completely.*

She hurriedly replaced the photo as Coral walked in, smiling. "So, you're from a magazine. The Bayou? Can't say that I've heard of it, but I don't get much time for looking at magazines."

"Really?" Jane asked.

"Okay," Coral said. "You got me there. I am a little obsessed with self-help articles and such. Guess I've always wanted to figure out where I went wrong in life."

"It's all right, Ms. Buchanan. I know you've had a lot to deal with lately. I'm so sorry to hear of your loss," she said, holding Coral's hand.

Coral's eyes welled up again. "Thank you for that miss, what was your name again?"

She smiled. "Jane Wheeler, ma'am, but you can call me Jane."

"Oh fiddlesticks," Coral said. "I must've totally forgotten. I haven't been myself lately. You'll have to excuse me."

"It's okay, ma'am. You have every right. You've been through a lot."

"Daryl Rae?" Coral said. "Can you go check on that stew in the crock pot? I'm worried about it drying out."

"Sure. I'll leave you ladies to it," Daryl Rae said with a lingering glance at Jane's legs.

"I know I just said we have a kitchen full of casseroles. I don't care for the taste of the casserole very much. Don't matter what kind it is. Don't like 'em at all. Guess none of my neighbors ever noticed that about me."

Coral looked at Jane. "Have we met before?"

Jane shifted in her seat. *What's she playing at? She can't possibly know me.*

"No, ma'am. I'm quite certain that we haven't. However, I've been to many of New Orleans' finest social events. Perhaps we've met at one of them? You, being a Buchanan, must have had your fill of those."

Coral giggled and blushed. *She really does want to be a woman of prestige. Wow! Look at her, forgetting her own son, to giggle at my compliment.*

Jane watched as Coral's eyes practically twinkled, marveling at how fast she grabbed on to the chance for some recognition.

"Well, maybe that explains it. I guess I have been to a *soiree* or two," Coral said.

Daryl Rae stuck his head in. "Hey, that stew's coming along. It smells finger lickin' good, baby. Are you gonna put it in the specials at the restaurant?"

Coral blushed. She put down her coffee. "Excuse me."

"Take your time," Jane replied.

Coral jumped up and even though she tried to whisper, her voice carried into the room. "Daryl Rae, I need you to stay put in the kitchen for a while so I can conduct my business. Do you hear me?"

"I was just trying to help," Daryl Rae replied, lowering his head. "Maybe I'll just go get a beer at the bar. See ya later."

Coral entered and took a seat on the couch again. Daryl Rae zipped through the living room and out the front door, taking one last peek at Jane's legs. *What a creep*, she thought.

Jane directed the conversation. She flipped out a small note pad and pen from her purse to take notes. "Now, Ms. Buchanan, how was it being married to one of the most powerful men in America? Tell us about the love story between you and

Jack Buchanan II." Jane prompted. She smiled wickedly. *Bet that's gonna make you forget the redneck.*

"Ha! Well, I wouldn't call it a *love* story. It was more of a *lust* story actually," Coral said, nodding her head at the memory.

"I don't understand," Jane said, tilting her head.

"Well, darlin', you know the drill. You get a job waitressing at a fancy New Orleans hotel, and you take it. You take it because you need the money, and because you never know *who* you're gonna meet at such a place. Lord, I swear, I have never seen anyone like Jack."

She smiled and her eyes softened. "He was a charmer from the start. Such a smile! Oh my."

Coral gulped and sighed at the sweet memory. "Not that I don't love Daryl Rae. Please don't get me wrong."

Jane smiled. "No, it's fine. I want you to be candid in your answers. Maybe it's better that he's not here right now."

"What's better if I'm not here?" Daryl shut the front door behind him.

"Nothing, darlin'," Coral sputtered. "Don't worry about it. I'm glad you're here. What happened to you going out?"

"Couldn't get the truck to start," he murmured. "Guess you gotta put up with me. Sorry."

Coral reached out to take Daryl Rae's hand. He sneered, then looked away. Jane cocked her head to one side. "How long have the two of you been together?"

"A long time...yeah, before daddy big bucks came along," Daryl Rae scoffed.

Coral winced. "Oh, I should explain. You see, Daryl Rae and I go way back. For a long time, he kind of switched between being my boyfriend and being with my friend, Stella."

"Stella? Really?" Jane had to resist the urge to wince.

"Yes, she was my best friend for a long time, until Daryl Rae decided he only wanted to be with me. That's when we started going steady." Coral poured herself a glass of iced tea, then continued. "But Jack was the infatuation of a lifetime. It was the one night with him that gave me my son, Brian." Coral sobbed.

Daryl put his arm around her and said, "Shh...Shhh...It's okay, baby."

"Didn't mean to upset you, ma'am." Jane said.

"No, I know. It's fine. I just can't believe he's gone. Jack and I got married for only a short time, just to legitimize Brian's name, to make him a *real* Buchanan," Coral said. She smiled. "I'm so proud of the man he became, but now that he's dead...I..." Coral sobbed. "I'm sorry, it's so hard to talk about my boy. God, how I loved him!" Jane feigned a tear, then made eye contact, forcing herself to look sympathetic. *I can't believe he rejected my mother only to accept...**this**.*

Coral gulped. "I can't help but wonder if I should have kept him. Maybe he would be alive today if he'd grown up with me instead of Jack? I don't know...In that house, his life was about being a boss, being strong...but in my house, he would have learned how to love...But, hey, he would've been dirt poor, and that ain't...I mean...isn't, any fun. That's why I agreed to Jack taking him after the divorce, so he could have a better life."

Jane leaned in to hear her better and muttered, "Agreed to give him to Jack? What exactly does that mean, ma'am?"

Coral said, "Well, in exchange for the start-up money for my restaurant, I agreed to divorce amicably and walk away from Brian's life. That's how I started the *Coral* restaurant. It's a big success in New Orleans now, and we've even got a chain coming up. Our second restaurant is going to open in Baton Rouge soon," Coral said, smiling. The tears were in her eyes, but clearly the thought of a new restaurant had perked her up. Her demeanor changed. *Success agrees with her.*

"And a fine establishment it is! We're planning a photo shoot there soon, to accompany the story. I hope you'll agree to be in many of the shots?" Jane asked.

"Oh, of course I will!" Coral beamed. She eagerly smiled as she shifted in her seat and crossed her legs. "It would be an honor."

Daryl Rae smiled. "See, baby. I told you your ship would come in."

Jane cleared her throat, forcing herself to stay in character. *What a phony!*

"All right then. I think I should be going. I won't take up much of your time today. I really just wanted to meet you in person and get a sense of things before doing the story on your baby."

Coral's mouth dropped open in shock and dismay. Jane quickly corrected herself. "I mean your flourishing business."

"Oh, I see." Coral said. She exhaled. "Well, thanks for dropping by, and let me know when you wanna take those pictures!"

Jane nodded and smiled, walking out the door, then to her car. She got in, cranked up the engine and waved goodbye to Coral, who was still watching from the doorway. Once she was a block away, she took off the brunette wig, revealing flowing blonde locks.

"Morons. Why did he pick *them?*"

# LARRY

IT WAS EARLY MORNING WHEN LARRY CHECKED IN ON LAURA, WHO was still asleep in her room. The small hotel suite they occupied wasn't five stars, but he was grateful for the fact that it was clean and comfortable. Between his cancer treatments and Laura's bailout, cash was tight, so it was the best he could do.

He stood in the doorway for a moment, watching her breathing. He sighed and smiled. *Rest now, sweetheart. God only knows what's in store for us, so you go on and rest up while you can.*

He let the feeling of gratitude wash over him like a warm summer breeze. For the moment, he took solace in knowing that she's safe and comfortable, and for now, that felt just fine.

Larry realized it was time to go visit Delta Dawn's aunt, Susan McFarland. Hopefully, Susan would shed light on who this young woman was, and how she came to know his son-in-law.

After leaving a note for Laura, and following an overly complicated set of directions, he arrived at Susan's house, although "house" may have been stretching it a bit. She lived in a trailer park, a very dilapidated one at that. Larry parked the car, then made his way to the door.

Susan's trailer was old, rusty, and weather-beaten. Larry jumped when he heard the snarl of a dog close by. "Holy shit!"

Thankfully, the pit bull terrier was tied to a tree. He looked more closely and realized that this poor animal was only lashing out due to its living conditions. His brow furrowed and his lips pressed into a hard line. *You scared the shit out of me... poor thing...tied up like that. You're looking kinda poorly too. Bet you haven't been well fed for ages. That's so wrong.*

Patchy bits of grass were growing all around, completely unattended. There was even a broken car in her yard, with no wheels, propped up on cement blocks. He removed the handkerchief from his breast pocket to cover his nose. The smell of raw sewage permeated the air, causing his eyes to water.

Susan opened the door, revealing a home ensemble of bedroom slippers and a cheap China town robe loosely wrapped around her bloated overweight body. She was holding a half-smoked cigarette that needed flicking. The ashes were hanging precariously, and a puff of putrid smoke propelled its way out of her lungs, revealing her yellow crooked teeth. *What the Hell is that? God damn, that's a face only a mother could love. And what is that fucking smell? Is that her cooch? Reminds me of my public defender days and all those "working" girls. God give me strength.*

She smiled. "Well, hello there. I'm Susan. It's really nice to meet you in person...Should I call you 'Mayor', or 'Your Honor', or just Mr. Beauford? You said on the phone that you're a mayor in Alabama."

He smiled back, lips tight. *Good God Almighty, her breath reeks!* "Oh, just call me Larry, ma'am."

She smoothed her wrinkled fingers through her outdated poofy beehive hairstyle, something that was popular a decade ago in the 60's. She grinned even wider. "Larry... well, well, do come on in. Make yourself at home while I get some clothes on."

Larry shuddered. *Why am I imagining her naked right now? Uff, I don't wanna lose my breakfast. Come on Larry! Let's get in and out of this lair before she eats you for lunch!*

He cleared his throat. "Yes ma'am. I appreciate you taking the time to see me today. Just have a few questions about your niece, and I won't take any more of your time."

She shouted from inside the bedroom, "Oh, Larry, it's fine. It's not every day I get such a handsome gentleman such as yourself at my door. A fine mayor like you is always welcome to set a spell."

She came out, wearing a skin-tight leopard-print jumpsuit with flip flops that showed her freshly pedicured feet. The outfit may not have been so inappropriate for a much younger woman. Larry started sweating as he felt her predatory glance take in his body from top to toe, crotch included. *Sweet Baby Jesus, please get me out of here without needing to touch any of that.* He prayed. Beads of sweat formed on his forehead, and he patted it with the handkerchief. Struggling to regain his composure, he carried on with the interview. "Susan, I'd like to share my condolences for your loss. I understand Delta Dawn was your niece and that you are her only living relative... Can you tell me more about her? Were you two close?"

"Oh, we weren't too close at first," Susan said, blinking back tears from her eyes. "Her mother was my sister, and she got killed when a bunch of junkies broke into her trailer, trying to find her stash."

Larry gulped. "Susan, do you mind if I record this? I promise this isn't for any other purpose except for trying to build a profile of Delta Dawn, so we can learn all we can about how she came to know my son in law."

"Oh, no. I don't mind. It's fine." Susan said.

Larry started the tape recorder. "You mentioned a stash? Did Delta Dawn's mother have drugs at her place?"

"Yes, she sure did! Oh Larry, she was a hooker, and she'd sometimes get paid in *product.* Poor Delta Dawn was about the skinniest thing I'd ever seen because she wasn't fed right most of the time."

"Poor girl," Larry said.

"Yeah, it was terrible. Her daddy could have been any of my sister's Johns. She wasn't the most *careful* in the world. Guess it wasn't a big surprise when Delta Dawn started tricking herself. Like mother, like daughter you know," Susan said.

She blew a smoke ring, watching it lazily float up towards the stained ceiling.

"I reckon so," Larry said, temporarily mesmerized by the smoke ring.

He shook himself out of it and paused, tapping his chin. *Pictures...that's what I need now.*

"Do you have any pictures of Delta Dawn?"

"Yeah, reckon I've got a few. After you called, I went on and found some that weren't too mangled up. Here ya go," she said, handing him a few worn photos.

There were only a few, and most were inconsequential, a few childhood shots of her with her mother, and one or two from grade school. But one photo caught his eye. One photo showed Delta Dawn as an adult with some other women. It looked like a reunion of some sort; Larry surmised. "What's this picture of?"

"Oh, yeah. That's when she met her friends from Juvie Town," she said.

"Juvie Town?" Larry asked. "She went to Juvie?"

"Oh, I keep forgetting how sophisticated you are, darlin'. Yes, that's right. They were detained in a rehabilitation center instead of going to jail."

Larry looked at the photo. *This girl next to Delta Dawn looks oddly familiar. I'll bet my kidney that Delta Dawn was set up by this woman, but why?*

"Can I keep this one?"

"Sure, you can, darlin'. You can have *whatever* you want," she said, giving Larry a little wink. She leaned forward to give him the photo and purposely leaned too far, so that she'd show her wrinkled cleavage. Larry gasped. She smiled and licked her lips suggestively.

"Thank you, ma'am," he said, weakly, dabbing the handkerchief at his brow.

*I now have a newfound understanding of women who feel in danger of being raped. I gotta get out of here, fast, before she throws that putrid body on me!* She almost purred as she stared at him with hungry eyes. *I gotta get her off my trail.*

"Well, now, how do you think Delta Dawn met Brian?"

As soon as he asked, he felt a stab of regret, and braced himself for her answer. *Oh God, please don't say Brian was her client.*

*Brian wouldn't chase down some cheap hooker.* It was unthinkable. Why would he? He had Laura, a beautiful and sophisticated woman who loved him dearly.

"Someone hired her to meet Brian at a hotel lobby. Don't know which one, or who hired her. But she rushed out saying how making this much money would set her up," Susan said.

Larry exhaled as though he'd been holding his breath. "Oh, thank God!" Susan did a double take.

"Sorry ma'am. Didn't mean that the way it sounded. I'm just glad my son-in-law isn't the one who hired her."

Susan took a drag of her cigarette, staring him down like a piece of meat. Larry felt the predatory nature of her stares but tried to carry on ignoring them. She smiled like a cat who's just seen a bird.

"Well, I didn't say who hired her," Susan said. "Her exact words were, 'I'm getting paid to meet a rich guy, Brian Buchanan. I've gotta go. Hotel's in New Orleans so I've got a way to go.'"

"But that doesn't sound like Brian himself hired her," Larry said. "Or at least I hope not."

"You're probably right," Susan replied, eyeing him from head to toe again.

Larry tapped his feet, shifting in his seat. She was looking at him again, and to his horror, she unbuttoned another button. He could see she was not wearing any brassiere. He gulped and pulled at his shirt collar. "Um...I...uh...anything else you can remember about that night?"

She paused, then clicked her tongue. "Now that you mention it, I do remember she threw some clothes in an overnight bag. When are the cops gonna give it back to me?"

"No, I have not heard any mention of Delta Dawn's things."

Susan grinned and moved closer to Larry on the sagging couch. His body screamed for her to get away. "Would you like to stay for lunch?" She whispered. "I make a mean bowl of chili! I'll bet you're a real strong 'chili' man, ain't ya?"

He noticed that now her breath reeked of not only tobacco but whiskey as well. It took all his willpower to avoid heaving. He smiled as politely as he could. "Oh, no ma'am. Gotta get home to my daughter. She's feeling poorly and needs me nearby these days."

She backed away a little, looking at him from head to toe. "Ain't you sweet? You're a good daddy, and you're good looking. Where've you been all my life, you stud?"

*I've been away from trash like you!*

He smiled, clearing his throat to disguise his revulsion, then got up and hurriedly shook her hand. "Well, thank you ma'am."

"Susan."

"I beg your pardon."

"Call me Susan, you good looking thing. In fact, you can call me anything you want," she said, winking.

*Dear God, I think I know what the deer feels like now. I feel positively stalked!* He reached for his tape recorder with his left hand and caught a glimpse of his wedding ring. *She doesn't know I'm a widower. That's my ticket!* He left the recorder alone for a moment and put his left hand over their clasped hands. She stopped shaking his hand to look at the ring more closely.

Larry feigned a sigh. "Yes, my dear Susan, if I weren't already sworn to another, I'd sit right down and have that chili, but I'm a good Christian man, and I do love my little woman, so I'm afraid I gotta go!"

"Uh, okay then," she sighed, defeated.

Larry took his chance and bolted back to his car. After he'd driven off a bit, he loosened his bow tie, then let out a big sigh. Finally able to breathe normally, he was relieved to have escaped her clutches. He let himself have a little chuckle as he thought of Susan.

"Good God Almighty! Whoo! Glad to be out of there."

*What she said about the overnight bag was odd though,* he thought as he drove. *Who took that? There was no bag found at the scene. Very odd indeed.*

# LARRY

LARRY REACHED THE HOTEL SUITE AND FOUND LAURA ON THE PHONE with yet another witness. She gave him a thumbs-up. "Yeah, okay. You're sure that's all you remember... Okay, what time did you say we can come over? Yes, very good. That works for us. We'll be there shortly. Thank you."

"Who was that?" he asked.

"Hey Daddy. How was your trip?"

Laura got up and gave him a warm hug. Larry snorted, "Well darlin', I barely got out of there with my life. That Susan is quite the huntress!"

Laura sniggered. "Huntress?"

"It's nothing, honey. That *lady*, and I use the term very loosely, was just trying her best to *bed* me. But I managed to make my exit without her attaching herself to my wallet."

Larry touched Laura's belly. "My wallet is all for this little guy or girl."

He looked her in the eye, hand resting on her shoulder. "How are you feeling today?"

She shook her head. "I'm better. Got me some crackers and Seven-Up for the morning sickness, so that's helping a lot."

"That's really good." Larry smiled. "Did I hear you on the phone with some of the hotel witnesses?"

She threw her hands up and exhaled. "Yes, and so far, nothing useful."

"But there's one odd thing," she said, tapping her chin.

"Odd?"

"Yeah. That night, I could have sworn I saw someone not on this list. All the witnesses are here in this file, and I have pictures of every single one, but there's a woman missing." Laura handed the file to Larry, and he started flipping through it.

"Who's missing? How do you know someone's missing? Don't forget you were distraught that night. Your memory could be faulty," Larry said.

Laura folded her arms. "She was so very sad…There was something about her eyes, so…forlorn. I ran into her once while we stayed there. Then, I remembered her face, even though I was far away when I noticed her. I was being hauled away, but the way she looked at me. She looked…I dunno, guilty? Like she had been crying. Like I said, there was something about her eyes, deep blue, like the ocean."

Laura scoffed and looked at him. "I know I was out of it, but I remember she had dark hair, and there's not a single brunette in this pile."

Larry got up to pour himself a glass of water. "That could be significant. Give that some more thought and maybe you will remember some more later?"

"You could be right. Well, tell me, did you find out anything important from Susan? Or was she just chasing you around her living room?" Laura asked with a sly grin.

Larry chuckled a little. "Other than how to protect my bank account and my virtue, I found out someone hired Delta Dawn to meet Brian at the hotel, and she packed an orange overnight bag trimmed with white that she took with her. Evidently it had big white daisies on it and was packed with a macrame vest, bell bottom jeans, and a halter top. That was the change of clothes she brought…Oh, and a pair of orange platform shoes too and lots of sparkly makeup. This gal was a real character evidently."

"No one mentioned an overnight bag as an item found in the room or anywhere else," Laura scoffed. "I certainly would have noticed something so ugly. Orange? Big white daisies?"

"Exactly," Larry said. "I want to return to the crime scene and look around myself. I'll interview the officers on duty that night. If anyone could make evidence disappear, it's a police officer, don't you think?"

Laura's eyes narrowed. "Still think it was Jim, don't you?"

"You gotta admit, it's the most logical choice at this point." Larry said. "But I dunno. They did have a certain affection for one another... but we are talking about millions of dollars."

Larry looked at the papers in Laura's hand. "I suppose we'll have a better idea when all the interviews are done. How far did you get?"

"About halfway ...But I'm thinking I should go to the hotel myself tomorrow to check the guest records, if they'll let me," Laura said.

"They may not. Those records are confidential unless the police order it. I'll have to take care of it. As your attorney, I've got the right to see all evidence gathered against you, and I'm betting they already compiled this list from guest records."

Laura folded her arms. *I've got every one of those faces etched in my memory. I should be there.* "Can I still come with you though?"

"I think that should be just fine. You're the only one who can identify that mystery woman you just told me about," he said, smiling.

Laura returned his smile. "So, you were listening."

"I was indeed!" Larry said. "Now, more importantly. Has my 'expectant' daughter eaten anything today?"

Laura shook her head and Larry saw the heap of cigarette butts in the ashtray. *What is she trying to do?*

He shook his head, lips pressed into a hard line. He gave her one of his best fatherly scolding looks.

"I know. I know," she said, feeling the weight of his stare. "I'm just holding on by a thread, Daddy. My husband was violently murdered, and I can't take five minutes to mourn him, not really. Not when I'm defending myself. I never thought in a million years I'd end up in this scenario. God knows how much I loved him."

Tears rolled out of her eyes as she reached for another cigarette. Larry couldn't take it anymore. He had to speak up.

"Sweetheart, please don't smoke...Every time you light up, think of that sweet little baby inside you. I just came from that old crow, Susan. God knows, every time she opened her mouth it smelled like an ashtray. Your mother used to smoke, as did I. I just don't have a good feeling about it." he said as he removed the ashtray.

Laura looked at the floor. "Fine, I promise. No more. Not one more smoke."

Larry cleared his throat and abruptly dumped the cigarette butts in the trash.

"All right then...So, come on. Let's go to this appointment you set for us, and we can grab a bite to eat on the way."

Laura nodded and got her purse. Before she left, she threw the remaining cigarettes in the trash. Larry grinned. She rushed to him and he held the door open for her as they left. On their way out, Laura paused. "What's wrong?" Larry asked.

"I forgot to ask...were any fingerprints taken at the scene?"

Larry cleared his throat. "Well...yep."

He looked away from her. "The only prints they found were yours. Other than that, they found a boot print on the balcony, but that could've been a window washer."

"A window washer?" Laura's brow furrowed. "Well, okay. I had to ask. Let's go."

# LAURA

SINCE BRIAN'S MURDER, THE LIFE OF A WEALTHY SOCIALITE WASN'T IN the cards for Laura. Mary Grace, who was Jack's secretary, then Brian's, regretfully informed her of her dire financial state shortly after her arraignment. Not only was she forbidden to leave the New Orleans city limits, her and Brian's assets were frozen until the trial came to an end, and the Buchanan Oil lawyers even sealed up her house for the time being. Buchanan Oil was operating under the leadership of Jack's Deputy Director, Harrison Howard III, a mealy faced balding man in his late sixties, a man without gumption, certainly a pale echo of Jack or Brian, but at least he was loyal. She felt confident that, for the moment, the company was in safe hands. She was free to worry about her freedom and her good name.

She had no choice but to stay with her father in the small hotel suite he'd paid for. Thankfully, he'd found something fairly affordable in New Orleans, so she could stay with him and ensure he took care of himself properly. She also needed to mourn the loss of her husband, something that her current predicament scarcely allowed her to do. Since the murders, she couldn't lay her head on a pillow without seeing Brian's face, the love of her life. By the time morning came, her blanket was awash with tissues. Even though it broke her heart, lying down with

Brian's memories and the love in her heart for him helped her feel his presence, even now. Alas, the morning always followed.

She poured the morning coffee as Larry finished his phone conversation. "Yeah ... Okay. I see. Yep, I'll be down there to pick it up today. Thank you."

"Who was that, Daddy?" Laura asked.

Larry took a cup of coffee from Laura. "Oh, that was the coroner's office. They have the results of the autopsy, and we need that to help build our case."

"What did it say? Anything helpful?" Laura asked.

"Well, he wouldn't tell me much on the phone, but there's a few things I found interesting." Larry said.

"Like what?" Laura asked, crunching into a slice of toast.

"So far, no news on Brian's autopsy results, but at least we know that Delta wasn't raped. Also, she doesn't have any living parents. Her only living relative, her aunt, is going to testify for the prosecution. So, we need to get the chance to interview her. Go ahead and put her at the top of the list," Larry ordered. He took a sip of coffee.

"What's her name?"

"Susan McFarland. She lives in Baton Rouge, so I'll have to go see her. You're ordered to stay here in the city, so I don't want you to violate your bail conditions, sweetie pie."

She noticed that her father wasn't acting his usual self. He gazed at her and looked a bit *misty. Oh no. Please don't cry, Daddy. I'll fall to pieces if you do.*

"What's up, Daddy? Are you feeling okay?"

"You're the light of my life, baby girl. Don't worry. I'll be fine, but in the meantime, I want you to compile a list of the witnesses in the hotel and their addresses. When I come back, we'll get to them and find out who else the DA plans on bringing to the party."

"Way ahead of you, Daddy! While you were sleeping, I was doing exactly that. I called for the list, then tried calling a bunch of them. Most people on the list said they remained in their room, even when they heard a scream. No one seems to have heard any gunshots, so that's weird."

Larry raised an eyebrow. "What kind of gun was used in the shooting?"

"A .38 caliber. The same service revolver most cops use around here, I reckon," she said, tilting her head. *What's he thinking?*

"You remembered your training, didn't you?"

She grinned. "Of course I did! What kind of proper Alabama debutante walks around without a decent knowledge of firearms?"

"That's my girl," he said.

He paused for a moment and raised his eyebrows, opening his mouth. "Jim ... Can we find out if that was Jim's gun? Did they find a serial number?"

"Surely, they have to tell you that. Anything less would be withholding evidence," Laura said.

Larry picked up the phone receiver. "I'm gonna ask about this before I forget."

Moments later, he plopped down on the chair and sighed. "Well, it just got stickier."

"How so?" Laura asked.

"The serial number was scratched off," Larry said, folding his arms. "I guess if Jim did such a thing, he'd know to destroy the serial number, but to tell ya the truth, I just can't see that boy hurting Brian. He's crude and rude most of the time, but murder? There's gotta be another explanation."

She nodded. "I'm just as confused as you are about that...Well, as for those who did pop out of their rooms when they realized something was happening, the prosecution has a list of thirteen names. I'll call them up and book us an appointment with at least four per day. Then we can start comparing their stories for clues."

"That's perfect, sweetheart. But don't forget we gotta find out everything about Jim and Ike's whereabouts at that time, all about their relationship with Brian, and how it progressed and...let's not forget about the other victim. Delta must have had colleagues, friends, or someone in the hotel must have seen her, someone we could talk to. We have to find out what her story was, and how she even came to know someone like Brian."

Laura nodded as her father spoke, writing it all down. She loved making *to do* lists. They made her feel there was order in a world of chaos. Each day, she happily checked off items, one by one, as they were completed. Larry knew he needed to interview her first, before the other people's recollections clouded Laura's memories. It was also near the top of her list. Learning about the most intimate details would shed light on the case.

"Daddy?"

"Yes, darlin'?"

"Can we get my interview out of the way now?" Laura said softly.

"Okay, sure thing. If you think you're up to it."

Larry started the tape recording and paced the room while speaking. "How would you describe your relationship with Brian Buchanan?"

"Well, we were made for each other. I didn't know that at first, but it became clear to me after a few years together in college and six months of marriage. Even when we fought, we were drawn to each other like magnets. We just 'fit' in every way. We were like pieces of a jigsaw puzzle that just filled in each other's empty spaces. I loved him every day, and he loved me," Laura said, a tear welling in her eye.

Larry paused, then went on. "Who did Brian spend his time with when he wasn't with you? *How* did he spend his time? Especially in the last months of his life."

Laura cleared her throat, then sat up straight. "Well, when he wasn't with me, he was working. He spent long hours at the office, but I just figured that's what it's gonna take to run his father's company. He was tremendously committed to making Jack proud of how he'd handled things while he was away in the Middle East."

"Long hours? Did Brian ever talk about the people he ran into at work? Who he ate lunch with? Who he golfed with?"

"Mary Grace was the main one he was in contact with. She used to be Jack's secretary, but she performed the same duties for Brian when Jack left. She's a sweet person, and if anyone would be able to comment on his habits at work, it'd be her. But with me, not so much. When he was home, he was *home*. He just wanted to get down to doing regular things. Every time I'd try to bring up work, he said he'd rather not bring work home. He wanted to keep *our* time as a relaxing time. Sometimes he'd call and say he needed to stay late because he had to go to work functions and such, but he never told me what they were," she said, scrunching her forehead. Her father's eyes widened.

"Did that upset you?" He asked.

"Sort of ... I mean, it didn't make me happy at all to know the man I loved was skulking around with God knows who," she said, lowering her head.

Larry's mouth dropped open a bit. He pulled a chair closer and sat down squarely in front of Laura. "Honey, was he cheating on you?"

Laura's mouth pressed into a hard line, and she thought for a moment. "Not that I know of for sure. Honestly, I don't think so. It was a little weird that he was out a lot and sometimes very distracted from spending time with me, but I have no proof he actually did anything. I was trying to give him the benefit of the doubt.

Gosh, we were even trying to get pregnant, and we succeeded. If I was gonna have this man's child, I certainly didn't wanna think of him playing around on me."

"Makes sense," Larry said.

He watched her take a sip of coffee. Abruptly, his eyebrows rose. "Should you be drinking so much coffee? You just said earlier that the baby was kicking up a storm."

She was about to take another sip, as the same thought entered her mind. She put the cup down and looked at it. "I don't know. Do you reckon I'm keeping him awake?"

Larry looked at her quizzically. Laura thought for a moment "Daddy, do you really think coffee would hurt the baby? I haven't had any chance to visit an obstetrician since I got out. My regular doctor didn't ever say anything about coffee. Gosh, I'm out of vitamins too. I hope he or she is okay."

*Oh God, this poor child. I really don't know the first thing about being a mother. I don't even know if drinking coffee is gonna hurt my baby.* She tapped her chin with a finger.

"You know, I know we're limited on time here, but I think a trip to the doctor is unavoidable. I have so many questions and I wanna do right by this child."

Larry nodded.

"We need to push again for more time till the trial," he said. "We didn't make a big enough stink about you being pregnant. We need more time to work out who did this and gather evidence. Oh, my Lord, darlin', we *have* to get you free. Do you realize this baby could end up being raised by Coral? You wouldn't want that, would you?"

Laura slammed her empty coffee cup on the table, turning towards him. Her hands shook at the thought of such a horrific possibility. *Coral? A mother to my child?*

"No, not her. Anyone but her! Oh God!"

Laura ran to the toilet, feeling the coffee coming back up. After she'd cleaned herself up, Larry took her to a doctor. The doctor confirmed that the heir to the Buchanan fortune was healthy, despite the stress Laura was experiencing. Of course, this stress was compounded by the fact that her doctor and his office staff were so obviously trying to maintain a professional attitude but failing spectacularly with all the side glances and poorly hidden looks of disgust. She was all over the papers, after all, branded as a gold-digging husband killer. It broke her heart. Only her inner circle would ever know how much she loved Brian, or how she wondered every night if she could live without him. There was one thing keeping her going and one thing only. This child. The only thing left of Brian on this Earth. She had to stay strong to make sure this child didn't grow up without a mother as well.

*My baby is gonna be one of the richest babies in America. Every one of them is gonna want to claim him or her. Daddy's right. I need to be freed. I have to prove I didn't do this.*

She recited this declaration to herself many times. Larry entered the examination room, sitting on a chair near Laura, who still hadn't changed out of her hospital gown. The look on her face was hard to decipher. She smiled, but it was grim, knowing that a part of Brian would live on beyond them, beyond all this terrible predicament. Her eyes showed her sorrow at the situation, the despair she felt knowing she may die shortly after she gives birth, leaving a very vulnerable, extraordinarily rich baby to Coral's manipulations.

"It's gonna be okay. You'll see," Larry said.

She got off the bed and hugged her father. "I don't know what I'd do if you weren't here. How am I supposed to live without you? You've always been my rock."

"You'll be just fine, my girl. You come from good stock. Don't forget that" Larry assured her. "I'm still here, so let's just focus on what we do have right now, okay?"

She nodded. "Okay. I'll go change, and let's get back to work"

"That's my brave girl."

# JIM

A FEW DAYS AFTER BRIAN'S MURDER, JIM PLANNED ON WORKING, BUT it was a rough day. He did have his first good night's sleep though, thanks to a certain sleeping tablet, so he came to work ready to face the day. He looked at himself in the mirror. *No one expects me to be there today. It's still too soon. Heck, there's a lot of them that wouldn't want me to come back, ever. Fuck them.*

He figured that now is probably a time for positive thinking. *That's what everyone keeps telling me. I'm positive all right. Positive I'm gonna find the fucker that did this to my brother and that poor girl and make them pay!*

That horrible night had haunted his dreams. He somehow knew that it had burned itself into his memory forever. His waking moments were spent remembering Brian as a kid. Since he was the oldest brother, Jim had taught Brian to ride a bike, how to shave, and how to flirt with girls. When he closed his eyes at night, he went back to that crime scene. The bits of bone and brains splattered on the velvet headboard. His heart pounded every time his dreams took him back to that horrible night. Would anything ever make this right again?

# JIM

"ALL UNITS. 10-76 AT CHATEAU VERSAILLES."

He drove at high speed, the siren going full tilt. He hoped that he was wrong, only to have his worst fears confirmed by a paramedic outside. They were waiting for the forensic team to finish with the evidence before they could remove the bodies. Brian was dead. And an unidentified woman. The detective knew that Brian was his brother and ordered Jim to stay away from the crime scene.

His heart broke at the thought of how Laura would cope. Then he saw her, his sister-in-law, deathly pale, handcuffed and crying as an officer loaded her into the back of another squad car leaving the premises. *What the fuck? How?* Jim clenched his fists. "That bitch. I'll kill her."

He put on his siren and drove to the police station where they were processing Laura. As he walked up to the counter, she looked at him with pleading eyes. This really pissed him off. How could she? Pretending to be innocent...the nerve. He lunged at her, only to be held back by his fellow officers. "You bitch! Why did you do it? You killed him!"

"No! I would never! I didn't! Please Jim, you have to believe me." She wailed, crying so hard that lost her voice.

Her face was pale, and tears streamed down her cheeks, smudging her mascara into black streaks. Her sobs became shallow. "I loved him with all my heart. I'd never hurt him." She declared in a broken voice.

Jim unclenched his fists and his jaw enough to shout, "The murder weapon was right there, and you were right there holding it. There was a woman in bed with him. Sounds like jealous rage to me!"

Laura sobbed. "I didn't see her until I saw her tonight, already dead in that bed with him. I swear by Christ I'm telling the truth...Somebody is setting me up! I didn't do it, Jim!"

"We'll see about that!" He smashed his fist into a desk. Laura jumped back, her hands shaking and her breathing rapid.

Officer Dan pulled Jim's arm back with an iron grip. "Take it easy ... Maybe you should go home and be with your family right now? We'll let you know when we find out more."

The other officers took Laura back to the cells to process her arrest, and Jim turned to Dan. "How can I go anywhere? I gotta help. I gotta do something! My baby brother...He's...He's dead."

Jim imagined Brian's face over and over. What his expression must have been when she killed him. His last thoughts, the disappointment, the heartbreak. *Did he call out for me? For Ike? My poor brother. He deserved better. God help him.*

He sobbed and Dan gave him a dry shoulder to cry on, patting Jim on the back. Jim forgot his pride and collapsed into his friend's embrace. As the tears flowed, Dan spoke soothingly "It's okay, buddy. Let it out. It's okay."

Jim sniffed, calmer. *Straighten up, man! Don't be a pussy.* Hating to show vulnerability, he stood up straight, wiped his tears and said, "I'm sorry."

"For what?" Dan put his hand on Jim's shoulder. "I could use some help on this, but I need you to be clear headed. Can I count on you?"

"Yes," Jim said. "But ... well maybe I should go see Mama and Ike first, just to break the news and make sure they're okay?"

"I think that's a fine idea," Dan said. "Do what you gotta do. We're gonna be up all night in paperwork and keeping the press away. This thing's going to make national headlines, the Governor already called to crack the whip on getting this wrapped up. Just come back in the morning, after you've sat with them a while."

"Yeah, okay," Jim said. He straightened his uniform, cleared his throat, nodded at the others in the room, and left the station.

———

LATER THAT MORNING, Jim couldn't stand being in his apartment. He returned to the station and was all business, having recently been made a detective, and ready to make Laura pay. *Now, where does the case stand so far?* Dan was at his desk, a coffee cup in hand, and crushed dixie cups all around his typewriter, as he'd been up all night.

"Hey, buddy." Dan said, looking crumpled.

"Hey, Dan. So, tell me what we know so far?"

Dan finished his coffee, walked over to the pot on the cabinet, poured himself a fresh one and one for Jim. Handing Jim the cup, he sighed. "It's looking bad for little Miss Debutante. She was holding the weapon, the same weapon used to shoot your brother and Delta Dawn."

"Delta Dawn? Was that really her name?" Jim asked, raising one eyebrow.

Dan nodded. "Just like the song...I know. I love that song."

He sighed and shook his head. "Well, it looks like Delta Dawn was a prostitute. They were found naked in the bed, but they didn't have sex."

Jim squinted. "Really?"

"That's the gospel truth," Dan said. "Coroner examined both him and her and they hadn't done a thing, or at least nothing that would leave a mark or anything. Trace evidence found no hairs on each other, no skin particles under the nails, no nothing. Still waiting for the toxicology report though. It was like they were in that bed like a virgin couple that just met. She was wearing makeup and a red lipstick that was not smudged at all."

"That makes no sense," Jim said, scratching his sideburn.

Dan picked up a sugar donut and took a bite. Dropping powdered sugar on his platform boots, he replied, "I agree. Looks like there'd be something going on, at least some heavy petting by that point, but the room wasn't suggestive of anything like that...No wine, no sign that clothes had been peeled off in a seductive way, none of her lipstick on his face or anywhere else on his person, if you know what I mean."

Jim's nose crinkled. "Arggghh...please..."

"Sorry," Dan murmured.

"What else was found at the scene? Any other evidence?" Jim asked, pinching the bridge of his nose.

The medical examiner did find a small mark on Brian's backside. At first, it seemed like a bug bite, but a pellet of some kind was found. We're looking into that as well. Could have something to do with all this.

"Interesting," Jim said. "Anything else?"

"Only one thing. A partial shoe print near the balcony window, and a bit of strange dirt on the floor...We did explore the idea that someone broke in from the balcony, but there were no signs of the window lock being broken, and it was locked from the inside. Also, why just one print? Why not more? Even if it was a window washer. Surely, he'd leave his prints all over that balcony. But, as it turns out, the entire room was wiped clean. No prints anywhere, not even for the residents. I don't know your sister-in-law well, but she doesn't seem like the criminal mastermind type. She didn't seem like she'd know to wipe the room down."

Jim thought for a moment. *Could she be telling the truth?* He paced a bit, back and forth. "Hey, Dan? Can I see the paperwork on the case?"

"Sure. I'll take all the help I can get."

Jim took the papers from Dan, then sat at his desk and began to read them over. He stopped and traced words with his finger, then noticed something peculiar. There were no clothes found for Delta Dawn. Brian's clothes were there. Of course, he and Laura had clothes in the suitcases as well, but nothing was found that obviously belonged to Delta Dawn. She *didn't just walk in there buck naked. This smells of a cover up gone wrong.*

He needed to go talk to Laura about this. She might have more answers. Calling the desk sergeant downstairs, he asked for Laura to be brought to an interrogation room. After another coffee, he went downstairs. There she was, handcuffed, sitting at a bare metal table. He took the empty chair opposite. "How are they treating you?"

Her eyes were bloodshot, and her skin was pale, but her eyes blazed with fury. If looks could kill. She lifted her cuffed hands, red at the wrists. "How the hell do you think I'm getting treated?"

"Sorry 'bout that, but rules are rules," Jim said. "Can I talk to them and try to arrange some better food for you? Maybe an extra pillow?"

Laura rolled her eyes "Gee, that would be swell. But you know what would be better?"

"What?" Jim asked.

"Gettin' me the hell out of here! You *know* I didn't do this, Jim. You saw with your own eyes how much I loved your brother, how devoted I was. Why would I do this? There's no reason at all," Laura pleaded, raising her hands to her face.

"Oh, I don't know Laura, maybe you had a few million reasons?" Jim said. Her face reddened even more. She was obviously insulted.

Laura edged forward and grabbed his hand. One of her long red nails dug into his skin, and he shifted back in his seat and flinched. "If I were gonna kill somebody, it wouldn't be my husband," she said, slowly and deliberately. "I adored him, and we were happy! Stop holding it against me that I was raised in a mansion and not a trailer park! I'm just as real as you, okay?"

She released his hand swiftly and he grabbed his wrist and rubbed it, to ease the sting. "I came here to give you the benefit of the doubt, to hear your side of things, but you can forget that now."

"Right," Laura snorted.

"Whether you wanna believe it or not, I could've helped you, but now I believe you may have had something to do with this!"

"I just told you, I didn't!" Laura snapped.

Jim stood up and pointed at her. "You don't get to talk to me anymore." He looked at the floor and laughed, shaking his head. "We always thought you were a snooty bitch, you know."

He looked at her, sneered. "Well, I didn't know if you were capable of such violence, but I guess I got the answer to my question."

Laura's eyes darkened. He felt a chill as her eyes bore a hole through him. *This bitch is crazy. What's goin' on in that mind of hers?*

She slammed her hands on the table and stood up to confront him. "You son of a bitch! It was you! I'd bet a million bucks it was you! Bastard!"

He gave a little nod to the attending officer, and without a word, the young officer came to escort Laura back to her cell. Jim cracked a smile. "Have a million bucks to bet? Well sister, I wouldn't bank on that after your trial."

Her brows were furrowed, and he could feel the rage coming from her. She put her hand over her mouth. *She acts like she's wanting to say more but stopping herself. Wonder why?*

Frowning, Jim watched as she was taken away, and once she was out of sight, he exhaled. *Damn! I wanna blame her. God knows I do...but, she had always been so sweet to him. She's got money and prestige of her own.*

Something wasn't right about all this. There had to be more to this picture, but he'd have to be careful about Laura. She made it abundantly clear she thought of *him* as suspect number one. The last thing he wanted or needed was the tables to turn in *that* kind of a way. Shit, he forgot to ask about the clothes. "Hey Laura! Wait!"

"What?!" she blurted as the officer allowed her to stop.

"Did you notice any clothes for Delta Dawn?"

"Who's Delta Dawn?"

"The dead girl that was in the bed with Brian."

Laura sighed. "No. I didn't exactly have time to look around, but now that you mention it, there weren't any strange clothes that I could see."

"And no other bag or purse?"

"Nope, not that I can recall."

"Thanks," he said.

She nodded, shoulders drooping as the officer took her back to her cell. Jim scratched his head. *Fuck this...now I'm more confused.*

He went back to his desk, shuffled some papers around, but couldn't shake his hunch that something more was behind all this. He tapped his chin. *Why didn't Delta Dawn have any clothes with her? Time to pay a visit to the evidence locker.*

A careful inspection of the inventory confirmed that indeed, there were no obvious clothes, shoes or purse belonging to Delta Dawn. Laura's and Brian's suitcases and all loose possessions were neatly labeled and sorted, as confirmed by hotel staff.

He went to Forensics and spoke with the technician who had examined the crime scene. He was a tiny little man, with thick Coke bottle bottom glasses and a wispy thin mustache. He had obviously grown it out to look more masculine, but it wasn't convincing, at least to Jim. His name was Ernie Sanders, and as soon as Jim came in, he looked up from his microscope. "Can I help you, Jim?"

"Yeah, actually you can," Jim said. "The gentleman who was murdered in the hotel double homicide was my brother."

Before Jim could finish, Ernie put his hand on Jim's arm. "Oh my God! I'm so sorry to hear that. That's gotta be so rough."

Jim nodded, "Yep, it sure is. My brother was a good guy. That's why I wanna figure out who did this to him. They've got my sister-in-law for it, and as much as I'd like to blame that snooty bitch, I have a gnawing feeling that something's just not right."

"Well, what do you have in mind?" Ernie asked.

"You were there last Friday night, when all the evidence was brought in. Was there anything unusual about the dirt that was found on the floor? Or the shoe print?" Jim asked.

"Well, as a matter of fact, there was one thing." Ernie said. "The soil was most probably dropped from someone's shoes; we didn't find any more of it. Also, the soil wasn't from any location near the hotel. It was from much farther away."

"Oh yeah? Where was it from?"

"This soil was red, most likely from Alabama, Texas or out North Carolina's way. We thought that was strange, seeing it at the hotel," Ernie said.

Jim thought for a moment, tapping his chin. "That makes no sense at all. That kind of farming dirt is brought in specially for certain kinds of lands here. It's more fertile and the crops grow better, faster."

"How do you know that?" Ernie asked, impressed.

"Me and Ike own a farm like that. We bring in fertile dirt."

"What size shoe do you wear, Jim?" Ernie glanced down at Jim's feet.

"Huh?"

Ernie smiled nervously, but it did not reach his eyes. Suddenly, the atmosphere in the room went cold and Jim realized he fucked up. An interrogation was inevitable. *Why can't I keep my big mouth shut? Fuck!*

"I wear a ten. Do you think I was on that balcony, Ernie? Huh?"

"No...come on Jim. I don't mean anything by it. We just have to look at everything though, right?"

"Yeah," Jim said, smiling. "I get it. So, what about the shoe print? What else can you tell me?"

Ernie rifled through some papers and produced a photograph of the shoe print with a ruler next to it. "It was only partial, but looks like a workman's boot, certainly not the small print of a woman's shoes."

"Somehow, there was a man other than me involved," Jim said. He smiled at Ernie. "But how? I know one thing. This feels all too staged for Laura to have done it. I don't think this was a crime of passion. I think this was premeditated. Set up to frame Laura."

He put the picture down and asked, "Also, why were there no clothes for Delta Dawn found at the scene? That's the strangest part of all this. Did they search Laura's car? Her home? Delta Dawn's clothes didn't just jump up and walk away on their own, and she sure as shit didn't go in there naked!"

"We did," Ernie said. "All those places have been searched. The court order was issued and every nook and cranny was searched for evidence...all clean. I agree it's strange though."

"Yeah," Jim said.

"Of course, the dirt and the shoe print could belong to any workman from a few days prior. It could be that the maid didn't have a chance to clean up the mess," Ernie offered.

"True...but a hotel workman that's got red dirt on his shoes?" Jim said as he sat down. He held his head in his hands, massaging his temples and his sideburns. He slapped his hands on the desk, alarming Ernie.

"So! We're looking for a murdering farmer pretending to work at a hotel...I'd say that was a long shot," he said, looking at Ernie with a side glance.

"Ha! Yeah, I guess you're right," Ernie said. "That's not gonna be easy to find."

Jim leaned on the desk, tapping his fingers, then stood up straight. "Well, I'll be back if I can think of anything else."

Ernie waved goodbye and got back to work. As Jim made his way to the door, he accidentally bumped against a table, stubbing his toe on the large table legs. "Ow! God damn it!" He sat down on a nearby chair and took his shoe off to rub his foot.

Ernie looked up. "You okay over there?"

"Yeah. All good! This is a big ass table you've got in such a small lab!" Jim blurted, putting his shoe back on.

"Oh, sorry 'bout that."

"See ya Ernie!" Jim said, walking carefully out the door.

# ERNIE

*February 1977, New Orleans, LA*

ERNIE WATCHED JIM LEAVE, BUT THE DOOR WAS STUBBORN AND didn't close properly. Tut-tutting, Ernie walked over, closed the door, and turned to go back towards his workstation. He noticed a few clumps of dirt that must have fallen off Jim's shoe when he took it off.

"What do we have here?"

It was red and looked similar to the mysterious farm dirt found at the scene. Grabbing a plastic bag, he scooped it up and sealed it, noting the details on the evidence tag. *I hope I'm wrong. I have to be.*

# JIM

*February 1977, New Orleans, LA*

AFTER REVIEWING THE NOTES AND PHOTOGRAPHS RELATED TO THE murder, Jim didn't feel like being at work after all. He popped into the station chief's office and asked for the rest of the day off. Dan, typing up a report at his desk, saw Jim packing up. "Hey buddy. I don't know why you'd come in today at all. I got the funeral notice from Coral. I'll be there for y'all this afternoon."

"Thanks man. We'll be glad to have you there...Just can't believe that he's gone. My baby brother," Jim's eyes filled with tears, but he looked up at the ceiling and swallowed hard, so they'd disappear.

Jim left, and once he got in the car, he cried. He pulled over into an open parking lot and wept for the younger brother he'd reconnected with recently, the younger brother who had everything to lose. A montage of memories bubbled up. Childhood pranks they played together, fishing trips, bars they'd visited, and family Thanksgivings and birthdays. They may not have been the world's most perfect family, but they had their loving moments.

He looked at his own image in the rear-view mirror. *He was always the best one of us.* He thought. *Only God can save the bastard that took him from me. I'm gonna kill that fucker if it's the last thing I do.*

# LARRY

*Late February 1977, New Orleans, LA*

AS THEY PULLED UP TO THE ENTRANCE, LARRY GRASPED LAURA'S hand. "Sweetheart, I have to tell you something, but let's get inside first.

She nodded and they went inside. Larry sat down and pulled out his handkerchief, wiping the forehead sweat away.

"Okay Daddy, what is it?" Laura asked.

"I know you're not gonna like this, but I've been in communication with Coral, regarding Brian's funeral. It's later today." He looked down at his hands.

He could feel her staring, so he took a deep breath, then went on. "Since your and Brian's bank accounts are frozen by the Court, and the treatments have taken their bite out of my money, I've agreed to let Coral take care of the funeral. We're invited, of course, but she can't guarantee we won't be *hated* there, or at least that's how she put it."

"Bitch."

"Yeah, she is, but...are you okay?"

"Yeah, I'll be fine. And of course, we're going, no matter what. I have to say goodbye to Brian."

"Of course! He was your husband. You have more right than anyone else to be there...except...maybe Coral herself."

"I know. Damn right I have a right to be there," Laura said, squeezing his hand, trying not to cry right then.

"Daddy?" she said as she was just about to get out of the car. "Yes, darlin'?" Larry asked.

"Did they do an autopsy?"

"Yeah, they did. They had to, because of the gunshot wounds."

"Well, did you hear anything about the results? I wonder," she said, "if it was something else."

"This all just seems weird, like they were propped on the bed," she said, clasping her hair back. "It's like they were on display or something."

"Is there a reason you're thinking of this now?"

Her brows furrowed and her forehead crinkled. "I kind of just remembered... you know...Brian was sick the morning after we arrived. On the first night, we went to dinner in the French quarter, a lovely little bistro, and then the first of the live shows began. We stood on the street corner, really enjoying the opening spectacle. We enjoyed the music and the dancing, and the next morning, he felt super tired and out of breath."

"That's strange. You didn't mention that before," Larry said.

"I know. I guess I didn't even think anything about it," she said, wincing.

Her lips formed a hard line. "My head wasn't screwed on straight, I guess," she said, scratching her temple. "But you said that they didn't do anything *sexual*, that's probably because he was barely able to stand when I left him. And though it was horrifying and gruesome, the gunshot wounds were aimed a little too precise, like someone with experience, you know?"

Larry nodded and exhaled deeply. He put his hands on his hips and thought for a moment. "Okay, if we're gonna make this inquiry, we'd better move fast. You go in and start asking questions here. I'll get on that payphone over yonder and give them a call. I'll see what I can find out. The autopsy results must have come up with something.

"Aces! I'll head out to see the hotel manager now. I called him yesterday to make an appointment."

"Okay, see you back here soon," he said.

Laura grabbed a bag and the keys to her father's truck. She waved goodbye to him as she darted out the door. He watched out of the window and waited until she was in the car before he made a call.

"Forensics Department, Ernie speaking," a man answered.

"This is Larry Beauford, the attorney for Laura Buchanan. I'll be brief. Regarding the Buchanan murder...Was a toxicology report prepared for both victims? We've got cause to believe that the victims in the Buchanan shooting were poisoned prior to the incident."

Ernie raised an eyebrow. "Poisoned? We did actually find something curious. Why don't you drop by today. As Laura's attorney, you have the right to see our findings."

"I'll be there soon," Larry said as he hung up, then reached into his breast pocket to get his handkerchief. He blotted the beads of sweat forming on his forehead. *Good God, I need to get to bed and lay down. Did I eat today? Fuck cancer!*

Later that day, as Laura came back to the hotel, she spotted her father returning at the same time. He walked slowly and his face was too red. Her heart ached as she feared for his safety. She parked the truck and got to him.

"Daddy? Did you go out?"

He smiled, relieved to see her. "Yes, I did. Got some information too."

"Let's get you out of the sun, Daddy. Then, I'll be glad to hear all about it," Laura said, as she led him to the suite.

Larry sighed. "I know you're pissed off at them, but I gotta tell ya, I don't think they did it. The boys, or Coral, I mean. They may be rough around the edges, but they're no killers. I've seen my share of killers. God knows, I have."

"I hope it's not them," she murmured. "But if they didn't do it, our lives get a whole lot more complicated. Why do you think they're innocent? Did you find something?"

"I did," Larry said, as he sat down and started wiping his face. "The toxicology report. I went to see a man at the police station, the guy who ran the tests, name of Ernie. Turns out, they found a pellet of some kind under Brian's skin, something the size of a BB. They noticed he had an enlarged liver, some intestinal bleeding and fluid in his lungs. The odd thing is that they can't tell what caused the symptoms, but everyone believes that it was delivered through that pellet."

"Really? That's so far out and so freaky," Laura said. "A pellet?"

"Yep. So that means, he was targeted by a professional. This had to be a professional hit. Coral and those boys don't fit the profile."

Larry's eyes started drooping and Laura insisted that he lay down for a while. He nodded. "Well, maybe I'll just rest my head for a spell."

He laid on the sofa. His eyes began to close when he remembered something else. "Oh, and it seems that Delta Dawn had some heroine in her blood. Maybe she was a junkie hooker? I don't know. Lord, have mercy. What has this world come to?"

"I don't know, Daddy," she said. "What on God's green Earth are we involved in?"

# LAURA

LARRY DOZED OFF AND LAURA HAD A QUICK LOOK THROUGH THE guest profiles. Thankfully, that particular Mardi Gras was considered a game changer in terms of security. Just a year prior, a major drug bust had happened in one of name brand chain hotels in town. Since the perpetrators used hotels to find unsuspecting mules, thanks to the tourist season. Laura's research produced photo after photo of security shots of previous investigations.

She flicked through the photos, sipping on a fresh glass of iced tea, until she stopped on one photo that nearly made her spew tea out of her mouth. The hair color was different, but the face looked awfully familiar. Her memory flashed back to that terrible night. There she was in the picture. It was the woman she'd seen that night. In the picture she was blonde, but that was her. Laura was sure of it. The woman with the ice from that night.

She was listed as a second guest of a man. They were registered as husband and wife, Mr. and Mrs. Wheel. *That's an odd name.* She thought. *Wheel?*

Mrs. Wheel wasn't as she'd remembered her, not exactly. The woman in the picture not only had blonde hair, but very little makeup. The brunette with the ice had been made up to the nines. Laura traced her face with her fingertip, every curve. *That has to be her.* She thought. *I just know it.*

"Hello there, mystery woman," Laura said.

Larry, who had been fading in and out of sleep, perked up when he heard this.

"You found her? The woman in the hall?"

"Yes, I believe so. Take a look at this," she said. "It's her. Different hair color, but it's her."

This woman had blonde hair, light brown lipstick, and a pale complexion, but those piercing blue eyes were remarkable. Mr. Wheel looked like a considerably older man with a salt and pepper beard and brown eyes. The hotel records didn't provide much information, other than the fact that the couple stayed in the hotel that night. "There's an address for this couple, in Bridge City," Laura said.

Larry looked intrigued. He paused, tapping his fist over his mouth. "Huh, well, I'll have to go there. This is in Bridge City, so you can't accompany me. I hope we get your travel ban lifted soon."

*He's so cute sometimes.* She thought. Laura smiled and patted her father on the shoulder. "What would I do without you? I couldn't be getting through this otherwise...I should be squirming in fear for what's to come, but I just know that somehow you'll make it alright."

Larry smiled and blushed. "I will darlin'. I've just got to."

"Not before you sleep at least one hour," Laura insisted. "I have to have you strong out there. Besides, you and I need to know everything that was in that toxicology report first."

Reluctantly, he sat back down and took off his shoes, then laid down, "Okay, Miss Bossy."

"Good man," Laura said, smiling.

He closed his eyes and Laura took another look at the woman in the picture. "I just know you're involved, but how?"

She sat down and looked intently at the picture of the man. She examined his hair. *It could be a wig.* A fake beard. "You two don't look like you belong together. I smell a rat."

———

LAURA WAS busy for most of that day, interviewing half of the thirteen witnesses from the night of the murders. Those she couldn't see in person; she called on the phone. While she chatted with the last of them, her father entered, looking exhausted, plopping down on a recliner. He exhaled loudly, then shut his eyes for a moment. She tried to wrap up her call quickly. "Okay...yes, fine. Thank you for your time. Bye."

She hung up.

"Daddy? Are you okay?"

"Yes, I guess I'm okay, just tired," he said. "I saw the toxicology report with my own eyes. Basically, it's everything I told you before, and I saw the pellet. Whoever did this was no amateur."

Laura sat down, her mouth forming an O. Her brow furrowed as she thought it over. "Huh...how about that..."

Larry put down his papers and sat next to her. "This is a huge breakthrough... But I want you to think now. Really go back to that night. Did you notice anything different, anything that would indicate he was poisoned?"

Laura tapped her chin and her brow furrowed. *Okay, what did I do the first night at the hotel?* "I was so excited the night we got there. I remember telling him how happy I was that we're taking the trip together. He had some business to take care of, and both of us love Mardi Gras so much, we thought we'd make a fun trip out of it. Kind of an extended date, you dig it?"

"Indeed, I *dig* it," he said, smiling.

Larry tapped her belly. "I'm so glad you'll have the best part of him with you, and those memories are good to have."

"Will I always? Have the baby with me, I mean," Laura said, lowering her eyes in despair. "Oh Daddy...It's so hard making myself think of that night. All this stress can't be good for the child."

Larry put a reassuring hand on her shoulder. "I know. It can't be easy, but you really need to remember everything you can about that night. I'm sorry."

She looked at Larry, a tear rolling down her cheek, as she continued. "We checked in, and Brian couldn't wait to...well, you know." Laura blushed.

"I know," Larry said. "Go on."

She smiled. "He was so cute. So sweet to me. Afterwards, we just held each other. His eyes were so soft...I can't believe he's gone!"

She leaned into Larry's shoulder and sobbed. Her father stroked her hair just as he'd done so often when she was small. "I know, hun. This is all so hard, but we're gonna get through this. I promise. You'll have all the time in the world to mourn him properly."

For a few moments, he let her cry and she was grateful. She needed that, as she'd been avoiding thinking of him all day. Eventually, she started to come around. Larry tightly smiled and nodded. "Sorry for this. But we do need to carry on. Can you talk about what happened later?"

Laura sniffed and sat back up. "After...We went downstairs to the restaurant and had dinner early because we wanted to go to a party that night. We had blackened red snapper with a few side dishes, some seafood gumbo, but I ate the same thing he did, so it wasn't the food. He seemed fine at the party."

Larry patted the sweat from his forehead with his handkerchief. "I don't get it then. Where did the pellet happen?"

"For the life of me..." Laura started but stopped. Her eyes widened and her voice went up. "Oh my! Wait...as we were walking on the street towards the party, he flinched once and said somebody must have bumped into him."

"Really?" Larry asked.

"Yes. At first, he was fine, but later that night, he started feeling sick. He had trouble breathing and his color was so bad. He got through the party, but once we got back to the room, he could hardly move. He laid down, but wanted to be propped up a bit, to help him breathe better. I thought he may have been getting bronchitis."

She looked up, forcing herself to recall the details. "I asked the closest M.D. to stop by and pay him a house call...well, a hotel call, I guess. He looked at Brian and said he thought it was probably bronchitis. He prescribed him some medicine to ease the symptoms, so once we heard that, we didn't get overly worried."

Laura got up and started pacing as the memories flooded back. "Later the next day, Brian remembered that we had an important dinner party at the hotel arranged by a charity organization but felt that there was no way he'd be able to go, so he asked me to go alone. I tried to nurse him to health all that day, but he just got worse and worse. We never saw a single Mardi Gras float, but I didn't care. All I could think of was Brian. I agreed to go to the party, but I didn't want to," she said, as she began to sob. "I tucked him into bed and sat his water next to him because I wanted him to stay nice and hydrated. He told me he loved me and kissed me on the cheek".

Her eyes streamed tears. She threw her face into her hands and heaved, sobbing uncontrollably. Larry held her as she snivelled and cried. She found it difficult to form words, but she carried on.

"He didn't wanna kiss me on the lips because he didn't want me to *catch* anything...God...Oh Daddy, I wish I'd had an inkling that he'd been poisoned somehow! Those people kept me at that damn dinner so long! It was night-time before I got back, but by then, it was too late..."

She pushed away from her father. Her bottom lip quivered, tears rolling down her cheeks. "Why didn't I see it? Why?"

Larry winced. "You couldn't have known! This is *not* your fault...Do you understand me?"

He got up, then hugged her tight. She let herself be comforted, trying to stay strong for the sake of her child. *Don't worry my sweet baby,* she thought. *I'm not gonna let them get away with this, but I want you to be born healthy. You're all I have left of him. Your daddy was so amazing. God, how I loved him so much.*

"The good Lord wanted him early," Larry said. "That's all we can do, is remember that. If he didn't pass this way, he would have passed in another way. When it's our time, it's our time. That's all there is to it."

"I reckon...but still."

"I know, darlin. I know. It doesn't seem right. A lot of bad things happen to good people though. I don't know if we're meant to make heads or tails of it," Larry said, smiling. The phone rang.

"Hello?" Laura answered.

Laura's face crinkled. "Well, I'm sorry you feel that way, but I'm going to my husband's funeral. I don't care how y'all feel about it."

Larry could hear Coral yelling through the phone.

"You don't care? Land sakes, girl. What's more important than letting the people who loved him say goodbye properly? You're a selfish girl, always have been."

"I beg your pardon!" Laura snapped.

"Don't think you can come there looking like a little Miss innocent!" Coral blurted. "You can't buy your innocence. You stay away and leave him to his *real* family."

"But Miss Coral...ma'am...I have a right to be there!"

Larry grabbed the phone from Laura and blurted, "I'm gonna ask you to stop bothering my daughter and upsetting her in her delicate condition."

There was silence on the phone. Larry and Laura looked at each other. "Huh?" Coral whispered, "Sorry" he mouthed to Laura.

"Larry? What do you mean by delicate condition," Coral whispered. "Is Laura pregnant? My son told me, but I didn't wanna believe it, and we heard that you announced it in court. I didn't know if it was a plea for sympathy or not, but now I think it may be true."

Larry frowned. "As her attorney, I should warn you to cease contact with my client until further notice."

He hung up the phone.

"Daddy! What did you do?" Laura asked.

"I'm sorry baby. I swear I wasn't thinking." Larry answered, lowering his gaze.

She pulled herself together for the moment. The problem at hand was more important than what he'd just done. "Okay, let's leave that for now. Let's talk about what's more important. Tell me what you found out about Mr. Wheel?"

Larry face palmed. "Dang it all. I forgot to tell you!"

She shifted and gave him her full attention. *He seems really excited about this. I wonder...please be something good. He looks like he's sitting on something explosive.* She smiled. "Gosh Daddy. Tell me."

"Well, as soon as I got there, I realized the address that 'Doug Wheel' gave the hotel was a fake," Larry said. "Or at least that's what I thought at the time. The address was for a storage facility. Initially, I thought of just driving away, but I'm really glad I didn't."

"Why? What did you find out?" she asked.

Larry grinned. "I found out that Mr. Doug Wheel did, in fact, rent a locker there."

Laura sat down and started biting her nails. Her eyes grew wide with anticipation. "So? What was in it?"

"At first, I couldn't get in, even though the payments for the locker were more than a year overdue, but then the proprietor, Bruno, saw fit to invite me to a storage auction that was taking place this very afternoon!" Larry boasted with a smile.

"Oh, tell me you won." Laura's breath hitched. "You have the contents of the locker, right?" She waited with bated breath.

Larry smiled. "Yes, I do, young lady! And you're gonna like what I have also."

Laura exhaled and smiled. "Whew!"

"Mr. Doug Wheel was using a fake name. This guy had a whole mess of different names he's gone by through the years—Frank Glass, Frank the Tank, but the original name on this joker is Vladimir Petroski, A.K.A., Vlad the Impaler. We've all heard of him. At least, any lawmaker worth his salt across the Southeast," Larry said.

Laura's mouth opened and her brow crinkled. "Vlad the Impaler? Seriously?"

"Yep," he said. "So, after I realized what was in there, I called Jim. After all, we're talking about hard evidence. And man, oh man...when Jim got there, his eyes went as big as saucers! I thought that boy was gonna kiss me like I was the goose that laid the golden egg!"

"Then what happened?" Laura asked.

"Then," Larry continued. "I hung around while they were dusting for prints, even though I'm pretty sure they won't find any. I mean come on, this guy is a pro. He knows how to be a ghost...Once they finished, they told me I'm not allowed to take any of it, but I got an eyeful. Passports, ID's, money in many currencies."

"Jeepers," Laura said. "So, is this guy a spy or something?"

"More like a mob hitman," Larry replied. "Question is, why on Earth would he be after Brian, let alone that poor Delta Dawn. She was a nobody. Why her? Why him?"

"So many questions," Laura said. "The more answers we find, the more questions we have. Did you notice that?"

"I did today," Larry said as he shifted in his seat, trying to get more comfortable.

"How does a professional criminal like Vlad make the mistake of not paying up the storage locker fees? I don't get it," she said.

"I asked Jim about that. He said according to his classified informants, VLAST, their mother front organization, now considered him a target. For the first time in his notorious criminal career, he was on the run. I don't know *how* they know that, but it makes sense why he wouldn't show up in a place he's expected."

She sighed. "Huh...wow! So, what does this mean for the case?"

"Well, it means that there was a known hitman staying in the room just opposite yours on the night of the murders, but sadly, we can't really prove he committed the murders...him or the supposed 'Mrs. Wheel'. We need more time to gather more evidence and wait to get copies of the forensics reports on the locker contents. I informed the forensics team that I was the attorney of record in your trial and that the two cases were linked, therefore I insisted on getting copies of everything they found out. At least we now know that even the great Vlad the Impaler has someone even worse than him to be afraid of. That's something, but let's try not to meet him."

"Yeah, let's stick with the devil we know," Laura said, as she shook her head and looked at her father. "We're almost out of time. The trial starts in three days."

Larry thought for a moment and looked at Laura with a scrunched face. "I think we need some help...Some 'official' help?"

"Jim?" she asked.

Larry nodded. "Sweetheart," he said. "I know this is upsetting, but let's talk to him at the funeral. It's tomorrow, so we'll have a chance to talk about what we've found. At least he'll stop thinking that you've done this if he hasn't already."

"That makes sense," Laura said. "Ok, Daddy."

# CORAL

*Late February 1977, New Orleans, LA (Brian's funeral)*

CORAL WAS THE FIRST ONE TO SHOW UP AT THE FUNERAL. SHE WORE A simple black tea length dress with long sleeves and a black sheer veil over her face, topped with a pill box black hat. It was an exact replica of what Jackie Kennedy wore to her husband's funeral. Coral believed that no one in attendance could question the grace and style of Jackie Kennedy, so her class in society would never come into question.

Despite her extraordinary effort to look the part of funeral elegance and grace, she sobbed uncontrollably for the loss of her son, looking at Brian's face one last time. "The funeral home did a good job. I can't even tell..."

She whimpered, holding a Kleenex over her mouth. Daryl Rae put his arm around her, allowing her to nuzzle into him. She groaned as the grieving mother she was, shaking with grief and touching Brian's hands. *Those little fingernails.* She remembered. *I had to always keep them trimmed or he'd scratch his face.* "Look at these hands. I hoped these hands would hold up my grandkids one day. Now, he's going into the ground. Oh God, why?"

She cried. Daryl Rae hugged her tight.

Her tears streamed down, smudging her mascara, and her heart felt that it would collapse into her chest. She put her hand over her chest and held on. Her boys approached, nonchalantly pushing Daryl Rae aside.

"It's okay Mama," Jim said. "It's okay to let it out. We're all gonna miss him."

Ike kissed her on the cheek. "We love you, Mama. We're both here for ya."

"Thank you, baby. I can't get through this on my own."

"You got me, Ike, and Daryl Rae. You're not alone," Jim said.

Daryl Rae kissed her on the cheek, and they formed a group hug. The group broke apart when some new arrivals caused the low buzz of conversation to stop dead.

# LAURA

*Late February 1977, New Orleans, LA (Brian's funeral)*

LAURA WALKED IN, WEARING A BLACK SHIRRED SILKY CHIFFON MIDI dress, flowing and loose fitting, large black sunglasses, with a black beaded bag. She looked chic, but comfortable. Her father was by her side. They both took a moment to notice Coral, and her classic look. Laura tipped her sunglasses down for a brief glance. Coral stopped sobbing long enough to notice them as well. She sniffed and wiped away her tears, as she watched Laura walk forward.

Laura felt everybody's stare and instead focused only on the open coffin ahead. *Guess she's gonna get obsessed with this baby now...Never mind that. She'll just have to wait. Now's not the time for that discussion.*

She walked straight up to the coffin. She didn't know how seeing his face was going to affect her, but she never imagined the impact it was going to have. Her knuckles gripped the coffin edge, helping her stand strong. Sobbing, she noticed the faint mark where the bullet pierced his skull. *They really covered it well...Thank God.*

The baby fluttered in her womb. Laura caressed her belly as she continued to look at her lost love. Even six months in, the pregnancy was barely noticeable. She had just started to show, and being near the end of her second trimester, the baby was quite active inside.

"You're really pregnant, aren't you?" Coral asked.

"Yes, yes I am, Ms. Coral," she said. "I think you've known that for a while."

"Who's the father?"

Laura's jaw dropped. Her face remained as neutral as possible after such a snide comment, but her mind was on fire. *Bitch!*

She turned to face Coral eye to eye. "Your *son*...Before he passed, we were trying for a baby. Apparently, it worked."

"Why didn't either one of you ever tell me right away? Why did I have to hear it from Jim?"

"We didn't tell many people because I'm very superstitious," Laura said. "My mother had many miscarriages before she gave birth to me. I begged him not to tell anyone, except for his brothers. He was pretty close to them."

"Miss Coral, with all due respect on this terrible day, I think you only have to remember him and his life...Am I wrong here?" she said, almost choking on her words. She dug deep, deep in her soul to explain to Coral, to make her understand the level of her grief.

"We had so many plans, and I know he would've wanted his whole family to be part of this baby's life...We were gonna be such a great family."

Laura's eyes began to water. "But now that he's no longer with us, I'll have to raise this child alone."

"You can't raise a child from prison," Coral said, snidely.

*Look at that face! This is her son's funeral, and she wants to do what she can to get her money-grubbin' paws on my baby before he or she is even born! No...no...I'm not gonna cause a scene at Brian's funeral, no matter how much she deserves it.*

As the organ music chimed through the chapel, she only let herself reply, "We'll see about that. There's still justice in the world, and innocent people don't go to prison. At least they're not supposed to."

She turned back to Brian's body and touched his face one last time. The ice-cold hard flesh shocked her. He was truly gone. Sobbing, she said, "I'll always love you, sweetheart. I wish we had more time together."

As she turned to re-join Larry for the service, she purposely didn't turn to look at Coral, but felt the heat of her stare. She saw her father nodding. "Good that you didn't react," he said. "We're not here to talk to her. We're here to pay respects and to talk to Jim."

"I know...It took everything I had to not spout off at that horrible excuse for a mom, though." She cleared her throat and settled in her chair.

She looked at the minister, Brother Bradley O'Keefe. He gave her a sympathetic look and approached her. "My dear girl, I can only imagine what you're going through right now. We were all shocked. Brian was a dear boy, and my heart was glad when I saw the two of you together. He loved you dearly."

Laura teared up. "Thank you. He was a special man. One of a kind."

"Indeed, he was. I'm so sorry for your loss," he said. "The Lord works in mysterious ways, and sometimes He takes the good of this world early. Let faith help you to be strong during this painful time."

He gave her a hug and walked to the podium, as he was about to begin the service. Everyone hushed down and listened. Laura peeked at Coral who was already whispering to her sons. That woman could never keep quiet about anything. Always gossiping.

"Nothing is sacred to that woman," she whispered to Larry.

"Yup," he said.

The minister said, "We came together this afternoon to say goodbye to a wonderful man. A pillar of the community, and a true man of God."

Laura strained to hear, but it sounded like Ike and Jim whispered something to each other, and Ike softly sniggered. Many eyes turned his way. The minister said, "It's okay my son. Brian was quite a character! He'd rejoice as people remember the happy moments. I remember him as a very young man with a lot of questions. He really made me earn my place as a reverend by asking about the Trinity and how it works, about the nature of God...Oh, a thousand little things. Brian had a unique mind, and he found happiness with the love of his life, his father, his brothers, and even his mother."

Laura's tears fell as she witnessed Jim well up. *Poor Jim. I don't really believe you could hurt your own brother. How could I have doubted you? Look at you now.* Look at him she did. He broke down and wept, an act so frowned upon by Southern society. Men are to suffer their lives in a quiet show of strength so that everyone around them stays calm.

# JIM

JIM COULDN'T STOP THINKING BACK TO BRIAN'S FIRST NIGHT AT THE university when they hung out. The way Brian's face looked when he realized that he was for real in his intentions, the first hug after so long apart. His heart swelled as he thought of his baby brother and the moments they'd spent playing together as kids. *That little guy sure did love his colors. Always coloring outside the lines. Ha... God, how I miss him.*

He looked over at Laura. *Did she do this? I swear to God...I don't see it. Maybe she's innocent?* He noticed how she caressed her belly. *Surely, she wouldn't put that child at risk. She loved him.* He thought.

As the minister led the prayer, the sounds of weeping permeated the chapel. The organ music began as the congregation sang, "How Great Thou Art" as the casket was closed. Coral screamed out, "My baby boy! Oh God why?? Why did you take him from me? Lord, God in Heaven! Oh God!" she sobbed uncontrollably.

Everyone seemed to cry after that. Coral always did know how to stir up the emotion of any given situation.

None of the other mourners stood a chance against Coral. Jim could see that she wanted everyone to know that she was the only person who lost someone. Part of him resented his mother for this. *I lost a brother. Does she not have any feelings about me right now? Or about Laura? Look at her over there,* he thought. *She must feel so alone and isolated.*

For the first time, he was truly ashamed of his mother, and found that he had unexpected feelings of sympathy for his sister-in-law. He'd make this right. Somehow, he'd make this right.

# LAURA

*Late February 1977, New Orleans, LA (Brian's funeral)*

"OLE CORAL IS THROWING AN AFTER-FUNERAL PARTY AT HER HOUSE. Good God Almighty. I really don't wanna go," Laura said.

She wouldn't get a better opportunity to speak to Jim about the materials confiscated in the locker. "But I reckon we have to," she sighed.

Larry agreed. "I was shocked she invited us also, but I guess she's trying to show she's a classy lady. That's why she mentioned it to you in passing when you were talking to the minister after the service." He put his jacket back on, as he'd taken it off due to the terrible heat in that chapel. "Come now, let's get this done."

———

THE YEARS HAD NOT BEEN KIND to Stella. However, despite being more wrinkled and a little chubbier now, she still had a friendly demeanor, at least to Coral. She worked for Coral now and helped her cater for the after funeral gathering at Coral's home. Stella made sure the drinks were full and everyone had cake and other treats. There was a solemn feel to the place, as everyone seemed to be quietly reflecting. Stella spotted Laura and her father. "Well, hello there. What can I get you?"

"An orange juice for me," Laura said.

Larry tapped his chin and grunted. "Whiskey, neat."

"I'll be right back with that," Stella said.

*Well, what do ya know? She's keeping it classy so far.* Laura thought. "I've heard a lot about Stella from Jim," Laura said. "She really seems like she's trying to make a good show of it for her friend. Maybe she's not so bad."

It occurred to Laura that Stella may have never had any other family than Coral and the other trailer park friends. She looked at Larry and realized how blessed she'd been to be so loved all her life, so protected. Poor Stella may have never had that, not in her whole life. Laura held on to her father's arm and he put his arm around her shoulder reassuringly.

The buzz of conversation was all anyone could hear, all talking about Brian and what a wonderful life he would have had, if he'd lived. Laura had held her emotions in check, but felt herself slipping, especially as she let herself imagine what their life would have looked like, if Brian were spared. Family dinners, vacations, more children, school recitals. It was the picture of a perfect American family, like something you'd see on a Christmas card.

"No one's ever gonna see that picture now," she sobbed. "But I'll make your killer pay, ma' darlin'. Oh Lord, yes. I surely will."

# JIM

*Late February 1977, New Orleans, LA (Brian's funeral)*

JIM SPOTTED LAURA. HE APPROACHED HER SLOWLY. *THIS LOOKS LIKE a woman mourning her beloved, not a killer. A scared little girl holding on to her father.* He remembered how much Laura used to smile with Brian. She beamed. She had to have loved him very much, and whomever killed Brian was quite cold blooded. The girl he was staring at didn't fit that description.

"Guess I'm not so surprised you turned up, but I gotta say, it took courage to walk into this lion's den. I'll give you that much."

Laura smiled and looked down at her shoes. A tear ran down her cheek. "Yes, well, I have a right to say goodbye to the man I loved."

"And the father of your baby?" Jim replied. "I'm sorry for my mother's rudeness, by the way."

Laura stirred. "I appreciate that, Jim."

"I think anyone could tell you're expecting. You're glowing." He smiled and took a sip of his coffee.

"Jim...I..." Laura started.

Before she could finish, a few police officers came into the party. They were obviously on official business, as their badges were showing. They approached Jim with caution. Jim turned and said, "What's up guys?"

"Sorry to have to do this, Jim. We're all sorry. But here it goes. Officer Jim Sanders, you're wanted for questioning. Come with us," The lead officer blurted.

"What the fuck?" Jim asked.

Another officer put his hand on his holster. "It wasn't a request, sir."

"Fine." Jim said. He looked at Laura and shrugged his shoulders. "What were you gonna say?"

She eyed the cops all around him, and her heart started beating faster. "It can wait. Looks like you have all you can handle now."

He nodded. "Okay, well I'll call you when I'm free."

Her eyes softened. "Yes, please do. We really do need to talk, and I'll check on you."

# LARRY

*Late February 1977, New Orleans, LA (Brian's funeral)*

LARRY WAS TRAPPED IN A CONVERSATION WITH CORAL WHEN HE spotted cops pulling Jim away. Coral didn't notice straight away as she was hyper-focused on Larry, shouting by this point.

"So don't you think you and your murdering daughter had better go?"

Larry glared at her. His eyes darkened and he balled up his fist.

"My daughter is NOT a murderer! Do you understand me?"

Coral smiled slyly. "Well, I guess I've got me another baby to raise after they take it away from her and put her to sleep for good."

"I...no," Larry became red in the face and gasped. He fell to the floor, half-dazed.

Coral screamed. "Lord, God Almighty!"

Laura must have heard the commotion. Larry was blinking in and out of consciousness. He opened his eyes to find Laura cradling his head in her lap. She was shouting. "Oh my God! Help! Someone, help us please!"

Larry opened his eyes again, saw police officers around him. One of them was checking his pulse, while another was loosening his tie.. He heard a man shouting that he was going to call in a 10-52. Larry closed his eyes again. Moments later, he was jostled into awareness by paramedics loading him into an ambulance. He heard Laura's voice following as they closed the ambulance doors with a bang. "Oh, dear sweet Jesus, not yet. Please, not yet".

———

Larry woke up in a hard hospital bed, the steady beeping of machinery the only noise. He tried to recall the events that led up to this moment. He remembered his heart pounding and sweat oozing from every pore as he and Coral got into an argument. He remembered taking out his handkerchief to blot his forehead, but his throat felt tight and his collar was choking him. He was about to shout right back at Coral, but then the room went dark. The rest was a blur. The next thing he knew, Laura sitting next to him, clutching his hand in the quiet room.

"Where am I?" He asked in a raspy voice.

Laura patted his forehead with a cool cloth, and he closed his eyes, enjoying the reviving effects of it. "You're awake! Oh, my poor Daddy," she said, "I really wish you could be just enjoying this time, instead of helping me. You should be having some final adventures right now."

He touched her arm, cleared his throat. "Nonsense. Making sure you and your little one's okay will make my life complete. I'll be able to die in peace. Besides, I'm a soldier, and there's nothing sweeter than fighting tyranny."

That statement made Laura sniffle, and she feigned a smile. But he knew a real smile from a fake one any day of the week and twice on Sunday. He tried to be firm "Now sweetheart, don't you worry. Not everyone gets to plan how they leave this world and set their own terms. In a strange way, that makes me lucky."

Laura smiled, then winced. "What was Coral talking to you about? Right before you collapsed?"

His eyes drooped and he scoffed. "Oh, that miserable old bitch!"

Laura was taken aback. "Daddy! Oh my God! What did she say? I've never heard you talk like that before. At least not in front of me. She's got you using profanity."

Larry shook his head and put his hands up as someone who was caught in the act. "Let's just say, she knows the whole deal, and she knows what that means if you don't make it." Laura's face went white as she contemplated Coral raising her baby.

"Well, in hindsight, I wish we hadn't gone, even though...I had to say my farewells," she said, regaining her composure.

"Did you talk to Jim?" Larry asked, hoping to change the subject.

"No, I didn't manage to. The police came to take him in for questioning."

"Questioning? Jim? Now, that's odd." He squinted and swiped his face.

"I thought so too," Laura said.

His daughter picked up his hand and squeezed gently. "Daddy, I think I'll go check on Jim. Come to think of it, it's been a while, and he said he was gonna call me as soon as he was free. So what if he's *not* free? What if they're holding him for some strange reason? Or they really have something on him?"

"That is odd," he said. "You go on, darlin'."

"Daddy, if I leave you now, are you gonna be alright?"

"Yes, yes of course my dear girl." He smiled. "You go find out what's happened to that big redneck. We need his brawn. But be careful about what you reveal. He's in custody and you're not his attorney, so nothing is privileged."

Laura kissed him on the cheek. "I love you."

"I love you too, darlin."

# VLAD

As Laura exited from the main entrance of the hospital, she did not see him lurking outside, standing in the dark near some tall shrubs. If she had glanced his way, she would have noticed his eyes glinted through the leaves like a wolf. He took a pull of his cigarette as Laura passed him, on her way to the parking lot. He looked at her ass and smirked, his pearly white teeth gleaming in the night.

He crushed out the cigarette under his boot heel, put on a pair of sunglasses, and made his way into the emergency room, his purposeful gait reminiscent of a powerful predator. When he reached the main desk, he asked the receptionist in a distinct Russian accent but mellowed down with his American raising.

"Excuse me, a friend of mine was just admitted here. Big American fellow, dying from cancer. Name is Larry. I'd like to pay him a visit if that's permitted."

The receptionist bit her lip, instantly awestruck by his presence. He used his most disarming smile as he noticed her admiring his muscular six-foot cut figure, dressed in a black suit with matching shirt. He lowered his sunglasses and stared at her hungrily with his coal black, piercing eyes. Almost instantly, she was his, and they both knew it.

He saw her eyes drift lower, glancing over his neck tattoo, Cyrillic letters. He doubted she'd still be smiling if she knew it spelled out Death Incarnate. His long dark hair was pulled back into a ponytail, with a few stray locks hanging down around his face. He smoothed his hand over his well-kept mustache and beard. Her cheeks reddened and she practically drooled at him. He slowly slid off his sunglasses, making sure that she noticed him looking at her generous cleavage in the tight uniform. She giggled and sputtered. "Where are you from, if I may ask?"

"I'm from Eastern Europe, darling. Have you ever been there? A beautiful creature such as you? Surely." he asked.

The receptionist blushed, quite floored by his magnetism. "No, I haven't ever been anywhere."

He leaned in and whispered, "After my friend gets better, maybe you and I can go see many places together? Hmm, what does my beautiful darling have to say?"

She giggled. "Oh my, you're just a charmer, aren't you?"

He winked at her. "I'm anything you wish."

"Well, I suppose I can tell you what room your friend's in," she said, as her breath hitched. "It's Room 556, down the hall and to the left. Please don't tell anyone I told you."

He took her hand and gave it a sweet kiss. "Shhhh...no darling. Don't worry. I'll never betray your trust...I'm coming for you later."

She giggled and he winked again, leaving her breathless, then he turned to go see Larry. He put the sunglasses back on, rolled his eyes. *All the same, wet now for the bad boy but waiting for boring prince charming. Dumb bitches.*

He got to Larry's door and carefully walked inside. Larry was sleeping, so he leaned in close to Larry's face and said, "Larry...wakey wakey...eggs and bakey"

Larry opened his eyes slowly. His eyes widened in recognition, and he immediately shot up, scorching back against the headboard. The heart monitor started beeping faster.

"Vlad...the Impaler," Larry stammered.

He smiled upon hearing his favorite nickname. "Yes Larry, that is me, but I don't actually want to impale you, so don't worry...I don't enjoy killing *dying* men...There's no sport in that."

Larry's jaw clenched. "Umm, all righty then. I think that's good that you don't wanna kill me. I can't reciprocate, but you understand."

"Waa haa...good one!" Vlad smirked, slapping Larry on the shoulder. "I'm relieved to see that I am dealing with a man of...how do you rednecks say? *Backbone.*"

Vlad saw Larry's dinner tray on the metal trolley near the bed and scooped up half of his sandwich. He stood close to Larry as he took a bite, then said, "Mmmm, not bad for boring hospital food."

Larry stared. His face got redder by the second. Vlad chewed, swallowed, looking amused at Larry's anger. "No Larry, I don't want to kill you, but your pregnant ass daughter would be like the sweetest nectar…"

Larry balled his fists. His teeth clenched, struggling to avoid saying something to antagonize the Russian. Vlad knew how hard it was for Larry to hold back. Every fiber of his being felt it. He looked at Larry speculatively. "Are you sure you'd like to maul me, papa bear? You sure you don't want to cry for the bastard in her belly?"

"If you hurt a single hair on her head, I will kill you," Larry snarled. "Do you understand?"

Vlad nodded thoughtfully and took another bite of the sandwich. It tasted surprisingly good. "All you need to do is keep officer Jim out of this and steal back my personal items, then she will be as you say, A-okay"

"Are you gonna kill me, or are you *only* here to threaten me?" Larry blurted; frustration clear on his face.

He half-sat on the bed, putting his arm around Larry's shoulders, and whispering in his ear.

"Believe me, Larry. You are so frail and pathetic. I would take no pleasure in hurting you, even *indirectly*…But you must realize I won't be going to jail for anything. Besides, I had nothing against your son-in-law. No hard feelings, *da*?"

"Did you kill him?" Larry asked, nervously.

Vlad smiled. "I told you; it was nothing personal. None of my hits are. They are just jobs to us."

Larry's mouth opened in shock. "Why?"

Vlad leaned in to look at Larry deep in the eyes. Those black piercing eyes cutting into his psyche. "Don't speak of this ever again if you love your daughter."

Then, his mood changed. Vlad smiled at Larry with a mouthful of sandwich and a few crumbs dropped to the bed. Larry looked at him with ever widening eyes, too overcome with rage to even reply. "Larry, do we understand each other? We do, don't we, Mishka?"

"I understand you just fine," Larry growled.

Vlad slapped him on the shoulder. "Good, this is good!"

He grabbed the juice from the meal and the straw. He plunged the straw into the cup, then turned to walk out of the hospital room but couldn't resist turning to flash Larry a big smile. "I know you *were* a war hero and all this *der'mo*, but don't try to be a hero here, Larry. You're old now, and sick. I truly don't want to kill you, but I *will* kill her...and all my men and I will fuck her first. Make no mistake."

He raised the juice cup as a toast. "To your good health, Larry!"

# LARRY

*Late February 1977, New Orleans, Tulane General Hospital*

As soon as Vlad was out of earshot, Larry exhaled as though he'd been holding his breath for a year.

"Mother fucker," Larry growled. "I'll kill you, if it's the last thing I do."

His face got redder as his blood pressure rose, when suddenly, he replayed Vlad's voice in his head when he said, "they are just jobs to us."

*Us?* He thought. *What did he mean by that?*

Larry pressed the call button, and a nurse quickly appeared. A sweet lady with a kind face, just what he needed at that moment. He didn't get a clear look at her at first, as his blood pressure began to spike.

"Oh Lordy," she said. "I know that look. Let's see what your blood pressure is, dear."

She took his reading and was indeed alarmed at how high it was. She left his room for only a moment, to retrieve a syringe. She shot a medicine into his lead and he felt immediately at ease. He exhaled and began to have a hard time staying awake.

"That's it," she said. "You need some rest now. Get some sleep."

Larry hadn't wanted to sleep when he called the nurse. He wanted to warn everyone about Vlad, but sleep took him, perhaps for the best, at the moment. Maybe the kind nurse was right. Sometimes rest is the most important thing.

# LAURA

*Late February 1977, New Orleans, District Three, NOPD*

LAURA ARRIVED AT THE NEW ORLEANS POLICE STATION, DISTRICT 3.
Jim was easy to find, but not easy to see. She would need to finesse this situation to
gain access to him. She claimed to be Jim's lawyer and demanded to confer with
her client. An officer went to confirm her identity with Jim, and miraculously, he
went along with the charade.

Jim was in an interrogation room, and he didn't look happy. He sat with his
forehead resting on his palms, and for a moment, she only felt pity for him. But his
mere presence there was a red flag. She didn't want to consider it, but she had to,
seeing him there.

*It couldn't be true. I saw the look on his face. I saw how he was with Brian. He
loved him. What the hell is going on? Something's so wrong here,* she thought. Jim
spotted her and called out. She couldn't hear him. "The glass is soundproof, Jim!
Wait!"

As Jim's legal counsel, all conversations between them were not on official
record, but she wasn't stupid. Many cops were crooked, on the take, bought and
sold to the numerous criminal elements that were in play, including the Russian
mobsters. She knew the whole conversation was being observed and recorded. Her

father warned her that would probably be the way it was, so she knew she had to be very careful about what she said.

She sat down and sighed. "So, they think you helped me?" She put her fingers over his lips. "Wait...Daddy wanted me to remind you that nothing you say to me right now is safe, especially with so many crooked elements in this case. Also, you need to declare me a part of your legal team. We may have convinced them that I'm your lawyer now, but they may want to kick me out of here at any time."

"It's okay, Laura," he said. "I know.  I don't care cuz I ain't got nothing to hide."

"Okay, just be careful," she said. "So... They think you helped me, huh?"

"Yep! I can't believe it! I've worked with these men for years. They should know better than this...to think, they really believe I could murder my own brother? I loved my brother. Me and Ike hung out with him all the time, and we had a great time. You know that. You saw how we were.  We never asked y'all for anything.  All we wanted was to spend time as a family."

Her eyes watered. "I know, Jim. I *did* see how close y'all were. I believe you, okay? Just know that."

"Well, I'm glad to hear that someone does. They're searching my house as we speak!"

Laura shook her head. "How do they propose that you've done this?"

"They found a footprint on the balcony of the hotel room.  They say it matches the boots I wear, and they found some 'farm dirt' on the floor that came from the boot print," Jim said.

"Okay, farm dirt? What does that mean? How's that different from regular dirt?" Laura asked.

Jim shook his head, "Well, this type of dirt is often imported from more soil rich states like Alabama, just for farming purposes.  I think between that and the shoe print, and the fact that I didn't have a solid alibi that night, except for patrol duty...And I suppose they think I would be in it for the money somehow? Well, you know."

"Can they hold you on such flimsy evidence?" Laura asked, looking offended. "It all seems very circumstantial. If my father taught me anything, it's the need for much stronger proof. So, how long can they hold you?"

"Not long.  Only twenty-four hours.  Then, they'll have to let me go."

Laura looked at him, and her eyes softened.  She remembered all the memories of childhood that Brian shared with her, and how happy he was to reconnect with his brother. *No, Jim couldn't have done this.*

"Seems we've both been wrongly accused," Laura said. "And...I think we've been wrong about each other as well."

Jim nodded. "Maybe."

"Daddy may be on to a lead as to who really did this," she whispered.

Jim looked up in surprise. He put his finger over his mouth, indicating that she should not reveal too much. She nodded and looked him in the eyes. "Maybe if we work together, we can figure out what's happening?"

Jim nodded. "Okay, sounds good to me. But wait for a second. Has that got anything to do with the contents of that place we went to?"

"Definitely," Laura said.

Jim asked Laura to ask the officer outside the interrogation room to bring him a pad of paper and a pen. Once the officer brought the pad and pen, Jim smiled. They went way back, classmates in the academy. Brick Landon seemed both overjoyed and sad to see Jim in such a predicament. "Hey Jimbo. I heard you were here. I'm sorry man."

Jim nodded and smiled. "It's okay, man. Listen, I need you to do me a solid right now. Can you lend me a buck?"

Brick didn't hesitate. He took a dollar out of his wallet right away. "Here ya go. Whatever it takes to get you proved innocent. You're no murderer. It's bullshit that you're in here. It's gotta be."

"I appreciate that. I won't forget this," Jim said, holding the dollar up between two fingers. "This may be what turns it all around."

Jim wrote a declaration of Laura and Larry as his legal defense team and signed it. He handed Laura the dollar. "Now you sign it."

She smiled and sighed.

"She's on my legal team now! You all know it's not allowed to record at this point, right? Not that I'd know if you were. I declared her father as my primary attorney yesterday!"

"Now, everything we talk about is privileged," Jim said to Laura. "So, tell me what you know."

Before she could respond, he leaned in so that he could whisper. "But don't forget that the criminal elements in this department may not serve justice. Careful with what you tell me."

Laura nodded, then told him about the woman at the scene, how she had shared a room with a known Russian mob hitman, Vladimir Petroski. Jim's eyes widened. "Wow! We got all kinds of shit on that guy, thanks to your pop. That fucker is going down when we get him. Problem is, he's a ghost! He's good at disappearing and he's a master of disguise." Jim thought of the picture of the blonde woman next to him at the hotel. "And so is his partner, evidently. I guess she was wearing a wig when she met you in the hallway."

He couldn't deny it, he was impressed. "Little gal, that's some pretty impressive detective work. You and your dad are amazing. We've been after Vlad for years. He's a pro. I'm just surprised he's left any trail at all. Like I said, he's a ghost. This is really unlike him. He must be slipping...wonder why?"

Laura nodded. "I know! I can't believe we've managed to uncover this much. Daddy figures that at least it will be enough to justify a *reasonable doubt* in the jury's minds. At the very least, the case will be opened again. But now, we gotta figure out what we're gonna do."

"Go tell Larry that I'm in. I don't believe you did it either." Jim smiled. "And I know I didn't." He looked at her tummy. "Besides, I want to protect my little niece or nephew."

"Ah...I see." Laura said, smiling.

"Once I'm out of here, I can help you guys. I'm sure it'll be anytime now. I know how this works."

"I'm sure you do," she said, getting up to leave. She sat back down when she saw the lead officer come back to Jim, looking angry. He entered the interrogation room. "Ma'am, I must insist you leave now."

"What if I don't want to?"

"We'll have a problem," he blurted in a threatening tone.

Brick intervened. "Maybe it's best if you came back later? Or, if you want, you can wait in the main reception. I could bring you some water?"

"Right, okay," she said, looking at Jim. "Don't worry, I'll be back."

She wasn't left a choice. She had to leave and watched in horror as Jim was shoved over the table and handcuffed. The officer began reading him his rights. "Jim Higgins, you are charged with the murder of Brian Buchanan and Delta Dawn Fergeson. You have the right to remain silent. Anything you say can and will be used against you in a court of law. You have the right to an attorney. If you can't afford an attorney, one can be provided for you. Do you understand these rights?"

"Yes," he snapped.

He looked at Laura. "Laura, I didn't do this! I've been framed! You know this. Please help me!"

She looked at Brick with pleading eyes. "Why? How can they arrest him now? As his legal counsel, I have a right to know what evidence they have against him."

"They confirmed that some soil samples matched from his boot at the crime scene with the dirt on his farmland," Brian said, lowering his eyes.

All she could do was nod, shaken by the turn of events.

As he was led away, Jim yelled at Laura. "This smells like Vlad! Watch out Laura! He's onto us and he's trying to make it look like *we* did this. The question is...why? Whatever his reason is, that's what he doesn't want anyone to know...be careful. He'll come for you!"

Her eyes grew as big as saucers. "Daddy...I've gotta check on Daddy! Oh my God!"

Laura bolted from the station and got in the car. She tried to keep to the speed limit, and this desire to be safe wasn't due to her, but her baby. She told herself to stay calm. "He's fine. There are guards at a hospital and nursing staff. They wouldn't let someone like that through, surely! I'm probably just worried for nothing."

She swerved into the parking lot and rushed to Larry's room. Her heart swelled with relief when she saw him. The nurse was taking his blood pressure. Larry's face was red, and his wrists and ankles were swollen. Before Laura could say anything, the nurse held her arm.

"Your father needs to keep his stress under control in his condition. His blood pressure is still through the roof. Never fear, though. We're giving him something in his IV to bring it back down."

The nurse stepped out.

"Hi Daddy. I'm here now. What happened?" Laura asked, sitting down.

"We'll talk about it later, little girl," Larry said. "The lady's right. I gotta get right as rain so I can be at full strength for what's coming next."

The nurse entered, carrying a cup of tea. She said, "I usually don't make tea for patients from my own supply like this, but I could see that your father needs to relax. This should soothe him."

Larry took the tea and sipped it. He sighed, making the nurse smile contentedly. She was a chubby middle-aged woman with a really caring personality. *She's super nice, like someone's mother.* Laura thought. *Thank God she was here.* She took the kind nurse by the hand. "Thank you."

The nurse smiled and put her hand on Larry's shoulder. "Now just relax. See, your daughter's here, and she's fine. Sip your tea and take deep breaths. I'm gonna go do my rounds, but I'll be back to check on you."

Larry kissed her on the hand. "Thank you. You're as sweet as you can be, darlin'."

She blushed a bit and made her way out. Laura watched and smiled as the nurse left and shut the door. "Okay, now tell me. What really happened?"

"Vlad paid me a visit."

He calmly took another sip of his tea. Laura's mouth dropped open in shock Larry went on to explain, "He threatened to kill you if I didn't stop trying to dig things up about him. Said he's never planning to go back to prison."

Laura gulped. "So, what that tells me is that he's guilty, right?"

"Yep! He pretty much told me so. But..." Larry sighed. "We can't prove it yet."

Laura nervously crossed her arms. "I'm sorry to have to tell you all this. But we can't ignore this threat...Sweetheart, I'm an old man on my last leg. I'll use everything I've got to protect you and the baby, but honest to God, I'm not sure what to do right now."

"I thought I had a plan, but something's happened," Laura frowned, "Jim just got arrested! He thinks Vlad framed him too. But a bit of good news though, he signed me on as his legal representative, alongside you. He even paid me a dollar!" Laura laughed nervously.

"Every dollar helps, sweetheart. Do they have any evidence?" Larry asked.

"They have one of Jim's farm boots, and some soil from the balcony matches soil taken from Jim's farm," she said, then sighed. Her heart was heavy.

"It had to be planted," Larry said. "We'll find a way to prove it."

"I agree," Laura replied. "But not until I get you out of here. I can't leave you alone again."

"I guess I can call that security guard you asked me to hire," he sighed.

"I'm glad you brought it up because I was just about to. Well, anyway, you do that tomorrow morning, because I may need to help Jim get out of jail. Knowing about this threat should help...but honestly, I can't face anything else until I've had some coffee and a snack."

The two of them decided to make the best of their evening in the hospital. Laura went to the gift shop and bought a deck of cards and all the candy and peanuts she could find in the vending machine. As they laughed and reminisced about the past, Laura smiled, relieved that Larry was looking more normal. Larry said, "I'm glad we're doing this. We needed this break, right?"

"Yes, sir. We did. God knows, we've had some curveballs thrown at us lately."

"Well, maybe we need to get some sleep? I had them bring in a cot for you. I hope it's comfortable?"

Laura yawned and stretched. "It'll be just fine. I'm so tired I'm about to pass out. I swear I could sleep on a pile of bricks at this point."

# LAURA

*February 1977, New Orleans, Tulane General Hospital (Next Day)*

THE NEXT MORNING, LAURA WAS TERRIBLY SORE FROM SLEEPING ON the cot. *Maybe I spoke too soon last night*, she thought. She'd never really been used to sleeping on her side before. She'd always been a stomach sleeper, but now that she had a little passenger, it was too uncomfortable to sleep in that position. She groaned and stretched, trying to work the kinks out. Larry woke up. "Your mama used to have trouble sleeping when she was carrying you."

"I'll bet she did. I was a big ole thing, wasn't I?"

"Ten pounds and three ounces!" Larry grinned. "Yep, you were like the Michelin man alright."

She touched her belly and winced. "Ouch..."

They waited for what seemed like forever for a nurse to come check on him. Finally, after their shift change, the nurse came through to check Larry's morning vitals.

"Yep, you're doing great now, Mr. Beauford. I think you may get to leave here today."

Larry's eyes lit up. "When's the doctor coming to confirm that?"

A smartly dressed man with silver sideburns and a crisp white overcoat entered. "Good morning, Mr. Beauford."

"Doctor, I'd like to introduce you to my daughter, Laura." Larry said.

Behind them, a hulking man in a black suit approached the hospital room. Larry rolled his eyes. "And that's Zeke. He's a *friend* of the family."

The doctor smiled. "Pleased to meet you both. Now, let's see if I can discharge your father today."

After a short examination, the doctor deemed Larry to be in acceptable health for someone with terminal cancer. He was cleared and Laura got him ready to leave. They went to check on Jim at the station. Zeke followed in a separate car, always at a distance as per Larry's orders.

Larry and Laura were surprised to find out Jim had already been released. Laura leaned on the counter, glaring at the duty officer. "Excuse me, how did Jim Higgins get released?"

"That's a police matter, Ma'am."

"I know that, but as his legal representative, you should follow the proper procedures," Laura said. "Frankly, I'm glad to know he's out because we have something to report as well. Last night, my father was threatened in his hospital room by Vladimir Petroski. He threatened to kill me if my father kept investigating this case."

"We know," the officer replied with a sigh.

"What? How?" Laura looked from her father to the officer.

"Your father informed us last night. This morning, we allowed Jim's mother to post bail for him."

"Hun, maybe you'd better start practicing a little non-disclosure in your *legal* practice?"

Laura chuckled softly and smiled at her father. He grinned. "What? You didn't think I could let that big redneck sit there any longer than he had to?"

"Big softie," she said, lightly shoving his arm.

# LAURA

WITH THE HAPPY NEWS THAT LAURA'S BAIL CONDITIONS ONLY KEPT her within the state of Louisiana for now, she made the trip with Larry to visit Jim at his farm in Ponchatoula, about an hour's drive from New Orleans. The drive was pleasant all along the way, the lush green backdrop with just the right amount of spring mist in the air. Louisiana wasn't all sweetness and charm, however. For all the fresh air, charming small communities, and greenery, there was a faint smell of rotting swamp along the back roads leading to the farms. Only in states like Louisiana would one find street signs warning motorists of alligators and snakes crossing the roads. The swamps sometimes had quicksand spots, trapping all kinds of unsuspecting living beings in the inviting sandy pit. Struggling would only make you sink faster.

Laura thought about how New Orleans was the epitome of this, almost a characteristic feature of Louisiana. Sweetness on top, but darkness at its core.

Indeed, it wasn't safe to go out there without a guide and the right equipment in the swamps, and it was beginning to feel that way in the cities also. Without a guide to keep you safe, you may get caught in something that you can't escape from, and the more you struggle, the faster it pulls you in.

The two were not planning such a harrowing journey today, however. They were going to the strawberry capital of the world, Ponchatoula.

"I wonder if Jim grows strawberries. He never actually told me what he grew out there," Laura said.

"Well, I'm sure we're about to find out," Larry replied.

They arrived by midday to Jim's house and found him, sitting on his porch swing, taking in the fresh air.

Larry carefully ascended the porch steps. Jim nodded and took off his cowboy hat. "Mr. Beauford, Laura. sorry to hear you were in the hospital, sir. I hope you're feeling better now?"

"Oh yeah, I'm much better, thanks...I gotta say, Jim. I know we've all had our differences, but you don't know how damn glad I am to see you right now too."

Jim smiled. "I take it that's your bodyguard?"

"Yep. On the orders of my new young legal associate here. She doesn't feel that I'm safe without him," Larry groaned.

"You're not," Laura groaned, rolling her eyes.

"Oh, so now that your daddy's an old fart, he needs a babysitter. Huh?" Larry blurted.

"Oh fiddlesticks! You are a stubborn old coot, aren't you?" Laura said.

"You love me anyway," he snorted.

"Yeah, I do. Now just ignore it and let's get on with things, shall we?"

Jim chuckled. "Let him come on in and we'll get him something to drink."

"I'll send him in a bit later. Lemme get him busy for now," Larry said. He waved Zeke to the door. Zeke stood at attention. Larry grunted. "Go on to watch the road leading to the house. We got some private business to discuss."

"Yes, sir!" Zeke said.

Jim smiled. Larry noticed the corn field. "Looks like a good yield this year. You boys are skilled farmers. I admire that."

"Oh yeah?" Jim asked.

"Yes," Larry said. He folded his arms and looked around. "It's a great thing to do. I've always been an Alabama man, but I'm ashamed to say I never had a green thumb. Can't grow anything to save my life."

"Well, thank you, sir. It's always been natural for Ike and me. Once Mama decided she was going into the restaurant business, Ike and I decided to invest in this land...figured we could increase its value by growing crops here. She gets a lot of the produce from us."

"It's a fine farm, son. You've got a lot to be proud of here.

Jim looked visibly pleased at the compliment. "Over there, see, we have corn, tomatoes, potatoes, and that's just here at the edge of the property. There's a lot more down the way. Oh, and you may not know this, but Ponchatoula is considered the strawberry capital of the world. Before y'all leave, I want you to help yourselves to a bushel of 'em."

Larry whistled appreciatively.

"We've also got peaches and watermelons too! I'll set y'all up with a basket of those too when we're done talking."

"That would be much appreciated, son. Thank you, but let's not put so many in there. Remember, Laura and I are staying in a hotel, so we don't need a lot."

"Oh yeah, that's right! I clean forgot. Sorry...Come on in, y'all. Let's see what we're gonna do about this situation." Jim said, opening his front door. Once they were sitting in the living room with some sweet tea and pound cake, Larry decided it was time to talk.

"I think we can all help each other, and if we work together, *both* of you will have a good future ahead."

"What about you? You don't have a future?" Jim asked.

Laura shook her head. Jim looked confused. "I, uh...don't get it."

"He's got cancer, Jim. My poor daddy doesn't have much longer with us."

Jim winced. "Oh Larry, I'm so sorry. Would you forgive me? I saw you collapse at the bail hearing. I didn't know it was something that serious though. I just thought it was the stress of it all wearing down on you. Damn, I just put my foot in my mouth over and over it seems. After a restless night on those darn uncomfortable prison cots, Laura, you have my apologies for the poor treatment you endured."

Larry nodded. "It's okay, son. You didn't know. But now that you do, you know the most important thing in my life now, or what's left of it, is protecting my daughter and that little baby."

Jim sighed. "I gotta say, I do like the sound of *Uncle Jim*."

"Aces! I like the sound of that too," Laura said, beaming a sweet smile. "Jeepers, what about Ike? Do you think he's gonna enjoy being an uncle?"

"Oh yeah! I think he'll love it! He's a funny dude, ya know. That kid is never gonna be bored." Jim said, smiling.

*This small talk isn't gonna cut it.* Laura thought. *We've gotta use every second. God, I hate breaking the mood.*

Laura cleared her throat. "Jim, um...we really need to talk about..."

Jim stood up in a non-threatening manner, with one hand up, then interrupted, addressing Laura first and then Larry. "The evidence they think they have on me won't stick, ok? No disrespect, sir, but I've already talked to my regular lawyer and he's gonna take care of this. That boot went missing a while back, along with some other items. I filed a report at that time, thank God, so there's a paper trail. I mean, I didn't report a boot missing, cuz that would be stupid. I just thought I lost it somehow. But I did report some missing watches and a diamond ring I got for a girl I was gonna propose to at one point...anyway, now I think whoever got in here then must have taken the boot to frame me later."

Larry nodded. "And he found out what kind of gun you carry."

"Most probably."

"Okay, that all sounds promising." Larry nodded. "So, Vlad, as we assume, killed them, and wanted to frame the two of you, make it like you did it together."

"But, why?" Jim frowned. "It's not his M.O., and it's downright sloppy! It's not like him to be involved in a cover up. He's usually very proud of his work... And, to leave that locker up for grabs! That was downright stupid. I can't figure out for the life of me why a slippery character like him would make a rookie mistake like that."

"You're right. None of this makes any sense at all. We're missing something," Larry said. "And now he's gonna come after us, not to frame us, but to kill us."

"Do either of you know any more about this guy?" Laura asked. "Is he really that bad?" Larry nodded grimly. "I know he was full of big talk when he threatened me, but hard asses like that usually are full of shit."

Jim's mouth dropped open, shook his head, and held his forehead in his hand. "What the fuck?"

"Language, young man!" Larry snapped. "A lady is present."

"Sorry, sir." Jim looked down and put his hands in his pocket.

"I was just saying though, y'all don't seem to have any idea how dangerous that fu...I mean, that asshole is. I didn't wanna say anything when you brought it up before, but the Feds have been looking for that bastard for years. He's connected to a lot of open investigations, all Russian mob related. His signature M.O. is a crossbow bolt through the heart, hence his handle, the Impaler."

Laura's mouth dropped open. She turned to look at Larry, holding her hands protectively over her belly.

"Don't worry, darlin'," he reassured her. "We're not gonna let him get to us. I'm sure Jim can come up with a plan."

"I'm working on it," Jim said. "But at least for now, I think we have enough here to at least cast doubt in the minds of any jurors."

"Hmm, you sure about that?" Larry asked. "It's really my word against his. I mean, we've got the fake I.D.'s and passports and all to pin on him, but that doesn't prove he murdered Brian and Delta Dawn. We need more than a confession to me that no one else overheard."

Jim put his hand on his chin. Thought for a moment. "You're probably right. I'm a cop. Not a lawyer like you."

"Well Jim, as your lawyer, I'm telling you, we need more than this." Larry paced the room, with his hands behind his back.

"This is the *Russian mafia* we're talking about," Laura sputtered. "We don't know who they have in their pocket. Cops, detectives, even the FBI. You know that better than anyone!"

Jim nodded.

"Who do you know that we can trust?" Larry asked. "Someone who is undoubtedly not being paid off by the mob?"

"Daryl Rae. My mother's boyfriend. He wouldn't even be smart enough to know things like that are out there, and I tell you what else... He may be dumb as a stump, but that guy is a loyal friend. I'll give him that much. At least he can be fully aware of what's happening and where we are on everything."

"So, you don't think your regular lawyer is up to the task?" Larry asked.

Jim nodded. "Um, he's probably fine. It's old Harry Bechamp on Main Street New Orleans. Pretty good guy but getting kinda long in the teeth now."

"Harry? Haha! I'll say he is," Larry chuckled. "What's that old fart been up to? I'm surprised he didn't check out yet. He must have one foot in the grave and another on a banana peel. But hey, I'm not one that should point a finger. He may last longer than me at this rate."

Jim snorted. "I'm sorry for laughing sir. I know that ain't a laughing matter. It's just the way you said it."

"Don't worry about it, son. If we don't have laughter, we don't have nothing," Larry said, putting a hand on Jim's shoulder.

Anyhow, if it means anything, I don't wanna take any chances right now. I'll stick with you as my legal counsel if that's alright."

"Smart man," Larry said.

"I'll need everything you've got on Vladimir and this mystery woman you told me about," Jim said.

"Absolutely. I really want to see if you recognize anyone. Let's sit down and get comfortable. It's a beautiful day. This sunshine is good for us." Larry pointed at Jim's lawn furniture, so they all went to sit down and look over the evidence carefully, especially the picture of the woman.

Laura handed him the pictures and the other documents. Jim looked at the blonde Mrs. Wheel's picture for a while, pausing thoughtfully

"Jim?" Laura couldn't contain her curiosity.

"I've seen this woman before. I'm not exactly able to place where, but I know I've seen her. She looks so familiar." Jim took a harder look at the photo. "Know what? I'm gonna borrow this stuff. I need to talk to Daryl Rae and see if any of them have seen her too."

"Delta Dawn's aunt had a picture of her niece with a bunch of girls..." Larry said, looking harder at the picture. "I'll be damned. I think that's her. They were in Juvie together, her and Delta. Look, she's got blonde hair here too."

"Oh, my sweet baby Jesus." Laura blurted. "Vlad may come back. He may be watching right now, and if he knows my father told me everything...told you...he may..."

Jim patted her hand and nodded at Larry. "Don't you worry your pretty head about that. I'll get a few boys from the precinct to guard you, and you've got Zeke. The others won't mind looking after you when I show the captain these pictures."

"But didn't you say you didn't know who you can trust?" Laura asked.

"Don't worry. I'm not gonna share this with *everyone*," Jim said. "Just a few men only, those who would never betray me, not for anything."

"Ok. Just know that my father and I are putting our lives in your hands right now. We've come a long way on our own, but we seriously need this help."

"You got it," Jim smiled, looking at the floor.

Larry put his hand on Jim's shoulder. "I'm proud of you, son. All I want..." he said, choking on his words, "before I check out of this world, is to see my family safe and happy. Then, I can leave here a happy man. So...you, see? You're helping to make a man's dying wish come true."

Jim shook hands with Larry and stood back. He put his hands on his hips and took on a serious tone. "Mr. Beauford...Larry, I hope you and Laura know how wrong you've been about us all these years. I *know* how wrong I've been about you, Laura. I'm sorry you even once thought of me as an enemy. I loved Brian, and when he went to the university, Ike and I made regular visits there."

Laura nervously bit her lip. Larry nodded at her. This was a perfect opportunity to mend broken fences.

Jim held both her hands, looking her directly in the eyes. "I know you thought we only went there to get him fucked up and distract him from his studies, but you're wrong. Pardon my French."

Larry patted Laura on the back encouragingly. She cleared her throat. "Actually, I knew that you guys were close," She exhaled and shook her head. "My father reminded me many times back then that it's good for Brian to be close with the down to Earth people in his life. Jack's lifestyle wasn't exactly normal. God love him... We all loved him! But, yes, I was glad he had someone grounding in his life, even though I didn't seem to like it sometimes."

Jim smiled and sighed. Laura put her hand on his shoulder. "I'm so glad you're on our side now. God knows, we need you so much." She teared up and caressed her belly. Larry put his arm around Laura, and together, they all embraced.

"Okay, let's break this up," Larry said. "We're hugging like a bunch of hippies now."

Laura and Jim laughed.

"Oh Daddy," Laura chuckled. "You're such a character."

Jim and Larry sat down to strategize and decide on which officers on the Force were trustworthy. Jim made a list of which ones he would start phoning first. Larry organized all their evidence and wrote some notes to present to the team.

Laura was feeling restless, probably the baby hormones causing it. "Hey Jim, sorry to interrupt. It is getting late in the day and as we might be here for a couple more hours, would it be okay if I rustle up something in the kitchen for us all?"

"Mighty kind of you to offer, Laura. I'm sorry I'm such a poor host to y'all. This case is so huge, I don't wanna mess up any of it. I do have some fresh steaks chillin' in the fridge. Just holler if ya need anything in there, ya hear?"

Laura gratefully busied herself in the kitchen. Luckily, Jim's fresh produce gave her a wide choice of ingredients and she started humming while preparing dinner.

Larry called Zeke over to join them for dinner. They ate juicy blackened steaks with a garden salad on the porch as the sun was setting, and it was indeed a beautiful day. Jim's colleagues would be arriving shortly. Jim stood on the porch steps, cigarette in hand, surveying his property. He looked picturesque there with his cowboy hat and bell bottom jeans. She regretted that she and Brian hadn't made the effort to get to know him in such a charming setting. *Stop dwelling in the past, girl. Keep looking forward*, she reminded herself.

# JIM

JIM MADE HIS PHONE CALLS, AND SOON AFTER DINNER, A FEW OF HIS most trusted colleagues arrived; including his captain, who didn't live too far down the road from him. At this point, it was a given that all phones were bugged and meeting at a place like Jim's farm would be more secure. Jim and Larry filled in the assembled officers on what was going on. The captain looked grim as more details emerged. His years of experience soon triumphed, however, and he split the group into two: a task force to work with the FBI and another to protect Laura and Larry.

Jim was given some leeway by his captain, but not much. He was placed in charge of securing Larry and Laura's safety, but he felt rather like an imposter. He hoped he was making the right decisions but felt unsure of himself. This was the biggest case he'd ever worked on, but he tried not to let his insecurities show. He gave his fellow officers orders, as though he knew what he was doing.

At least he felt like he was doing something useful, something to avenge his brother, and maybe unite the family. "You fellas understand what's at stake and who we're dealing with. It won't be long until the Feds want a piece of this, especially now that they're into the locker evidence, so let's not screw up. We're dealing with one of America's most wanted right now."

Jim folded his arms and looked down. A JFK pose if you ever saw one. He really stepped up to take charge of things. First things first... everyone was assigned their duties. He grinned when he heard Laura whisper to Larry. "It's hard to feel anything but safe with the looks of them."

Jim agreed wholeheartedly. After all, his boys were the best. New Orleans' finest. Larry's guy, Zeke, looked like a badass, but Jim believed his guys to be the absolute bomb, as far as hard asses go. They were all very capable officers. Charlie was over six feet tall with a buffed-out chest, jet black hair and a pointed chin. The guys called him Chuck. The second guy was blonde and shorter and went by the name Bruce. He was only about 5 and a half feet, but harsh in appearance, ripped, complete with tattoos, an earring, and a gold tooth. The third guy was also buff and brash, a Cajun named Roy. Bald as a cue ball and missing his front teeth after he got the wrong end of a pool stick during a bust.

---

JIM AGREED to meet up with Laura and Larry later that evening, after he and the captain had a chance to go over all the material again. Tension was mounting from every angle, and everyone involved felt it. There was something ominous in the air. The dark underbelly of New Orleans was coming to the surface.

# LAURA

LAURA AND LARRY RETURNED TO THE HOTEL SUITE AS IT GOT DARK and the four officers followed closely, trailed by Zeke in his own car. "God, I never thought I'd need to be guarded like this," Larry whispered. "But I'm surely glad they're accompanying us right now. We'll need to discuss sleeping arrangements of course and shifts."

She nodded and looked over her shoulder. There they were, keeping close, and at least for that moment, she felt safe. Chuck had decided that going to their room as soon as they arrived was the safest course of action.

*We're here. Thank God.* She thought. Larry gave the car keys to the valet, and stood waiting for the rest of the caravan to pull in. There were also two unmarked police cars parked near the hotel entrance.

Chuck handed over his keys as well and turned to Larry. "We can't protect you if we're standing in the lobby. We need to remain in close proximity and get you inside. Do you understand?"

Laura nodded. "Whatever it takes. I'm just so glad y'all are here!"

Chuck followed behind as Larry strode ahead into the lobby. Laura took her time getting out of the car, standing in between Roy and Bruce on the hotel steps. Suddenly... a strange sound whistled through the air. WHOOSH!

Blood splattered from Bruce's chest, staining his shirt red. He fell to his knees, wide-eyed, gasping as he grabbed his chest. Laura couldn't breathe for a moment, but then let out a scream that would burst ear sockets. Roy pushed her through the glass doors to the safety of the hotel lobby. She tumbled to the floor, curling up around her belly, doing everything she could to protect her baby. She whimpered, trying desperately to stay low on the ground. *Oh, dear merciful Jesus, please help us live through this and get us to safety. Oh please!*

"Over here! Now!" Chuck shouted at her, gun drawn and a determined look on his face.

Whimpering, she half-crawled towards him. Chuck reached out and grabbed her, then pulled her behind the front desk where Larry was already hunkered down, pale but unharmed. "Okay, you two, stay here and stay down! Got it?" They both nodded. Larry shielded her shaking body with his, holding her tight. Curiosity got the better of her though. She couldn't help but peek at what was happening.

Chuck and Zeke crept toward the door, both with revolvers cocked and ready. Zeke checked his perimeter...

WHOOSH!

Zeke fell face down, shot through the chest with a crossbow bolt. Laura was frozen in place. Larry struggled to relax her legs so that she could keep her head down, but she was in a state of shock, incapable of moving a muscle. Another gunshot whizzed by, then hit the front desk. Roy signaled that Chuck should call for backup, then reached in his front pocket to pull out his walkie talkie.

"Laura! Get down!" Larry snapped, pulling her off balance.

The movement jarred her into action. She dropped down, struggling to breathe normally. Her heart was pounding, and she could feel the blood draining from her face, leaving her dizzy. She turned as she heard one of the men radio for help.

"All units, 10-33! We have a 10-77 on 311 Main Street. Active shooter in front of the Hotel Royal. Request backup and 10-52, officers down."

Larry held her tight. "We're gonna be okay. Be strong now, you hear? They know what they're doing."

She tried to believe him. Her back ached, reminding her of the baby. She managed to take a deep breath and sobbed into her hands.

# CHUCK

*March 1977, New Orleans, Royal Hotel, same day.*

CHUCK CRAWLED BACK TO CHECK ON LAURA AND LARRY. "HEY, everything's gonna be fine. We're gonna get you two safely out of here and into protective custody. If someone wants to kill you this badly, you must either be very guilty or very innocent!"

"Innocent! Like I've been telling y'all!" Laura blurted in a panic, her voice cracking. Her face was pale and splotchy from shock and crying hysterically. She clutched her belly with shaking hands.

More gun shots swooshed through the air, making popping thuds wherever they hit. Larry shuffled closer, to sit half in front of Laura. He nodded grimly at Chuck, appearing quite calm under the circumstances.

Chuck slithered on the floor alongside the large desk, then made his way to the front entrance. The front doors of the hotel were all made of glass, which gave Vlad and his men great advantage as they could see everyone inside.

Chuck remembered that they all put on bulletproof vests under their plain clothes before heading out on this mission. He touched his chest to reassure himself that he was wearing it, then peeked outside. He saw Roy laying on the ground near the car with a bolt in his chest. Chuck sweated profusely and he pressed his lips into a line as he murmured, "A bolt? That's definitely the Impaler!"

He looked at the tall buildings around, hoping to spot where the bullets and bolts were coming from. No shots had been fired back because they didn't know where to shoot.

They waited tensely ...

Backup arrived in the form of the SWAT team and a helicopter to give the cops eyes in the sky. Chuck listened to his walkie talkie. The pilot reported, "Suspect is not in sight. That's a negative. Got some empty gun stands. No perps in sight."

The SWAT team swept the area and reported that there were at least two shooters, no confirmed sightings either.

Meanwhile some of the cops rushed into the lobby, guns drawn, speaking to the staff who were coming out of various hiding places. Everyone heard the screeches of tires pulling up and the *wee-ow, wee-ow* sound of the ambulances that blocked the entrances. A flood of emergency workers arrived on the scene to attend to the wounded and the traumatized.

Laura and Larry were finally cleared to leave their hiding spots. Chuck made eye contact with Laura. He tried to give her a reassuring nod, but he couldn't tell if she accepted it or not. *She's in shock. Leave her be*, he thought.

"A crossbow," Jim said. "Who the fuck does this guy think he is? Dracula? Jesus Christ."

"Yep, a crossbow. Whoever clocked Roy must have hit him from a moving vehicle as it crossed paths with the scene of the crime," Chuck sighed. "I'm really ashamed to say I don't know if this clown was lying in wait for him or what. Everything just happened so fast."

Jim nodded, folding his arms. "Anything else you can tell me?"

"Yeah, as a matter of fact, there is," Chuck said. "The gun stands were military grade, nothing that a civilian would have. But this... *this* had to have been full on Mafia. And that crossbow? Signature move of Vlad the Impaler. So yeah, chances are, he knows by now that you've found his stash of ID's and stuff, and he's making good on his threats.

# JIM

BACK AT THE STATION, JIM TOOK A LONG DRAG OF A CIGARETTE, THEN his brow furrowed.

"How can you be sure?" he asked.

Eddie scoffed as he examined the feathered bolt. "It's from a steel crossbow, Romanian made. One of the historical Vlad the Impaler's favorite weapons. It's from a three fingered draw crossbow. In Transylvania, the three-finger draw may have been used and that bows were both longbows and smaller Tartar bows. He must have wanted to send Larry and Laura a message, or just straight up kill them then and there. No prints, but that was expected. He's a professional, after all."

"Wow. You're like a walking encyclopedia, my man," Jim said. "I'm impressed."

Eddie smiled and nodded but looked away when he saw the look on Laura's face.

Jim peered at Larry and Laura. Laura cried and Larry wiped the sweat from his forehead with his handkerchief. *The old boy is trying to be strong but look at him. Motherfucking bastard!* Jim cocked his head to one side and said, "Look at 'em. They're both unglued. I think they got the message."

His heart went out to them. He had to help them. It was all too much, and Jim felt completely out of his league. It wasn't only that. He was genuinely scared, scared of losing anyone else. This fight was win or die for Jim, as nothing else would do.

———

EVERYTHING CHANGED for Jim and the Beaufords after that day. Laura was right about the current state of things. The official stance on her accusation of killing her husband was that she was most likely not guilty, but still a person of interest in the investigation, which was now officially reopened. Her trial date was cancelled.

Jim shared the same status. This meant that Larry got the bail money back and Laura's accounts and properties were officially accessible again. However, she was still under a travel ban, forbidden from leaving the state.

The FBI was now involved. Since Jim brought the incriminating evidence to light against Vladimir and the mysterious woman from the hotel, he led the local team of investigators, as long as he agreed to report to the FBI at every step. The other benefit was that the FBI was more than happy to cooperate with his team's investigation by allowing them access to previously restricted resources.

Nothing prepared Jim for the movie-star statuesque, blonde man in his thirties, Agent Bernard Smith, lead agent on the FBI team. At ten AM the next morning, they rolled in, the whole team dressed in black suits and ties.

There were a few receptionists at the thirty-first precinct, and one head secretary. They all watched Agent Smith as he walked by. He didn't seem to notice the cascade of sighs and swoons as he entered the meeting room. "Good God Almighty," Jim muttered. "Like a cock in the henhouse."

Agent Smith was there to gather all attending officers to discuss the case, and he clearly meant business. Jim entered and approached him to shake hands. He looked Jim over and smiled. "I'm Agent Smith. Glad to meet you, Jim."

"Hey there," Jim said. "Glad to meet you too."

Agent Smith nodded. "Go on, grab a seat so we can get started."

"What are we gonna do about nailing these bastards?" Jim blurted. "I mean, what's the connection is to my brother's murder?"

"God love you country boys," Agent Smith smiled. "I can always count on some fine manners.

"Our mamas raised us right," Jim said, smiling cautiously.

Agent Smith nodded, "damn straight. First slide!"

The first image was of Jack Buchanan. Agent Smith announced, "Gentlemen, somehow this all starts with this man, Jack Buchanan, whereabouts unknown. Now, our task is to find out what Buchanan Oil has to do with the Russian mob and Vladimir Petroski, also known as Vlad the Impaler."

The next slide showed one of Vladimir's blurry photos from the hotel. Alongside him was the brunette female with the blue eyes, who had checked into the hotel with him as his wife, Mrs. Wheel. Jim sat up straight in his chair, certain there was something odd about her, something not quite right. He spoke up. "Excuse me, but do we have an ID yet on the woman?"

"No," Agent Smith answered. "Why?"

"I've seen her. I don't know where, but I have seen her for sure. She's not his wife."

Agent Smith cocked his head to one side. "Yes, you've made that known to us. Would you be able to recognize her again if you saw her?"

Jim nodded. "Pretty sure."

"Okay, that's a good start. Let's meet about this after the briefing."

Jim sat in the back of the room as Agent Smith explained what else they already knew, thanks to Jim and Larry's investigation on behalf of Laura Lynn Buchanan. The team saw photo after photo of Vlad's fake passports and IDs, along with what the testimony Susan McFarland had disclosed regarding Delta Dawn, that she was likely a pawn placed to frame Laura.

Laura had also given them the recordings of the conversations that she'd had with the witnesses from the hotel.

Jim asked, "Where's Laura and Larry? Are they safe? The Mob won't lose any time finding them again."

"We've got it under control, Jim," Agent Smith said, putting his hands in his pockets.

Jim winced. He didn't like the sound of that.

"Under control? What does that mean, exactly?"

"After the briefing!" Agent Smith snapped.

A short, chubby, ginger haired agent tried to be discreet as he reached for a glazed donut from the common tray. When the men noticed him, he grinned, revealing dimples and bucked teeth.

"So, gentlemen...is the DA gonna drop the case against Ms. Buchanan? I suppose this Vlad guy is the primary suspect now?"

"Not exactly, Agent O'Connor," said Agent Smith. Ms. Buchanan is still a person of interest. She was caught holding the murder weapon, right in front of the victims, when she was arrested."

"The gun had literally just gone off minutes before she was taken. The gunshot wounds were still fresh.

However, her contribution to this investigation and her being targeted by the mob has cast doubts."

Gulping down the donut, Agent O'Connor pointed at Jim. "Do we still consider *this* guy a suspect? Mr. Farm Dirt? Maybe he plugged the poor bastards and hung out on the balcony while Miss Daisy May took the blame?"

The other agents chuckled softly. Agent Smith's lips pressed into a hard line, and he folded his arms. He glared at them, and they cleared their throats, murmured amongst themselves, and shifted in their seats. *This guy's got 'em scared to death.* Jim thought.

Agent O'Connor must have thought no one could hear him when he turned around and whispered under his breath, "Suit yourself, pretty boy." Jim didn't let on that he had heard.

"The victim's brother has been cleared of suspicion, and that's all any of you need to know right now. If he were a suspect, he wouldn't be on the team at all," Agent Smith said, looking back at Jim.

The meeting went on for a good while. Agent Smith led the group by setting out a strategy to stake out known mob hangouts in and around New Orleans and put pressure on their informants.

"I want all of you to find out everything you can about why Buchanan Oil was a target. Were they using the shipments to smuggle drugs? Women? Were they stealing the oil shipments to sell them on the international black market? There must be a reason. This also may go *beyond* the mafia. There could be KGB involvement as well."

Agent Smith also tasked Agent O'Connor with researching Buchanan Oil's past employees to look for a possible connection. Additionally, each agent received a copy of the blurry picture of the mystery woman with Vlad at the hotel as well as the juvie picture of Delta Dawn and the mystery woman.

Jim took notice of Agent Smith and how he had mastered the ability to look confident, no matter what. At least that's what Jim thought. He tapped Agent Smith on the shoulder.

"Hey. I gotta say, I like the way you delegate authority," Jim said.

Agent Smith smiled. "I know I'm missing something, but this feels like the right way to go."

"I agree," Jim replied.

He watched them all, digesting their assignments, discussing amongst themselves.

The briefing finished, and the agents dispersed to begin their work. Agent Smith sat down near Jim. The precinct secretary poked her head in and asked, "You boys want some coffee?"

Agent Smith looked back, flashed his pearly smile at her. "Yes darlin'. That would be sweet. Milk and sugar for me. How do you take yours, Jim?"

"Doreen knows, thanks," Jim said.

Doreen barely noticed Jim as she stared at Agent Smith. He appeared to be fully aware of her stares, but pretended he wasn't. Jim waited until Doreen left.

Bernard smiled at him. "I've never found that it was a good idea to encourage women that I work with. Just bad business. Better to keep work and private life separate."

"I suppose," Jim said.

Jim rolled his eyes as he watched her still swoony through the window in the next room. "Boy, you aren't gonna let any of our girls get any work done, are ya?"

Agent Smith lit a cigar and pulled an ashtray closer. He raised one eyebrow. "Look, Jim, I know how attractive I am to women, but I don't shit where I eat."

Jim scoffed. "Well, they're all drooling for you. Why don't you leave some for the rest of us?"

Agent Smith enjoyed a soft chuckle as he thought of it. He took a drag of the cigar, winked, and said, "Well, I'll keep that in mind."

Doreen delivered the coffee and sat Jim's down without even giving him a backwards glance. Jim chuckled softly and Agent Smith smiled wolfishly. Doreen stood still for a moment as Agent Smith said, "That'll be all, sweetness."

She gulped, smiled, and blushed. She stepped backwards a bit and made her way out. Jim cleared his throat. "Now, all foolishness aside, tell me where Laura and Larry are."

Agent Smith took a sip of his coffee. "On their way to a safe house."

"What?!" Jim blurted. "Do you know how risky that is? Don't you think that Vlad can find them? He's got spies everywhere! How do you even know your own men aren't working for him?"

Jim's brow furrowed and he let out a long sigh, before continuing in a softer voice. "She's pregnant with my brother's baby."

"Don't worry Jim," Agent Smith replied. "I'm confident in my men. They've got safe houses all over the country, and they know how to travel without getting tailed."

Jim nodded. "I hope you're right. Mama's already sick about losing Brian."

"Speaking of your mother...You need to interview her about Jack Buchanan's life, the office, his staff. Anything she can remember. Anyone suspicious. You'd be surprised at what tiny details we notice every day that don't seem important at the time but turn out to be crucial to cracking a case," Agent Smith said as he blew a smoke ring towards the yellow stained ceiling.

"I'm on it. I'll see her tonight. But she hasn't been in real contact with him for years."

"Oh, one more thing...Be sure and show the pictures of the woman. We need to find out if anyone's seen her. Be discreet. We do *not* want her getting wind of the fact that she's a suspect. She is simply a person of interest right now. Quietly. Got it?"

"Yeah, Roger that. I'll go round Mama's house tonight and see what I can find out. I sure hope I can find something useful," Jim said. He sipped his coffee.

Jim took a long look at the picture. "I know I have seen her. Where? This is gonna keep me up all night..."

# LARRY

*March 1977, undisclosed distance from New Orleans, on route to the safe house*

THREE AGENTS ACCOMPANIED LAURA AND LARRY TO THE SAFE HOUSE. The road was bumpy. Felt like they were taking all the back roads to get to where they were going. *Smart,* Larry thought.

"How ya doing, kiddo?"

Laura seemed relatively comfortable on the bench seat in the van with black tinted windows. They couldn't see anything outside. "I wonder if we stand out more because we're in this vehicle that's obviously trying to cover up the fact that we're in it," Laura snorted.

"You read my mind." He grabbed her hand. "No sweat. We'll be at our destination soon."

Laura rested her hand on her belly and smiled. *God, that does a man's heart good.* He hadn't had much to smile about lately.

"The little rascal is acting up, huh?"

"It's like little butterfly wings flapping. But sometimes he gives me a solid kick and sits on my bladder. I already have to pee, and I may throw up at any time. Must be my anxiety. I hope all this trauma isn't gonna give him a complex or anything." She smiled.

Things were good and they were going to be safe.

A violent impact hit the van, spinning it around before coming to a juddering halt. Larry held on to Laura, preventing her from falling onto the floor, but she slipped from his grasp and ended up near the sliding door where the third agent was sitting.

Larry did a quick visual check on everybody. Laura was curled up in a fetal position, but appeared to be okay, as she started getting up. The agent in the back with them, patted himself, before assisting Laura back to her seat.

"What the fuck was that?!" growled one of the agents from the front, in a deep whisper.

Larry was suddenly reminded of his days in World War II. He suddenly felt an old, but familiar gut instinct snap into action. He grabbed a gun straight off the holster of the agent sitting across from him, cocked it and took aim at the door. The agent tried to reach for it and Larry hissed, "Get off me and shut up! Pull your head out of your ass! This is an ambush."

Somebody knocked on the driver's window. "Hey, y'all okay in there? Can anyone hear me?"

The driver wound down his window two inches and replied, "Step away from the vehicle, please. I will call for help."

"Hey buddy! No time! I've got my wife in the car out here and she's banged up pretty bad. Anyone in there got any medical training?" The man asked.

Larry pointed to shadows passing the tinted windows of the van, they counted the silhouettes of at least four people as they surrounded the van. "I told you," he whispered. The agent nodded grimly.

The speaker outside approached the driver's window. Larry hid his gun arm and peered in between the driver and passenger seats. The man outside had a small cut on his forehead that oozed blood. He seemed nervous but looked harmless. The agent in the front seat groaned with pain from his whiplash. "It's your call," he said to the driver, pulling his gun out. Larry's gut twinged when he saw the agent in the driver's seat visibly relax. "I'm not gonna let a woman die on my watch."

Larry snapped, "Don't roll that glass down! We're all dead if you do! Just drive!"

"Listen to my father," Laura begged. "He knows what he's talking about. Please, let's just go. Please."

A woman's voice from outside suddenly cried out in pain, "Help me! Help me! Honey please..."

The agent turned briefly back to Larry, "Old man, you've lost your damn mind." He rolled down the window. The man outside stepped back, raised his arm, and pointed a gun inside the van, smiling as he said in a Russian accent, "Spasiba!" Everything happened in a blur.

"Noooo!!!" Larry shouted.

Shots came in through the driver's open window, deafening everyone inside. Larry watched as the agent in the driver's seat collapsed sideways, his head blown open and spraying blood, bone, and brain matter across the interior. The agent in the passenger seat was thrown against the side door as he took a bullet between the eyes as well.

Laura screamed. Larry spared her a quick glance. Blood and gore splattered on her face, arms, and dress. He briefly thought he must look worse, as he was closer to the action. Then instinct kicked in again.

Larry pointed the gun at the windows, ready to kill anyone who tried to get them from the back, trying his best to shield Laura. However, the attackers were swift. They pulled open the doors and shoved the dead agents out, then slid into their seats, all with guns pointed at the occupants in the back. With another loud bang, they shot and murdered the agent sitting across from them, leaving only Larry and Laura. "Baby girl, cover your eyes, okay?" Larry didn't want her to go into shock.

A familiar voice shouted from outside in a sing-song voice. "Oh, papa bear! Drop the gun, or my men will make kishka out of your daughter and her bastard."

Larry grunted. He knew that voice, it had threatened him in his hospital room not too long ago. "My daughter didn't do anything! So let her go! You can kill me if you want! That ought to make you happy. I'm asking you as a gentleman."

Vlad snorted with a chuckle. "I told you Larry. I take no pleasure in killing a dying man. I warned you not to talk, or your pretty daughter will pay the price."

Before Larry could reply, Laura blurted, "Mr. Petroski, let's talk about this. I'm sure there's something we can work out. There's gotta be a way I can convince you that my father and I are worth more alive than dead. Please..."

She was shaking but determined. Larry was terrified and proud at the same time. Vlad thought about it for a moment. He grunted. "Come out and let me see you. I'll decide if you can live, if only to pleasure my men."

Many muffled snorts ensued. Larry's face turned red, and he gritted his teeth. He started to say something, but Laura put her hand over his mouth. "Shhh... Daddy, it's okay. Trust me."

# LAURA

*March 1977, undisclosed distance from New Orleans, after the car crash.*

LARRY OPENED THE SLIDING DOOR, CAREFULLY CLIMBING OVER THE dead agent's legs. He helped Laura out. The two of them stood in the midday sun, exposed. There was a Cadillac and a Ford pick-up truck, both had crashed into the FBI's van. But the immediate threat was the group of men standing around the area, all of them holding various guns at the ready.

Laura finally saw Vlad up close. She smoothed her face and hair, getting her bearings. Her makeup was running somewhat as the shock took its toll on her emotions and she could barely stop the tears leaking from her eyes. She felt disheveled, with blood splatters on her face and dress. She could feel it on her skin and in her hair, sticky and unpleasant. She shivered as she clutched her baby bump and lowered her gaze, then slowly looked up with wide doe eyes.

Southern women of a certain breeding were all well aware of how to make a man feel as though he were in charge, even if that were not the case. Vlad's a man. As any man, he will appreciate a show of submission and flattery, she figured.

"Sir, I find myself at your mercy, and I know you're a very intelligent man," Laura said with a trembling voice.

He smiled; head tilted. "I'm listening."

Laura studied his face, but it was difficult. Vlad had been at his trade for many years, so he knew what a poker face was all about. Laura needed to rely on other instincts, everything she'd been taught about political negotiations by her father, her knowledge of money, and her instincts as a woman.

"My husband was worth millions of dollars. I don't know who you had working on this, but I'm sure that I can give you more ... and ..." she paused with a cheeky smile, "I'd be willing to bet you a dime to a dollar that they were not as cute as me."

All the men laughed, and Vlad cracked a smile. "I think you've earned a chance to talk. After you, my beauty."

He pointed to the Cadillac. One of his henchmen opened the back door and motioned her to enter. Vlad chuckled softly as she walked past him. She smiled. "I just knew you were special ... much more intelligent than dumb Southern boys."

She looked back at her father. "Daddy, are you coming?"

Vlad said, "Yes, come papa, you may join us for now. I may still have use for you."

Laura winced as she watched Larry grit his teeth as he got out of the van. She also spotted him sticking the gun in the back of his pants, which made Vlad chuckle.

"Oh Larry, don't think the Impaler is stupid. Drop the piece on the ground...*now.*"

Larry exhaled, exhausted, Laura could see that he was in pain. Tired, but not beaten. He tossed the gun and gave Vlad a piercing look. Vlad cracked a sideways smile and said, "Yes, you are probably going to regret this. You don't think I can read your thoughts?"

Stumbling a bit, Larry walked towards Laura who was perched on the back seat. Taking a painful breath, Larry looked Vlad dead in the eye. Laura would never forget what he said.

"You'll never know what it's like to give your last breath to ensure the survival of the ones you love. No matter what you do, you cannot take that from me. All I do, I do for them."

Larry closed the car door behind himself, and Laura wondered if Vlad was thinking about what her father had just said. For all the times Vlad kept his emotions in check, he seemed to be taken by what Larry said. He peered at Larry and gently nodded.

She shook her head. *That man isn't pure evil, but he's close.*

Vlad scoffed. "You'll be taking your last breath soon, papa bear," he murmured. "But after I taste some honey."

His smile slowly turned into a leer as he slid into the car next to her. Laura smiled sweetly but cringed inside. *I was wrong. Pure evil.*

Another talent of the Southern lady. She knew she had to keep flirting with him, at least to be sure they would not end up dead. But would that be enough? Only time would tell. The most important thing now would be to remain calm and be strong for her father. She couldn't let herself believe that this was the end.

# JANE

*March 1977, New Orleans, LA*

JANE WHEELER WAS ON HER WAY TO A VERY GRAND HOME IN NEW Orleans, in an exclusive area of the French Quarter. The snaking driveway took her under a canopy of very large oak trees, not that she could see it at night. She arrived at three AM, the night's darkest hour, as instructed.

This wasn't her first time visiting this address. She had a sinking feeling in her stomach. This wouldn't be good, no matter what happened, despite the charm of the location.

The Baroque style of the home was the pinnacle of elegance in the South, and her heart began to beat rapidly as she stopped the car at the main entrance. Her instructions were to meet with Alex at this address, at three AM. She did as she was told, arriving on time.

A tall well-built doorman awaited her. She rolled down the window. "I'll park your car while you meet. The Don is waiting for you."

"All right," she replied, putting on the parking brake and leaving the car to idle.

She had a handgun in her clutch purse, which she carefully tucked under her arm, as she swung her legs out and stepped onto the neat driveway. She wore a red sequined crepe jumpsuit, paired perfectly with her red lipstick. The doorman stared her down with a steely look. His brow furrowed and she felt his eyes boring their way into her head. Finally, she couldn't stand it and blurted, "Is there something I'm forgetting?"

"Gun," he said, holding out his hand to take her purse.

She rolled her eyes and handed it over. "Spread your arms out and face the house," he commanded.

"What?"

He continued the death stare, so she did as he asked. He patted her down swiftly, checking for weapons of any kind. He found her knife holster, around her upper thigh. With one swift move, he took her blade away, satisfied she wasn't packing more weapons.

"Wait in the front living room," he said, walking ahead to open the front doors for her.

Struggling to keep her cool, she walked into the living room, where a butler entered. "Would you care for a drink, madame?"

She looked around and her shoulders relaxed a bit. *Mr. Alex must not want me dead, or I would be wearing a toe tag already.* She smiled at the butler. "A scotch on the rocks please."

Her drink was soon served to her in a cut crystal goblet with a small linen napkin. "Thank you," Jane said, taking a deep sip. She was admiring a particularly elegant painting by Botticelli, when she heard a soft voice behind her.

Her breath hitched and she hastily gulped the mouthful. She knew that voice, and who he was. It all made sense now. She'd met him when she was a child. Until tonight, she didn't understand who the notes were from. The "Don" as he called himself, always sent hand delivered notes via messengers. As she understood the story, he wasn't one to be trifled with, given the nickname and title, "Don" by the Italian mob, due to his deep connections with their inner circles and his admiration for their culture.

*He covered up his true identity. He couldn't have anyone finding out that he's connected to all this, not just connected, but central to everything. I remember him by the name V used to call him, Mr. Alex.*

"Good evening, Natasha."

"Good evening, Don Alexander."

Alexander Arsenyev was an attractive man, despite the fact that he was in his early sixties. Some may describe him as a silver fox, deep blue eyes with a full head of hair and sideburns. He dressed impeccably, always in a suit of the finest cloth, tailor made, with a Rolex and Amedeo Testoni shoes. Nothing but the best.

He was the current head of Vlast Incorporated, the mob's front company. The official business of the Vlast group was real estate, and according to the books, Alexander Arsenyev was an upstanding businessman in the community who was rapidly acquiring many hotels and businesses in the French Quarter and subsections of Baton Rouge. He had strong ties to the Odessa family that wished to expand from New York to the Southern states. They were products of the U.S.S.R, Ukrainian to be exact, but Alexander never really embraced his heritage as other bosses. He admired the Italians and their corner on the cocaine market and was reported to be in good standing with them, hence the handle that they respectfully gave him, "The Don."

His own people called him "Glava Semi", or the head of the house, but that never had quite the same ring to him. Natasha remembered the stories. A part of him always wanted to be Italian.

What only his small inner circle knew was that Natasha had brought him to power. Natasha Krykon, also known as Jane Wheeler, had been given the task by her commander, Vladimir Petroski, also known as Vlad the Impaler or when he used his American pseudonym, James Wheel. Now, she was faced with meeting the face behind that transaction.

Jane fought every urge to run, but she remained cordial. Alexander sensed her unease. "Relax. You're here to discuss a different sort of...employment. This is a friendly meeting, or at least it can be, if you behave yourself."

"Employment? Sorry Don Alexander, may I ask what that means?" she asked as she took a deep sip from her drink to steady her nerves.

He put a reassuring hand on her shoulder, looking deep in her eyes. "It means that you won't be working for all of the Southwest groups. You'll work only for me."

He smiled, and at first glance, one wouldn't think of him as dangerous. He looked good. His hair was still full, considering his advanced years. The same couldn't be said for his skin, in spite of his obvious efforts to keep himself young. He still smelled like an old man, and Natasha resisted the urge to wince. *You'd think he could afford a better cologne, not the shit he's wearing.*

His eyes were the deepest blue, gorgeous, like sapphires. They almost masked the criminal mastermind behind them, the dark father type that Vlad told her about, many years ago. He had the eyes of an angel, but the soul of Satan. No matter how nice he pretended to be, this was a cold-blooded butcher, known for his violent and unexpected kills.

He once took out a snitch with an ice pick straight through the eye, right after shaking his hand and telling him that he was free to go. Nadia shook her head and forced herself back into the moment. *Why did I question him just now? Fuck. Is he gonna kill me?*

"Exclusivity? That's what you're asking?" she asked, politely.

"Asking?" he said, smirking.

"No, no," she stammered. "Of course, you never have to *ask* for anything, sir."

"Exactly," he smiled, taking her hand, kissing it gently. "Please, my dear. You are an angel to look at. Sit down and make yourself comfortable. We have much to discuss."

Once they were comfortable, he summoned the butler with a wave.

"You may serve dinner in the dining room," he said.

"Yes, sir," the butler replied, then left.

Alex looked at Jane, not moving. He reminded her of a patient predator, like a snake waiting to strike. She struggled under his gaze. *What is he planning now?*

"Why me?" she eventually said, softly.

He rolled his eyes. "Milaya, I should think that the answer is obvious...I'm only here *because* of you. Your skill set is to my liking. Much less messy than your previous commander."

She exhaled and sat the glass down on the marble-topped side table nearby. "Speaking of him, won't he be angry to learn that you're poaching me? He's not exactly known for being understanding. What if he kills me?"

Alex's smile faded, and his face became deadly cold. "Let me worry about the Impaler. Besides, he's got enough to deal with now."

Natasha smiled and nodded, "Cheers to that."

Alex held out his arm to accompany her to the dining room.

For now, she'd have to play nice. The food was exquisite, if served at a very unnatural hour.

*Thank God for the small things...At least I don't have to act like I'm enjoying the meal.* Truly a culinary delight. The main course was lobster with creamed potatoes. With every bite, glance, and light conversation, she made sure to woo him, just as her mother had taught her.

She could still hear her mother's voice in her head. "Men need to feel like they're teaching you something. Let them feel powerful, and you can have power over them."

She did not let slip that Vlad had spent many hours sharing details of his connection with Alex. She'd known for years that Alexander had taken in six-year-old Vlad after he had been kidnapped from his family in Romania, and also that Alexander was most likely responsible for the kidnapping.

Poor Vlad, trained by Alexander, kidnapped from Romania to the USA to be a killer. Alexander wanted a protege, an heir. No one knew why he never fathered his own son. Perhaps he was sterile? Or perhaps he simply liked the idea of taking a helpless boy from his family and training him to do whatever he commanded.

While Vlad knew Natasha as a child, he never told Alexander of their friendship. Natasha knew that the omission had been for her protection. They were only five years apart in age, but she knew Vlad would break free of him one day.

How better to hurt him though, by taking what he loves the most? Now she understood the motivation for tonight. It was all a power play over Vlad because he finally broke free.

Alexander must have an idea that Vlad loves her, but she needed to be sure to pretend that her loyalty was to Alexander.

Vlad must have tried to keep Alexander from knowing the full extent of his feelings for her. He knew what Alexander would do if he found out that Vlad actually cared for or let alone loved someone. Emotion, especially love, was something denied to the young Vlad. For the moment, she had to put these thoughts out of her head. For tonight, she had to pretend to *desire* this monster that beat a six-year-old kidnap victim into submission, until he was a murderer with no connection to his humanity.

Vlad would understand she had no choice but to come when summoned, to do whatever it took to survive this meeting. Her mother taught her how to switch off her own humanity, to use her body and beauty as powerful weapons. *Vlad will get it, and he'll get us out from under his boot heel.* After all, he told her what Alexander did to those who displeased him. *He'll know I had no choice.*

Throughout dinner he seemed to be enjoying her company, laughing at her jokes, responding to her subtle flirtations, falling under her spell. *Just another man at the end of the day, ruled by one thing.* She chuckled to herself.

"Natasha, you are a surprise, but in many ways, you are your mother's daughter," he said, puffing out his cigar.

She looked at him quizzically, then smiled, peering at him from underneath her brunette bangs. Blue eyes gleaming. "What do you mean?"

"Tsk, tsk, Milaya... don't pretend to have forgotten your training," he said as he gave her a little wink.

She felt foolish. *He knows. The son of a bitch knows I was playing him. Shit! How could I be so stupid? Any other man...I'm a fool.* Somehow, she had to recover from this. "I understand. I'm sorry if I have offended you, Don Alexander. I'll be more mindful."

He rolled the cigar in his mouth, wetting down the end for a better drag, as he stared at her. *Mother fucker sees right through me. Fuck! This is bad. Wonder where he's keeping the ice pick?* She didn't move at all or object. She knew better, as she was sure that she'd already offended him by attempting to charm him. *What the fuck is wrong with me?*

He got up, stood over her and carefully tucked a wisp of her hair behind her ear, stroking her cheek lovingly. Then, he put his fingers around her throat.

He didn't squeeze, but Natasha was afraid, nonetheless. He sighed. "This beautiful neck. What a shame it would be if anything happened to it..."

He stroked her neck and then ran his fingers down her jawline to her chest. Her skin formed goosebumps under his touch, and she forced herself to hide the shuddering feeling. As she was repulsed, at least Alexander believed that she was under his power. He was the kind of man that needed to make sure she'd never forget that she's now *his* property, so she let him think just that.

He reached into her strapless bra and cupped her breast, pinching her nipple painfully. She gasped. He smiled, satisfied with her reaction.

"Now, little sparrow, go to my bedroom and prove your loyalty to your new master. Be obedient to me always, and you'll never be harmed. I take good care of my property, as you can see."

She looked up at him, then silently turned to walk towards his bedroom, the same bedroom that she used to play in when the old bitch would take her there to play.

Fighting back a tear, she swallowed and put her body into the task. She remembered what her mother had said, all those years ago.

*They are only using your body, but you can't ever let them into your mind or your heart. When it's time to perform for survival, switch those off.*

She remembered this as she sat on the sumptuous king-sized bed covered in gold satin. He closed the double doors, put out his cigar in a solid gold ashtray on the bureau, and unbuttoned his shirt. *It's just your body*, was the thought she repeated to herself over and over, like a mantra.

———

WHEN THE DEED WAS DONE, and she was standing in the foyer once again, she smoothed her hair one more time and took a deep breath. In her mind, she had changed her mantra to, *just get out of here in one piece.*

Alexander approached her and leaned in closer to whisper, "Agent O'Connor, FBI."

Her breath hitched slightly as she was terrified at the thought of icing a Fed. Alexander pulled back and smiled. He cocked his head to one side and said, "Oh, don't be afraid, my little princess, you are a born killer, as was your mother. You won't let me down."

He kissed her hand, and just when she thought she was getting away, he pulled her closer to him again and whispered. "One more...Richard Parker."

Her mouth dropped open as she tried to pull back. He smiled and said, "We can't have loose ends, little princess. These loose ends could prove tricky for you if they're allowed to keep drawing breath. I'm only thinking of you... If *he* wants to take responsibility, let him. Once they have him in custody, I'll make sure he never talks. Don't worry. Didn't I tell you that I take good care of what's mine?"

She nodded and managed to crack a small smile, leaning in towards him. He seductively kissed her on the cheek and slipped a  blood-red ruby ring on her finger, which made her skin crawl. Her thoughts kept her satisfied for now.

*Vlad is gonna slice you into mincemeat. You fucking pig. Wasn't he once yours too? Now, you wanna put him down like a rabid dog, just because he wants to take the fall for me? You suck! ...Just get out of here alive, Natasha.*

The doorman gave back her gun and knife. Starting the car engine, she glanced at Alexander. He smiled sweetly. She managed to reply with a similar smile, while trying to remain serene.

She drove at a reasonable pace as she left his house, not wishing to appear as though she was fleeing.

As she drove, her nose twitched as she still smelled him on her. A tear made its way down her cheek. Her bottom lip quivered, and she sniffled.

She reached into her car's console to retrieve a perfume bottle and sprayed it on herself, then put down the bottle and breathed in deeply. The perfume helped, but it didn't stop her from having painful memories of her mother, one memory that she thought she'd suppressed.

She vividly recalled one evening, when she was four. She woke to the sound of

Nadia crying while taking a bath. Tiptoeing quietly to the half-open door, she saw her mother brutally scrubbing at her skin, as if she were trying desperately to get dirt off. She couldn't see any mud or dirt, but Nadia kept on scrubbing, despite her skin being red and raw looking.

It had puzzled her at the time. Now, Natasha felt certain what her mother was trying to wash off... guilt, and the smell of self-loathing.

Natasha's tears flowed freely now, so she let them come. Over the years, Natasha had learned how to suppress her emotions, especially when she was fully into her alter ego, Jane. This was essential for self-preservation. It felt good to let everything out, especially at a critical time like this.

She exhaled and switched on the radio. She cringed when she heard the lyrics to "Do Ya Think I'm Sexy?" by Rod Stewart blare through the speaker. Not exactly what she wanted to hear at that moment. She turned the tuner button, looking for a better station. "Dancing Queen" by ABBA turned out to be much more soothing.

# JIM

AFTER INTERVIEWING THE OTHER HOTEL WITNESSES WHO WERE present the night of the murders, Jim sat in his car and let his body rest against the steering wheel. He sighed and looked up at himself in the rear-view mirror. The dark thoughts flowed freely. *Loser...why can't you find one lead? Something you can use. Jesus Christ!*

Jim knew it wasn't all his fault. People didn't tend to remember much. Half of them were drunk, high or both, and the rest only remembered seeing Laura dragged out the hotel after she was arrested. Whoever this "Jane" woman was, she knew how to blend, how to be invisible.

*Mama's house is gonna be a sight for sore eyes now.* Daryl Rae would certainly have some beers available, and why not? Time for active duty today was long past.

As soon as he drove onto the gravel pathway, Coral came out to greet him. He smiled as he saw her wearing only her house dress and flip flops. He rolled down the window. "Hey Mama! You could've waited two minutes. I'm coming inside to sit a spell with ya."

"I know, my sweet boy. I know. I'm just so glad you're here."

He got out of the car, and she hugged him. "My boy! Come on in. I've just made dinner for me and Daryl Rae. You better say you're gonna eat with us, cuz I made enough to choke a pig."

Jim nodded and grinned. "I was hoping you'd say that. I miss your cooking, Mama."

Coral replied, hooking her arm through his, "Well baby, you're gonna love what I made tonight. It's my jambalaya!"

They went inside and Daryl Rae called out from the bathroom, "Hey baby, who is that?"

"Don't call out while you're sitting on the goddamn toilet, Daryl Rae! That ain't classy."

There was a flush, then the rushing of water at the sink. Daryl Rae came out, drying his hands on a hand towel. "Okay, sugar, I'll try to remember my fucking manners next time."

Daryl Rae rolled his eyes and Jim chuckled. He slapped a hand on Jim's shoulder and said, "Hey, buddy! Your mama's been wondering when you'd come over to visit. She was real happy you called."

"This investigation is taking it out of me," Jim sighed. "Now that there's reasonable doubt that Laura didn't do it, we've got a huge case, and there's a whole lot more angles now."

Coral started setting the table. "Like what, darlin'?"

"Aww, don't worry about that Mama. That's my job, and believe me, I intend to do it. At least for that 'lil baby on the way." Jim said, holding her hand.

Coral gave his hand a little squeeze, smiled, and got dinner on the table.

As he bit into the juicy shrimp and rice, Jim remembered the picture of Jane Wheeler. He kept it in his pocket to remember to ask around, and besides, he needed to jog his own memory of her.

Licking his fingers before he wiped on the napkin, he fished the photo out of his jacket and handed it to Coral. "Mama, have you ever seen this woman? She's wanted for questioning."

Coral swallowed a bit of her food and took a big swig of iced tea before looking closely at the photo. She nearly choked.

"Wanted for questioning?"

Jim patted her on the back and looked at Daryl Rae, who grabbed the picture and said, "Hey! She's that lady from the magazine!"

Jim's jaw dropped. He put his napkin by the plate and cleared his throat. "Magazine? What magazine?"

"Yeah, this lady came to the house once, just after Brian got killed. She said she was a reporter and wanted to do a piece on Coral for a magazine. You know, cuz of the restaurant and the fact that she was married to that snooty falooty asshole."

Coral nodded. "Yeah, it's true darlin'. She's a reporter. But you know what? She never called again to take all the photos she promised. I did wonder about that."

Coral looked at Jim and cocked her head to one side, looking a bit flustered at the lost opportunity to feature in a magazine. Jim scoffed, "Mama, you don't see anything wrong with that?"

Coral squinted at him. "Huh?"

"She played you, Mama."

Daryl Rae laughed uproariously. "And you thought you was gonna be famous! Ha!"

Coral's lips pressed into a hard line and her brow furrowed. "Shut up Daryl Rae! She looked so fancy and all. I thought she was for real. Lord, how stupid I am...Maybe I am just an ignorant hillbilly after all." Coral quietly began to sob.

*God, here we go...Miss Coral and her legendary hissy fits.* Jim thought, as he squeezed her hand. Daryl Rae patted her on the back and stroked her hair.

Jim tried to comfort her. "Oh Mama. Don't do that to yourself. I don't blame you for being bamboozled by her. I don't know much about her, but it seems like she's pretty darn slippery. Probably a pro."

"Like a hooker?" Daryl Rae asked.

Jim shot him a dirty look. Daryl Rae lowered his eyes, chastened.

"No. That's not what I meant. I mean that she's probably a professional con artist of some kind. Mama, you're gonna need to tell me everything she did and everything she said, okay?" Jim took out his notebook and a pencil.

Throughout dinner, Coral revealed all that Jane had talked about, but Jim didn't feel any closer to finding out who she was or what she was up to. The whole visit seemed like it was an excuse to meet Coral, but why? Jim tried to make sense of it, but he only ended up frustrated. Was she interested in Brian? Admiring her handiwork? *What did she want, coming here? Is Mama safe?*

# JIM

THE NEXT MORNING AT WORK, JIM REPORTED EVERYTHING HE'D found out to Agent Smith. "I have a feeling that this is bigger than we know. This involved Brian, Jack Buchanan, and even my mother, for some reason. Something's not right, man."

"We've been checking her picture against all known felons and found nothing so far," Agent Smith said. "However, if she's in cooperation with Vladimir, she's most likely Russian mob. We've got an informant in there, and one undercover agent, but they haven't reported anything yet. Will let you know if there's anything significant."

Agent Smith sighed. He really didn't want to tell Jim the worrying news. He put a hand on Jim's shoulder. "Speaking of which, we haven't had a report from the agents that were transporting your sister-in-law and her father to witness protection."

"What!? What the fuck!" Jim shouted. He threw Agent Smith's hand off his shoulder. "What do you mean no one's *heard* from them?"

Agent Smith put his hands up defensively. "We've sent agents to trail them, and we found the bodies of the agents, all dead. Also, the van's been shot to shit, but so far, no sign of Laura or Larry."

Jim inhaled and exhaled a few times to calm down. He nodded. "Okay, so that obviously means they've been taken."

"Most likely by Vlad, I'm assuming." Agent Smith said. He showed Jim a folder filled with large photographs of the scene. Jim hoped Laura and Larry were okay. The black and white photographs were grim enough, but he could tell by all the blood splatter that Laura must be going through Hell.

Agent Smith continued. "We've dusted the van for prints, but it's been wiped down, of course. The tire tracks are there, and it seems that the van was sandwiched in between two vehicles. One of the sets of tire tracks here would indicate a large car, like a Cadillac or a Buick drove away from the scene. The other tire tracks are made by the two smashed vehicles here. We're also searching the area, going door to door, but it's backcountry and they could be pretty far by now."

Jim's eyes darkened. "This has to be the work of Vlad. He's holding them somewhere, otherwise we'd find their bodies here. We've gotta find a way to get to them. I can't let anything happen to her baby. I owe my brother that much."

"We'll get 'em. We've put out a nationwide APB on all of them. Vlad won't get anywhere in public without getting made."

"Good," Jim agreed. He thought for a moment and scoffed. "Well, unless he's in disguise!"

He thought for a moment, his brow furrowing. "What does he want with them? Why didn't he just shoot them?"

"Good question," Agent Smith said. "That's what we need to focus on. What purpose do they serve? Look, we'll figure it out. That's what we do ... at the very least, we can be positive your sister-in-law is clear of this. We know it in our gut, but of course, we still need that concrete evidence."

# NATASHA

*March 1977, New Orleans, French Quarter*

NATASHA WOKE IN HER LUXURIOUS HOTEL BED. SHE SAT UP AND admired the sunrise over the French Quarter. *How beautiful. A good day for someone to die.* She cracked a small smile, then the memories of Alex resurfaced and her expression turned sombre. She got out of bed and stretched. As she walked towards the bathroom, she caught a look at herself in the mirror and lingered for a moment. "You're a killer, after all. Aren't you? So, what if you're a whore also? Like mother, like daughter."

After freshening up, she was enjoying a hot black coffee to get the blood pumping. A knock at the door disturbed her pensive mood. Her breath hitched and she smoothed her long hair into a roll and stuffed it in a stocking, then quickly grabbed a red wig from the suitcase. She needed to get ready early for her day of hunting, disguised as someone far less threatening, complete with fake freckles to accompany the red wig she'd chosen.

The APB hadn't come as a surprise to her, but she was impressed by how quickly someone had identified her as an associate of Vlad. Now, she would be able to move freely again.

She called out, "Who's there?"

"Madam, it's housekeeping. You want your room cleaned now?" A woman's voice called out.

"No...Come back later, please," Natasha said.

She breathed a long sigh of relief and continued enjoying her morning coffee. She took another peek at her clever disguise in the mirror and smiled. Her mother had been a master of disguise and taught Natasha everything she knew.

As she stared out over the horizon, she thought of her mother *Not exactly a normal childhood. Pretty fucked up.*

---

SHE'D NEVER FORGET the first day she allowed herself to realize that her mother wasn't exactly the popular "June Cleaver" type. It was a scorching summer day in 1957, and she was only nine years old. Nadia took her by the hand to cross the street in downtown New Orleans. They reached the other side, but her mother stopped to watch a very tall handsome man get out of a limousine. He looked like a very important man. Nadia stared intently at him while he entered the nearby office building, not even glancing their way.

At the time, Natasha had no idea who he was. Now, looking back on it, she felt that it must have been so obvious, the love Nadia felt for him. There were practically stars in her eyes.

Jack Buchanan was beloved by her mother. They spent a lot of time together, and Nadia always looked at Jack with an affection that Natasha had never seen before, certainly not from the other killers her mother spent time with. Even at nine, Natasha could understand her mother didn't want to harm Jack.

On the contrary, she loved him very much, even though he only saw her in secret and never spoke to Natasha as a daughter. He never acknowledged her at all.

On a different occasion, two years later, mother and daughter were approached by a "not so friendly" face. Her mother had a handler. Natasha only knew him as "Uncle Nik." He didn't seem like a typical uncle. He was bald with a huge scar across his cheek, always dressed in black. Natasha thought he looked more like a mortician than an uncle. He never seemed concerned that Natasha was there, or that she would hear everything discussed, leaving Nadia concerned after all of his visits.

One day, Uncle Nik approached them as they sat on a park bench, but stood facing the other way, then he and Nadia both fanned out newspapers in front of them, while conversing in low voices.

"You have to finish the job," he said. "That's the only reason you're alive."

"Exactly," she said. "Please, I want to just leave. You can replace me. He did, so why not my country?"

"No one leaves us, not the K.G.B. The only way you leave is in a body bag," he said.

A tear streamed down Nadia's face. "He has doubts about you. He'll ask too many questions."

"No, he won't. I've taken care of it. You must trust me. I'd never put our operation in danger. He knows nothing about it. I swear to you. His impression of me is personal, not related to business. He thinks I left the company for personal reasons. I doubt he even remembers me now," Nadia said, holding back tears as she held Natasha's hand.

"You had better be right. You were one of our best, and you're throwing away everything for *this*."

Nadia snapped, "You mean for her? I've been living in hiding here for years, living on what I saved from working at Buchanan Oil, but now, there's no more. I need a stable job to support her. I need a new identity."

"Keep your voice down, Comrade. I can make it seem that you were killed, at least for now. Afterwards, I will try to get you out without harm coming to you, but she may get taken away from you. I can't guarantee. This is not the best time to go back to our home. Too much turmoil and political tension. It is best you hide here, as long as you can. I will send new papers for a new name."

"Thank you. But please, I can't let anyone take her away from me. She's all I have."

She had looked down at Natasha with a tender smile. The man folded up his newspaper and walked away without another word.

Afterwards, things seemed to get more difficult as Nadia strived to stay one step ahead. Even with new papers, she couldn't find steady work. The U.S.A. wasn't the best place for an unwed Russian mother to find a job.

Spying and killing for the K.G.B. were her most polished skills. At least they could not simply eliminate her. A hitter of her reputation wasn't someone they wanted to deal with. For now, it was more prudent to allow her to blend in with American society, then call on her later, if need be. Better to keep her loyal. She understood that.

Nadia shared her fears with Natasha, despite her age. She couldn't really grasp the adult situation, but she tried to comfort her mother. She would never forget Nadia's worst decision. Especially that fateful day.

There was only one place that a disavowed agent could go to earn a good living, enough money to keep her and her daughter out of shoebox apartments and filthy neighborhoods.

Nadia did her research and knew the Ragimov family was the first of the Russian crime families to make an entrance to the Louisiana scene. They were no match for the Italians or the Mexicans. They'd beg for her mother's services.

Nadia not only found work, but more than she could manage, which meant Natasha was left with babysitters more often than she liked...Mob babysitters.

Natasha remembered looking at her mother with pleading eyes asking her to stay at home more often, but Nadia had no choice, or at least that's what she told her daughter. All Natasha heard about, it seemed, was Jack this and Jack that, and when his son came along it was all about Brian, and how Brian had stolen a life that was meant for her.

"I must work now, my love. What I do, I do for us. We'll leave this place one day, just you and me. We won't need anything from *him* at all. He can go ahead and give it all to that bastard child."

Natasha enjoyed the goodbye hugs she'd get, and the treat she'd get afterwards, when her mom came home. Once Nadia was done with each of her jobs, she'd bring something special for Natasha: toys, books, candy, art supplies, and stuffed animals. She had many lovely trinkets around her when she was small, but nothing could substitute for a mother's attention.

Over time, she became acquainted with a boy. He was slightly older than her, and he was often brought with her regular babysitter, an old woman that liked to chain smoke and watch TV most of the time they were together. he boy liked to play, but his games were destructive. The two of them would often sneak outside to smash plates, throwing them against the walls like frisbees. She only knew him as "V." He referred to the babysitter as the "old bitch." He taught Natasha how to fight and how to lie. V looked out for her. She thought he was cool, and so much fun.

As she got older, around thirteen years old, Nadia strived to spend special mother/daughter time with Natasha. They did fun things together like having their nails polished and painted, shopping for pretty clothes and eating at different restaurants. It was a fun time, and her mother seemed to genuinely try to form a strong bond with her.

Young Natasha only saw the mystery man only once more, before she finally figured out how important he really was to her mother. The two of them were eating ice cream on Bourbon Street watching a street performer do magic tricks. The weather was sunny and picture perfect. Nadia's smile was as warm and bright as the sunshine...then...*he* came. It was as if someone put out the sun and all the lights switched off. The look on Nadia's face changed. Especially when she saw a then eleven-year-old Brian walking with his father, Jack Buchanan.

Nadia's face dropped, and her smile turned into a pained grimace. Tears appeared in her eyes as she looked at Natasha. She leaned closer to whisper. "Sweetling, they will revere us one day. You'll have more than that Buchanan *mu-dak*."

Nadia's expression changed to something sinister. Her expression darkened, especially when she watched them going into an expensive clothing store. They continued eating the ice cream in silence. When they emerged, little Brian was dressed in clothes so costly they'd take Nadia a month to afford, despite her lucrative work. Natasha's eyes followed them. She sighed and looked at her mother with a puppy-like expression.

"Mama...who are they?"

"People we'll meet again one day, but for now, they aren't important. Don't worry about it darling."

Nadia took her by the hand and insisted it was time to go. Natasha's curiosity heightened and from that day forward, she enlisted V's help in discovering the truth. He would find out, by any means necessary. She never wanted to know how, but V always came through.

Over the next year, Nadia refused to talk about it, and became angry each time Natasha brought it up, especially if she dared to mention *his* name. V later confirmed what Natasha had suspected all along. Armed with this knowledge, she was determined to confront her mother.

"Mom, when will I meet Jack? He is my father, after all."

"Drop it!" Nadia snapped.

"And Brian? He's my brother, right?"

Nadia grabbed her by the shoulders and shook her. "Never talk to them! Never go near them, do you understand?"

"All right! All right! I get it!" Natasha said, tears forming in her eyes.

Over time, Natasha learned that bringing it up never resulted in anything but a fight. V's revelations didn't stop there. He helped her realize what her mother did for a living, so she figured that her father must be why they lived in secret, in shame, secluded from everything they had a right to. The resentment slowly built into rage. Rage became something empty and still, something...*darker.*

The Ragimov family was gaining strength, thanks to Nadia. They'd managed to expand their operation from simple prostitution and drug smuggling to protection scams, counterfeiting, and identity theft. The Italians cornered the market for cocaine, and the Mexican Cartel controlled the flow of marijuana, but the Russians had the most beautiful prostitutes, who only tended to high-end consumers.

All the business was protected by the enforcers. The muscle of the organization. The intimidation. Tattoo covered bruisers on motorcycles. They made a fortune selling their own brand of *insurance.*

Nadia was well paid for her services as an exterminator or a black widow hitman, but her income was nothing compared to the millions the Buchanan name was worth. Natasha saw the regret in her mother's eyes from time to time. There was something in the way she looked at her, a certain remorse.

Less than a year later, Nadia disappeared, leaving teenage Natasha with an orphanage in Baton Rouge. Her mother had placed her in the care of the state, under the name Jane Wheel. For years afterwards, not knowing if her mother was dead or alive, she finally got her answer.

The package came with her former babysitter, the old bitch. On Natasha's eighteenth birthday, on her last day at the orphanage, she arrived.

"You're too late," Nadia snapped. "If you're here for my mother, tell her to save it. She can fuck off for leaving me here. You tell her that."

The old bitch squinted her eyes and said, "Child, you don't know what you're talking about. Your mother put you here to protect you."

"Ha! Protect me? Protect me from what? Her prostitution?"

"How dare you!" the old bitch glared.

"How dare I?" Natasha snapped. "That whore left me so she could screw her johns without a kid getting in the way."

The old bitch slapped Natasha across the face, stopping her tirade. Natasha froze, rubbing her cheek. "Wha...what? Why?"

The woman handed her a box. "Your mother left you here to give you a choice she never had, a chance to be something more."

"More than what?" Natasha asked.

"A killer," the gruff woman said.

She turned and left Natasha standing with a box of Nadia's things. She looked down at this cigar box, the only thing she had left of her mother.

Natasha only opened it when she reached her cheap room for rent, temporarily provided by the orphanage. Inside, she found her mother's passports, her IDs, her memoirs, and a letter for Natasha.

As Natasha read it, tears fell.

My Dearest Natasha,

I know that you must have had many questions about why I left you there. Let me start by telling you this. I have never stopped loving you, not for one single day. My love for you is why I had no choice but to leave you, to protect you from becoming just like me. If you're reading this, I'm already dead, so there's no point in looking for me. My profession has undoubtedly caused my death, as I've caused death to so many others.

My dearest, I have been a professional killer my entire life. I was trained to take out anyone who opposed the KGB or got in their way, depending on what their objective was at the time. I also spied for the KGB when my skill set was needed. I was a sparrow, trained to use sex as a weapon for weakening a man's defenses and obtaining what I wanted from them. My last mark was Jack Buchanan II, your father.

Yes, I know this must come as a horrible surprise to you, but I was leaking information about oil shipments from Buchanan Oil to Mexico so that the shipments could be intercepted by Russia, and so that contraband could be smuggled into the USA. I also sabotaged his business in many other ways, to hinder the American oil industry. During my assignment, I was required to become very close to Jack. I tried not to care. I was trained not to care. But there was something about him, something wonderful. I loved him, more than I ever thought it possible to love anyone. He loved me too, or so I thought.

Truthfully, he was taking a break from his wife, and really had no intention of ever marrying me, even when I got pregnant with you. For years after you were born, I tried to get him to know you, to accept you, but he refused. I never told you because I never wanted you to be burdened with any of this. You are and always have been, my whole world, the reason I've kept going.

Even when I refused to kill Jack, it was for you. Maybe one day, you can meet and form a relationship as father and daughter. I don't want to do anything that would take that possibility away from you, my love.

When I refused to kill Jack, the KGB barely let me go with my life, and I was able to disappear with you. However, we needed money, and this is all I know —killing. The Ragimov family has been good to me, considering my options. All was ok, until they suggested that you should begin your training to work by my side.

That was not the life I wanted for you, and that's why I hid you and changed your name, to keep you safe and let you have choices that I didn't have. Please make a good life for yourself. You deserve a clean slate.

With all my heart,
Your Mother, Nadia

# NATASHA

*March 1977, New Orleans, French Quarter*

NATASHA LOOKED AT HERSELF IN THE MIRROR AND SIGHED. *A CLEAN slate.*

"She never wanted me to be like her... I'm sorry Mama. I must be such a disappointment."

She wiped a tear from her eye and brought herself back to reality. After all, she'd need to be a hundred percent focused to prepare for the two targets she had to eliminate. Parker wouldn't be hard to find, or difficult to kill, but Agent O'Connor would be different. *Both these targets are to cover up for me. My poor V. Where is he?*

She was applying her makeup when she heard a knock at the door. "Who is it?" she called out.

She looked through the peephole. No one. She felt a chill. The knocking continued.

"Who is it?" she said, forcefully.

She listened, standing next to the door. Goosebumps. *Is someone screwing with me?*

"This is the hotel manager, ma'am. I need to speak with you about the identification you've given us at check in," a male voice said. "May I please take a moment of your time to clear this up?"

Natasha put the gun in her carry bag, smoothed down her wig, exhaled, then opened the door. Vlad's associate was standing there, smiling. Natasha asked, "You? What do you want?"

The man stepped aside to reveal Vlad standing behind him. Natasha stammered, "Uh...Um...Wha...What are you doing here? I thought you were done with me."

"Never, my love," Vlad smirked.

He nodded to his associate to indicate that he should leave. Once they were alone, Vlad walked into her room and shut the door behind him. Natasha scoffed. She backed up slowly and quickly tied her robe tighter considering that underneath, she was only wearing her underwear. Vlad chuckled softly. "You aren't covering anything I haven't seen."

She blurted, "What are you doing here? I thought we talked about this. No one can see us together or they'll suspect I had something to do with the murders. I thought you wanted to protect me from...how did you say it? My own stupidity?"

He laughed out loud. She cringed and looked around, as though she could see if anyone heard him. In one swift move, he got awfully close to her face. She trembled. "Dorogaya, you *did* have something to do with the murders. A lot, actually."

"You know what I mean," she said, trembling.

"Yes, I do know, my dear. You want them to think it was the pretty wife."

He began to walk around her. "Tsk, tsk, tsk...As a killer, you are *pathetic*. How did you plan to blame the little woman for your ridiculous rice poison, huh?"

"It was ricin. A bean, and I was planning to anonymously report her after he and the hooker were dead. I managed to get her fingerprints on everything."

"How?" Vlad enquired.

Natasha smiled. "I posed as a manicurist when she went to the salon... managed to get an impression of all her fingers as she drifted off into a relaxed slumber. That's how I got it into Delta. I slipped a voucher for a free manicure into her bag. When she went to claim it, I was there. I knew her well enough to know that even feeling sick wouldn't keep her from a good paying gig. She turned up, just as I thought, and I was waiting. Once they were close to passing out, they were malleable. Brian was already in bed, but I talked Delta into getting into that bed herself. She took longer to pass out, so I had to inject her with a little heroin."

Vlad grunted, "Huh. That's pretty good."

"My mother's journals and your trainers taught me everything I know," Natasha said, smiling darkly.

"Did they teach you to feel like confessing? To try and revive the bastards you killed? Which was impossible! There's no coming back from what you gave them, but you and I didn't know this." He walked closer to her. "I made a mistake, but I still cleaned up your mess. You should have been sure, before you killed them. Your mother was a legend, and I'm shocked you attribute your failure to her teachings. You insult her."

"So what? The thing is, when I saw Brian and Delta Dawn there, I thought there must be another way, a way I can be a part of his world, for real...I didn't know about the poison. How certain it was."

*He's staring at me like I'm an idiot,* she thought. *I hate it when he does that. I feel six years old!*

"Yeah, I admit it. I wanted to pull the plug. Delta Dawn was stuck in that same shit hole as me for many years. We were friends. I hate that I've done this to her, even if she was just a low-class prostitute. Even that wasn't really her fault."

Vlad took her by the shoulders and shook her with one sharp shake. "I never knew you to be stupid. You can't be anything other than what we are. Stop making me responsible for you. You're the one that can't let me go. I asked you to just let me take care of it, my way. You refused. Now, I can't go back!"

"I'm sorry. I'm terribly sorry. You're actually right. My V, my Vladimir. You've been the only person who's always been there for me. I know that now. The way you swept in and took care of it all. You are my knight, and always will be."

Vlad turned away from her and shook his head. "I have the little wife and her nosy father."

"What do you mean? You *have* them? Where?"

"I always mean exactly what I say! I have them in a safe house."

Natasha narrowed her eyes and put her hands on her hips. "What was your plan? To keep them as pets?"

Vlad grabbed her by the neck and slammed her against a wall. Her eyes bulged and her heart pounded. She gurgled, "No. No. I didn't mean it. V...please."

He laughed. "No...No Vlad...Please...Poor little bunny. You know how much I'd enjoy snapping your neck, after all I've been through for you!"

"I know what you've been through. I'm sorry," she whispered.

"Now I'm on the run from not only the police, but Alexander's men as well. I had a good life here, but no more. Finished!" he said. "I blame you for making mistakes, but I made the biggest of all."

For a moment, he looked at her tenderly. His grasp on her neck loosened and he turned so she couldn't see his face.

She gasped for breath as he eased his grip on her. "I'm sorry. I just don't know why you didn't kill them. The father and daughter."

He sighed. "Yes, I suppose you're right. Eventually, I will *have* to kill them. However, the daughter is pregnant, and her baby will bring an exceedingly high price, not to mention the amount of ransom *she* is worth."

"Ah yes, she's pregnant," Natasha said, massaging her throat. "I had tried to forget that little detail."

Vlad smiled. "Yes. I understand why you'd want to forget. Ah, well that makes sense now."

"So, you're keeping her to sell her child," she said. She turned to the window and sighed. "So why the old man?"

"Larry is an old man dying from cancer. I don't get pleasure from killing someone already near death. The daughter's pregnancy will progress smoothly if her father is with her. Once the baby comes, I will get rid of them, but with only a bullet to the brain. Quick, painless. I only take pleasure in killing the guilty. You know that about me."

She nodded. "So why are you here? To what do I owe this pleasure? Was it just to keep me informed? You act like you don't even care for me anymore." She caressed her neck. "And you just tried to kill me."

"Kill you?" He turned her to face him. "I was being dramatic. I would never kill my *dorogaya*. You are what's left of my heart."

"Really?" she cracked a small smile. "Your heart?"

"Yes...so imagine how it felt to leave my prisoners to see for myself if Alexander is stealing you from me."

He stared, waiting for a reply. "I came all this way, after covering for your stupidity, to find out that I'm right."

He stepped menacingly closer, his face devoid of emotion.

She felt her neck and shoulders clenching. He could kill her right here and there'd be nothing Alexander or anyone could do about it. Vlad was untouchable in their community, or so she thought.

Even the heads of the families were far too afraid of him, although they'd never openly admit it. Everyone except Alexander. With each step, he became increasingly intimidating. Again, he backed her into a wall, but this time he put one hand on the wall next to her face and peered into her eyes.

"Fine kitten, do as you wish. But never think you will get far from me. After all, I truly know you."

She gulped, nodded, and managed a small smile. He felt validated and backed off. She put her hand on her chest and said, "So what do you want me to do now? I know you. You didn't come all this way for anything less."

Vlad smiled facetiously. "Yes kitten, I've come for two reasons...number one, to ask you nicely to forget about one of your marks."

"Which one?"

"Agent O'Connor."

"Why? Why do you need him?" Natasha asked. His face changed from a light-hearted grin to a deadly stare. She felt a cold shiver down her neck. After all, Vlad wasn't a man to be toyed with. One wrong word and she'd never see it coming. She cleared her throat. "What I mean is, how is he useful to you?"

"Alexander isn't the only one who uses him. He's providing me with intel as well. You can report that to your new boss. The other idiot can go. Richard Parker. I approve. He's a loose end that needs to be removed."

She felt his eyes boring into her soul in a way only *he* could do. She lowered her gaze. Natasha held her head down and sighed. "I recruited him for his role in everything. It's my fault he's got a target on his back now. All he did was arrange for Delta Dawn to be there. He's not even sure of the full scale of what he's done."

"And you said Delta Dawn was one of your friends from Juvie, yes?"

"Yes."

Vlad blinked and nodded. "Cold, even for me."

Vlad lifted her chin with his fingers. "As for Richard, make it a good death. If he was wicked, make it hurt. If he was an innocent lamb, duped by you, make it quick and painless. This is a gift from those of our kind."

"Our kind?" Natasha asked.

Vlad smiled. "Killers."

She broke free from him and scoffed. He chuckled. "Admit it! A part of you likes it."

Natasha gave him a look that would burn through his soul if he had one. Vlad found it amusing. "Yes, sorry to burst your bubble, *dorogaya*, but you are a stone-cold killer, just like me. You like it when the life leaves your prey. Just like me. That's why we're perfect for each other. Why no one understands you, like I do."

She couldn't take it anymore and slapped him for saying that. Caution be damned. He smiled seductively, licked the corner of his mouth, then grabbed her. She struggled, but he didn't relent and kissed her hard, feeling up her bra. She struggled to wriggle free and slapped him a second time, but it only seemed to arouse him more.

"You didn't ask about the second reason I'm here," he groaned.

"I think I know."

"You do know. Pretend all you want. I know you, and what turns you on. I know you like domination...and you like being *mine*."

He threw her on the bed and jumped on her, stripping off her robe and underwear. She groaned in pleasure and gave in to the dangerous passion that she'd never been able to resist. She hated herself for this lack of control, but there was something about him, something...*primal*.

———

AFTERWARDS, Vlad stood up to get dressed and smiled at Natasha. He blew her a kiss and she grinned. The look on her face changed swiftly, however, once reality set in. She looked away. He smirked and finished tucking his white shirt into his black trousers. "Watch your step now, alright?"

She smirked. "I'm not the one who shot them, so tell yourself to watch your step. If one of us goes down, so does the other."

He nodded, flipping on the kettle. "All the more reason to work with me, not Alexander."

She sat up in bed. "I can't cross him. Do you know what he did to the last person to cross him?"

"I slit his throat at dinner. The food he was eating slid out on the plate. It was almost as satisfying as watching innards fall to the ground, but not quite as much," he said, while making himself some instant coffee.

Natasha's mouth was open. "You...How?"

He sighed, shook his head, and put the coffee cup on the table. He stroked her cheek. "Yes, ...me."

He looked at her for a lingering moment, then stood up to retrieve his cup. He took a sip.

"Alexander is a fool, especially to cross me. You are *my* protégé. How dare he come between us," he said, shaking his head. "I won't allow it."

Vlad noticed Natasha shiver. "Don't be afraid. I will protect you. Go ahead and take care of Parker. I don't care about him. The world will be better without another spoiled rich white American *durachit*."

"A what?" Natasha asked.

"A fool." He answered. "You don't remember any of your mother tongue."

"All right," she said. "We'll do this your way. I'll find Parker today, and you make sure Alexander knows I'm *not* his girl."

# LAURA

LAURA WAS LAYING ON THE CREAKY BED, ONE HAND SHACKLED WITH handcuffs to the ornate brass bed post. She had convinced her captors to let her have some mobility, so she could use the bucket they had left in the room as a toilet. After letting her wash off most of the blood and remains of the agents from her face, hair and clothing, the gruff guard told her she must be locked in the room for her own safety.

At her stage of pregnancy, she had to pee about every half hour. Larry wasn't so lucky. He was sitting on the floor, handcuffed to the chifforobe. For his toileting needs, a guard accompanied him to the bathroom down the hall.

They were somewhere in New Orleans itself. During the drive they had been told to shove their heads down and with cold steel pressed against her belly, Laura had not tried anything. She could hear faint city noises coming in through the grimy window, but large tree branches scraping against the glass obscured any view and made the room dark. The window was also nailed shut. The house itself was single-story, brick and that's all she could make out before she and Larry were shuffled to the back room.

There were a number of guards in the front parlor, watching noisy television.

She guessed there were some sports matches but sometimes she imagined they were watching movies too.

At least four days had passed, judging by the number of meals that had been served to them. For breakfast, they were given what tasted like buckwheat porridge with honey and a fruity tea.

Lunch and dinner were almost always greasy sandwiches with soda. There wasn't a cook amongst them, so that made sense. A bunch of goons that had no idea how to boil water, let alone fry an egg. They did, however, agree to bring Laura extra water to drink, since she was pregnant. She tried to be thankful for the small miracles.

Some things were far from miraculous, however. Larry's depression had gotten so hard to deal with, he did not speak much and mostly communicated through the occasional grunt. *What's gonna happen to me if he dies right here? Oh God, poor Daddy. He's never once let me down, not in my whole life. At least I gotta try to keep him from slipping away.*

"Daddy?"

Larry looked up. "Yeah?"

She fought every urge to give into despair but refused to cry. "I felt the baby kick just now, Daddy. He's really in there! Or maybe her? I just wish I could get you free somehow so you can feel this."

He cracked a small smile. He sniffed and cleared his throat. "I'm gonna get us outta here, sweet girl. Just lemme think for a second."

"You do that, Daddy. I believe in you."

In that moment, she felt her father's spirits lift, seeing his amazing brain at work, his never-give-up attitude. *He's got something up his sleeve. I just know it. He wouldn't leave me to deal with this on my own.*

# LARRY

LARRY THOUGHT ABOUT HIS DAYS IN WORLD WAR II, HOW THE German regime had captured him once. They held him and a few other soldiers' captive in a general's private holding cell. They were lucky that this particular regiment wanted to interrogate them before transferring them to the general facilities designed for prisoners of war. This general had a private residence, fixed with his very own torture room, for just such an occasion.

He and the others hatched a plan where Larry feigned having a convulsion. Each man had already picked the locks to their cells and managed to find medical supplies that could be used as weapons. This particular general was fond of performing experiments on some of his prisoners, so poisons were the dealer's choice.

Once the guard entered the room to check him, the others jumped him and snatched the gun and the keys. They broke the guard's neck and managed to make it to the study, where Larry found a secret passage, perhaps designed to help Nazi war criminals hide to avoid capture. One by one, they made their way through the escape route to the grassy lawn. Larry received a medal of honor for that, and remembering such bravery gave him the courage he needed. He looked at Laura and realized they only had one chance at this. *God help us. I hope she's up to this.*

During his toilet break, Larry pretended to throw up in the toilet. It was easy enough to do, the greasy sandwiches they were fed were disgusting. While making retching sounds, he investigated every nook and cranny of the bathroom, hoping to find something to use as a weapon.

Crawling on the floor to check underneath the clawfoot bathtub, he spotted a piece of broken tile. Jubilantly, he quickly pocketed it. He felt cool air coming up from underneath the bathtub. He felt around on the floor and discovered a trapdoor covered in tiles! *I knew they had to have a way to run. I just knew it!*

The broken piece had come off a corner and he was able to gently lift it with one hand. This was a goddamn miracle, and he couldn't wait to tell Laura about it.

"I'm gonna need you to listen carefully, darlin'," Larry whispered, as loud as he dared, and told her of what he had discovered and the beginnings of a plan to escape. Laura's face was a sight, she was smiling from ear to ear and tried not to yelp from excitement.

"Daddy, that is the coolest damn news!" She whispered. "I wonder what's down the trapdoor. Is it a secret tunnel? What if it's only a secret place to hide valuables?"

Larry felt his hopes crumble as he remembered something. "A tunnel would flood in this part of town, honey. The water table is too damn high. But I'll try looking again in a few hours. I'll just keep on pretending I'm gettin' sick again from the crap they're feeding us."

He tossed the tile shard to Laura, who tucked it into her bra for safekeeping.

A few hours passed and Larry felt it was safe enough to try getting back to the bathroom. He started calling the guards. An irate "What the fuck now?" emanated from somewhere deep in the house.

"I can't be shitting in here, pregnant woman and all, ya know? Quick, I need the toilet!" Larry tried his best to act sick with stomach cramps.

The exasperated guard grumbled under his breath, but dutifully dragged Larry to the bathroom again. This time, Larry tried moving the bathtub quietly. It appeared to be especially prepared for a situation like this and slid smoothly across the floor.

Lifting the trapdoor, he saw ladder rungs disappearing into darkness, surrounded by old brick walls. *Aha! Vlad you bastard and thank you, this is gonna piss you off big time."*

He shifted the tub back into position and washed his hands. Now to plan part two of the Great Escape. He felt almost young again. Back in the room, he shared the good news with Laura. He reckoned he could push the guards for one last toilet break before they clocked out for the night.

# LAURA

*March 1977, somewhere in New Orleans*

LAURA HAD TO TIME IT VERY CAREFULLY. LARRY WAS IN THE bathroom, guard standing in the hallway, keeping a bored watch. He was grumbling about missing the game in progress but stood half out of sight of the bed. She heard Larry whistling a tune loudly. This was her cue. She carefully pressed the tile fragment against her palm. It was very sharp and instantly cut through the skin. She quickly tucked it back into her bra, then rubbed her bleeding hand all over her underwear, down her thighs and gave a loud groan.

"Help!"

# LARRY

*March 1977, somewhere in New Orleans*

LARRY WHISTLED, SLIGHTLY OUT OF TUNE, AS IT WAS LAURA'S CUE TO put their plan in motion. As he stepped out of the bathroom, Laura groaned and cried for help. It sounded very realistic. He half shoved the guard ahead of him into the room, towards Laura. She was holding her belly. Larry could see blood on her panties, running down her thighs and staining the coverlet. The guard panicked and forgot that Larry was behind him, so he didn't notice when Larry grabbed the gun from the holster. The guard had no idea what to do.

"It's okay, lady. Please calm down. Fuck! Let me just..."

Larry knocked him out cold with the butt of his gun and quickly shut the bedroom door. Rifling through the guard's pockets, he found the keys and uncuffed Laura.

Once Laura was up, she quickly cut a strip of cloth from the bed sheets and tied it around her bleeding hand. Larry had grabbed a pillow and with all his might, smothered the guard until he stopped twitching.

"Fuck you, asshole. Rot in Hell."

Laura winced but didn't say a word. She grabbed the two sets of handcuffs and the keys, stuffing them into her bra as well.

Larry pushed open the door carefully, gun ready. The guards in the front parlor were cheering for a particularly good goal and had not noticed their comrade was missing just yet.

He pulled Laura behind him and put his finger on her lips to indicate that they should both be very quiet. So far, so good. Laura quietly closed the bedroom door behind her, locking it and taking the key with her. They slipped into the bathroom without anyone noticing.

"Good thinking, sweetheart!" Larry whispered inside the bathroom after Laura closed that door too. It was a tight fit, but he pushed the bathtub against the door while Laura quickly washed the blood off.

She looked nervous when he lifted the trap door and motioned to her to climb down the ladder. It was pitch dark in the tunnel, but it was their only choice.

"It looks very old. We don't know where it goes," Laura whispered frantically.

"It's the only chance we've got. Be careful down there. Now, let's go!" Larry said, shoving the gun in his waistband.

Hopefully the other guards would not notice they were missing for quite some time. He hoped it was enough. The bathtub blocked the door for now, but just in case, he also looped his belt around the door handle, tying it to the nearby towel rail. *Let them try and get through this!*

Larry's WWII training kicked in and suddenly, he was *that guy* again, a man of action, now also motivated by a father's protective instinct. The tunnel was tight, clearly built for smaller people. He and Laura had to half-crouch as they walked with their hands stretched out into the dark. Every hundred feet there was an occasional glimmer of dim light, God only knew from where. He could smell fresh air permeating the musty tunnel, hear water dripping and they sometimes stumbled into half sunken puddles. They forged on. A rat scuttled past, and Laura whimpered as it brushed her leg.

"Stop, honey. Let's rest for a while. How is your hand, is it still bleeding?"

"I think so, I don't know if the moisture is from the walls or if it's blood. It doesn't hurt, at least."

"That'll do just fine. I'm so proud of you, my baby girl, tough as any of the brave souls I've marched with."

There wasn't any room for them to switch places. Neither of them had a clue where this tunnel would end, or even if there was an end, but they had to keep moving, no matter what.

At least it stayed reasonably dry, and Larry hoped there wasn't rain coming. He didn't want to scare Laura with more bad news. For now, it was enough to keep her calm and moving forward.

They started moving again.

# LAURA

*March 1977, somewhere under New Orleans*

AFTER WHAT SEEMED LIKE HOURS, LAURA STOPPED. "I GOTTA REST, Daddy, just for a minute." She peered up at the pipe leading up to the sky. It was a bright dot, but hard to tell if she saw blue or gray. She needed to pee badly but was holding it in with all her might.

"No...Keep going," Larry said, gasping. "I don't want us passing out. No one would even know to look for us here. We gotta get out."

Laura strained to see Larry clearly in the dim light. He was panting, clutching his chest, but still managed to give her a reassuring smile. She remembered that same smile from back when she was little ... every time she was in trouble, when she scraped a knee, or got an injection at the doctor's office. He was always right there, holding her hand.  He gave her courage and made her feel that everything was going to be alright.

She sighed. "Daddy, I can't go any further without resting my legs. My belly hurts. We didn't bring any water or anything, and I gotta rest, even if it's just five minutes, okay? I'm worried that I'm hurting the baby."

Larry's eyes looked puffy. Both of them were covered in dirt.  "I just don't want either of us to lose consciousness. That can easily happen in these circumstances. We've been through a lot and don't have any supplies to keep us alive."

"I know," she said, as she sat down, stretching her legs, rubbing her back and belly. The baby was quiet, worryingly so.

"Who knows if there's more of Vlad's men waiting at the other end of the tunnel?"

Laura inhaled and exhaled, trying not to breathe the musty air too deeply, enjoying the peace of sitting, even if for a moment. Larry sighed, then joined her on the floor.

"Take a few breaths, and then let's keep pushing on. This has to end somewhere, and we didn't bust out of there just to die in the ground, did we?" Larry said, looking at her with wide eyes.

"Okay, Daddy, just a few breaths more. I wish we'd been able to break out some water with us. Guess we didn't think this through properly."

Larry rolled his eyes. "Ya think?"

"Well now, there's no reason to be mean," Laura said, clicking her tongue and giving him a sly side glance.

Larry looked down at his grimy hands. "I know. I'm sorry darlin'. I'm just anxious for us to get outta here."

"Shhhh..." Laura said, putting her hand on his arm.

"You heard something?" he whispered.

She looked up, straining to hear better. Wherever they were, it wasn't far under the ground. Her eyes opened wide and she gasped when she heard men's voices coming down through the pipe. She kept listening. *Were they speaking Russian?* She couldn't tell. The voices blended into each other, impossible to discern.

"I can't make it out," she said, softly.

"Me neither. Let's keep going," Larry said.

She nodded. The two of them got up and they shuffled forward. Neither had any way of keeping up with the time. All their personal belongings had been taken by their captors, including watches and also Laura's diamond ring. Laura felt like it had been at least a few hours of half-crouching/half-crawling on their hands and knees. She didn't even have the strength to look back at her father to check if he was okay. She also thought that she had peed herself, but in the damp and muddy conditions, she couldn't really tell either way. Ladylike manners be damned, this was life or death now.

There was an unspoken agreement between them to conserve energy, so now and then, they stopped to catch their breath and provide each other with needed encouragement. However, with their weakened state, spirits started to wane, and their breathing started to slow. They stopped one last time. Larry could barely hold his eyes open. Laura wasn't much better. "Daddy?"

"Yes?" Larry murmured.

"Don't give up, Daddy. Please stay with me. I can't do this alone. Just a little further. Please!"

"I can't," Larry faintly whispered. "Go on without me. I beg you, leave me."

Laura was too defeated to argue. Instead, she sat down, holding Larry's hand. The next puddle of light had a different shape. After so many monotonous beacons of hope, this immediately piqued her curiosity.

She crawled towards the light, this was much lower and there was a short wooden ladder leaning against the end wall. They couldn't go anywhere except up!

"Daddy, I found something!"

Larry felt one last burst of energy, allowing him to crawl to Laura. Laura climbed on the ladder, feeling a wooden door above her. She grabbed the handle, while pushing upward as hard as she could.

"Ahhh...gaa!!" *Yes! Thank you, God! We're out!* She crawled up into a small dusty room of some kind, the setting sun illuminated the space with long shadows. Larry needed her help getting up there.

She winced and grunted as she pulled him, trying not to hurt the baby or tear something in her stomach. She dropped the trapdoor, sealing the tunnel once more. They weren't alone. There was a coffin on a stand. She was horrified, but too exhausted to scream.

Larry laid down on the floor of the little room and took a moment to catch his breath. Laura explored the walls, avoiding the coffin. She noticed that there were vertical slits in the walls, covered on the outside by decorative iron grills. A matching large iron gate covered the doorway but was boarded up with wooden planks. She heard a commotion nearby.

Larry weakly stood up, leaning on the coffin, peering through one of the grills. Laura could see a small crowd of people gathered around a fire. They were chanting something.

"I can't hear what they're saying," Larry said softly.

"Are those drums?" Laura whispered. She tensed. "What kind of sick shit is this? At least it isn't the Russians!" She was hesitant to reveal her and Larry's whereabouts, so she watched the scene carefully.

There was a guide wearing a T-shirt with the words "Voodoo Tours" standing on a ledge in front of the group. He silenced the group and announced that they were standing before the tomb of the Great Madame Marie Laveau, New Orleans' most famous Voodoo Priestess.

There were tourists mingling all around, some with little drums hanging from their necks. Others were taking photos.

"Madame Laveau was known to turn people into her zombie servants, if they crossed her in any way. She was both feared and revered by her people, and it's said that if you come to her grave and write three X's on the wall whilst saying her name, your wish will come true.... Well folks, it looks like she was as close to a *genie in the lamp* that we'll ever have here. Feel free to leave a tip if you like. Much appreciated, thank you. Have a wander around and we will gather back here in 20 minutes."

They all clapped at the end of the presentation. Laura finally got up the strength to peer at the casket behind her. The lid had cracked open, and she could see decaying bones inside. Laura whimpered in fright and her voice caught the attention of a few people close to the tomb. The crowd was dispersing as people started to snoop around the area. Some poked their cameras through grills and gates to photograph the caskets inside.

The Voodoo tour guide wandered over to the nearest group and said, "Many of the tombs are in sad shape and due to missing stones, you can see the decaying skeletons of those that have passed."

Laura yelped in fright, but Larry clasped his hand over her mouth. She recoiled, disgusted, and blurted in a loud whisper, "Your hand smells disgusting! Eww!"

"I've been crawling through shit, just like you," he whispered loudly. "Now can it or we're gonna get caught."

Her high-pitched yelp caused a stir among the tourists and more of them made their way towards the tomb with their cameras. Laura saw eyes everywhere, peering in to see her and Larry covered in grime, looking very disheveled.

"Ahhhhh!!!!!" screamed a young woman, and this set off a chain reaction of screams. Larry burst forward, pulling Laura along and their combined weight ripped the gate from its crumbling frame in the wall. They stumbled out of the crypt as the crowd pulled back in horror.

"Zombies!!!!" screamed a young man, dropping his polaroid camera. The people ran away as fast as their legs could carry them.

As Larry and Laura fell to the ground, she noticed the tour guide stayed behind to film the event. He had a Kodak Super eight home movie camera on his shoulder, and he couldn't stop smiling. Laura had no energy to say another word.

Both of them were exhausted from their ordeal. Laura was overcome by it all and collapsed in a heap on the ground, barely able to stay conscious.

"And that's the money shot! My tours are gonna be sold out forever! Wow! What a night!" She heard the tour guide talk to himself.

He came closer, picked up a stick and poked Laura. She had had enough drama for one day and could only whisper. "Fuck off you moron... call an ambulance."

# JIM

*March 1977, New Orleans, LA, same night*

A VOICE BLARED THROUGH JIM'S POLICE RADIO, "10-5 FOR OFFICER Higgins. Acknowledge. 10-18, repeat, 10-18. 10-86 located and *en* route to Tulane Medical Center. Acknowledge."

Jim hastily swallowed the donut he was eating and sputtered into his car radio, "10-67, Higgins here. On my way to Tulane now! 10-30, repeat 10-30, requesting backup. Over."

The operator replied, "10-4, copy that."

Jim put on the siren and sped away.

# IVAR

IVAR THANKED GOD THAT HE MADE IT TO THE CEMETERY BEFORE THE bitch and the old man could escape. When Vlad had called the house to check on the prisoners, they had reluctantly admitted their fuck-up. It was only after the football match that they realized that Pavel was not back with them.

After breaking down the bedroom door, they discovered his body. Chaos ensued.

"Dammit!" Ivar screamed.

He slapped one of the other men with a loud thwack. "Pavel is dead because of you! Your negligence! Vlad is coming back at any moment, and Stephan will inform him of what you've done."

Ivar had hoped to be gone before Vlad arrived, but he didn't have much luck in that regard. He burst through the door, looking satisfied and smug. "How's this night for all of you? Huh? I'll be right back. I need to go see my favorite papa bear," he said.

"Um, I'm sorry, sir. They've escaped," Ivar said.

"What?" Vlad asked, his eyes boring into Ivar. "Let me understand you. You allowed a terminally ill senior citizen and a pregnant blonde socialite to escape and kill one of your men in the process?"

Ivar looked down, unable to muster an answer. *He'll kill me now. What will my daughter do?*

"Find them," Vlad commanded. "NOW."

Ivar nodded, then left, happy to still have his life. He followed the trail of the tunnel, knowing full well where it led. He got there just in time to see Laura and Larry being loaded into the ambulance.

He followed the ambulance until it stopped. He laid low, out of sight, to witness the patients being wheeled into the emergency room. A police cruiser raced around the corner and two officers rushed inside. He spotted a pay phone nearby and hurried towards it.

"*Da*. They are at Tulane. I can't go in. *Nyet*! Pigs already arrived. Send someone fancy looking. Fuck you too, asshole."

He hung up, then got in his car. Another police car arrived as he was pulling out into the road. Ivar ducked down in his seat, just in case, but the cop must have spotted him. The cop made a U-turn and blasted his siren. Ivar stepped on the gas, and since he was driving a Maserati, he jerked forward like a racehorse. "Fucking pig!"

# JIM

*March 1977, New Orleans, LA, same night*

"ALL UNITS! THIS IS OFFICER 7453 OF THE THIRTEENTH PRECINCT! 10-94, repeat 10-94! Black Maserati. Headed down 16th towards Lafayette! Over."

Jim stepped on the gas. He felt it in his gut. This was no accident. This car was here for a reason, and he was pretty sure he got a glimpse of a suspected member of Vlad's gang. "You're not getting away, fucker! I got ya now!"

The suspect sped through a red light, causing a collision behind him. "Mother fucker!"

Jim avoided the collision by veering up onto the sidewalk, though he knocked down some newspaper dispensers and clipped a hot dog stand. He wasn't giving up. *No one runs like that unless they have something massive to hide.*

The suspect sped up, shifting between cars with the precision of a dancer. Jim's patrol car was no match for an Italian muscle car. Jim winced and breathed shallow bursts, mastering the steering wheel. The driver took a hard right onto Pinhook Road. The siren blared. Jim blurted, "Ah! Now you've fucked yourself! Ha! You're in my territory now! You gotta be a Ruski. I'd bet my left nut on it."

"All units! 10-94! Black Maserati on Pinhook Road headed toward the Southwest Evangeline Thruway. 10-38B! Yellow!"

He plowed forward, unrelenting. Jim's eyebrows furrowed as he dug his heels into the floorboard and white knuckled his steering wheel. "You aren't going anywhere, fucker."

The driver of the Maserati must have spotted the roadblock from far back. Pinhook Road was wide and flat, so it was a long shot on the best day. Jim knew he'd seen the police roadblock when he took another hard right on Chag Street.

"Son of a bitch! All units! Perp saw you coming! Repeat, all units! 10-63P! Maserati made a right on Chag Street! 10-65."

A voice was heard through the police radio. Maybe backup was finally on the way?

"Officer 7543, what's your 20?"

Jim grabbed the handset. "Headed West on Chag, still in pursuit, coming up on the Church of Christ."

He listened for a reply as he continued his high-speed chase of the Maserati. The muscle car turned right toward the church. *What is he doing?*

The Maserati came to a screeching halt on the gravel road in front of the church. The perpetrator took off on foot. Jim swiftly followed; revolver drawn. "New Orleans police! Stop! I order you to stop and put your hands up!"

The man ran towards a thicket of bushes but was apprehended by another officer that heard Jim's call for a perimeter. The perpetrator head-butted the officer and managed to get about thirty feet before Jim roundhouse kicked him, causing him to fall. Other officers forming the perimeter appeared, guns drawn to reveal their locations. Squad cars arrived, sirens blaring.

Officers pounced on him, cuffed him, then took him to a squad car. The man was bald, with a tattoo of a sledgehammer and sickle on his neck. He had one earring, a missing tooth, and an expensive leather jacket. As tough as he looked, he dropped his head down and sighed. He looked defeated.

Jim felt satisfied and exhaled, as though he'd been holding in his breath for a very long time. *You're gonna talk for me, Baldy.*

Jim told the other officers, "Take this piece of shit downtown and book him for resisting arrest, causing a crash and property damage. He's wanted for questioning in a kidnapping. I need to go check on my sister-in-law."

Jim made his way to the hospital. Larry and Laura were in a double room, both on fluids via IV injection, and both fading in and out of sleep. Jim entered as silently as he could, but Laura woke up, and smiled when she saw him.

Tears streamed down her face. "Oh Jim, I'm so happy to see you. It's been horrible. I didn't know if we were gonna survive."

He squeezed her hand and nodded. "Be strong, Sis. You've got this. We're gonna keep you guys nice and safe till you're better, okay?"

She smiled. "Okay...But I should tell you everything we saw there, right?"

"Yes, for sure, but not now. Right now, I need you and your father to rest and recover. You need to listen to the doctors and get better. Get strong, cuz we got some bad guys to take down. Now, not another peep out of you. Sleep, and don't worry. I've got four officers, two right outside the door, and two are gonna be in here with you. When their shift is finished, I'll put in four more. The Feds also have people watching the hospital from outside."

She closed her eyes and soon fell asleep. Jim stroked her hair and looked at her growing belly and smiled. He leaned in and whispered, "I don't know if you're my nephew or niece in there, but I'm gonna get you to this world safe, for my brother."

His eyes became moist as he thought of Brian. He had a momentary vision of Brian as a young boy, standing next to him, wearing his cute boyish grin. Jim wiped away a tear and cleared his throat. He went out to have a word with the guards to leave orders.

"No one but authorized medical personnel gets in here. Got it?"

They nodded. "Yes, sir."

Jim cracked his knuckles as he left, preparing for his appointment with the bald man in black.

# JIM

DOWNTOWN, OFFICERS HELD IVAR FOR QUESTIONING, AND BERNARD was already there to manage the situation.

"Jim! Hey there," Bernard said, placing a file in Jim's hands. "This was your win. You don't know yet who you've got in there."

"Enlighten me," Jim said.

A henchman of Vladimir, Ivar Volkov," Bernard said, smiling. "Your hunch paid off, so I'm leaving this one for you to finish questioning."

"Groovy," Jim replied.

He stood in front of the interrogation room, getting a preliminary look at Ivar. His face had a suspicious new bruise, which made Jim irate. He glared at the officers in charge. So, that's what Bernard had meant by *finishing* questioning. *These dipshits know that operatives like this only harden once the beatings start! I'm surrounded by idiots.*

He would try another tactic. He looked at the file Bernard gave him and was happy to see that the Feds had done their research and hit the mother-load. Ivar had a weak spot, a daughter, Svetlana. She was only seven years old and lived with her aunt in New York.

Knowing this, Jim entered the interrogation room with a big smile on his face.

He knew the Feds were in the observation room, watching and recording everything, so he had to choose his words very carefully. The two cops guarding Ivar were not a problem.

Ivar gave him a deathly stare from dark eyes glinting with malice. He was tense, cuffed with his hands behind his back. *He's rattled. Must be looking me up and down for anything he can use right now.*

Jim wasn't bothered. He sat down, then threw the file on the table. "I'm gonna save us some time here. We've got Svetlana, and on my orders, she'll go straight to an orphanage...I doubt if she's got any chance of getting adopted though, being the daughter of a thug like you."

Ivar remained silent, glaring at Jim. *Tough bastard. Alright Baldy. Time for the big guns.*

Jim pressed harder. He reached into the file and pulled out a paper and began to read. "Svetlana Volklov. Date of birth January 5, 1970. Long brown hair with blue eyes," he smiled and held his hand over his heart. "Aww, she sounds delightful. Look, there's even a picture of her. So beautiful..." Jim looked at Ivar and hardened his eyes. "You *do* know what happens in state orphanages to young girls, right? People like you kidnap them and traffic them all the time, don't they?"

Jim smiled. "Actually, I can't think of more poetic justice for a piece of shit baby stealer like you to have his own daughter sold off to the highest bidder, but I suppose I'll just have to look the other way when it happens. You know what reputation we have down here in New Orleans, and you know we have all the contacts for many organizations all over the country, if you get my drift..."

Jim's eyes bore into Ivar's. "And I *will* make it happen. Make no mistake. Unless you start singing, *right now*, little Ruski."

Ivar jumped across the table in a violent rage. "You mother fucker! I will kill you! Fuck you!"

The two officers restrained him. His chest heaved and Jim could almost hear his teeth grinding. "If you tell me everything you know about Vlad, his men, their plans, their involvement in the murder of my brother and Delta Dawn, I'll help you."

"He'll kill me if I talk," Ivar muttered.

Jim clenched his teeth. "The sex traffickers will fuck and kill your daughter if you don't."

A small part of him was dying inside. Saying that made him sick to his stomach, but he had no choice. One of the cops behind Ivar paled but stayed poker-faced.

This guy had to be broken down enough to talk. Jim had to convince this guy that he meant every word. He hoped Ivar would crack soon though. *Either he'll crack or I will. Let's see.*

He began to see victory ahead as Ivar slumped in defeat, a tear rolling down his face. He sighed.

"Okay, I'll tell you everything, but you must protect my little Svetlana."

Jim nodded. "I'll do you one better. I'll protect both of you. You give me what I need to put away these pricks and I may be able to give you amnesty and witness protection for you and your little girl."

Ivar thought for a moment. "You mean that everything I've done will be...*gone?*"

"If what you say helps me bring them all down, *yes*. So, make it good, okay?"

What Ivar said was better than good. It was gold, everything that their investigation needed. Indeed, Ivar sang like a canary and gave up everything he'd ever known about the organization, the families in charge, their crimes, and finally, their involvement in the murder of Brian Buchanan and Delta Dawn. It was everything the Feds and he needed, but now he had to keep this man and his kin as safe as a box of kittens.

"I want you to know that the next call I make is gonna be to the NYPD to send a squad car to pick up your aunt and your daughter. They're going straight to protective custody, and so are you. But this kindness isn't free."

"Nothing is ever free," Ivar said. "What do you want?"

"You'll have to testify. That's why we need you all alive," Jim said.

Ivar scoffed. "The way you kept your sister-in-law and her father safe?"

"No, we're not gonna let our guard down again. This case is our top priority now. It's just too big, and we're counting on a *lot* of arrests. This isn't just about my brother and Delta Dawn anymore. It's way bigger."

Jim gave him a reassuring look. They would keep him in a holding cell for now, to keep him safe. On the streets, he'd try to do a runner or become a dead man, and everyone knew it.

Jim asked, "What are they gonna do if they don't hear from you now?"

"Probably assume I'm captured or dead." Ivar replied.

"So, someone will come looking for you?"

"No. I'm not...how you say...'asset'. I'm only a little man."

Jim put his hands on his hips and thought for a moment. "Well, that's a good thing. It makes getting you, your aunt, and your daughter to witness protection easier. It's always harder with someone more high profile."

He looked at his watch. "Speaking of which...I'd better get to Tulane."

Jim exited the room and made the call to protect Ivar's family. He opened the door and found Ivar looking anxious for good news.

Ivar asked, "So you have my family? Yes?"

Jim put a hand on his shoulder and looked him in the eye. "Got them the moment you got here. No worries. Just stay here and know they're safe."

Ivar exhaled, looking relieved.

# JIM

JIM WENT UP TO THE ELEVENTH FLOOR, THE MOST REMOTE AND secure hospital ward to protect Larry and Laura. As he walked around the corner, his heart almost stopped when he saw the bodies of two officers outside Larry and Laura's room, and a wounded doctor, crumpled down on the floor, slipping in and out of consciousness. Blood was running down the front of his white coat.

Both the officers had visible bullet wounds to the head. Blood and bone were splattered on the wall where they had been standing. There was no time to ID them. He would deal with that sorrow later. He hoped the officers inside the room were alive. Jim pulled out his gun and backed against the wall. A frightened nurse approached from a side corridor. He motioned to her to phone for backup, showing his badge and gun. She nodded and backed away. He moved forward slowly, watching for surprises. The room door was slightly ajar. He took a deep breath. *One...Two...Three.* He jumped into the room, pointing his gun, only to discover the two officers busy detaining and cuffing the perpetrator. Larry was asleep, but Laura was sitting upright, wide-eyed, but safe. He swore, exhaling in relief.

"What the fuck, man?"

Officer Branson replied, "We got him! Jumped him when walked in. Guess it was a good idea for there to be four of us, huh? He never expected more of us inside."

Officer Branson pointed to Laura. "He was gonna kill them. His gun has a silencer. It's a good thing we wore our vests."

Jim looked at the well-dressed man who was cuffed with his hands behind his back and lying on the floor, with officer Starling standing guard over him, gun drawn. *Damn! This was close.*

"Who did he hit out there?" Jim asked, pointing to the door.

Officer Starling bowed his head slightly. "That was Officer Harding and Officer Salinger. Officer Harding, Rick...he and his wife just had a baby daughter last month. And Salinger just got promoted from traffic duty. This was his first assignment."

Jim's face turned red, as he looked at the perp. His fists balled up and he took a deep breath.

"Take this scumbag downtown and put him in holding," Jim said. "I'll question him later. God damn it! This shit is never gonna end, is it?"

Officer Branson did as he was instructed. "Officer 8117, NOPD, code 10-63, reporting a 10-15, requesting assistance."

"Copy that. Officer 8117. 10-16, Tulane hospital," a voice replied.

Jim ran back to the wounded doctor, giving the all-clear to the rest of the staff. "I am officer Jim from the New Orleans Police Department. The suspect has been apprehended. The situation is under control. Please assist the wounded!"

Within minutes, the hospital was crawling with NOPD. The officers were asking questions, taking statements from hospital staff, and the hospital staff checked on Larry and Laura under Jim's watchful eye. For a while, the hospital sounded chaotic instead of hushed. Jim was glad the Press were barred from entering. He had had enough excitement for one day.

Laura sat still as a nurse listened to her chest with a stethoscope. She thanked the nurse for her attentiveness and called Jim over after the crowd had dispersed from the room. "When is all this gonna be over? How many of these goons are gonna try and kill us today? Lord, God almighty! I don't know how much more I can take!"

Jim grinned. "Calm down now. No need to have a hissy fit. You need to think of the baby."

"I'll show y'all a hissy fit! These bastards better stop trying to kill me and my father! I'm just plum sick of it!"

Larry mumbled. "What's going on out here?"

"Nothing, sir," Jim said. "Don't you worry. I've got this."

Larry clunked his head back on the bed, mumbling. "They took away my pocketknife. I need that...I..."

Laura looked at Jim. "He's talking about his trusty Swiss Army knife. He never goes anywhere without that blasted thing, just like a good boy scout."

Officer Starling chuckled. "Your old man's quite a character."

"Oh, I know," Laura said, smiling.

She thought of Jack. Now that was a character. All this because of his last name, that and the money that went with it. *What happened to him anyway?*

# JACK

JACK LOOKED AT TYPED LISTS OF INCOMING SHIPMENTS FOR THE coming months. His secretary, Nadia Wheeler, came to his office. "You wanted to see me, sir?"

"Yes, just a moment," he said as he finished writing down the details and coordinates of next month's exports to Mexico.

He finished and put his pen down. He looked at Nadia and sighed. She wore a pencil skirt with penny loafers and a button-down white top. *What a cutie!*

She felt him admiring her, so she smiled, looked down, then fidgeted with her notepad.

"How long have you been working here, Ms. Wheeler?" he asked.

"About six months now, sir."

"Do you like it? Working for me?" He said with a grin.

She blushed, which Jack found endearing. "I do, sir. You've been kind to me. I appreciate it."

"You don't have to sugar coat it, darlin. I know I can be a big 'ole bear sometimes," he chuckled.

"A teddy bear..." She grinned with a side glance, then blinked.

He got up from his desk and slowly closed the office door. He kissed her, holding her tight to his body. She raked her fingers through his hair and moaned. "Are you sure this is allowed?"

He stroked her cheek and whispered, "I own the company, so I make the rules."

"Yes, that's true," she replied.

A sullen look swept across her face, and she pulled away from him, looking down at her feet. She frowned.

"Hey darlin'. Why the long face?" He pulled her chin up and brushed a few strands of hair out of her eyes.

She shrugged her shoulders and looked up at him with doe-like eyes as one tear streamed down her cheek. "You can't tell anyone about me because I'm a *Russian secretary*. I'll never be good enough for anything but a secret relationship."

He wiped away the tears and exhaled. "Oh sweetie. That's the kind of world we're living in. I wish things were different, but I'm engaged to a woman my father accepts. If I go around them, there's no telling what they'll do to me, maybe even take the company away."

Jack held her and whispered, "Let's just enjoy what we have right now. Why are we thinking too far ahead? Huh?"

They embraced and kissed passionately.

# NADIA

NADIA SAT AT HER DESK OUTSIDE OF JACK'S OFFICE. SHE WASN'T supposed to listen to conversations happening within, but she did. She didn't really have to herself, as a Soviet listening tower was nearby anyway. Her team picked up every word spoken in Jack's office, thanks to a recent delivery of special-order shoes.

Jack loved his custom wingtip Florsheim lace ups, and his secretary oversaw picking them up. Nadia's team had intercepted the shoes and adapted them, hiding a microphone, batteries, and a transmitter in his left heel, which sent every word straight to the listening tower.

Operatives from the tower recorded today's meeting as officials from the Pentagon were up in arms about the missing oil shipment on the way to Mexico. Buchanan Oil had recently opened sales to Mexico, and it was to be a very profitable venture. The Southwest USA refineries were already buying almost more barrels than they could supply.

All over the USA, oil companies were dealing with lost shipments, damaged and missing equipment, contraband material being smuggled aboard, and industrial accidents that kept them in litigation for months at a time. It was as if the US oil industry had been invaded by gremlins. There were too many unfortunate events, so many places. If they were only mere coincidences, the Pentagon's involvement wouldn't be a factor. Something much more sinister was at play.

Jack rang Nadia's office. She picked up. "Hello?"

"Nadia, little darlin', can you get my lawyer on the line?"

"Yes, sir," she replied, patching through one of the best corporate lawyers that money could buy. The officials left and Jack was practically barking, "I don't care what you have to do! I don't pay you this much money to cover my ass for you to sit on yours! Got it!?"

Jack slammed the phone down and put his forehead in his hands. Nadia peeped into his office to see if he was all right. He spotted her and said, "Hey there, why don't you come in here and close the door behind you?"

She began to close the door, and he stopped her. "Wait! Grab a bottle of my special stock and two glasses. Let's hang the 'Closed' sign on our door tonight, sexy ass."

Nadia grinned like a minx, grabbed the Scotch, and sashayed over to Jack Buchanan, after closing the door behind her as instructed. She poured him a glass and handed it to him. *He looks so vulnerable. I don't remember seeing him like this. I can't do this to him anymore.*

He gulped down a glass in one shot and grabbed her onto his knee and back into his arms. She squealed with delight. "Mr. Buchanan, whatever shall I do with you?"

He ran his hand up her thigh, squeezed her butt cheek, and said, "You're gonna have to do whatever I say, my little borscht."

She giggled and then kissed him deeply. He pulled back a moment to look into her eyes. "What would I be without you?"

One side of her lips went up to form a coy smile. "Maybe you'll never have to know?"

He grinned and hugged her. His brow furrowed and he pulled back again and looked at her belly. She narrowed her eyes and smiled. "What's wrong?"

"My little borscht has put on a few pounds, Huh?" Jack said as he felt around Nadia's waist. "Be careful, little darlin'. Americans get fat quickly. The food here in *Nawlins* is so damn good. No one could blame ya."

"Nawlins?" Nadia asked.

"New Orleans, darlin'. That's how the Yankees say it. But you're family here. I want you to say it right," Jack said, smiling.

Nadia pulled down her sweater and jumped off his lap. He shrugged his shoulders and asked, "What's wrong? Don't be like that, sugar. I don't mind a little extra padding. Come back here."

She smiled and tilted her head to one side. "Oh, sweetheart. No please. I don't feel well, and I forgot about my mother."

"Your mother?" he asked.

"Da...I mean yes, my mother. She is coming tonight, and I'm already late."

*He knows I'm lying. I can see it on his face.* She was grateful that he didn't call her on her excuse, but this was expected. He never wanted to know so much detail. He simply shrugged his shoulders. "Ok, sexy ass. You just go do what you gotta do. I'll see you at work tomorrow."

She folded her arms and shifted her weight to one hip. "Home to the little woman, yes?"

His shoulders dropped and he exhaled. He put his hands up defensively and said, "Darlin', how many times do we have to go through this? I *had* to marry her, but I'm not gonna stay married to her...at least it's not looking good."

"But you can't marry someone like me? A Russian."

He scooped up his briefcase, then looked at her, his eyes darkening. "No...and if I have to go over this again, we're over. Let me be crystal clear. We have fun together. I like you. I enjoy fucking you, and you enjoy my expensive gifts and attention. But that's as far as it's ever gonna go."

She nodded her head and looked down at the floor. "I understand."

He left, without saying another word on the subject. As soon as he closed the door, she caressed her stomach and said, "I'm sorry, my sweet baby. Your father is a miserable imperialist American pig...But I can't harm him, not anymore. ...And I can't harm myself by being near him. We need to leave...now."

She gathered up her belongings from the office and locked the door behind her. She started for home, but she was being followed. A tall blonde man followed her to her car. Before she could get inside, he slammed his hand next to her head and pressed her against the car door. She trembled and said, "Privyet...Please...I can't. I've been...*compromised*. The mission cannot be completed without exposing everyone, the whole team."

His nose and mouth were covered by a scarf, so she only saw his eyes and the blonde hair that poked out beneath his hat. His voice was robotic and garbled, with a thick Russian accent to boot. "Then you are finished and left cold. You will not return to the Kremlin. You are disavowed and on your own. If you're caught, we will not save you. If you are exposed, you'll be eliminated. You'll need to become invisible. Da?"

"Da," she whispered. "I am sorry."

"You should be. You have failed your country and lost your honor. Only your years of exemplary service compel us to allow you to live. You've never betrayed us, even under remarkable circumstances... Disappear now...Comrade. Consider this mercy a gift."

She closed her eyes and took a moment to catch her breath, got in her car, and left, quietly sobbing all the way.

# SHEIKH FAHED

*March 1977, Arabian desert, near Saudi Arabia*

SHEIKH FAHED, HEAD OF THE AL-JUBRAN TRIBE, ENTERED THE SIMPLE home he'd made for his family. Their tents were set up near an oasis, so that they, the camels, and other livestock could drink. The tents were adorned with embroidery and pom-pom tassels of many colors, but mostly red. Inside, there were cushions all around the edges, meant for relaxing while the sun was at its strongest. Men and women covered their heads to protect themselves from heat.

His wife looked at her husband, and even though he couldn't completely see her smile, he felt it. He felt lucky, for a short thin Arab man with bad teeth, a scraggly beard, and a thick mustache. She was there, veiled from head to toe, accompanied by three of his sons and three daughters. He took a deep breath and smiled. *Alhamdulillah, life is blessed.*

Everyone turned to the strange visitor they've been caring for, for months. As typical Bedouins, they were not trying to be rude. Being cut off from society and from technology, their only source of news was what they heard from other tribes. Badr, Fahed's son, stood at his side, as did Shams, his son-in-law. They sat on cushions next to the strange Western man.

Fahed's wife, Sarah, went to another tent and came out with a tray of Arabic coffee, called *qahwa*, and many tiny glasses that sat on tiny saucers. The Western visitor has become accustomed to this aspect of the culture.

"Shukran," he said.

As he sipped the coffee, he avoided direct eye contact with Fahed's wife and his daughters. *He's learned to show proper respect, and now he's looking healthy for the first time.*

Fahad looked under the visitor's bandages and nodded. "He seems to be recovering nicely...It's a miracle he's alive after his airplane went down...Did he tell anyone who he is?"

Shams smiled. "Yes, he did, and since he's been with us for a few months, he's picked up quite a bit of our language, haven't you, my friend?"

"He knows our language?" Fahed smiled, truly impressed.

# JACK

*March 1977, The Arabian desert, near Saudi Arabia*

JACK BUCHANAN, NOW SPORTING A THICK BEARD, HAD INDEED PICKED up functional Arabic skills, and could now hold simple Arabic conversations with the kind family who took him in all those months ago. He actually wanted to learn Arabic as fast as he could, not just to survive, but to be sure no one was lying to him or talking about him behind his back. He never realized how good he was at picking up a foreign language so quickly. Of course, Jack was always the first one to believe that there's nothing you can't do when you put your mind to it. He was living his wisdom.

He took a sip of the coffee and replied in Arabic, "Yes, my friend. I'm grateful that your family has cared for me all this time...It's what I get for being out there in a plane with a drunk pilot."

"Nothing good comes from alcohol. Now, you must agree with why we don't drink, yes?" Fahed smiled.

"You are right about that. I don't think I'm ever going to touch it again.  Look what it did to me."

"Ah...Allah works in mysterious ways, my brother," Fahed said. You are here, with us, and now you have a new family to add to your own."

Fahed touched Jack's shoulder which prompted him to smile and nod. "I can't thank you enough. You and your family, but soon, I will need to return to my own. I hope you'll help me get to Riyadh soon, so I can alert my embassy of my whereabouts."

Fahed said, "Of course we will help you, now that you're well enough, but you must understand that this is a long journey for us, and we must assemble a caravan to travel safely."

Jack nodded. "I would appreciate it, truly. I can be sure you and all your men are compensated for your effort. I can make that happen."

"My friend..." Badr blurted. "You're a foreigner here, so we will excuse you for your lack of knowledge."

"If I've offended any of you, please excuse me. You've been wonderful to me, and I'd be dead without you, if you hadn't found me and brought me here...It's just that I need to go home. I have a family there, and I'm worried about them," Jack said.

Badr smiled. "That's all you need to say. Of course, we will help you, but it will take time to arrange a safe caravan. You must know that there are other tribes out there, and if any of them find out you are valuable, you may be in trouble."

"Oh," Jack said. "I didn't realize."

Shams squeezed Jack's arm and leaned in. "You're fortunate it was *us* that took you in. Our father is an honorable man, and he'll never accept payment for taking you to Riyadh."

Jack sat the coffee cup down and looked at the two men. "What if I want to show my gratitude?"

"The traditional way would be to bring him a gift. Perhaps a fine sword? He would be pleased," Badr said.

Jack smiled and nodded. In all his life, he's never heard of such people. Of course, he had been briefed about Arab culture and the Bedouins extensively before his arrival, but nothing could compare to experiencing Bedouin culture up close and in person. It was hard to believe they were real, in the world he knew.

Where he came from, everything was about money. No one ever seemed to do anything without it. There he was, in the middle of the desert, with a strange family that didn't seem to follow the rules of *normal* society. Or at least what he always believed "normal" meant.

*This seems more normal than anything I've ever encountered. This is how it should be. How people should act. What have I done with all my time?*

He'd had a long time to recuperate from the accident, and this gave him an opportunity to reflect on his past actions. He wanted a family like Fahed, to be happy like they were, happy and loved.

He looked at Fahed and nodded. "Your kindness overwhelms me, my brother. I am forever grateful."

Fahed smiled, and Jack wasn't the only one who thought he looked rather charming when he smiled. His mustache curled up on both sides of his mouth and his crow's feet dug into his temples. Everyone tried to keep Sheik Fahed happy. He had a way of making one feel special when you're in his good graces.

He smiled and offered everyone a fireside poetry reading with music and wonderful food. Jack couldn't remember the last time he'd had a Scotch, but strangely, he wasn't missing it. He looked forward to the fireside poetry and feast tonight, and his pleasure and enthusiasm showed on his face as he offered to help. "Is there anything I can do?"

Fahed patted him on the shoulder and grinned. His mustache curled to reveal his bad teeth. "No. No. You are our guest. You need your rest so you can travel soon."

Marwa was a known poet in their tribe, so everyone looked forward to what she'd recite. Jack took in the sights and smells of the occasion. The smell of the fire, the sound of it crackling, stars in the sky like he'd never seen, and the peaceful silence of the desert. The kids passed out fresh dates and poured thick Arabic coffee into everyone's cup. The men cooked kebab skewers, and the ladies made fresh bread on round griddles heated by the fire. The smell of the food made Jack's mouth water. *Damn, I'm gonna miss this smell.* He licked his lips in anticipation. The scene was magical, set to the music of Fahed's cousins and their rhythmic drumbeats. *Talented guys. God, I wish I had a camera. No one's gonna believe me.*

The night pressed on, and everyone enjoyed a bellyful of delicious food, laughter, and storytelling. Jack had never known such tranquility. For months now, he hadn't touched alcohol or cigars, but he'd enjoyed smoking the hookah pipe with Sheikh Fahed and his enormous family.

Maybe it was the rest, the air, the food, or the hospitality. Who knew? Jack felt himself in better shape than he'd ever been in his life. When the night's festivities began, he was excited to be a part of something so exclusive. This kind of evening was only for honored family guests. Whether he'd ever admit it to himself or anyone else, this meant something to him.

*I almost hate to leave. Would it be crazy to stay? To be a part of this group? No. I have to see my son again. What's gonna happen to him without me there?*

Just when he thought he'd seen everything, the poetry reading began. The youngest daughter of Sheikh Fahed, Marwa, sat in the middle of the circle on her own cushion. She was wearing a beautifully sequined veil to cover her face, but it did nothing to cover the striking beauty of her eyes. Honey brown and large, lined in kohl. Jack had witnessed every manner of woman, every lady of society, every woman of the night, but no one captured his attention as much as the alluring Marwa.

*The most beautiful girl I've ever seen. God help me.*

This was a great tradition among their people, but it happened very rarely. Badr told him that they'd had a few during the months that Jack was in their care, but he had been far too weak to attend. Healing from his injuries took a long time. Jack didn't even know how long he'd been there or what was happening back home. The desert was nothing like the decadent streets of New Orleans, and he'd never felt so at peace in his entire life. Seeing Marwa was potentially upsetting to that feeling.

*He'd kill me if I looked at her in a desirous way. I better hide this well.*

Sheik Fahed spoke.

"My daughter, the jewel of my heart, has always been so eloquent with her words, sharing the light of her soul with her poems. She has written another for us."

Marwa began,

> *My eyes, my windows, open to see thee,*
> *Yet in sorrow am I.*
> *Sweet sorrow is all we must share,*
> *Our worlds apart and split.*
> *To the far corners thy shalt take night flight,*
> *I keep the fire aglow.*
> *Remaining is the memory of thee,*
> *My heart's fire burning bright.*
> *Return for me, my love.*
> *If ye will not, know the light will burn bright.*
> *Until the windows of our souls shall meet again.*
> *And intertwine as one.*

The fire crackled and Jack was speechless and in complete awe of this beautiful young woman, but he didn't dare say anything or move, especially since no one else was. The poem was, it seemed, inappropriate for her to read.

*Damn, is she attracted to me? That's not gonna make her daddy happy. Just look at his face! I've never seen him so rigid,* Jack thought.

Sheik Fahed's brow furrowed, and his eyes darkened.

"Go to your tent."

Marwa teared up and ran to her tent, as instructed. The whole family began to whisper and murmur about what was happening. Fahed glared at Jack. Jack, for once in his life, didn't know what to say.

"I have a daughter, but I left her," he blurted.

Fahed's face softened. His eyebrow was raised. "Left? How could any man leave something so special? Your daughter is your pearl, your heart."

Jack's shoulders dropped and he looked at the ground. For the first time, he truly felt ashamed of what he'd done. His voice shook as he replied, "I had a dark heart back then. I don't know what I was thinking. I'd just found out that her mother was a spy and had tried to sabotage my business. I could've had her arrested for espionage, but my affection for her kept me from it...that, and her pregnancy."

*And I couldn't find her anymore after she disappeared.*

The whole space went quiet. The music stopped. "It wasn't her fault. I should've known that...I tried to make up for it all with my son. I even married his mother, a horrible woman, but my Natasha is still out there, probably hating me by now."

Fahed asked, "And, what about her mother? What was her name?"

"Nadia..." Jack said. He gazed up at the stars. "I loved her. I was in such denial. I'm glad you didn't know me back then. I was such a terrible man."

Fahed patted him on the shoulder and said, "My brother, we make mistakes in life, but we are human. Allah can forgive, and so should we. We have a saying among our people... 'If you are not quick to forgive, Allah may take time to forgive you as well.' We live by this, but for human beings it's not always so easy."

Jack smiled and nodded. "I can't thank you enough for what you've done for me. I think you have a wonderful family and an extraordinary way of life, one of honor and such simple joy. Please don't let the modern world in."

Fahed sniggered. "So, we should stay simple men in the desert?"

"No...No, come now, that's not how I..." Jack blushed.

Fahed snapped his fingers and ordered. "Get my brother more food and tea. He needs his strength for tomorrow's journey."

The music started again. Once the extra helping was brought for him, Jack began to speak, but Fahed interrupted. "Don't worry. I know you love us. I was, as you say, 'pulling your leg'?"

The two men enjoyed a nice chuckle and dug into the delicious food. They played music with the traditional stringed rababa, almost like a violin; the guitar-like oud and the hypnotic drumming sounds of the darbuka. The smell of the food, the perfume, the hookah smoke and the sight of the fire and the stars... the sensation of being wrapped in warm hospitality. Jack felt he had all he needed. After the party, he slipped into the most restful sleep of his life. Just before drifting off, he surprised himself by shedding a few tears. Tomorrow, he'd leave these people. The months spent in their care had influenced him. He truly regarded them as family, and just before he fell asleep, he vowed to return to them one day, to make Sheikh Fahed feel overjoyed with a grand gesture of friendship and brotherhood.

# NATASHA

ON THE OTHER SIDE OF THE WORLD, NATASHA STALKED RICHARD Parker. Her mark, as ordered by *Don* Alexander, and approved by her mentor and on and off lover, Vlad. She was wearing a red wig, since Richard knew her as a brunette. She also wore much thicker makeup than usual, but much thinner clothes. Spending time with Richard had revealed to Natasha his penchant for "wild girls". He had graduated at the same time as Brian, but was always jealous that Brian was more successful, despite his lowly birth.

Richard, like Brian, took over the family business, Parker Insurance. They were known throughout the country. Over the years, they'd developed a close relationship with rival families of Alexander, helping them cash in on some exceptionally large policies, one of which was Frank Glass, another of Vlad's aliases. Vlad used the money to set up his army of professional hitmen. Crime bosses all over the Southeast began to rely on him for "extermination" services. In fact, that was Frank Glass's profession, on paper.

Now that Alexander officially claimed Natasha as his own, he felt that Mr. Parker was long overdue for his own life insurance policy to be cashed in. As Natasha thought about everything, she felt the weight of his stare. He was drunk, thankfully.

*This is too easy...pervert. Here he comes.*

"Hey, cutie. Dance with me," Richard said, smiling.

"Cutie?" Natasha said with a thick Southern accent.

He smiled, and even though he'd put on some pounds over the years, he still had dimples that made him look boyish. "Yeah, baby! You are as cute as a button. I just gotta dance with you now. Don't go breaking my heart, as the song says."

She smiled, relieved he reminded her of what a womanizing jerk he is. "Sure handsome. Whatever you want. How can I resist that smile?"

He slammed his hand down on the bar. "Exactly!"

She gulped as he clutched her arms to practically drag her onto a crowded dance floor with him. He put his arms around her and immediately started grabbing her bottom. She nuzzled into his neck and was just about to strike when she saw Vlad standing near the entrance, observing her every move. He smiled at her, nodded, then blew her a kiss. She smiled provocatively in return and as an unspoken moment of devotion to Vlad, she didn't break eye contact as she jabbed Richard with a small needle laced with batrachotoxin, the poisonous secretions of the rainbow multicolored frogs found in Colombia. Richard began to convulse immediately, falling to the floor and gurgling. Natasha stepped backwards, then screamed, prompting others around her to scream and run out of the nightclub. Vlad followed as Natasha slipped into an alley and took off the red wig to throw it in the trash. She grabbed a bag lodged between a garbage skip and the dirty brick wall of the building. She hurriedly stripped off the smutty outfit, dumping it in the trash and putting on a black jumpsuit. While the chaos from the nightclub was still spilling out onto the street, she removed a damp cloth from a plastic bag to clean the makeup from her face. On the other end of the alley, Vlad was waiting with his arms open. She slammed into them, and they kissed. He led her by the hand to his nearby hotel so that they could celebrate properly. They almost broke the door of Vlad's hotel room as they hungrily groped one another, kissing, and tearing each other's clothes off. The satisfaction came quickly, as it always did with them. The attraction was strong, even if the power dynamic of the relationship was off kilter.

After they finished, Vlad lit a cigarette and took a deep drag. He blew out a stream of smoke, then sighed. "Dorogaya, I missed you too much! We make a great team, my darling."

Natasha rolled towards him and took his cigarette out of his mouth. She took a deep drag as well. "I missed you too. Why does it feel so natural to be with you?"

He smiled. "Because we grew up together and we were both raised by killers. Don't you remember?"

Natasha put the cigarette back in Vlad's mouth. She remembered their childhood all too well. Nadia spent a lot of time with Vlad's caretaker. She only remembered her mother calling him "Al". In her mind's eye, she saw Al turn to face her mother, and it all clicked into place. Al was Alexander Arsenyev! Nadia sat up in bed. "You were Alexander's ward?"

Vlad smiled. "Now you get it, Dorogaya. I put that bastard into power. He's the head of Vlast now, because of me! Because of how well I trained you as well. But as usual, he only wants to take what's mine, what I have worked for and earned."

Natasha took his hand and caressed it. *What a bastard for a father figure! Poor V, no wonder.* She bit her lip and took a breath in. "I get that. I've also thought about what you said... I guess there's no denying it. We are two of a kind, aren't we?"

"Da," Vlad replied as he took another drag from his cigarette.

"I understand how the relationship between you and Alexander is... complicated," she said.

"I don't care anymore what he's done for me. He didn't raise me as a father. He raised me as his property. When he declared *you* his property, I declared that *he* would die."

Natasha smiled and nuzzled into him. "I hated being summoned to his house that night...I scrubbed so much it seemed I wouldn't have skin left." She looked into Vlad's eyes.

*Sometimes he's so warm. I could almost forget. Is this love?*

"Thank you for not letting him have me—well, at least permanently.... I remember how you protected me, when all those older boys in the family business wanted to have their way with me, you scared them half to death."

"You're my dorogaya. The only person I could ever love if *love* is something I can feel... for anyone."

Her brow furrowed. "Why do you think you can't love?"

He scoffed. "Do you know me? What I do? How many people have I done this to?"

She smiled. "Um, yeah. I've known you all your life."

He took a drag from his cigarette. "Do you know that I enjoy it?"

Natasha remained silent. The thought was profound. *Do I enjoy it?* She never really asked herself point blank before.

"I don't always like it. Sometimes it breaks my heart. I guess I'm like my mother in this. Nadia was supposed to kill my father, after he made her, but she just couldn't bring herself to do it."

"Ah! The famous Jack Buchanan!" he said as he blew a smoke ring. "What happened to him anyway? He is dead, right?"

"That's what they all say. He's been gone for almost a year now, but no one found the body. Search teams were out there for weeks...He went to Saudi Arabia for a diplomatic mission or something. That's all I know. Except no one's ever heard from him again, and then Brian inherited it all."

"Not anymore..." Vlad said, followed by a cold, dark stare.

"Yeah, but his wife is gonna get it now, we both know she's pregnant."

Vlad scoffed. "I tried to take care of that. I was going to sell that baby to the highest bidder." Vlad shook his head. "So many childless couples. They will pay anything for a healthy white baby."

Natasha cringed at the thought. "You don't sell them to people who would hurt them, right?"

Vlad's eyes opened wider, and he exhaled. "I try not to, dorogaya. But some of the clients I take...I can't vouch for them. That baby is technically your nephew. Maybe you would want him? I'll get him for you if it will please you."

Natasha smiled. "Me, a mother? Hmm...maybe, who knows? My mother had the same profession as I do, and I turned out fine."

"But with *daddy* issues!" Vlad said, snorting laughter.

Natasha smirked and shoved him. "Shut up, you!"

He pulled her over his knee and smacked her bottom. "Maybe daddy will spank you now, Huh?"

They giggled and tussled playfully. Natasha stopped for a moment to catch her breath. She pulled away, being serious for a moment. "Guess I don't really have a dad to think of anymore. He's probably buried face down in a sand dune somewhere now, after that attack on their convoy."

She got up and looked out the window. Vlad held her from behind. "It's okay. No matter what, you were and are cherished, dorogaya, by your mother, by me. I'm here always."

Natasha's heart warmed. Her eyes softened. This wasn't the cold-blooded killer she'd always known. This was her childhood playmate, V. Someone who genuinely cared for her, ready to turn his back and make an enemy of his former father figure and mentor. She smiled, then exhaled, relieved from her fears...for now.

The peaceful feeling was short-lived. The hotel phone rang. Vlad answered purposefully, as though he knew it would be for him.

"Da? What?! Nyet!!!" he exhaled, trying to calm down. "I'm coming. Don't move."

He slammed the phone down and began cursing in Russian.

"What happened?" Natasha asked, alarmed.

"Ivar has been taken. Uff! Idiot!"

He started dressing and muttering, "All messes are up to me to clean. One day, just one, things can go right? No, they can't!"

He turned to leave and kissed her. "I'll be back. I'll tell you our plan shortly."

She nodded and winked at him. He smiled and left. Natasha stared at the sunrise. It was so beautiful that she almost forgot about the mess she'd created.

*Will we ever get past this? Can I ever have anything normal?*

# JACK

*March 1977, The Arabian desert, near Saudi Arabia*

JACK GAZED AT THE HORIZON AS DAWN WAS JUST BREAKING IN THE desert. He took a deep breath, soaking up the beauty and atmosphere. Sheikh Fahed and his sons had the camels ready and were busy saying goodbye to the rest of the family that would remain. Fahed saw Jack looking sombre and approached.

"We've enjoyed having you here. Now, we must leave. These are the best hours for travel. Soon, it will be extremely hot.

Jack nodded and finished getting his gear into his bag. He approached Fahed's wife and daughters but kept a respectful distance. "Thank you for everything."

They nodded and smiled. He got on his camel and was hoisted high in the air. No matter how many times the men taught him how to do this, the sheer height of being on a camel's back was ever intimidating but exhilarating. He waved goodbye and shouted,

"Masalama! Allah ya salmak."

The camels began their swaying walk, carrying the procession of tribal elders and their sons, protecting Jack Buchanan. Soon, he couldn't see the tents anymore, as the last glimpse of the oasis faded into the desert sand, under the ever-brightening sunlight of the day.

# LAURA

*March 1977, New Orleans, LA, safehouse.*

LARRY AND LAURA WERE GETTING BORED WITH POLICE PROTECTION, quite fed up with being restricted to an FBI "safe house". Laura's pregnancy was progressing without any issues, but Larry's cancer was hitting him with a vengeance. He coughed deeply, and his tissues were spattered with blood from his lungs. It wasn't just the coughing; it was the excruciating pain that she could see in his face, despite his best efforts to hide it.

They had been promised a visit from one of the officers once a day, and so far, today, there was no visit. Laura waited by the window, hoping to see a car pull up at any time.

Larry had another nasty coughing fit into a fresh wad of Kleenex. Laura cringed at the sound.

*I can't stand seeing him in so much pain. God help him. He should be spending his last days at a resort, an island, and a trip around the world. But no...he's here with me, living the worst days of my whole life. It's so unfair.*

She concentrated on looking out the window even harder, as if it would make them come faster. Finally, she felt relief as she saw a car pull up, but a bit confused to see a different person coming to check on them. Instead of the young blonde agent that visited every day and brought them supplies, it was Agent O'Connor.

Laura opened the door. "It's about time! Where's our regular guy? I never caught his name."

O'Connor said, "He's sick today, so I'm filling in."

Laura folded her arms and tapped her foot. "Hmm, really? Well, where are the supplies he promised me?"

"Supplies?" O'Connor asked.

Laura's eyebrows raised and she clicked her tongue.

"Yeah, my prenatal vitamins and my father's pain killers. Can't you see he's in massive pain? I can't have his last time on Earth spent like this."

O'Connor winced as he looked closely at Larry. "Oh, yeah, he's really hurting, isn't he? Don't worry, we'll get him what he needs today."

"Well, thanks for that." She turned to walk away. "Here, let me get you a list of other stuff that's needed, and please, for the love of God, get a doctor out here to see him. There must be a shot they can give him or something to make him comfortable."

"Yes ma'am," O'Connor replied.

Laura handed him the list. He glanced at it. "I'll get a doctor over here today. Don't worry."

She nodded. "Okay, I trust you. But please hurry."

She watched him from the window as he walked away, and a shiver ran down her spine. She brushed it off as worry for her father and got on with his care.

# O'CONNOR

*March 1977, New Orleans, LA*

O'CONNOR TOOK THE LIST AND LEFT FOR HIS CAR. HE TURNED TO look at the house and spotted Laura staring from the window. He smiled and nodded. She stopped staring.

He went back to the gas station near the Interstate and made a call from a grimy payphone.

"Yeah. They are at house number ten, Elysian Fields Avenue, off Interstate ten...Okay I did as you asked, now can you let my wife go? Please?"

O'Connor began to sob quietly as he heard the answer. His wife shouted in the background. "Help me please, honey! He's lying to you."

The next sound was the thunk of something heavy hitting the floor. He shuddered.

"I'm not done with you," the voice said. "Don't worry, this will all be over soon. In the meantime, don't think of going to any of your colleagues for help. Keep your mouth shut, and I won't have to cut her pretty face. Understood?"

"Understood," O'Connor said, sobbing. "Please don't hurt her."

"That all depends on you. I'll be in touch soon. Within forty-eight hours. Be ready."

The man hung up and Agent O'Connor left, wiping his eyes.

# JACK

*Late March 1977, New Orleans, LA*

JACK BUCHANAN RETURNED, AFTER ALMOST ONE YEAR, BUT WASN'T prepared for what he found, in spite of his debriefing from the CIA. After so much time in the peaceful desert, he had to learn how to slide back into his own life, unfreeze his assets, and take control of his business and family affairs. He never expected such a sledgehammer to his heart, or the fact that everyone naturally assumed he was dead. Why? Surely someone could have looked for him a little longer. At least that's how he saw it.

He asked the taxi driver to wait for a moment as he looked at his house all boarded up; the front gates padlocked.

"What in tarnation is happenin' here?"

He got back in the taxi and asked to be taken to his office. When he got there, his long-time assistant, Mary Grace, fainted upon sight of him. An employee from the mailroom happened to be making rounds at that time and rushed to fan Mary Grace and attempt to revive her.

"Mary Grace? Are you all right, ma'am?"

The young man turned around to speak to Jack. "I'm sorry, but who are you?"

Jack pointed to the portrait of himself on the wall. The young man's eyes widened, and his mouth opened.

"You're Jack Buchanan? Oh my God, sir. We all thought you were dead! In fact, I remember the memo on that. You *were* dead. How are you here right now? I'm Zack by the way."

Mary Grace started to come around. She feebly looked up at Jack. "Is it really you?"

Jack smiled, although it was hard to see under his thick beard and mustache. "Hello Mary Grace. You are a sight for sore eyes. God, how I missed you, young lady!"

She smiled and her eyes teared. "Sir…"

"Here Mary Grace, please drink some water," said the young man.

Mary Grace took a sip and a deep breath. She looked at Jack and began to cry. He scooped her up in his arms and took her to the employee lounge.

*They changed everything in here with me gone. Good God almighty! As soon as I'm back on top, this new-fangled shit is all gonna go…poor Mary Grace. Look at her. Like she's seen a ghost.*

She sobbed and Jack got her a tissue. "Darlin', I wish you'd stop crying so hard."

"Oh Jack…I'm thankful to the good Lord that you're okay. We thought you were dead. We even had a funeral."

Jack smiled. "A funeral, huh?"

"Yeah…But as much as we're all happy to have you back, I'm afraid I have terrible news. I didn't think you were alive to know about it, but now that you're here, I have to tell you something… heart breaking."

He swallowed and sat straight. "Spit it out."

"Your son, Brian…He's…"

Jack narrowed his eyes, and his breathing became rapid. "He's what?"

Mary Grace blinked the tears back. "Dead…I'm so sorry to have to tell you."

For a few moments, Jack froze. The department secretaries, Janet, Kelly and Charel peered around the corner, looking at Jack with sympathetic eyes. The office was quiet enough to hear a pin drop.

"I'm so sorry, sir," Janet said.

Other curious staff entered, to see what the commotion was. Soon, the office was buzzing with whispers, gasps, and sighs. Jack felt the weight of their stares. He didn't know what any of them wanted from him, or how they could just assume he was dead all this time. How could they say his son was dead? Surely that's not true. The State Department would have informed him.

*It's like they didn't know me at all! Or care. How long did this so-called search last anyway? It really doesn't seem like they tried very hard. They don't know their asses from their elbows! I bet Brian's not dead either, no more than I was.*

Soon, there were only the sounds of people gulping, sobbing, and sighing.

"Back to work! All of you!" Zack shouted.

Finally, Mary Grace whimpered, "Jack, are you okay?"

Jack walked out of the room, leaving everyone to murmur and whisper once again. They weren't doing a great job at keeping that quiet, because he could hear everything they were saying.

"Oh my God, poor man. I can't believe he's back, and to hear such news. Sweet merciful God. I hope he's gonna be okay," one of the secretaries, Jennette, said.

"He's a lot taller than I thought he would be," her colleague, Betsy said.

A third voice, Patricia, grunted. "You're so bad. Poor man's having the worst day of his life, and you're thinking about how he looks?"

"What? I've always had a little crush on him," Jennette said. "He's still handsome. I wish all men aged that well."

"Shhhh...here he comes."

Moments later, he returned with his arms folded, wild-eyed. "My son...is... dead? Is this literally what you're telling me? Dead?!" He shook his head, grunting and pacing back and forth. "No...he's not! He can't be! My son is my legacy. He can't die. Do you understand?"

"Sorry Jack, but he is!" Mary Grace blurted, sobbing.

Jack winced and formed a fist with one hand and held his heart with the other. He slammed the coffee table and growled, "How?"

Mary Grace sat up, sniffling, and whispered, "Murdered."

He snapped and threw a chair against the wall and smashed it completely. When he looked around, the fear in everyone's eyes made him pause. Mary Grace whimpered, tears streaming down her face.

Jack's face contorted as one would expect for a grieving father. Crying wasn't going to be an option for Jack, or at least that's what he thought. He fell on his knees and his chest heaved. As much as he wanted to prevent it, he couldn't keep tears back completely.

His eyes burned, as he looked up at the ceiling, forcing the tears back. He would have no more of that, at least not in front of his subordinates. He struggled to catch his breath. "Take care of Mary Grace...Someone tell me where I can find my daughter-in-law."

Mary Grace said, "None of us can get to her. She's in witness protection somewhere. That's what we heard. At first, she was accused, even arrested, but as it turns out, she didn't do it. It wasn't her."

Jack pulled himself up and slammed his fist down on the desk. "Of course, it wasn't her! She loved my son...Why does she need witness protection?"

A familiar voice answered. "Because it was the Russian Mafia. Laura and her father have testified to that effect."

"What?" Jack asked, realizing that this could only be the voice of Jim Higgins. *What's he doing here?*

"Sorry to just show up, but the Feds were informed by homeland security that you're back. I'm sorry that they didn't fully inform you of everything. I was hoping I'd get here before you heard. But I reckon nothing makes hearing that any easier," Jim said. "I'm sorry for your loss, sir."

"And I'm sorry for yours," Jack said.

He turned around to see Jim, who looked shocked by Jack's overall haggard appearance. "Jack Buchanan, as I live and breathe. Where the hell have you been?"

Jack put his hands on his hips and breathed in and out, pulling himself together. "Well, if it isn't little Jim Higgins. You did it. You're a cop. I gotta say, it really suits you."

"Thanks, "Jim said, folding his arms. "Oh, and it's *Officer* Higgins, if you don't mind." Jim folded his arms. "Now that you're back from the dead, and by the way, I take back my question. I don't really care where you've been. What's important is that we need to take you downtown to answer some questions. You must know something about the enemies that my brother faced. Somehow, I think they would have rather taken *you* out instead of him."

Jack scoffed and forced his fists to come unclenched. "Jim...After what I've been through, I am indeed a changed man. But don't think that I didn't notice your little innuendo that I'm somehow to blame for my son's untimely death, something I literally just found out minutes before seeing you."

Mary Grace stopped crying, smoothed down her hair and stood up straight. "Why don't you let me help Jack get some business items attended to and he'll be right over?"

Everyone looked at Mary Grace and Jack smiled, thankful that she was still as efficient and considerate as ever. Jack nodded. "I'll see you downtown, Jim. Let me pull myself together and I'll be right there, promise."

Reluctantly, Jim agreed and left. Jack watched him go and remembered a long-ago summers day. He had dropped Brian off after a visit before he was awarded full custody. Jim and Brian ran off to play in the woods together, laughing, and happy. At the time, he resented the two brothers and believed they were white trash and bad influences on his boy, but he realized now that what he was really seeing was love. Brian loved his brothers.

*God, what a selfish prick I've been.*

# JACK

*March 1977, New Orleans, LA, 13th precinct*

When Jack reached the police station, he looked much more like his old self. Shaven, wearing one of his suits and a swagger to match, he felt much better. So, what if the suit hung a bit loose. Mary Grace had found it hanging in a storage closet, still with the dry cleaner tags on. He'd soon get back to his old physique with his beloved New Orleans cuisine.

*Whoever did this is gonna pay with their lives. I swear to God, I'm gonna string this fucker up for all the world to see.*

One could hear him coming from quite the distance. "I'm here to make a statement, as instructed by Officer Higgins. Who's gonna take my statement?"

The precinct's receptionist, Betty, nodded. Without looking up, she dialed a number. "And who are you, sir?" She asked Jack.

"Jack Buchanan II, at your service," he said.

"Sure thing, hun'. I'll be right back."

"All righty, Miss Betty," he said. "I'll be here."

Jack watched her walk away. He looked at his watch and began to feel fidgety as he wondered if Betty had gotten lost. He watched cop after cop go in and out, men in suits that he presumed were lawyers, and a few perps as well. The desk staff all seemed busy taking phone calls or typing reports. Maybe a statement from him wasn't as high a priority as he'd imagined?

Finally, a young officer approached, holding a clipboard. He said, "Who are you, sir, and what case are you referring to?"

"Are you fucking kidding me?" Jack blurted.

The young officer's mouth opened, and he held the clipboard close to his chest. "What?"

"I go away for a year, and this is what I come back to? My son is dead, and everyone's forgotten my name. No one even comes to take my statement. Good God!"

"I'm sorry, sir. Let's start over. My name is Frank, Frank Glasshouse," said the young man, as he reached out for a handshake.

Jack shook his hand. "Hello Frank. I'm Jack Buchanan II. My son was the young man that was murdered. I believe there was a young woman found dead as well, but I can assure you that my boy had nothing to do with that gal. He was as faithful as the day was long."

Frank was writing it all down. Jack waited until he made eye contact. "Let's find the prick that did this."

Frank smirked. "Yep, sounds good. Right this way, Mr. Buchanan."

"I am wondering, if you don't mind, how you've come back," Frank asked. "Were you captured?"

"No," Jack said. "Nothing like that. I went out with a colleague of mine to survey the oil fields of Saudi Arabia. Some are in remote areas, so we could only get there by private plane. After the accident, it did occur to me that I didn't know this fella very well, but he was recommended by colleagues of mine. He took me out on a plane ride, and we made several stops. On one of them, he picked up a little contraband. You know, a little whiskey. So, we both had a shot, but that was all! One shot. So, I didn't understand why he just fell over the control panel like that. He tried to land it gently, but we touched down pretty hard."

"Wow, what happened next?" Frank asked. "What were you doing in the Middle East anyway?"

"That's classified," Jack said. "As for the accident, I got out, but just barely. He told me he had to find something before he got out, something sentimental to him I guess, but the poor bastard didn't have time. The plane exploded and I was knocked out on the sand."

"Do you think someone somewhere wanted you dead, Jack Buchanan?"

There was something about the look in his eyes that caught Jack's attention. *What a sick guy! He's either taking pleasure in my suffering or he's up to something.* Jack looked at his badge. *But he's a cop, and here we are, surrounded by cops. I must be imagining things.*

"I hadn't thought about it, until now," Jack said.

Frank smiled dismissively. "Well, it was probably just a tragic accident. Let's get to the office so we can finish off this statement. Shall we?"

Jack nodded, but his eyes narrowed. The men went to a private office and spoke for less than five minutes about Brian, Brian's relationship with Laura, and whether or not he knew anything about Delta Dawn. Jack emerged, then walked out the front door, standing next to the street, feeling relieved that he'd gotten that part over with. Still, he had an uneasy feeling, gnawing at his gut.

Jack made his way out of the station to hail a cab. He intended to see his lawyer next in order to get his assets unfrozen. If he was going to help Laura, he'd need the best private investigators money could buy. He bit his bottom lip to keep it from quivering, especially as he remembered his father. *Real men don't cry. Isn't that what the old bastard used to say? Heartless old prick.*

He looked at the sky and remembered a rare day that he had with Brian, one of his best memories. Brian had just made a bad grade in science and had tried to cover it up. He was worried that Jack would be disappointed. Jack remembered that day, the day he took his son to learn how to shoot a gun instead of yelling about a bad grade. Yelling was something Jack the first would have done.

In his mind's eye, Jack saw them there, on the horizon, shooting empty cans off a log. The sun was brilliant that day, and for a brief moment, all was right with the world. Jack felt his cheeks. He quickly wiped away the tears that had managed to reach them.

*Oh, sweet Jesus, what shit is he gonna stir up now?*

He exhaled as he saw Jim pull up in his police car and get out quickly. Jack put up both hands and said, "Hey Jim! Been there already to give my statement. Now, I really need to hire a good PI to crack this case so my daughter-in-law can come home."

"Great! Who took your statement?" Jim asked, plunging his hands in his pockets.

"Um, let's see..." Jack tried to remember his name as he tapped his chin. "Oh yeah, how could I forget! Glasshouse. His name was Frank Glasshouse."

Jim gasped. He put his hand on his hips and tapped his revolver. "What the fuck? Frank Glasshouse? Oh God.... Is he still in the building?"

Jack shrugged, nobody else had come out with him through the main doors. He had no idea who Jimbo was so upset. He could only watch helplessly as Jim darted into the precinct; gun drawn.

Jack rushed in after him. He saw Jim peer around the main reception hall before quietly informing the desk staff of a code 10-30, 10-48 in progress in the building. "Secure all exits and search room by room."

Jack was unsure what to do next. Jim motioned to him to wait near the doors. Suddenly the PA speakers blared out rapid instructions and a wailing siren accompanied it. The whole precinct erupted into chaos.

After a fruitless hour, Jim returned to the front area and instructed the reception staff to put out an APB on Frank Glasshouse, last seen right here, impersonating an officer.

"What the hell, boy?" Jack asked.

"That was one of Vladimir Petroski's men! They all use the name Frank Glasshouse when they are undercover, except for Vlad himself, who uses the name Frank Glass. He's the Russian Mafia hitman implicated in Brian's murder."

"He's the bastard that did it? There's no one else involved?"

Jim called Jack into the nearest empty desk, while another officer brought over a file of photographs. Jack described the man. "He was about yea high with sandy brown hair, blue eyes. He looked like a good kid. How was I supposed to know he wasn't a real cop?"

Jim held up one of the photographs.

"Oh yeah! That's him."

Jack was relieved that at least his short-term memory worked just fine. Jim tapped the picture. "That's Dimitri the Doppelganger, a damn infiltrator. Gathers intel for Vlad and his men. God damn, they're good! If I weren't working my ass off to bring them down, I'd admire the hell out of their methods."

Jack scoffed, "They aren't that great! You figured out who he is, fast as greased lighting!"

"Ha!" Jim snorted. "Believe me, we found out who he was because he *wanted* us to know. Vlad is fond of rubbing our noses in our failures to catch and incarcerate him."

"So, what are we gonna do now?" Jack asked.

Jim went to the precinct phone and dialed a number. "We need a car to check on the assets. Yeah, the widow and the lawyer... What?!..."

Jack blurted, "What's wrong? What happened? Why do you need another car? Something wrong with yours?"

Jim rolled his eyes. "So, no one around their safe house will know it's me. That's why."

Jack's eyebrows jumped up in recognition and he nodded. Jim listened to what the person on the phone was saying. Within moments, his mouth dropped open and he took a deep breath. He gritted his teeth while clenching his fists.

"Bastards! How could you all let this happen, again? Who knew they were there? ...What?... Well, you find that motherfucker before I do, or I'm gonna do something violent to him. I don't wanna go to prison! You hear me! Find him!"

Jack waited for an explanation. He folded his arms. "Okay, what happened?"

"We have to find Laura and Larry. They've been kidnapped again." Jim sighed.

Jack looked up at the ceiling, then huffed. He put a hand on Jim's shoulder. "You do your job and I'll do mine. I'll use everything I've got. Let's get to work!"

"Yes sir!" Jim blurted.

"Again! Jesus H. Christ," Jack said. "If you want something done right, you do it your Goddamn self."

# JIM

JIM WINCED, THEN ORDERED OFFICERS TO FIND AGENT O'CONNOR. He was one of two, other than Agent Smith, who knew their whereabouts. It stood to reason he was an informant. O'Connor had family in town, so that was a stop to make as well.

*Someone must know something.*

After watching Jack storm off to battle, he got into his squad car. He sighed, thinking of all the times Brian stood up for him to his snotty college friends. He heard Brian's voice in his head.

"He's my brother, my flesh and blood, and I will not let you or anyone else disrespect him. Got it!"

Jim sniffed. His eyes narrowed as he allowed himself to feel the full force of his anger of the situation.

"You deserved so much better, Brian. You had a good heart, and this is what you got for it." His eyes grew solemn and his breath slowed. "I don't know if you can hear me brother, but I'm gonna make this right. I promise, no matter what."

# BERNARD

*March 1977, New Orleans, LA, O'Connor home*

AGENT SMITH WAS THE FIRST TO ARRIVE AT O'CONNOR'S HOME. HE knocked...no reply. "Mrs. O'Connor! Federal Bureau of Investigation, Agent Smith here. I have a warrant to search the premises. If you don't answer, I'm authorized to enter by force. One last chance!"

Agent Smith gave the signal to the accompanying officers to bust into the residence.

CRASH!!

Once inside, they realized that Mrs. O'Connor was missing. Although there were no signs of a struggle, the back door had been forced open and there was half-eaten food on a plate on the table. Flies buzzed around. He used his handkerchief to gingerly pick up the phone and call the field office. He noticed a photo of O'Connor and his wife on the shelf.

"Let's get an APB out on O'Connor and his wife. She's a redhead, about five feet tall, one hundred forty pounds. I want officers combing the area and any known properties of Vlast." He looked around again. "And get someone down here to dust this place immediately. I doubt if it'll do any good, but we can't leave anything to chance."

# JACK

JACK FOLLOWED UP ON A HUNCH TO FIND LAURA AND HER FATHER. He went to Nadia's former apartment because sometimes you need to start at the beginning of everything to understand the end. As soon as he'd learned that the Mafia was involved, he had had a suspicion about Nadia.

Getting in was easy once he bribed the doorman. Nadia had lived in the Garden District, near Lafayette Cemetery. Jack knew several prominent members of the Russian community lived in this area as well.

He knew that Nadia was presumed dead, but he also knew that Natasha was out there somewhere. He felt a pang of guilt for that. When he was younger and still married to wife number two, he wanted nothing to do with legitimizing the Russian lover he'd taken. At the time, he thought she was just a secretary, but over time, he began to understand she was so much more. He tried to keep tabs on them through the years, but lost track of Natasha. The only thing he knew, on good authority, was that Nadia left a safe house, an apartment, there for Natasha, just in case.

When he got there, he'd hoped to find Natasha herself, although he knew there was little to no chance of that being the case. Her mother must have taught her to stay hidden, and all the other tricks of the trade. Jack was suddenly gripped with a wave of heartsickness, making him feel quite helpless.

*I don't even know what she looks like now. What kind of pathetic father have I been?*

He snooped around the apartment, fishing for any information that could lead him to Natasha.

*Come on Nadia. You had to leave something here to lead me to you...or at least our daughter. You're at the center of all this. God knows, I can't prove it, but I feel it in my bones.*

As he searched, he felt an odd sensation, something he hadn't felt in years. Was it dread? No. He smiled as he realized it was excitement. That's what their relationship was based on, at least for him. The thrill of it, the sneaking around.

*Lord Almighty! It turns out I really was an asshole. I hope it's not too late with Natasha. If I can help Laura and Natasha from getting mixed into this, I may at least make my boy proud when he looks down on me.*

He used the doorman's telephone to call his office. Mary Grace didn't ask any questions, but simply instructed one of the assistants to meet him at the apartment to help him sift through all of Nadia's old things. She was there in the trenches with him, searching for any clue. However, try as they might, the search seemed to be futile, and Jack started to feel powerless. He sighed.

*No. No! I am not giving up that easily. Push on, old boy. You'll find what you need.*

# NATASHA

*March 1977, New Orleans, LA. Same day*

AROUND THE CORNER, IN THE HALLWAY, NATASHA WAS APPROACHING the apartment, but stopped in her tracks when she heard Jack's voice. "I wish I could tell you what we're looking for, just anything to lead me to my daughter."

"Umm, yeah." A woman muttered. "I wish we could find something. An old bill, a business card, anything."

"Yeah. Well, just keep looking," he said.

Natasha strained to keep listening. Jack grunted, then threw a box of Nadia's things. "Son of a bitch!"

"Sir?"

He turned and said, "This is about as useful as a fart in the wind! I have someone, a good PI who may be able to track her better than me. I mean hell, no one's ever even found proof that Nadia's dead!"

"You think she's alive?"

"Well, all I know is that this woman was one of the best Commie spies that ever was. She had me convinced for years she loved me and would do anything for me. She had my child, kept her hidden from me, and all the while she was spying on Buchanan Oil for them! Classic honey trap, and I was the bear!"

Jack looked down and shook his head. "I just wish I could find her, see if I can help her out of this mess."

"Nadia?" The woman asked.

"No! Screw her for keeping that sweet girl away from me! Lying bitch ... I mean my daughter. Nadia mentioned her name was Natasha, but who knows if she changed it or what. She was so small the last time I saw her," he said, remorsefully.

"God help us.... anyhow...I gotta step up the search on Laura and her father. I can't believe those idiots lost them a *third* time! I gotta get back and get on that right now."

He smacked his lips and put his hands in his pocket. "Well, I'll tell ya what. I want you to keep looking through all this, but I can't leave you here alone."

"Sir, I'm a big girl. You can go ahead if you want to."

Jack huffed. "Oh no I won't! You don't know how many of her former *comrades* are living around here. God knows what kind of goons she's got lurking around. I'll have one of my boys come by here with you later."

She rolled her eyes. "Oh, all right. Just lemme get my purse."

"Well, shake a leg, sugar!"

Jack winked and held his arm out for her.

She giggled and they started to walk out. Natasha darted into another hallway to avoid being seen. Jack and the woman left the building, and she slid down to sit on the floor. She couldn't believe her ears. Her father...after all this time. The regret over what she'd done started to burn at her heart. All this time... All this time she thought he was dead, and now he sounded concerned. *Did Mama keep me from him? Could it be true?*

Then it hit her...Laura and Larry, missing again? "V...Oh God, what have you done?"

# LARRY

ON A MISTY SPRING MORNING, VLAD TIED THE NYLON ROPE AROUND Larry's wrists. He tried not to wince and show weakness. Laura and Larry were being held in one of the many offices of Vlast, back-to-back, in one of the real estate fronts, RAG Real Estate, owned by none other than the Ragimov family.

Larry mumbled and struggled, while holding Laura's hands for comfort and reassurance. "Mmf! Mmf!"

Vlad huffed and pulled his gag out for a moment. "Yes!! What do you want, Larry? Huh?"

Larry coughed up some blood, making Vlad wince. *Okay, that's good. At least he's squeamish, and I may be an old fool, but it seems like this psycho likes me.*

"Please. Just let my daughter go. Like you said...I'm dead anyway. Why not let a pregnant woman walk free?"

Vlad leaned into Larry's face and held a large hunting knife against his throat. Larry grunted and Vlad said, "Shhh...papa bear...Do you have any idea how much a healthy white baby can sell for on the market? Even more, if it's a girl. Quiet now, and I'll let you keep this gag off. No more spitting blood, da?"

Larry bit down hard to keep silent and clenched his fists. He nodded once.

*Mother fucker! He knows that shit makes my blood boil. He's just fucking with me.*

Vlad's mouth curled into a leer, as he turned to start a fire in the free-standing gas fireplace in the office. Larry closed his eyes, struggling to keep control over his rage. He opened his eyes. "You're going to burn in hell, so hot it makes that fire seem like a vacation."

Vlad laughed. "Don't take it personally, Larry."

Larry's eyes darkened. Vlad chuckled.

"I know you want to help her. Every fiber of your being wants to rip my face off right now, da?" Larry nodded, gritting his teeth.

Vlad chuckled. "Don't be the hero, Larry. You'll only die faster, huh?"

He noticed Larry's burning eyes, the hatred roaring inside them and sighed.

"Maybe you've talked enough for now," Vlad said as he reapplied the gag.

Laura sobbed uncontrollably. Vlad growled in disdain. "Shut up, you entitled bitch!"

He slapped her. Larry flinched. "Daddy's special little girl...pfft! My girl never got such a privilege, and she's a hundred times the woman you are!"

"Don't listen," Larry mumbled.

Vlad moved close to her face. Larry could feel how close he was as he also felt the disdain in his voice and the tremble in Laura's hands. *Hang on darlin'.*

Larry stroked her fingers with his, trying to keep her calm. It wasn't working.

"She's strong and beautiful," Vlad blurted. "You're a pathetic sniveling bitch. Soon, I'll be done with you. Trust me, it hurts me to kill your father more than you. You, I'll enjoy it."

*As I'll enjoy killing you when the time comes,* Larry thought.

The phone rang and Vlad answered. Larry could see Vlad again when he went to the phone. He cringed as Vlad winked at Laura and made a kissing gesture before picking up the handset. "Da?"

As he listened, he visibly tensed more and more. "Why are you questioning me *now*? After all I've done for you? Because Jack Buchanan is back? The same bastard that left you for dead?"

Larry struggled to control his emotions and stay silent. Vlad listened and began carving something into the desk. His breathing became louder and louder as he grimaced. "Nyet!!"

He slammed the receiver down. "I have to go out for a while. You'll both excuse me, I'm sure." Vlad said, grabbing a gun and a jacket.

# LAURA

*March 1977, on the top of the Plaza Tower in downtown New Orleans, same day*

LAURA WAITED BREATHLESSLY FOR A FEW MOMENTS, LISTENING FOR sounds he had left. She shuffled backwards, feeling for Larry's hands. He squeezed her hands and then Larry began to tap on her fingers, in a specific rhythm. *Morse code! Clever Daddy....*

He tapped one firm and three short taps. *J.* He continued with one firm and one soft tap. *A.* He continued until he spelled out, *Jack is back. Help me get untied.*

Laura struggled with the nylon binding behind Larry's back, and began tearing her nails into the restraints, managing to get one of Larry's hands out. He used it to pull the gag out of his mouth. "Don't worry, darlin. We're getting out of here."

He broke free and started to work on Laura's restraints when he spotted exactly what he needed.

*Is that a letter opener? How foolish.*

He grabbed it, and after a bit of frantic sawing, Laura was free. "Oh my God!" she gasped. "What about the other offices here? Can we make a run to one of those?"

"It's Sunday," Larry said.

"Ah," she nodded.

"Shhhh," Larry whispered. They heard footsteps, and her heart fluttered when she pointed to the revolver Vlad had carelessly left on the desk. *Whoever called him sure did rattle him! He got sloppy.* Larry grabbed it and checked the chamber. Only two bullets. *Not much. Make 'em count, Daddy!*

He motioned for Laura to get behind him. She did as she was told but grabbed a fire poker she found in the corner. They braced themselves.

# VLAD

*March 1977, on the top of the Plaza Tower in downtown New Orleans, same day*

VLAD WENT TWO FLOORS DOWN, USING THE EAST STAIRWELL, TO another office fronting for Vlast, an ice sculpture design company, only to find out that Agent O'Connor was dead. Dimitri showed him a polaroid picture of the body. Vlad gritted his teeth. "How?"

Dimitri clicked his tongue and folded his arms. "It seems one of these idiots let him drop by his home to *grab a few things*, as he put it. He must have grabbed some pills. He asked for a glass of water when we gave him his lunch. We didn't know he was going to swallow a handful of pills with it. His body's in the trunk."

Sirens wailed outside. Vlad unholstered his gun and peeked out the window. The streets were crawling with pigs. His eyes turned steely "What have you done? Did you check him for bugs?"

Dimitri and the others looked at each other blankly. Vlad rolled his eyes. "I'm dealing with fools. Fools that are gonna get us killed."

"We checked him when we took him. He wasn't wired," Dimitri said.

Vlad growled. "And after you let him *grab his things*? Did you check him again?"

More blank looks. "Durak!" shouted Vlad, as he swiped all the glass models of sculptures off the bar, smashing them against the wall.

Dimitri stood perfectly still. "Shh"

"What?" Asked Vlad. "What's going through your idiot mind now?"

"I hear footsteps. Someone is out there, near the West stairwell."

Vlad led the others, revolvers drawn, outside to see who was creeping around. Vlad was no stranger to surveillance. He could sense his target and become invisible, until it was too late for his victim, who would often find themselves at the deadly end of a crossbow or a knife. He didn't care much for guns. He only used guns when he didn't have time to be *creative* with his kills. After all, he had a reputation to uphold.

# LAURA

*March 1977, on the top of the Plaza Tower in downtown New Orleans, same day*

AFTER SHE HEARD THE SIRENS, LAURA CREPT BEHIND HER FATHER, as he searched for a way off the floor that wouldn't attract attention. A stairwell was their best bet now, it seemed. They walked silently but quickly to creep down the stairs.

Laura was so focused on getting out that she didn't notice Dimitri. Failing to check her corners, he grabbed her from behind. She screeched. Larry turned quickly and pulling Laura out of the way, spun her into the wall, almost clunking her head. She heard a shot. *That's one bullet down.* She thought. *One to go.* Turning around, she saw Dimitri slowly collapse to the ground with a loud thud.

Larry motioned for her to come over to him. She stood up and gathered herself, smiled with relief and was almost within reach of Larry when Vlad grabbed her by the neck and promptly pressed a blade against her throat, hard enough for blood to drip onto her blouse. She squirmed.

"Let me go!"

Vlad clicked his tongue. "Larry...oh my friend. What have you done? Dimitri is dead because of you. But you know what? You are a particularly good shot, Larry!"

Vlad tightened his grip on Laura. She felt the tightness of her abdomen as the baby squirmed inside her. Tears started rolling down her cheeks and she felt flushed.

"I didn't expect this. Perhaps I've underestimated you?" Vlad said. "Hmm?"

He sniffed Laura's neck and licked her cheek. She squirmed and winced. "No, please...let me go, please!"

"Speak again, little bitch, and I cut an artery!"

She whimpered, struggling not to open her mouth. He smelled her hair and exhaled loudly. "Larry...papa bear! You never told me your cub smells like honey! I think I need to taste this honey before I kill her. What do you think, Larry? You won't mind if I taste it?"

Laura squirmed as Vlad felt her up. Larry drew his gun and fired. Her ears rang from the sound of the gunshot. In slow motion, she saw Larry drop the gun as he winced and held his hands over his ears. She wondered if Vlad was dead. It had happened so fast, she was not sure when Vlad had let go of her. Stumbling to regain her footing, she tried to walk over to her father, who was shaking his head to clear his ears.

*He can't hear right now. Neither of us can.*

"Daddy, Daddy, can you hear me?"

Neither of them had heard Vlad getting up until he pulled Laura back, with a knife in his other hand. She shivered when she saw the evil look in his eyes.

"Larry, you shot me. Tsk. Tsk. Tsk."

Vlad pulled away his jacket to show a bullet proof vest that he wore underneath. Laura felt her hope drain away.

Larry exhaled but remained silent.

"I know. Yes, you'd never usually see me wear one, but there's more out there than you who want to kill me. They may even reward you!"

Larry held his stance. Vlad grabbed Laura by the waist, pulling her close against him, even though he was talking too loudly because he couldn't hear.

"But, hey! If I wasn't protected, you would have ruined my day...More than most can say! Ha!"

Laura screamed as the shock hit her, "Daddy! You could've shot me!"

"What did I tell you about speaking, bitch!" Vlad grazed her upper arm, but he did not cut too deep. The arrival of two more underlings interrupted his fury. She whimpered, collapsing into him.

"Consider that your last warning," he said.

Vlad's mouth curled into a leering smile. "Drop that gun right now, Larry."

Larry kicked the gun towards Vlad and glared. "Mother fucker! You're going down!"

Vlad quickly retrieved the gun. One of the men sniggered. Vlad turned and struck one of them with a loud THWACK!

The object of Vlad's rage fell to the ground, gripping his jaw in pain, the other standing by, watching in silence.

All Laura could do was try to remain calm. She fought to hold back her emotions. It was a curious thing to see Vlad defend her father so much. He'd just struck one of his own posse for her father's honor. She struggled to keep a poker face, but the pregnancy hormones made it difficult. One thought rang through her mind.

*This psycho actually likes my father. Far out. Who would've thought? I just wish he could use it now, somehow.*

"Don't laugh at this man! Never laugh at this man! Understood?" Vlad yelled, reprimanding the group.

Vlad whispered in his ear, "Larry, don't let these idiots get to you. What you did took balls, balls of steel. For a dying man, you are a bear! Don't forget this."

# JACK

JACK STOOD IN HIS EMPTY HOME, STARING OUT AT THE ONCE manicured grounds, cigar, and scotch in hand. He took a sip and wondered, *what do I do now? I have no one. No family. Nothing that holds any real value. That baby is all that carries my blood...except for a disturbed daughter I can't find.*

The phone rang. He didn't want to answer, but who knows what could be happening now. He prayed for good news for a change.

"Jack Buchanan here. Hello?"

Jack listened and felt as if he were waking up for the first time in years. He crushed out the cigar and blurted, "Yeah, okay...Yeah."

He scribbled a few notes on a piece of paper, holding the phone between his shoulder and cheek. "Okay, I'm on my way...Hey, Jim? Um...Nothing, just thanks."

Jack hung up and smiled. He looked at himself in the mirror, at his swag appearance, fresh shaven with a white smile.

"Come on, you handsome son of a bitch. Let's go be a hero."

# JIM

JIM SPED TO THE SCENE, SIREN BLARING. HE ARRIVED AND STRAPPED on his bullet proof vest, then found Agent Smith. "So, what's this all about? Laura and Larry are up there?"

"Yeah." Agent Smith grunted. "The bastards are holding them hostage."

Jim nodded. "So, what's the play?"

"We've got every entrance and exit guarded, but the sorry son-of-a-bitch is demanding a helicopter to land on the building's helipad to transport them elsewhere."

Agent Smith bit his bottom lip and balled his fist. "Scumbag! A pregnant woman. You just *know* why he wants her."

Jim shrugged. Then the implication hit him, punching him in the gut. "Oh my God! That's vile."

"Russian mafia. Trafficking is a big business for them." Agent Smith said, patting Jim on the shoulder.

Jim's forehead scrunched and his face turned red with anger. He breathed in and out, actively controlling his temper. "We have to stop them. They can't take Brian's child; I owe him that."

"We won't. This is gonna turn out all right. I promise you, okay?"

Jim turned to look at Agent Smith. "Thanks, man. If we all get out of this unharmed, we'll all get our shit together, but let's look at what we have going on here. A professional hitman with, I don't know how many underlings."

"Two underlings," Agent Smith said.

"How do you know?" Jim asked.

"We have helicopter reports that Laura and Larry teamed up and killed one, then another gunshot was fired, but we don't know who shot who. At that point, our visual confirmation was blocked. They pulled the blinds tight."

"Son of a bitch, that old man is a hard ass!" Jim smirked. "Well, what about now?"

"Our eyes in the sky say that they are moving up and we can see that they've stopped a floor higher than before. We are in position and snipers are all around the neighboring buildings. This office doesn't appear to have blinds, so we've got eyes on them now," Agent Smith said, looking through his binoculars.

"Suspect in the office with two armed suspects, one guarding the old man and one for the woman..." the pilot said.

"Copy that," Agent Smith replied. "Easy does it now. We don't want those hostages getting shot."

"Female hostage appears to be writing something under duress," the pilot said. "She dropped it in what appears to be a satchel."

Suddenly, Laura opened the office window with her hands up, with something in her hand, possibly the satchel. Agent Smith watched intensely with binoculars.

"All units stand down. Hostage moving forward. Let's keep her safe," Agent Smith said.

All eyes were on Laura in the office." Jim winced. "What's she doing?"

"Hell, if I know. Looks like something's in her hand?" Agent Smith said. "There, she's done. She's dropping it over the edge in a satchel, and it's clear that he wants me to see her."

Agent Smith's team was standing by. "Go! Go! Retrieve the package!" he commanded.

One of Agent Smith's team picked it up and rushed it over. Bernard and Jim looked at each other. Bernard motioned for Jim to open it. Jim opened the satchel and the note inside said,

Bring me a Bell 206 Long Ranger helicopter with a full tank and extra fuel in 8 jerry cans. Be here by 6pm. Bring 500,000 unmarked, non-sequential

American Dollars in a briefcase. The pilot will stay behind. I do not need him. Disobey my instructions and I will decorate the pavement with him, the pretty widow, her unborn child, and her dying father. Do not test me. You will lose.

Sincerely V

*p.s. Once we are safe, I will release the debutante and her father. I give my word.*

Jim calmly handed the letter to Agent Smith, then punched his fist into his other hand with all his might, suppressing the urge to swear to the heavens.

Agent Smith frowned, "Who would give us that kind of money? And in an hour?"

"Jack, that's who. He knew Jack was back. That's why he changed his strategy."

Jim shifted to face Agent Smith. "Don't you get it? He knew that asking too much would take too long but asking for too little wouldn't mean he'd be taken seriously."

"How the fuck did Jack get access to funds so fast? Unfreezing his accounts must take a while," Agent Smith asked.

"Jack's got his ways. He must have had some money hidden somehow. A secret account, maybe? Who knows, really. But I wouldn't put it past him."

Agent Smith nodded. He looked at his watch. "Well, the clock is ticking. Let's get a move on this. I'll get on the helicopter, and you get on Jack."

Agent Smith grunted, frustrated. "That Commie son of a bitch. He's gonna get a helicopter all right, one that comes with a transmitter attached."

"What?" Jim asked.

"A transmitter...You didn't think I'd just let him go, did you?"

"No," Jim said. "But if he doesn't feel safe, wherever he is, he won't let them go. You saw the letter."

Agent Smith clicked his tongue. "Oh Jim. You must know that we won't activate it until we have Laura and Larry in hand. We just have to pray he won't find it himself before that."

"Ah, I see," Jim nodded. "Okay, meet you here in twenty."

"You got it buddy," Bernard said. "Don't worry. This will all turn out okay."

# LAURA

VLAD LOOKED AT HIS WATCH AS HIS MEN, VIDAM AND SERGEI, PACKED up more provisions, such as cash and diamonds stolen from the office safe, passports, a little food and water, as well as some sort of files. Since Vlad was down one man, he called for Vidam. Laura watched carefully. *I'll bet those files contain proof that Vlast is a sham, a cover for the mob. He's not stupid. He knows he needs leverage, so that they won't come after them.*

Laura was gagged, her eyes leaking tears of rage. Larry wasn't gagged, as Vlad thought of it as a reward for his display of bravado to let him speak freely. Laura leaned against Larry, tapping out in Morse Code that she was hungry. She shuffled around, shifting her weight to get more comfortable.

Larry waited a few minutes. "If you wouldn't mind, my daughter needs to eat something. She's pregnant and she hasn't eaten or had any water all day."

Vlad loaded the gun and took the safety off. He turned to look at Larry, smirking. "Men like us don't *ask*. We *tell*…Try again."

Larry cleared his throat. "My daughter needs a goddamn sandwich and a glass of water…NOW. She's pregnant for God's sake!"

Vlad took a long drag off his cigarette and smiled. "Yes, that's better."

He threw a knife into the wall and growled, "Sergei! Get her a sandwich and some water, right now! I saw some vending machines down the hall."

Sergei looked behind him at the knife sticking out of the wall. He gulped and left the office, slamming the door behind him.

# VLAD

*March 1977, Plaza Tower in downtown New Orleans, same day*

MINUTES LATER, THERE WAS A SCRATCHING SOUND AT THE DOOR. Vlad was still checking the weapons. He snapped his fingers irritably. "Vidam, go!" He kept a watchful eye on the door.

Vidam flung the door open, but Sergei wasn't there. In the dim light, he saw a crumpled garbage bag on the floor. "Get it."

Vidam shrugged, then went to pick it up. Vlad put out his cigarette on the tabletop and moved towards the door. Fast as lightning, Natasha jumped out of the garbage bag and grabbed Vidam, pressing a blade to his throat. Vlad laughed and slowly clapped his hands.

"Ah! The student has learned every lesson that the master has to teach. Is that how it is, dorogaya?"

"Don't flatter yourself, V."

Vlad looked at Vidam, clicked his tongue. "You are a fucking idiot. You know this, right?"

"I came here to save you," she blurted indignantly, releasing Vidam, who had the grace to look embarrassed. "How is it that you're here, and no one from Vlast is here with a machine gun, plowing you down? I know they're after you. Alexander wants you dead."

"My comrade at the FBI called in a bomb threat for me. Not only is it a weekend, but no one will also dare enter because of the danger and the cops outside."

"I noticed them," she said. "I thought they were here for you."

"They are here for me now, but the bomb threat got them here," he replied.

"Fine," she said. "But we should go, V. Right *now*."

"Oh, course we will," he answered slyly. "We're about to order our ride." He pointed towards Laura and Larry. Laura mumbled and struggled, obviously wishing to say something. Vlad stepped over and lowered her gag. Laura spoke hurriedly, "Lady, I know you from somewhere. Don't I?"

Natasha scoffed. "Who knows what you know, stupid bitch! I've never seen you."

Vlad folded his arms, leaned against the desk, and said, "Tsk, Tsk...Liar."

"What do you mean?" Larry winced. "Have you seen her before? Where?"

"Never mind, Larry. Just be a good guest until Jack Buchanan's money gets here. Ok?"

"What?" Larry said. "My daughter has something to say. Let's hear it."

"Oh my God!" Laura blurted. "It's Jack, who's giving you money?"

"Yeah, yeah. Your rich father-in-law has returned from the dead. Just in time to pay for your safety." Vlad said, glaring at Laura. "If you don't piss me off, you may get a chance to see him again. Now, excuse me for a moment."

Vlad led Natasha out of earshot, or so he thought. Vlad grabbed her by the shoulder and whispered, "What are you doing here? I was going to send for you when I'm out of the country...How did you get all the way up here?"

Natasha kissed him. She whispered. "You taught me how to be invisible, remember? A few clever disguises and these hillbillies don't know their ass from their elbow. Besides, they were too busy focusing on you." She smiled, then frowned. "I never wanted this, for you to get caught up in what I did. All this is my fault."

Vlad took her in his arms and kissed her on her head. He embraced her and whispered, "Shhh, no. I can't let anyone harm my love, so you'll never be blamed for anything. Don't you see? This will be on me. The murders, the kidnapping, everything. They'll never catch me. When I'm secure, I'll send for you."

He noticed Laura staring intently at Natasha, and suddenly, there it was, a look of recognition that washed over her face. She must have realized that Natasha was the woman in the hotel that night. Vlad looked at Larry and shook his head. "What a shame...I was hoping I wouldn't have to kill them."

Natasha looked at Vlad. "What? Oh no, come on. We don't have to do that."

He growled and released Natasha, "You shouldn't have come here. Their deaths are on you! She knows your identity now."

Vlad looked over at Laura and Larry. Cursing, he strode to the outer door, shouting all the way. "Where the fuck is Sergei? Sergei! Get in here with that sandwich!"

# NATASHA

*March 1977, Plaza Tower in downtown New Orleans, same day*

NATASHA WALKED OVER TO WHERE LAURA WAS LEANING AGAINST A desk. Laura looked pale and drawn from exhaustion and malnutrition. Tears rolled down her cheeks. Natasha felt nothing. "Brian? My Brian? And poor Delta Dawn? Why? Just tell me, why."

Natasha replied scornfully, "Because *he* wasn't supposed to have *my* life."

"What! *Your* life?" Larry shouted.

"Yeah!" Natasha snapped. "My life! If Jack had acknowledged me and my mother, he would have never sought out that trailer tramp that bore *your* husband." Natasha pointed at Laura's stomach and gritted her teeth. "He would have never existed, and neither would *that* baby."

Natasha looked at Laura speculatively Laura's belly was growing, her straight A-line top hiding just how big her abdomen had grown. Her eyes grew dark. *That baby isn't supposed to be here.*

Laura cradled her belly protectively. "What do you have against me? All I did was fall in love with my husband and get pregnant with his child. I just wanted to live and be happy. I didn't do anything to you."

Natasha suddenly slapped Laura. Larry growled. "Hey! Stay off of her!"

"Shut up, old man! This has nothing to do with you!" Natasha snarled.

"She's *my* daughter! Who the fuck are you?"

Natasha ignored him and focused on Laura. Bending down, she pointed her finger in Laura's face. "You wanted to live your life? So did my mother!"

Natasha drew her hand back, to slap Laura again but restrained herself. "She fell in love with a man, had his child, and just wanted to live and be happy, but no." She began to choke up, and struggled to hold back tears, so she turned to make sure Laura didn't see how emotional she was getting.

Vlad pulled Natasha into a big hug and glared at Laura. "You don't know anything, princess. While you were growing up with a father as impressive as my friend Larry, my sweet Natasha grew up with men worse than me to learn from. Her *true* father will pay now. He has plenty of money and will now open that wallet for his blood, in more ways than one."

"Fuck you," Larry snapped. Laura didn't make any sound. *Good, she understands the odds now,* Natasha nodded to herself.

Vlad laughed. "Oh Larry, you're making it harder and harder for me to kill you. If only we could have met as friends," he sighed. "Too bad..."

Larry rolled his eyes.

Laura suddenly spoke, "Oh my God. My baby is your niece or nephew. Doesn't that mean anything to you?"

Natasha pulled out her gun and pointed it at Laura. "No! Now, I'd shut up if I were you before you piss me off any further."

Laura whimpered and hid her face in her arms. Vlad said, "She tried to stop it. You should know that. She tried to undo what she'd done, but the poison had already done its work."

"Why are you telling them?" Natasha blurted.

"They won't live to tell anyone. You don't have to worry about this." Vlad said, brushing some dust-off Larry's shoulder. "Although I really would like to keep this one."

"That's fucked up," Larry grumbled.

Vlad chuckled softly, dismissively patting Larry on the head, then turning back to Natasha. "Look, you shouldn't be here. I'm taking the blame for it all. Go now, and no one will be the wiser. When I've drawn all the heat off you, and it's safe, I'll find you again."

She hugged him and kissed his cheek. "V...you're the only one in my life who's ever really loved me. I love you. I really do. You should know that. You are loved."

"You're the only one I'd ever do this for. You made a mistake. You don't deserve to pay with your life for a mistake," he said softly, kissing her on the forehead. "Let them chase me. I can take it. They'll never find me."

Natasha looked toward the door. Her heart was beating rapidly. She had no more options left.

"Go on. Go now," he said.

Sobbing, she did as he asked. She looked back once more and mouthed the words, "Promise me, you'll be okay?"

He winked, stretching his arms wide in a typical Vlad move. "Hey baby. It's me. Come on."

She smiled and entered the hallway, turning to take one last look. Vlad had already snapped back into control, his smile replaced by a grim expression He looked at his hostages, then at his watch. "Only 20 minutes left. Tick tock."

She started to make her way out of the building, but a dark ominous feeling came over her, causing her to hesitate.

# LARRY

*March 1977, Plaza Tower in downtown New Orleans, same day 5:40pm*

THE SINISTER GLEAM IN VLAD'S EYES ALARMED LARRY. HE KNEW HE had to do something. Once Vlad got that money and had them in the air, there'd be nothing stopping him from murdering his *baggage*. He watched carefully as Vlad stared out of the window.

"Are you crazy? Get away from the window." Sergei ran into the room, with half a dozen sandwiches in his arms.

"Da." Vlad calmly lit a cigarette, took two long puffs, then walked back to a more shadowy area of the room. He watched as Sergei dumped the sandwiches on a desk.

"Give the meat sandwiches to the woman. Babies need food. Larry, you feed her."

Sergei approached, tossed three sandwiches on the floor in front of them. To his dismay, Larry heard his stomach growl loudly. *When last did we eat? No wonder Laura is all pale and shaking.*

Larry tore open the box with difficulty, then leaned closer to let Laura take small bites. He made sure she ate two whole sandwiches before he allowed himself to eat. The bologna was dry, but it tasted like the best steak in the world. Laura leaned closer to whisper to him.

"Thank you, Daddy, that helps. If it weren't for the baby, I couldn't eat anything. I wish I could go to the toilet and clean up. I had a little accident, and it is really awful to sit on a wet carpet."

"Vlad, my daughter needs the bathroom urgently."

Vlad gave them both a side-eye look. "Do you think I am stupid, papa bear? After last time, you can rot in your own piss for all I care."

As Vlad paced, Larry watched, trying to think of what he could say to buy a chance at freedom. *There's gotta be a way out of here. Think, Larry! Think!*

# JIM

JIM FOUND JACK IN HIS OFFICE. TIME WAS ALMOST UP, AND JIM COULD feel his blood pressure rising. He slammed the office door open, making Jack and Mary Grace jump.

"What the hell is your problem?" Jack blurted, looking irritable.

Mary Grace stood behind him, apologetic. Jim couldn't be bothered with their irritation. He had bigger fish to fry. His face was pale, stress causing sweat to run down his scalp and face.

"My problem? Oh, let's see, shall we? Your daughter-in-law and her father are trapped by Vlad the Impaler in one of Vlast's offices downtown, and we have very little time to deliver five hundred thousand dollars and a helicopter to get them out!"

"Way ahead of you, Jim. As usual," Jack grimaced.

Jim was momentarily at a loss for words. He folded his arms instead. This wasn't what he was expecting. Why the hell wasn't Jack panicking like the rest of them? Was there nothing that would rattle this old twister? He felt the panic rising again.

"And what does that mean, Jack? Talk, goddamnit, we are on a literal deadline here!"

"I've been coordinating the rescue with the CIA all morning, and we have it under control. The helicopter will be there, ahead of schedule...with extras," Jack said, still looking at the papers on his desk.

"What extras? And why were we and the FBI not informed? Damnit, we've gotta work together here!" Jim was furious.

Jack stood up, walked over and put his hand reassuringly on Jim's shoulder. "Son, I know you have everyone's best interests at heart, but you're kinda getting in my way right now. Leave it all with the experts."

Jim threw up his hands and snorted, "Oh well, excuse me Mr. Big Shot! I'll get out of your damn way then."

Jack grabbed the papers from his desk and headed for the door.

"Thanks!" he said with a smile.

When the door slammed, Jim tilted his head to one side.

"Huh? What just happened?"

Mary Grace simply shrugged.

# NATASHA

*March 1977, Plaza Tower in downtown New Orleans, same day, 5:59pm*

NATASHA HAD TAKEN THE FURTHEST OF THE TWO STAIRWELLS TO make her getaway. She was almost home free, nearly reaching the ground floor of the building, when she heard the dull thud-thud of the helicopter's blades. Part of her was relieved that she had gotten away, but she had an ominous feeling that Vlad needed her, a feeling she couldn't shake.

"Vladimir...I am coming, my love."

Fearing that she may be too late, she turned and ran back up the stairs. As she turned to the next set, she ran into an armed CIA swat team. They were too many to take on. The leader grabbed her, and within moments he had her gagged and handcuffed to the stair railing. He communicated through hand signals to the rest of the team. They moved up.

# LARRY

VLAD HEARD THE HELICOPTER COMING. HE APPROACHED THE window, checking the sky. He turned to Larry and smiled.

"Our ride has arrived."

"What did you mean by 'poison' earlier?" Larry blurted. "So, there was poisoning involved?"

Vlad smiled at Larry. "You are right, papa bear. Little Natasha infected both of them with the poison and then wanted to save them when she regretted her decision. I could not let that happen."

"Why? What does she mean to you?"

Vlad ignored him as he loaded more guns with ammunition and hid various knives away on his person.

Larry cleared his throat. "Hey! You said we were friends. Why are you hiding this information from me?"

Vlad huffed through his nose, blowing smoke out from his nostrils like a dragon. "Okay Larry, since it doesn't matter what I tell you, I'll be honest with you, but we must all get to the roof now."

Vlad looked at his watch. They were early. He nodded with a semi-approving smile. "Impressive...minutes to spare."

Sergei and Vidam grabbed Laura by her arms, lifting her to a standing position. "Come on, your highness. Let's move."

Larry took a while to stand unaided. He saw Laura looking at him with a concerned expression. He returned an encouraging nod, but in reality, he was hoping for a miracle.

The five of them slowly made their way up the stairs to the roof. The cops had cut the electricity in the building so that they'd be more likely to want to leave their hiding place, therefore, the elevators were no good.

Larry tried to keep up, but he felt weak, and was coughing up more blood than before. He sure hoped his sandwich stayed down! His handkerchief had fallen somewhere along the climb and eventually he just resorted to wiping the blood away with his forearm. His legs felt numb, as he'd been kept in the same position for far too long.

Vlad saw that he was struggling and hooked his arm through Larry's for stability. As they climbed, Vlad relayed the story of what really happened that terrible night.

"She told me what she planned to do. I told her it was stupid. She didn't have the stomach for it...not back then anyway."

Vlad continued to support Larry's weight as they went up the stairs.

"So, the poisoning was stupid?"

Vlad huffed. "Larry, for a sick man, you are too fat. You must know this."

"Ha. Ha. A real comedian..." Larry said. "Seriously though, what was stupid?"

"The killing in general. She needed to talk to him first, even threaten him, blackmail him...but kill him? There was no need and no benefit." Vlad grunted. "I never kill for emotion, Larry. Only purpose."

"What purpose do you have for killing me? Or my daughter? You said that you and I are friends. Friends don't kill each other."

Vlad chuckled. "Ha! True my friend. True. But you see, this is my problem. For Natasha I broke this rule, leaving emotion out of what I do...and you know too much now."

Larry studied Vlad's face. "You love her, don't you?"

Vlad conspicuously ignored him, focusing on every step to get Larry up to the roof. They finally made it.. Larry blinked in the brightness of the setting sun. The sky looked magnificent with pinks, oranges and purples streaking across the clouds.

The helicopter had touched down in a clear space on the roof. The propellers blew paper and dust around. Everyone had to brace against the wind as they approached the whirling blades.

Vlad thrust Larry in front of him, to use as a human shield. Sergei and Vidam did the same to Laura. The pilot spoke in a low voice through a loudspeaker from the small open window in the door.

"Keep your distance! I will come out with my hands up. I will bring the money and place it on the ground in front of you."

# NATASHA

*March 1977, Plaza Tower in downtown New Orleans, same day, 6:05pm*

NATASHA WAITED UNTIL THE LAST FOOTSTEPS DISAPPEARED HIGH UP in the stairwell. They must be close to the roof by now. There was not much time.

*Handcuffs. How pathetic. There's no handcuffs I cannot get out of. Idiots. Always underestimating women.*

She got the cuffs off in record time, even for her. That was the easy part. The door to the roof would be more problematic, she worried, as the SWAT team may cover the door too. She ascended the stairs two at a time, heart pounding.

Carefully easing open the door, she was relieved that the noisy helicopter prevented anybody from hearing her approach. She could see only one of the SWAT team members taking cover behind a walled-off area. He was staring intently at the group of people near the helicopter. She was safe, for now, observing the situation before deciding on her next move.

The helicopter pilot spoke through a megaphone. She could not make out the words, but the voice seemed eerily familiar somehow. *Who is that? Never mind, I must protect V right now.*

# LAURA

LAURA SHUDDERED. SERGEI WAS AN UNPLEASANT MAN, STINKING OF cheap cologne and old ashtray. His rough beard scratched her skin when he rubbed his face against her neck. He sniffed deeply, then licked her ear. She shuddered in disgust, repulsed by his lechery.

"Too bad we didn't have more time," he whispered. "I *love* pregnant women." He made slurping noises and laughed darkly in her ear.

"Pig! Stay back or I will throw up on you." she sputtered, her voice shaking.

"Oh, what's the matter, little pretty debutante?" he smirked, turning his attention to the helicopter. "Think you're too good for me?" He deliberately let his hand wander closer to her breast, giving her a painful squeeze.

She yelped as he pulled her along, fighting off her panic every step of the way. He bumped her belly with his elbow and suddenly she did feel nauseous. She hoped she wouldn't throw up in front of everybody. Her wet gabardine pants were chafing in the most tender places, and she was feeling thoroughly miserable. *Sweet baby, you just hang in there. Mama's gonna get you to safety, you hear?*

# LARRY

LARRY SAW THE GUN PRESSING AGAINST LAURA'S HEAD AND THE FEAR in her eyes. He slowly bent down to place the knife on the ground. He heard Sergei snigger and figured this was his only chance.

He forced all his strength into his throwing arm and launched the knife straight into Sergei's left eye. Sergei fell back onto the rooftop, gun clattering to one side. Laura broke free holding her bound arms forward for balance.

Larry stumbled forward. He had to grab the knife, it was his only weapon!

"Get the bitch! Get her!" Vlad screamed at Vidam.

Vlad's eyes darkened, as he lunged toward Larry.

There was no time to think. Vlad punched Larry in the stomach, knocking him back on the hot asphalt surface. Larry's belly exploded with pain, and he saw stars. He coughed, desperately trying to catch his breath. Vlad was angry.

"Larry! Why did you do this?"

Vlad punched him again, this time in the ribs. Something cracked. Larry heard Laura screaming.

"Huh? Tell me!" Vlad shouted at him. "I thought we were friends, Larry. Why would you kill Sergei?" Vlad hauled him upright.

Vlad was about to punch Larry again, just for good measure, when one of the officers got off a shot. It ricocheted off the ground near Vlad's feet. He pulled Larry in front of him for protection. Larry heard the pop-pop as Vlad fired back at the officers. He had a massive headache, and his vision was slightly blurry. He stumbled.

"Who did that? I told you to hold your fire, dammit! They have nowhere to go!" An officer shouted.

Larry groaned, and slowly got back up.

"One wrong move and Vidam will shoot the woman! Understand?" Vlad said. Vidam grabbed Laura in a firm grip in front of his body, the gun pressing hard against her head.

"Throw down your weapons and surrender! It's your only chance!" The lead officer said through a bullhorn speaker.

Larry was having a hard time staying awake, with all the injuries, but he struggled. Knowing what was at stake forced him to dig deep for that little extra burst of energy, something primal.

Larry tried to stand tall but could barely focus. His nose was bleeding, but he couldn't feel his mouth, as it was numb.

*Come on, you! You've come through worse than this, kicked the shit out of one Nazi bastard at a time. For Laura, for the baby, come on Larry! Do not fail! You have to kill this Commie son of a bitch!*

He moved forward, fists in the air. Vertigo struck him and he almost fell. He probably looked like a drunk, about to pass out. Vlad exhaled, exasperated.

"Larry...pass the fuck out. You are done, my friend. I didn't lie when I said I take no joy in killing you."

Relieved, Larry obliged.

# LAURA

WITH LARRY COLLAPSED ON THE GROUND, VLAD WALKED OVER, grabbing Laura from Vidam. He pointed the gun at her head. He shouted loud, very loud, so everyone could hear him, despite the helicopter noise.

"Anyone try anything, and I shoot the bitch! Vidam, grab papa bear and drag him onto the helicopter."

The pilot made a move towards the helicopter. Vidam fired a shot in the pilot's direction.

"Nyet! No! " he shouted at the pilot. "Back the fuck up! We're getting in that chopper."

The pilot moved further away, hands in the air. Vidam grunted, lifting Larry and half-dragging him towards the door. Laura was shocked at how old and vulnerable her father suddenly looked. It broke her heart.

The officers lowered their weapons. She stared at them, but their faces revealed no emotions.

Vlad dragged Laura with him. "Pick up the case. Careful!".

"See this, princess?" Vlad whispered in her ear, grabbing her by the hair. "I'll start a new life with this. Come with me now. Your life is safe until this baby is born. After that, maybe you'll find a place in my stables."

Vidam laughed as he pulled Larry towards the door.

"What a pretty whore you will make! Maybe I'll keep you to myself for a while when we get to Ukraine. Until I'm bored." Vlad said.

Laura fought down a scream, as she realized the horror that awaited her.

# LARRY

LARRY HAD BEEN BIDING HIS TIME, GATHERING HIS STRENGTH AFTER the beating. If they had thought a cancer riddled old man was done for, they didn't know Larry. He knew what he was made of, last leg or not.

He waited until Vidam let go of him in order to open the helicopter door. Vlad was standing very close to his head. This was a golden opportunity. Larry lunged forward, biting Vlad above the ankle as hard as he could, ripping and twisting his head sideways. He spat out flesh and fabric, feeling woozy from the sudden adrenaline pumping through his body.

Vlad screamed in agony.

"I will kill you, old bastard! Look at what you have done!" Vlad scrambled around the open door, shoving Vidam out of the way.

Larry felt the world spin as Vlad pulled him half-upright and dished out a flurry of blows with his right hand, still clutching the gun. He barely heard Vlad's angered shouting as everything faded around him.

# LAURA

VLAD PULLED LAURA TOWARDS THE HELICOPTER BY HER HAIR. His threat still rang in her ears. She held the case close to her body.

"Open the door and no bullshit, da?"

Laura struggled with the unfamiliar handle, shaking with terror. Suddenly, Vlad howled, bumping into her. Laura dropped the case. It burst open and dollar bills went flying through the air as the helicopter blades spun above them. She saw Vlad rush around the open door, swearing. She stood frozen, helpless, as money flew in the air around her.

"I tried to be kind! This is what I get! American pig! Fuck you! Fuck you, Larry! Vidam! Grab the bitch!"

Laura dropped to her haunches, ducking behind the open door. She saw Larry's body violently shuddering with each attack. On the far side, Vidam's legs disappeared towards the rear of the helicopter. He was going to come for her from around the back!

The thought had barely entered her head when a new horror unfolded. Sprays of blood, bone and flesh flew everywhere. She looked down at her arms and legs, covered in gore. The door had shielded her head from the worst of it. *What is that? Daddy! No!!*

Laura knew she had to make a choice. Larry or her baby. The sudden surge of love filling her heart gave her the energy to get up. She saw an officer beckoning to her. Locking eyes with him, she ran for her life. For her baby's life.

# NATASHA

*March 1977, Plaza Tower in downtown New Orleans, same day, 6:13pm*

THE TWO OFFICERS THAT HELD HER DOWN WERE NOT TAKING ANY
more chances on losing her. They had handcuffed themselves to both of her
hands. She was stretched out between them, the bullet wound in her shoulder
throbbing painfully. The makeshift bandage slowed the blood loss, at least. She
would live.

Natasha focused on the scene. Vidam dragged Larry to the rear door of the
helicopter. Vlad howled; Laura fell to one side. The case dropped and money
started blowing around. Natasha could not see what had angered Vlad. He lunged
around the helicopter's door, attacking Larry. Vidam looked confused, then
turned to run to the rear of the helicopter.

"Nyet, you moron, don't .... No!" Natasha shouted, in vain.

Vidam was a small bloody heap on the ground, or what was left of him.
Natasha could see streaks of red on the helicopter's side. There were a few bloody
pieces laying on the ground. The officer on her left turned away, vomiting. She had
seen her fair share of brutality in her life, but this was a horrific way to die.

Vlad stood upright, ignoring Larry. He turned towards the spinning tail rotor
with an incredulous look on his face. With lightning speed, he turned towards

Laura. She was running away, clutching at her belly. Vlad raised his arm to shoot her in the back.

Suddenly the air erupted into gunshots from the officers. Vlad jerked around as bullets thudded into his body.

"Noooo!" Natasha jerked upright, pulling the one officer off-balance." She tried to run forward, but the weight of the two men was too much.

"Vladimir! I love you! I always loved you. Don't die, please!"

Vlad collapsed against the helicopter. Somehow, he saw her across the rooftop. He coughed painfully, half-smiling at her. Then his eyes closed, and she knew he was gone forever. She sobbed, heartbroken, as a part of her died alongside him.

# LAURA

*March 1977, Plaza Tower in downtown New Orleans, same day, 6:18pm*

LAURA REACHED THE OFFICER AS SHE HEARD GUNSHOTS. INSTINCT kicked in and she rolled onto the ground, protecting her baby. The officer stepped in front of her, blocking her view.

After a few breathless minutes, she dared to sit upright and look around. The officers were all clustered around the helicopter. People were speaking on walkie-talkies, shouting orders. She started sobbing hysterically.

"Laura! Laura! I'm coming!".

It sounded like Jim. She looked up to see him running towards her from the stairwell.

# JIM

HE HAD RUSHED BACK TO THE SCENE, HOPING THAT JACK WAS telling the truth. Agent Smith looked up. "Jim, you are just in time! Things have been happening up there. I'll fill you in on the way. Let's go!"

*This was it!* Heart pounding, Jim ran up the stairs with the rest of the team. As he burst through the doors, it took him a minute to take in the scene.

The helicopter blades were still going full speed. Streaks of red painted the side. Paramedics were strapping Larry to a gurney. He looked in bad shape. Laura stood nearby, wrapped in a blanket.

"Laura! Thank God you are all right." He rushed over to her. She leaned into him, shaking. "Hush don't say anything right now. You are safe and the baby is safe." She was staring at Larry.

"Hey, Ryan. Glad to see you here, man. Is your patient gonna make it?" He called over to one of the EMTs. Ryan looked up, as he was shining a flashlight into Larry's eyes.

"Unclear, Jim. Head trauma and possible internal bleeding. Gotta get the doc on it." They rushed the gurney to the stairwell.

Everywhere around them, SWAT officers were busy checking bodies, removing weapons and shouting orders. Jim started walking Laura towards the stairwell.

Looked like they got all the perps, except one. A pretty woman was cuffed to two officers. *Goddamn, that must be Vlad's accomplice.* Jim watched her carefully. Laura stopped.

"She killed Brian and Delta Dawn. She wanted to kill me too. Jack is her daddy. She did all this because she hated Brian and his... *our* perfect life. Maybe revenge for her mother too, who knows? Oh God, I miss Brian so much!" She collapsed against him, sobbing.

*That bitch!* His hand itched to grab his gun and empty it into her head. She must have sensed his animosity, as Natasha looked at him. He silently mouthed at her "Fuck you." She shuddered.

A group of men in dark suits approached them. Showing a badge, the older man pointed at the helicopter and beckoned to the pilot. The pilot came closer. The older man addressed the officers.

"SAIC Wilkinson. Good job on capturing the suspect. These are your orders from HQ. You will accompany the suspect and three of my agents in the helicopter to a secure facility. I've cleared it with your CO. Keep an eye on her, gentlemen, she is highly trained and very dangerous. Supervisory Special Agent Nadia will fly you out here and supervise the mission. You follow her every instruction until she deposits you back in town, are we clear?"

The pilot took off his helmet and long dark hair tumbled out. It was a woman. The two officers looked surprised, but Natasha reacted as if she'd seen a ghost. She fell to her knees.

"*Mama? Ya sozhaleyu.*"

The pilot lifted her hand to Natasha's face, gently cupping her cheek. "Natasha, you disappoint me." And slapped her, hard. Natasha made no sound.

Nadia turned and ducked beneath the blades as she boarded the helicopter, her face expressionless. The group followed, crouching low to avoid the deadly blades.

This was getting interesting. He looked at Laura, who appeared equally confused. Maybe Jack could shed some more light on things. Then he gently escorted Laura down the stairs, to a waiting ambulance.

# JACK

JACK STARED OUT OF THE HOSPITAL WINDOW OVERLOOKING THE city. New Orleans, such a fine place. On the surface, charming, as most Southern cities are. However, as one observes the soft undercurrents, one may discover a darkness that is particular to New Orleans. Black magic, tales of lore, and all seven of the deadly sins as a staple of daily life.

*Rotten to the core, but I still love it.*

Laura was still under sedation, dangerously dehydrated and malnourished. The doctor reckoned she needed bedrest for at least another week, but that there was no long-term damage to the baby.

Larry had undergone emergency surgery through the night. He had suffered head injuries and internal bleeding from the beatings he had taken.

Jack, Jim, Ike, and Coral sat in the hospital cafeteria. They'd met for lunch, but no one could work up much of an appetite. Jack grunted as he looked out the window.

"They say he was bloody on the ground, beaten half to death after biting a chunk out of that Vlad's leg."

He turned to look at Coral. "Can you believe that shit?"

"He was a tough old bird, that's for sure." Coral said, dabbing her tears with a hanky.

Jim frowned. "Hey now, let's not talk about him like he's already gone. He may pull through yet."

"That's right," Ike said. "But yeah, Jack. He is one badass dude. Gosh, who knew he was that tough?"

"Amen to that, honey," Coral said, nodding.

Dr. Greene approached. "You're the family of Larry Beauford?"

"Yes, sir. We are," Jack said. "How is he?"

"He's awake, and...considering the circumstances, his advanced stage of cancer, he's doing well," Dr. Green said.

Dr. Green's face didn't match the cheerful looks everyone else shared. Coral's expression changed. She became somber as she approached the doctor.

"Dr. Greene, why do I feel like you wanna give us some bad news?"

Dr. Green put his hands in his pockets and sighed. "Yes, ma'am. I'm afraid I do have some upsetting news..."

"Spit it out then!" Jack blurted.

"Good God, Jack!" Jim said. "Settle down. Let the man speak."

"Larry won't last much longer. The cancer is just too advanced. The weakened state he was left in...I'm actually amazed that he's still alive at all. I think he's only holding on to make sure his daughter and his grandchild are okay."

Coral's eyes welled with tears. "Can we go in and see him? Maybe we can make him feel better?"

"I don't see why not," Dr. Green said. "I just want to be sure that none of you will say or do anything upsetting to this man. He's literally on his last days, so let's make sure they're spent well, okay?"

# JACK

*March 1977, New Orleans, LA. Tulane Medical Center, later same day.*

JACK AND THE OTHERS SLOWLY ENTERED LARRY'S ROOM. LARRY WAS very pale. He sat up and smoothed his hair, trying to look his best. Coral choked back tears. Jack put an encouraging smile on his face and firmly shook hands with Larry.

"My friend, I can't thank you enough for all you did over these last few months."

Larry smiled. "Aww well, it's nothing that any father wouldn't do for his little girl and his grandbaby. I just wanted to be sure they're gonna be okay...speaking of which, have you heard how Laura is doing?  How's the baby? I hope nothing went wrong.  Where is she?"

Coral started to speak. Jack squeezed her arm.

"Oww..." she winced. "Okay, you tell him."

"She's in the obstetrics ward, Larry," Jack said. "From what the doc said, things are looking promising. Laura's still asleep...but hey, I'm sure she's gonna be fine.  It's actually a good thing, to force her to get the rest she needs to heal, after all she's been through. Doc says that there's been too much stress on her system and she's spotting a little. He thought she'd do well to be under light sedation for a while so she can catch up on her rest."

Larry's eyes grew sullen. Coral held Larry's hand. "I swear to you, Larry. There's nothing I won't do for that girl or that baby. I'll die to protect them, and I'll treat her like she's my own daughter. I swear to God."

"I know, Coral. I just wish I could see her, that's all. I know she's got all of y'all. That does make me feel better," Larry gulped, swallowing back tears.

Jim's face brightened. "You know what? I think if I were you, I'd write a letter to Laura, just to be sure you say all you wanna say. There's not much else to do now, right? What do you think?"

"That's a good idea." Larry said, nodding. He smiled.

Ike grabbed a notepad and a pen from the chart cubby. He handed it over to Larry. "Here ya go. That ought to do."

Larry smiled. He looked at Jack. "I appreciate all this. Y'all being here makes me feel better, but I need to be alone when I write this. You get that, right old boy?"

Jack winked. "Say no more. We'll get out of your hair...well, you know what I mean."

Larry chuckled. "Yeah."

# LARRY

*March 1977, New Orleans, LA. Tulane Medical Center, 3:35pm*

ONCE THEY HAD GONE, LARRY LET HIMSELF SHED A TEAR. HE KNEW his once-strong body had taken a lot of punishment. He thought for a moment and started writing. He was strangely out of breath and had to pause a few times. *I used to have so much energy and now a simple letter is taking a lot of effort.*

My dearest daughter,

As I write this, I'm aware that I may not be here when you wake up, and I won't see your beautiful child come into this world. I'd give anything if I could be here to help you raise him or her, to teach them things, like my daddy taught me, but the good Lord has other plans. It looks like I'm gonna be crossing that bridge really soon, darling girl. I just want you to know how much I love you and how you made my life worth living. You were the sunshine in my life and I am so proud of the fine woman you've become. I know you're gonna be a wonderful mama, and this baby is lucky to have you and his grandpa Jack, grandma Coral, and his two uncles. See darlin', you're not alone. No matter what, you've got family, and when you have family, you're always rich. I know I'm leaving you in good hands.

Now, on the off chance that your baby is making the journey with me, don't you worry 'bout a thing, I'll take that child and protect it, no matter where we're going, but God knows, I've prayed so hard that he or she stays here with you. I know as long as you're here, I'm still here because a part of my heart is alive. I love you to the moon and back.

Your sa.......

LARRY'S HEART gave out and the pen dropped on the floor. As everything faded around him, he heard the beeping flatline noise. He heard frantic voices. And then... nothing. Larry Beauford was gone.

# JACK

JIM HAD TOLD CORAL AND THE OTHERS TO GO BACK TO THE cafeteria. He had hung back, wanting to speak to Larry privately after a little while.

Suddenly, many alarms went off in the room and various nurses rushed inside. Dr. Greene arrived shortly thereafter.

He followed Dr. Greene into the room, shock rooting him to the spot when he saw the medical team fussing around Larry. Dr. Greene spoke softly.

"I'm calling it. Time of death, 3:55pm."

The doctor pulled the sheet over Larry's face. He looked angrily at Jack.

"Didn't I ask that you people refrain from upsetting him? What did you say to him?"

"My stepson suggested that he write a letter to Laura, as Larry was scared, he might not be around that long.," Jack murmured.

"A letter?" Dr. Green asked.

They both looked around the room. Jack found the letter on the floor, thanking God that it was not torn in the chaos. He read it and choked up, forcing back tears.

"Um...here it is. Wanna read it?"

The doctor read the last words of Larry Beauford and he wiped a tear from his cheek.

"The good never last, do they?"

# LAURA

*March 1977, New Orleans, LA. Tulane Medical Center, 5 days later*

NEARLY A WEEK LATER, AFTER DRIFTING IN AND OUT OF SEDATION, Laura woke, thankfully still pregnant. Her hands went to her belly as soon as she was conscious and alert. Jack was sitting next to her, reading the New Orleans daily.

"Hey there, young lady. Welcome back."

Laura, groggily murmured, "Hey...how long...how long was I out?" *I can still feel my baby, thank God.*

"About 5 days, give or take. Its Friday afternoon." Jack said, as he held a glass of water for her to sip. "The doctors thought it safest to keep you sedated until all the shock had worn off your system. It gave the baby a chance to settle down and grow stronger. You were malnourished and severely dehydrated. They've been feeding you during your half-awake moments. It's a miracle you both came out of it unscathed."

"And Daddy?" Laura asked.

Jack got up and poked his head out the door.

"Excuse me, nurse?"

The nurse entered with a big smile and checked Laura. Her heart, her blood pressure, her baby, the baby's heartbeat.

"All seems well. Are you the grandpa?"

Jack smiled. "Yes, yes I am."

Laura hesitated, "You didn't answer my question."

Jack smiled a tight-lipped smile to Laura, then touched the nurse's arm.

"Ma'am. How is my daughter-in-law's health? My grandchild? Are you sure that they're healthy? Strong?"

The nurse touched his shoulder and gave him a reassuring squeeze. "She seems like she's come through this like a trooper. Now, excuse me while I get our girl a proper meal."

The nurse left. Laura's lip quivered. "He didn't make it, didn't he? You're trying to keep it from me, but I can tell."

"Yes," Jack said. "I'm sorry, sweetheart. He woke up for a while though, and he was okay. His last thoughts were about you. He passed with no pain or suffering at all. I promise you."

Laura sobbed. Jack stroked her head and held her hand. He pulled out the letter and handed it to her. "He wrote this for you, right before he ..."

As she read the letter, she sobbed softly. By the time she finished, she was crying with all her heart. Jack held on to her. "I'm here, sweet girl. I am here. I'm not going anywhere. I've got you. I've got you."

Jack stayed with her the rest of the day, encouraging her to eat well and making sure that she knew she'd always be surrounded by family. No matter what, she'd be loved and so would her child.

# JACK

*June 1977, New Orleans, LA. Buchanan home*

CORAL STARED AT JACK ACROSS THE DINING TABLE. HE TRIED NOT TO notice, but her eyes were boring a hole in his head. He finally lost his patience. "What?!"

"Oh nothin'. I was just wondering about that Ay-rab family you were living with all year before you came back." She said, tapping her manicured nails on the mahogany dining table.

Jack gave himself a face palm and shook his head. "I'll just stop you right there, woman. Why don't you keep your trap shut about them before you say something to display your ignorance?"

Coral jumped up and shot her finger out to wag at Jack. She was about to tear into him when Ike stopped her. "Mama, stop! Come on. He ain't worth it, remember? Let's get a drink before Laura gets here. We'll go outside to get some fresh air too. How's that sound?"

"Sounds nice, sweetheart. Thank you. It's good to know that someone's got some manners around here."

She got up to walk out but kept eye contact with Jack for a few moments. When he cracked a sly smile at her and winked, she huffed and turned to walk outside.

"That woman sure loves drama." Jack said to the room in general.

The phone rang and Jim grabbed it. "You don't mind, right?"

Jack shook his head. "Help yourself, Officer."

"Uh huh. Yeah. Okay, we can do that. I'll tell him," Jim said as he hung up. "That was the precinct. They're confirming Larry's memorial for tomorrow. Can we all be ready?"

"Poor bastard. He went through hell. Let's go give him a great tribute. God knows he deserves it. But today, I'm expecting my visitors from the Middle East. I guess they can join us tomorrow or maybe they'll be too tired. I dunno. We'll see when they get here."

"The rag heads?" Coral shouted from the foyer.

Jack's face turned red and he clenched his teeth. "I'm going to ask you one more time to be polite to my guests! This man and his family saved my life. They're my guests and I'll do whatever I have to do to make sure they don't get any flack, especially from you. Am I clear, woman?"

Coral entered the dining room again and stood unusually silent. She sighed and put her hands on her hips. "Okay, fine. I'll be good. I promise. I reckon it will be good to meet them. That is the *Christian* thing to do, after all."

"Amen, Mama," Jim agreed, grasping Coral by the shoulder. Like a good son, he led her off to relax in the living room.

*Maybe there's hope for these boys yet. Brian loved them. Guess I can try to love 'em too.*

There was a knock at the front door. Jack's butler opened the door and the driver handed off a rather large amount of baggage. Six brand large new suitcases and various exotic woven carry bags. Coral, Jim, and Ike stood very still to witness the entourage that entered Jack's luxurious home. Two men in robes with Arabic headdresses and three women with beautiful sequined kaftan dresses entered. The women's hair was covered with ornate veils, with just their black lined eyes peeking through. Heavy Arabic perfume permeated the air. It was a strange woody smell, but lovely.

Jack had missed it more than he realized. He looked around anxiously for his long-time friend. Finally, Sheikh Fahed himself entered, wearing an Arabic bisht and a full ghutra with agal.

Coral and her sons watched, awestruck as Jack greeted Sheik Fahed by touching noses with him and then exchanging kisses on each other's cheeks. Coral whispered, "Good God Almighty. What's he doing? Kissing men now?"

Jim elbowed her. "Shh. Let's just see what happens."

Sheikh Fahed approached and Jack introduced them. "My friend, this is my ex-wife Coral and my two stepsons, Jim and Ike."

Sheikh Fahed shook their hands and said, "Salam Alay Kum."

Jack whispered, "Say...Alaikum Salam."

When the boys answered with their strong Southern accents, the Sheikh nodded approvingly and said, "So, these are the boys you were mistaken about?"

"Yeah. I had them pegged wrong. They're not bad guys actually. I regret how I treated them. I have you to thank for giving me another chance to make it right, not just with them, but with everyone."

Jim and Ike were at a loss for words. Jack reveled in the sight of them standing there, motionless, and speechless.

*I love seeing those two dipshits speechless. Just look at those faces. They thought I was an asshole. Ha! How do you like me now?*

Coral didn't seem convinced. She cleared her throat conspicuously. Jack smiled. *Here it comes.* He walked to Coral and hugged her. Coral's breath hitched and Jack said, "Yes. You too, Coral. I haven't appreciated you, and I'm sorry for anything I've done to hurt you in the past. I hope we can always be friends now. We had a child together and we lost him. It was my child from another hurt woman that caused it all. As God as my witness, I'm gonna make it all good again now, and I have this man and his wonderful family to thank for it."

Daryl Rae entered just in time to hear Jack's declaration.

"May I take your...*cap*? Sir?" The butler asked.

Coral and Jack turned to look at Daryl Rae. She nodded at Daryl Rae, as he smiled at her.

Coral's eyes watered and her voice quivered as she said, "Jack, I've waited so long for you to say that. Thank you."

He pulled back and kissed her gently on the cheek. She smiled and squeezed his hand. "You are a changed man. Golly, I really don't know what to say."

"Sweet Jesus, somebody call the newspapers! Coral doesn't know what to say!" He couldn't resist teasing her.

Everyone sniggered. Coral blushed. Jack kissed her hand.

Sheikh Fahed looked on with a smile, nodding. Coral stepped forward to try and hug him. Jack took her hand and said, "No honey. Don't hug. One of those lovely ladies is his wife, and she may not take too kindly to that."

Coral stepped back and smiled. Her face turned red as she saw the women looking at her, curiously. "Oh. I'm sorry. I just wanted to say thanks to your husband...Thanks to all of you." She giggled nervously.

Jack suggested they all get settled into the guest rooms. "My servants can take care of you while we're out. I'd love for you to join us, but I think you must be very tired from your journey."

One of Sheikh Fahed's sons, Shams, agreed. "We are tired. I hope you'll excuse us as we rest and wash up. It's almost prayer time as well."

Jack slapped his hand on his forehead. "Oh, I'm sorry! I've already forgotten the prayer timings. Of course! Please, treat my home as your home. My butler can help you with the Qibla I've prepared. Be comfortable and we'll be back soon. We've got so much to catch up on."

Within moments, Jack ushered the group into the limo. They had many errands to take care of before the memorial service and a party fit for a true war hero.

# Natasha

Natasha blew smoke through the bars of her cell. She had never smoked much, but given her situation, there was not much else to do. The guard entered her block and opened her cell door.

"To what do I owe this pleasure?" Natasha said.

"Come on, smart ass!" the guard grumbled. "You have a visitor."

Natasha followed her to the visitor's area and on the other side of the glass, there she was, Nadia. She was in disguise. Feathered blonde hair wig with a shag cut. A rabbit's hair coat, hip hugger jeans, and blue sunglasses with matching blue platform shoes.

*What a getup! Either she's dumb to stand out like that, or a genius.*

Natasha fought back every urge to cry. She simply couldn't give this woman the satisfaction. With a cool and steady hand, she picked up the receiver. "Well, you look healthy for a *dead* woman, and so...*groovy*."

Nadia smiled. "The apple doesn't fall far from the tree. You're definitely my child, but you have your father's sharp wit."

Natasha snorted, "My father? How would I know anything about what he's like? I never got a chance to really know him."

"Was that the reason?" Nadia asked.

"For?" Natasha snapped.

"Why you hurt what he loved. You really wanted to hurt him, didn't you?" Nadia pulled down the edge of her sunglasses to make eye contact.

Natasha looked away, ashamed. "You're not wrong. When I thought he was dead, I killed what he loved the most because of how he treated us. Now that he's actually alive, I can't imagine he'd ever want to know me now."

"I wouldn't be so sure about that. He's been rather forgiving lately. He went on about his eyes being open now and his renewed appreciation for life..." She paused for a moment to study Natasha's reaction. Nothing. Cold stare. "Anyway, give him time. He may come around one day."

"Yeah, right. He's just gonna forgive me for killing his precious son."

Tears streamed down Natasha's face as she remembered Jack looking for her in the apartment. Could he have truly been there for her? To save her? What had she done now? Lost everything, even the man she loved.

Nadia lowered her voice. "There are some influential people who are very interested in your skills and experience. Your crimes would get you the death penalty under normal circumstances. You are fortunate. I will be on hand to personally ensure that you do not embarrass me again. But first, I think a few more months in jail will be a valuable lesson to you."

Natasha looked up, but Nadia was already walking away.

# ALEXANDER

*June 1977. New Orleans, LA. French Quarter. Home of Alexander.*

ALEXANDER SIPPED SOME FINE CHAMPAGNE AS HE LOOKED OUT OVER his lavish terrace. The sun was setting, and the garden looked magical. He smiled. After the drama a few months ago, life was finally good again.

The glass shattered in his hand as he felt a violent blow to his chest. He looked down. A crossbow bolt was protruding obscenely from his chest. Pain came in waves.

A masked figure in black silently walked closer. He could not find the strength to speak or shout for help. The person removed the mask. Nadia stared at him; disgust visible on her face.

"Nadia..." he gurgled.

"Yes, remember me?" she said, grabbing the end of the bolt to enhance the pain.

She smiled as he struggled to stay alive.

"Courtesy of Vlad the Impaler and Natasha, my daughter. Don't fuck with a lion's cub...Pig." She spat at him, then stepped closer. He could see the glint of a blade in her hand as she raised her arm. He barely felt anything as she slit his throat. His blood was warm as it gushed down his chest and he saw her turn and walk away as everything else faded.

# LAURA

LAURA CARRIED THE CUSTOM-MADE LEATHER BABY CARRIER INTO THE Thirteenth Precinct and carefully set it down on an empty table. Brianna looked up at her with those beautiful big eyes, so much like Brian's. Her heart swelled. She looked around the room, at all the pictures of Larry and flower bouquets and her breath caught in her chest.

*What a beautiful tribute! Daddy would be so proud. This is so much better than a funeral.*

Jack, Coral, Jim, and Ike entered, bringing the cake. Jack walked over to her and held her in a warm embrace. He peered into the carrier and his face lit up.

"Oh, my dear Lord, would you just look at that beautiful little bundle!"

He beamed as he pulled funny faces for Brianna.

"Hello Grandpop's, little angel. Yes, you are, oh, yes, you are, my beautiful little Brianna. Peekaboo!"

He didn't even blush as he cooed in a high-pitched voice. Laura suppressed a giggle. Jack stood up, cleared his throat.

"You must come by the house tomorrow and let me show her to my friends from Saudi Arabia. Sheikh Fahed and his family are gonna love her."

"I will, Dad. Don't worry," Laura said. "We're just so happy you're here."

Coral blurted, trying to push Jack away, "Now can I please have a minute with my sweet grandbaby?"

"Oh now, Coral. You're gonna get a lot of time with her. Just a few more minutes for Grandpop Jack!"

Coral huffed with her hands on her hips. Jim elbowed his mother. "Mama, what did we talk about? Don't make everything about you."

She rolled her eyes. "Fine."

Daryl Rae pulled Coral's hand. "Can I see you for a minute, baby?"

Coral followed him to a quiet corner. Daryl Rae pulled out a bouquet of roses from behind the door and dropped down on one knee.

"Oh, my sweet baby Jesus." Coral exclaimed. Everybody in the room turned to watch.

"Coral, my darlin'. I was gonna wait until we were alone at home to do this, but I thought with all the happiness going around here, I might just top it off... Will you marry me?" he said, smiling from ear to ear. Coral beamed and the tears began.

"Yes! Of course, I will!"

Daryl Rae held out a large diamond ring, and Coral looked taken aback. "Oh baby, where on Earth did you get the money for this?"

Daryl Rae simply smiled at Jack, who was standing behind Coral. Coral whipped around and her mouth popped open. "You?"

"I just figured he should give you the ring you deserve, Coral. Let's just call it a peace offering. I really do want what's best for you, and this dingus seems to really love you."

"Hey!" Daryl Rae blurted out, red-faced.

"Just joking, you big lug! Now come on! Get off your knees. The girl said yes," Jack smiled. "Let's celebrate. I snuck in some of the bubbly to go with this strawberry cake. Let's give everyone a party they'll never gonna forget."

Laura was genuinely happy for Coral; she'd been through so much. It was a great start to a beautiful memorial service. Many people shared stories of Larry, some who had even driven down all the way from Alabama. It was wonderful, but a bittersweet evening for Laura. When everyone left and Laura was getting ready to pick up the carrier with a sleeping Brianna, she looked around at Larry's smiling face all around her. She smiled softly as she cuddled Brianna.

"I feel him here, sweet girl.  He's with us. We love you, Daddy. Thank you."

### The End.

# ALSO BY DEDRA L. STEVENSON

You can also find the following books, also by Dedra Stevenson at an online source near you. These titles can also be found on the Blue Jinni Media website: bluejinnimedia.com

## The Revenge of the Blue Jinni

### The First Book of The Hakima's Tale

Phoenix Kassim and her family discover their great destiny as they prepare to defend the human world from the attack of beings from an unseen dimension, the Jinn. Benevolent, human-friendly Jinn assists the young Hakima every step of the way to keep her safe from the Blue Jinni and his loyal followers.

## The Rise of the Warrior

### The Second Book of The Hakima's Tale

The young Hakima trains under the direction of a mysterious old woman to learn the secrets of fighting supernatural forces. Along the journey, Phoenix Kassim acquires the tools of the Hakima, including the amber of the Enchanted Blue Whale, the Magic Carpet, the loyalty and assistance of the wolves, and the Ring and Glove of Ghalib.

## The Dawn of Redemption

### The Third Book of The Hakima's Tale

Humans from every corner of the Earth cower in fear as the twelve tribes of the Jinn unleash their wrath upon the world. The only hope for humanity lies in the hands of a young woman, Phoenix Kassim, otherwise known as The Hakima. The human army is joined by the benevolent tribes of Jinn, and together they strive to bring an end to the tyranny.

## Desert Magnolia

Daniella Suleiman left her original home in Georgia many years ago, and made a comfortable life in the Middle East, alongside her husband, Faisal, and her children. Suddenly, her life is turned around upon hearing the news that her father has been fatally struck down due to a hate crime in her small Southern town. She finds herself compelled to go back and attempt to exonerate her cousin, who has been accused of the crime. Going back will mean digging up skeletons from the past, however, and skeletons don't like living in closets.

## Breaking Bread Around the World

Breaking Bread Around the World provides easy meal plans for 30 different countries, and a bonus chapter with extra recipes for breakfast, side dishes and a few extra desserts. The book is also Vegan friendly, as there are a generous number of Vegan recipes included! There's photos of all the food available, and Dedra's personal notes on each country, thereby providing a bit of travel information as well.

## More titles are coming soon!

**Blue Jinni Media**

# About the Author

Dedra L. Stevenson is a multi-genre author, filmmaker, and a multi award-winning screenwriter originally from Alabama, USA, but now residing permanently in the U.A.E. Her novels include a fantasy fiction trilogy for young adults, known as The Hakima's Tale, a controversial courtroom drama called Desert Magnolia, a horror called The Skinwalker Resurrection, a collection of fantasy short stories called Tales of the Lantern, a children's book called Little Loud Beatrice and the Magic Painting, and a spy thriller called The Buchanan Bastard.

She's currently assembling a science fiction anthology called Human Horizons that's to be published in 2023. She's also Co-Authoring a new young adult series, S.P.O.O.K.S. with her long-time creative partner at Blue Jinni Media, Rodney Harper. The first of this series, Ifrit, has been released, and the second book, Aja the Traveller, is being written.

In addition to writing stories, Ms. Stevenson enjoys writing movies. She won Best Short Screenplay for Desert Magnolia, based on her novel of the same name, in Mediterranean Cannes, 2018.

She wrote the screenplay for the horror short film, Amunet, that went on to win many awards and distinctions.

She wrote several feature screenplays after that, including: The Skinwalker Resurrection (award nominated, 2018, along with many selections), C.U.P.I.D. (award nominated, 2020, along with many selections), and Earth Angels, an original horror (semi-finalist, 2020, along with other selections). She's currently writing a feature screenplay for The Buchanan Bastard and a feature screenplay entitled, Speechless in Sharjah.

Additionally, Ms. Stevenson has written two short screenplays, Kill the Writer and Kill the Millennial, winning eleven "best short screenplay" awards between them, with more to come. She's currently writing another instalment for this series, entitled, Kill the Planet.

With great aspirations of becoming a writer of television series, Ms. Stevenson has also written a pilot entitled, The Hakima's Tale, episode 1: Iretunar, the Blue Fire of the Desert.

Last, but not least, Ms. Stevenson is a playwright. Her stage play, Desert Magnolia, is currently being cast for a read at Berklee School of Performing Arts, Abu Dhabi.

Ms. Stevenson intends to keep on writing, if her genre hopping keeps her fresh and in the zone. Many more stories to come.

facebook.com/Hakimastale

twitter.com/HakimasTale

instagram.com/dedrastevenson

# About Blue Jinni Media

Blue Jinni Media is a publishing imprint for books and media created by Dedra Stevenson, Rodney Harper, and various cooperative partners.

Working with other independent authors around the world, Blue Jinni Media embraces a shared ideology to help other writers get their stories out and achieve their goals as successful self-published authors.

Please join our mailing list to receive information about new releases, author news as well as opportunities for joining our Beta reader program and receive advanced copies of new books for FREE. You may join by visiting the Blue Jinni Media website - http://bluejinnimedia.com

Thank you for choosing our books and please, don't hesitate to contact us with your comments and suggestions.

Dedra L. Stevenson (Sharjah, U.A.E.)
Rodney W. Harper (Raleigh, NC, USA)

facebook.com/bluejinnimedia
twitter.com/bluejinnimedia
instagram.com/bluejinnimedia